S.

EARTH ETERNAL

EARTH ETERNAL

EARTHRISE, BOOK IX

DANIEL ARENSON

CHAPTER ONE

The two mechas, humanoid machines the size of skyscrapers, flew through space, heading toward the solar system. Heading to Earth. Heading to war.

For long months we studied Deep Being, the way of peace, Marco thought. *Now we will fight again. Now, with these great weapons, we will defend our world.*

He thought of Durmia, the planet where he had studied Deep Being. He thought of Taolin Shi, the flooded planet where he and Addy had found these mechas. Two worlds in ruin. Two civilizations that had destroyed each other.

That will not be our fate, Marco vowed. *With these machines, we can win our war. We can defeat the grays. We can bring peace.*

He flew inside Kaiyo, the male mecha. Kaiyo was a colossal machine that would have dwarfed the Statue of Liberty. He had a lion's head, maned and proud, and he wore armor engraved with runes. Yes, Marco had come to think of Kaiyo as a *he* rather than an *it*. The legendary warrior held a mighty hammer the size of a building—a hammer that could crush gods.

Marco controlled the colossal robot's every movement. He stood inside Kaiyo's head, enclosed within a sensor suit. As Marco moved, the massive mecha moved in tandem. Marco almost forgot he had a body of his own. As he flew here in space, he *was* Kaiyo—towering, strong enough to shatter worlds.

"Eleven years ago, I left Earth for the first time, a scrawny boy," he said softly to himself. "I return home the greatest warrior Earth has known."

His communicator crackled to life, and a voice emerged from the speakers.

"What's that? You're talking shit, Poet. *I'm* the greatest warrior Earth has known. Me! Addison Linden, Goddess of War!"

Marco groaned. "Goddess of Hot Dogs and Freaks maybe."

Her voice thundered. "Addison Linden, Goddess of War, Hot Dogs, and Freaks!"

Marco looked at her—or at least at the mecha she was flying. She was inside Kaji, the female mecha, companion to his own machine. Her mecha wore golden armor, and she carried a sword the size of a tower. Her face was the face of a lioness, beautiful and fierce.

"I like you inside that mecha," Marco said. "At least you can't elbow me in the ribs this way, and—Addy? Addy! Stop!"

Her mecha flew closer to him. The metal elbow—it was the size of a truck—jabbed into Kaiyo's side.

"Boom!" she said.

Marco's mecha tumbled through space. He struggled to right himself, releasing puffs from his engines.

"For Chrissake, Addy. Can you *not* play with these colossal, ancient fighting machines of a forgotten culture?"

Kaji's golden shoulders, large as hills, rose in a shrug. "Hey, if they can't take a mere elbow to the ribs, how are they gonna fight the grays?" Her feline eyes widened. "Hey, Poet. Do you reckon these mechas have private parts?" She gasped. "Can they have sex?"

"We're not having mecha sex, Addy."

"Oh please! Can you check under your armor to see if you have a robo-willy?"

"Addy! For fuck's sake!"

"Let me check." She reached for his armor. "Come on, just a peek!"

"Hands off!" Marco slapped her giant metal hand aside. "Sex later. First saving the world."

She groaned. "You have your priorities all wrong, Poet."

Marco pointed. "Look, Addy. The sun. We're almost home."

From here, the sun was still small, a bright star shining ahead. The two mechas entered the heliosphere, the bubble-like region of space containing the sun's solar wind. They left the vast emptiness of the interstellar medium behind. Even the solar system, so small within the grandeur of the cosmos, was vast. They still flew at warp speed; with conventional engines, it would take years to reach Earth, even from here. They passed by the orbit of Pluto. The dwarf planet appeared as but a dim speck of light in the distance. Soon they saw Neptune ahead, a beautiful blue sphere.

Home, Marco thought. *We're finally home.*

"Only two hundred years ago," he said softly, "the orbit of Neptune would have seemed impossibly distant, a frontier beyond human reach. Now it feels like coming home."

Addy's mecha nodded. "And I think I see Earth ahead. That tiny dot like a blue star."

Marco saw it. "Earth. The cradle of humanity. Birthplace of all our art, science, and understanding. All that we humans have achieved, from Mozart to the wormhole—all came from that grain of sand."

"The cradle of hot dogs!" Addy said. "Of hockey and Spam! Of jalapenos stuffed with cheese and wrapped with bacon!"

Marco rolled his eyes. "Not everything is about food, Addy."

"Hey. I mentioned hockey! Hockey matches while drinking beer and eating nachos and spicy wings … in the, um, cosmic cradle of humans." She grinned. "See? I'm a poet too."

"Yes, Addy, that was beautiful."

They flew onward, and they finally saw Saturn ahead. Marco remembered flying by Saturn ten years ago aboard the *Miyari,* marveling at its beauty. He decided to take a detour now, to fly by Saturn again, to view its beautiful rings one more time before continuing on to Earth. Addy followed. Saturn grew larger ahead, its rings shimmering.

"It looks like a giant onion ring," Addy said.

"Not everything is about food!"

"Fine, fine. A donut then."

"Addy!" Marco groaned. "It's a wonder you don't weigh six hundred pounds."

"Oh, I weigh about six hundred *tons* in this mecha."

As they flew closer, Marco frowned. He narrowed his eyes.

"Do you see that?" he said. "By Titan. Saturn's moon."

Addy stared with him. She hissed, and her mecha raised her sword.

"Fuck. It's them. Those assholes. The grays."

Marco reached toward some of the holographic controls that hovered before him. He zoomed in on Titan. It was a large orange moon, larger even than the planet Mercury, with a dense atmosphere. It was a cold world rich with hydrocarbons, and methane rained from its clouds. Here was a harsh environment, but humanity had settled this world. Several towns dotted Titan's surface, home to miners and their families, and a handful of satellites orbited the moon.

And now the grays had come too.

Dozens of their saucers, maybe hundreds, were flying around Titan. As Marco watched, three saucers blasted their cannons, destroying a human space station. Debris rained into

Titan's atmosphere, burning up. Several saucers began descending toward the colonies.

If any human starships had fought here, they had already fallen.

Holographic alerts flashed before Marco. A message was coming in from Titan. Marco played it.

"If anyone can hear us, by God, help!" A man appeared in a grainy video image. His voice shook. "They're everywhere. They're slaying the last few men. They've taken the women. Help us. Help us please! They're coming. They're—" The colonist spun around. "No. Get back! I'm armed! I—"

Claws lashed.

Blood sprayed.

With a gurgling scream, the image died.

Marco forced a deep breath. The old terror of war rose in him again.

Breathe.

He had to breathe.

Addy's voice emerged from his speakers. "Poet, you picked that up?"

He nodded. "I did."

Addy's voice was strained. "You up for a good old-fashioned bar brawl?"

He nodded. "I am."

Addy's mecha raised her sword. "Let's show those fuckers what real soldiers can do."

Ahead, the saucers had seen them. A hundred came charging toward the mechas, leaving Titan behind. Several were motherships, large as football stadiums, built of dark metal and engraved with hieroglyphs. The others were small red fighters, spinning madly like throwing stars.

Standing inside his mecha, engulfed in a suit of sensors, Marco raised a small hammer. His mecha raised his own hammer, a weapon the size of a starship. At his side, Addy's mecha raised her sword, and the blade caught the sunlight.

The saucers stormed closer. Their cannons fired.

Plasma blasts flew toward the mechas. Alarms blared and holographic warnings flashed.

Marco swung his hammer.

A bolt slammed into the hammerhead, and the mecha jerked. Pain blasted up Marco's arm. More blasts slammed into his mecha's breastplate, denting the armor. Inside the machine, Marco felt the impact on his own chest. He was one with Kaiyo, fighting as the giant, feeling his pain.

The saucers kept charging. Lasers beamed out. Rays hit Kaiyo, and Marco cried out. The attack seared his armor, burned a hole in his hammer, and the giant trembled. Damn holographic displays kept popping up, obscuring the battle, and Marco cursed, trying to wave them aside, but they kept reappearing. A robotic voice kept speaking in Taolin, and he didn't know how to shut off the damn computer.

At his side, Kaji was taking a pounding too. Plasma bolts and lasers slammed into the female mecha, searing her armor, chipping off steel shards.

"That does it!" Addy shouted, swinging her sword. The jets on her back blasted out fire, and she charged toward the saucers.

Marco joined her.

The blasts slammed against them. The saucers swarmed. The mechas kept flying.

With blasts of light and fire, the two forces slammed together.

Addy struck the first blow, lashing her sword. The massive blade clove through a mothership. The saucer split in half, spilling out thrashing grays. A dozen smaller saucers slammed into Addy, knocking her back. Marco swung his hammer. The head drove into a saucer, crushing it. He swung again, hit one of the small buzzing ships. A hundred flew around him like hornets, blasting their guns, stinging, burning the mecha. The pain flowed through the sensors into Marco's own body. He spun, swinging his hammer in circles, trying to knock them back. The lasers flew everywhere, blinding him, stinging his mecha's eyes. Saucers drove against his armor, spinning like saw blades, cutting through him.

"Those fuckers are everywhere!" Addy shouted.

Marco couldn't see. He reached out blindly. Alarms blared and Taolin letters hovered before him, a language he couldn't read. He swung his hammer, trying to clear away the saucers. The holographic warnings kept obscuring his vision, and that damn robotic voice kept speaking. How could he fight like this?

Between the flashing holograms, he glimpsed one of the motherships charging toward him.

The enemy ship slammed into his chest.

Marco fell back, screaming.

Dozens of smaller saucers peppered him with plasma bolts. Above him, he saw Addy tumbling through space, blindly swinging her sword.

One of the motherships was flying toward her, prepared to ram into her head.

Marco activated his engines.

He flew toward Addy and grabbed the mothership meters away from her.

His metal fingers dug into the enemy hull. The giant saucer was blasting its engines, bathing him with fire, but he clung on. It was a ship the size of the Colosseum, and Marco gritted his teeth, pulling it away from Addy.

He hurled the mothership through space and slammed it against another saucer.

Both vessels shattered, peppering him with shrapnel. Burning corpses spilled out.

Another mothership flew.

Addy charged forward, swung down her sword, and cut the vessel in half.

Marco looked around at the battle. They had done the grays some damage, but many saucers still remained. The saucers regrouped and prepared to charge again.

"Addy, is your mecha blinding you with fucking holograms too?" he shouted.

"Yeah! And the computer keeps talking to me in Chinese!"

"It's Taolin!" he said. "I—Damn!"

Saucers flew at him, pounding him with plasma. He swung his hammer, but these were enemy starfighters, too fast to hit. They kept circling him, dodging his hammer. The damn holograms rose again, Taolin runes that blinded him. He waved at the pesky controls, struggling to brush them aside. A button flashed, begging to be pressed. With a groan, Marco pressed it, hoping it got rid of the hologram.

Blessedly, the orange holograms turned green, then faded.

His mecha thrummed.

Cannons emerged from his forearms.

Marco gasped.

The saucers charged at him, and Marco concentrated, moving his awareness to the cannons. With his mind, he fired them.

Blasts flew out and slammed into saucers. The enemy ships exploded.

"Fuck me!" Addy shouted. "How did you do that, Poet?"

"You see a hologram on your left, an orange one? Scroll down and press the button!"

A moment later, Addy too grew cannons from her forearms. She fired them, tearing through saucers.

The mechas hovered back-to-back, firing out an inferno, tearing through the saucers. Marco grabbed another mothership and swung it like a shield, slamming it into smaller saucers. Addy kept firing, shattering the smaller fighters.

With their cannons blasting, the tide turned. A few last saucers turned to flee. The mechas chased, their cannons fired, and the saucers exploded.

The battle was over.

Kaiyo and Kaji, ancient mechas of Taolin Shi, hovered in space among the wreckage of a hundred enemy ships.

"Poet?" Addy said.

"Yes, Addy?"

"Can you check under your armor for a robo-willy now?"

"No, Addy."

She sighed. "Such a party pooper."

He engaged his engines and flew closer to Titan. "Come on, Ads. There are grays down on Titan. And maybe still some colonists."

They flew down toward the moon. It was a rough entry; the atmosphere was thicker than Earth's, a dense soup of methane and organic smog. Hydrocarbon rain streamed around him, and soot swirled through the air. Marco couldn't even see the surface, just clouds and rain and ash.

Finally, farther down, he could make out landforms. A lake of methane shone below, and dunes rolled toward hills. Mountains soared in the distance. The land was yellowish and brown and wet.

"There." Marco pointed. "Look at Gandalf Hill, just below Erebor Mountain. I think that's a colony."

Addy flew her mecha at his side. "Gandalf? Erebor? Aren't those characters from your nerdy books for nerds?"

Marco rolled his eyes. "Well, we can't all be connoisseurs of fine literature like *Freaks of the Galaxy*. But yes, Gandalf is a character from *The Lord of the Rings*. Erebor is the name of the dwarves' mountain. The original explorers of Titan, all the way back in the twentieth century, named its landforms after characters and locations from Middle Earth."

"Nerds," Addy said.

"You'd probably name them after hot dogs."

"Not true!" Addy said. "I'd name the mountains after freaks. Pillowman Hill, Elephant Man Mountain, Lobster Girl Gorge …"

How easy it was to joke, Marco thought, when one fought wars from inside massive machines of steel. How easy it was to banter when death was just the press of a button. How different it was to face death up close, wearing nothing but tattered fatigues, armed with nothing but a rifle!

They landed on Gandalf Hill. Standing in the mechas, Marco and Addy towered above the colony. Tractors and bulldozers lay smashed and burned in the valley, and human skeletons still sat within them. Other skeletons, wearing mining helmets, lay scattered across the land. The colony sprawled across the hilltop, a complex of domes, tunnels, and bridges. It was the size of a shopping mall, large enough for thousands of colonists.

And thousands of grays, Marco thought.

"Are the colonists all dead?" Addy looked around at the burnt skeletons.

Marco felt queasy. "Remember the message? The grays killed the men and captured the women."

Addy's mecha clenched her fists. "Let's kill those sons of bitches, Poet. Let's kill 'em dead."

Marco nodded. "I'd like to. But if there are any grays on the surface, they're inside the colony. We can't fit inside while wearing these mechas."

"Then we go in ourselves," said Addy. "My mecha has an armory. There are rifles, knives, grenades. There's even armor. We go in and kill those gray fuckers. No mechas. Just you and me. Like the good old days."

"There might be hundreds of grays in there," Marco said.

"Come on, we can take 'em," Addy said. "We faced the scum and marauders, remember?"

"We had an army then," Marco said.

"We do now too," Addy said. "A two-human army."

"Ads, I don't know. Maybe we should call for help from Earth. Maybe this is too big for us."

She stepped closer to him. Her mecha placed her hand on his mecha's shoulder. "Listen, Poet. You know what happened to me while you were searching for the Ghost Fleet, right?"

He nodded. He spoke softly. "I know."

"I was so scared then," Addy said. "I was naked, my head shaved, bound, broken. But I rose up against the marauders. I did not back down. And I will not back down now either. I'm going in there, and I'm fucking shit up. Are you with me?"

It was madness. He knew it was. It was suicide. But he looked at her mecha's feline face, and he could see her fierceness there. He nodded.

"I'm with you, Addy. Always."

"Meet you downstairs, Stinky. Bring lots of guns."

Marco stepped out from his sensor suit, losing control of the mecha. It was a disconcerting experience, almost as dizzying as entering warp space. His consciousness shrank, pulling out of the mighty mecha and returning to his own— much smaller—body. For a moment Marco could only blink. He shook his head wildly, readjusting to his smaller dimensions, to being a mere man again. He stood inside the mecha's head, a control room filled with monitors, keyboards, and the control suit he had just vacated.

After finding his bearings, he entered the elevator. On the way down, he stopped by the armory, a chamber in the mecha's chest. He found an armored spacesuit. It was crimson and painted with golden runes, and when he put it on, he felt like an ancient Chinese warrior. The Taolians were a bit shorter than humans, and perhaps for the first time of his life, Marco was thankful for his humble five feet and seven inches. Addy had always teased him about his height, but at least that meant he could fit into this armor. From a weapon rack he chose a railgun; it too was dark red and trimmed with gold. Finally he grabbed a sword, its pommel shaped like a lion's head.

He stepped onto the surface of Titan. Rain was falling, thick with soot, and methane rivulets flowed across the mud. The atmosphere was so thick it felt like walking through soup. Scabby insects scuttled underfoot, the evolution of parasites humans had brought from Earth. Marco was reminded of Haven, the colony where he had spent two years; the air there too had been thick with haze and foul rain.

He met Addy between the mechas. She too wore an armored spacesuit. She carried a railgun and her backpack. They shared a quick embrace.

"Fuck, I could barely squeeze into this armor," Addy said. "Those Taolians were *tiny*."

They probably didn't eat as many hot dogs, Marco wanted to say but didn't feel like getting punched repeatedly in the face.

"You don't need your backpack," he said. "What have you got in there? Schoolbooks?"

She snorted. "You know I only read *Freaks of the Galaxy*. Just bringing some supplies."

Marco nodded. "All right, let's do this thing." He began walking toward the colony gateway. "We'll do it quick. We barge in, bullets spraying. We kill the grays. We save the colonists. Easy peasy. Good luck in there, Ads." He paused and looked behind him. "Ads? Addy! What are you doing?"

She had walked under his mecha and was peering upward. "Just trying to see if he has a robo-willy. But it's too dark up there. Got a flashlight?"

He grabbed her and dragged her away, shaking his head in disgust. "Come on."

They stepped through the smog and rain toward the colony. The walls soared ahead, dark and rising into nitrogen clouds. Barbed wire secured the installation, and a guard tower rose above, but Marco saw only a skeleton inside.

He and Addy kept walking, silent, scanning the area, guns pointing ahead. The old instincts kicked in. Marco had been away from the military for a long time, but a soldier remained a soldier. A soldier never forgot.

They reached the colony gateway and froze.

They stared.

Marco's heart thrashed, and cold sweat washed him.

"Those bastards," Addy whispered through clenched teeth. "Those goddamn sick bastards."

Severed human limbs hung from the gate like a Christmas wreath. A child's head was nailed to the door, eyes gouged out and stuffed into his mouth. Severed fingers filled the empty eye sockets. With blood, somebody had scrawled a message on the doorway: *Come in, apes. Treats inside!*

Marco stared, eyes burning. His chest ached. His head spun.

Deep Being. You are not your fear. You are fire over calm water.

"Let's kill those sons of bitches," he whispered, voice shaking.

He and Addy shouted and kicked open the doors. They stormed inside, railguns held before them.

A scene from hell awaited them.

A hallway stretched ahead, drenched in blood. Intestines hung from the ceiling like party ribbons. Human corpses were nailed into the walls, their ribs cracked open, the organs removed and placed on the floor. No. Not corpses. They were alive. It was impossible. Impossible! And yet the hearts were beating on the floor. The eyes were moving. The mouths opened and closed, whispering, begging for death.

Marco's head spun. He wanted to retch. The humans on the walls stared at him, missing limbs, their spines exposed, gutted like fish yet still whimpering. Addy stared with him, eyes wide, jaw clenched, face pale.

Marco and Addy walked through this nightmare, staring around, not sure what to do, how to save these people.

They were halfway down the corridor when the door slammed shut behind them.

Another door, at the opposite end of the corridor, slammed shut too.

Marco took a step forward. A boy hung on the wall ahead, his ribs opened like saloon doors. Just a boy. He was whispering to Marco. Tears in his eyes.

As in a dream, Marco stepped closer.

"Run," the boy whispered. "Run."

That's when Marco saw what was inside the boy's chest.

Wires. Pipes. A ticking timer.

"Addy!" he shouted. "Run!"

They ran down the corridor, under the dangling entrails, toward the far door. They fired their railguns, shattering the door ahead, and leaped toward the entrance, shouting, and—

A *pop* louder than a cannon.

Searing, furious sound followed by ringing like a siren.

Fire. White fire everywhere, blasting around him, and the hammers of gods slamming into his back.

Marco and Addy tumbled through the shattered doorway as the corridor behind them crumbled and blazed.

The colony—Titan itself—shook.

Marco slammed onto the floor facedown. Addy lay on her side, moaning, her visor cracked. Flames fluttered across their armor, melting the golden runes engraved onto the crimson plates. Smoke filled the chamber. Marco could barely breathe, barely move. Searing pain was clawing at his leg.

Nothing but ringing—deafening ringing, wailing, a banshee cry in his ears, and his mind seemed muffled, wrapped in cotton. His knuckles were crushed; he had landed on his rifle. Addy was shouting something. He couldn't hear.

And from the smoke ahead, they emerged.

Countless of them, black eyes filled with glee, claws reaching out like demons from the abyss.

The grays.

One of the creatures grabbed Marco, claws digging through armor and flesh. Marco screamed. He could barely even hear that scream above the ringing in his ears.

But he could hear the gray's words.

The towering, wrinkled creature gripped him tighter, his black eyes penetrating, searing, digging through Marco deeper than the claws. The gray's voice filled Marco's mind, guttural and demonic.

You ... will ... suffer.

Marco's consciousness unfurled. The colony peeled back. The vastness of space and time spread out around him like a blooming wound, rife with terrors. He saw Earth burning. He saw Earth black and dead. He saw himself and his friends nailed into ankhs, flayed, cracked open, screaming, growing old in agony.

The claws tightened. More grays leaned above Marco, grabbing, cutting, mocking. Their voices hissed, a cacophony in his mind.

You ... will ... beg ...

Their banners rose over the ruins of Earth, black and crimson, as the millions perished on ankhs, screaming under a blood-red sky. A new Earth. An Earth reborn, cruel and macabre. An Earth of humanity enslaved and wretched and crawling in the mud, begging for mercy from their masters.

The terror filled Marco.

The visions swirled through his skull.

The voices chanted, screamed, laughed. Everywhere— their laughter.

And beneath—cool water. A solid stone.

You are not your thoughts.

He breathed.

You are not your fear.

He grabbed his fallen railgun.

Breathe. Observe. Be.

He sank into Deep Being, letting the nightmares flow above him like storms in a sky. He saw the grays' eyes widen in shock. And Marco fired his railgun.

His bullets blasted out at hypersonic speed, far faster and more destructive than what a regular rifle could fire. They tore through a gray, pulverizing the creature's flesh and bones.

The claws pulled free from his armor.

Marco turned toward another gray and fired again, tearing through the beast, scattering bones.

He spun to his right. Several grays had grabbed Addy, were carrying her away. He fired. Again and again. His bullets sliced through the grays' legs, ripping them off, and Addy fell.

The creatures were everywhere. More kept emerging from the smoke. Marco loaded another magazine and fired again, slaying them. They fired back, aiming bulky black guns. Electrical bolts slammed into Marco's armor, and the pain was terrifying and white and all-consuming, and tears filled his eyes and his teeth rattled, but he kept firing through the agony. He kept killing them.

Because that's who I am, he thought. *A killer. That's what the HDF made me. That's what the scum made me. That's what the marauders made me. I was born to kill. I am a soldier.*

Addy rose beside him, panting, coughing, wounded. She fished her railgun out from the gore, and she screamed as she fired, pulverizing the grays that swarmed toward them.

"Keep tearing through them, Addy!" Marco said. "Forward! Let's get out of this gauntlet!"

She nodded. They walked through the smoke, blasting back grays. They found themselves in a towering, transparent dome, a plaza atop the hill. Once, perhaps, this place had been beautiful. Now death filled it. A statue of Yuri Gagarin, first human in space, lay fallen and draped with corpses. Somebody had broken off the statue's bronze head and replaced it with the severed head of a colonist. Alcoves around the plaza, perhaps once shops, now contained statues of Nefitis, twenty stone likenesses of the goddess, human hearts laid at their feet as offerings.

A few grays lurked in the plaza, hissing. Marco and Addy took them down with a hailstorm of bullets. They stood over the corpses.

"That's right, assholes!" Addy shouted, looking around, arms raised in triumph. She kicked one of the dead grays. "Nobody messes with Marco Emery and Addy Linden! We'll kill every last one of you fuckers!" She laughed maniacally, and tears streamed down her cheeks. Her hands were trembling. "Is that all you've got? Come on! Come on, assholes! Come face us! We've got more bullets for you! I'll kill every last fucking one of you!"

Marco placed a hand on her shoulder. "Addy. It's all right."

She was trembling, panting, sobbing. She gritted her teeth, whipping her head from side to side. The corpses of grays lay around them, some still twitching. From the ceiling hung other corpses—the corpses of human colonists, disemboweled, stretched wide, skin hammered into stone. The grays had made this place a temple of death.

They're a race of Josef Mengeles, Marco thought, nausea filling him.

"The dead colonists are all men," he said. "We have to find the women and children."

From deeper in the colony, voices rose, speaking in an alien tongue. Laughter echoed. Creatures cackled. Marco and Addy had slain many grays, but many others still lurked here.

Addy nodded and spat through her shattered visor. She sniffed and wiped her tears.

"Let's go kill those assholes."

They ran into a covered walkway, the glass ceiling affording a view of Titan's orange clouds. Methane rain pattered above, thick with organic ash. The walkway took them to another building, and they burst into a brick corridor lined with doors, perhaps the colony's living quarters.

Screeches tore through the air. The lights shut off with a *thud*.

Marco and Addy froze, guns raised, and activated the flashlights on their helmets.

Their beams fell upon dozens of grays.

The creatures emerged from the doorways, naked, hissing, claws red with blood. Marco and Addy shouted, firing. Their muzzles lit the shadows.

They moved down the corridor, but the grays were everywhere, emerging from bunks, scuttling along the ceiling, bursting out from vents below. Marco and Addy's bullets tore through them.

Screams rose ahead—these ones human screams.

"Come on, Addy!" Marco ran, cleaving a path before him with his railgun. "Forget clearing these rooms. Prisoners ahead!"

They raced through the gauntlet. From every door they passed, grays emerged, cackling, lashing at them. Claws tore off their armor. Claws tore their skin. Marco and Addy kept running. They reached the end of the hall, blew back a gray guardian, and burst into another dome.

They froze.

They had found the women of the colony.

They stared, for a moment too shocked to move. Addy paled, and her fists clenched.

The women were still alive, but barely. Hundreds crowded the chamber, living in squalor, their own waste covering the floor. The grays had cut off their feet, cauterizing the wounds, leaving the prisoners hobbled. Most of the women were pregnant, bellies swelling. A few were nursing babies with swollen heads, pinched faces, and oval eyes—hybrids. Some hybrids were already toddlers; one gazed at Marco curiously, chewing on a raw, severed foot.

How long have they been here? Marco thought, nausea filling his belly. Time was relative across space. He had been on Durmia for a few months, but several years might have passed here.

The women looked up at him and Addy. Tears filled their eyes.

"Help us," they whispered. "Help us …"

Several women lay on the ground. Grays had mounted them, were copulating with them, grunting, hissing, grinning at Marco.

He shouted and ran. Addy ran with him. Their bullets blazed out, shattering the grays. Marco knelt by one of the women, tried to help her up. She gazed at him with terrified eyes.

"Above you!" she whispered.

Marco looked up and screamed.

Hanging like bats, hundreds of grays coated the ceiling. The beasts leaped down, shrieking.

Marco howled and fired his gun. Addy fired too. They slew a few grays, but others mobbed them. Addy's gun ran out of bullets first. Grays knocked into her, cut her skin. She screamed, swinging her rifle like a club. Marco's railgun ran out of ammo next. The grays were everywhere. Many carried guns, and electrical bolts slammed into Marco, burning him, knocking him down. He lay on the bloodied floor.

And Marco knew he was going to die.

And he refused.

No. No!

As the claws grabbed him, stripping off what remained of his armor, he gritted his teeth.

No!

The grays leaned above him, smirking, drooling. One licked him.

"You are a precious toy," the creature hissed. "We cannot impregnate you. But we can try ..."

Marco clenched his fists.

"People of Earth!" he shouted. "Grab their fallen weapons! And fight! Fight for humanity!"

Across the chamber were dead grays, still clutching their guns. Among them cowered the human women.

"Fight them!" Addy shouted, struggling against gray claws. "Grab guns and rise! For Earth! For Earth!"

And across the hall, the women—pregnant, abused, their feet cut off—crawled toward the dead grays and wrenched the guns free.

And they fought.

And they rose up.

Some fired their guns from the ground. Others stood on stumps, howling, blasting out electrical bolts, tearing into the enemy. The fire slammed into the grays clutching Marco. He shoved their burning bodies back, grabbed a fallen rifle, and fired too. Addy howled at his side, firing a gray gun in each hand.

They fought—two veterans and a hundred mutilated women. They killed. They drove back the enemies.

The surviving grays shrieked. They began snatching up the hybrid babies. One gray, perhaps in a panic, began tearing into a baby with his teeth, sucking on the entrails. Marco fired, killing the creature. The other grays tried to flee, only for the bolts to knock them down.

The surviving humans stood among the carnage. Dozens of dead women and babies lay across the floor.

But the grays lay dead among them. And hundreds of humans still lived.

"Fuck yeah!" Addy shouted, raising her fist. "Victory! Victory!"

But nobody else was cheering. The women looked at one another, fear in their eyes. A child wailed.

A woman crawled up to Marco. She grabbed his leg and stared up with terrified eyes.

"She heard," the woman whispered, voice shaking. "She is coming."

Addy spun toward them. "Who?"

The woman trembled. She could no longer speak.

From deep in the complex—laughter. High-pitched. Demonic. The surviving women wailed.

Marco turned toward one of the survivors, a tall woman with black hair. She had managed to stand on her stumps, leaning on a rifle like a crutch. There was no mistaking the tattoos on her arms; she was a veteran, one who had killed scum. She met Marco's gaze. Her eyes were hard. Eyes that had seen much darkness, that had withstood it.

"Lead the survivors out," Marco told her. "You'll be able to survive a short dash on the surface. Lead them into our mechas outside. You'll know what I mean when you see them."

The inhuman laughter rose again, drawing closer. Cackling.

"Go!" Marco said. "We'll hold her off."

The woman stared into his eyes. "You do not know who you face. You cannot kill her."

"You'd be surprised what we can kill," Marco said. "Hurry! Go! Lead the survivors out."

The veteran nodded and began leading the women and children out of the dome. A few of the women managed to hobble on makeshift crutches. Most could only crawl. As they fled, the demonic laughter grew louder, closer. A voice sang, dripping with mockery.

Ring around the rosie
A pocket full of posies
Ashes! Ashes!
They all fall ... down!

And from a tunnel, she emerged into the dome, smiling crookedly.

Marco took a step back and raised his gun. Addy sneered at his side, a rifle in each hand.

The creature sashayed toward them. She was female, a beautiful woman flowing with curves. She had a human body, voluptuous and strong. Yet her head was massively swollen, twice the normal size. The head of a gray. Her eyes were oval and searing blue, her claws long. A string of babies' severed arms hung around her neck, woven like a daisy chain, still dripping blood.

A hybrid, Marco realized. *Half gray, half human.*

Smiling, the hybrid spoke. "The most precious jewels you'll ever have around your neck are the arms of your children."

Marco and Addy opened fire.

The bolts slammed into the hybrid and bounced off, doing her no harm. She kept advancing, her smile growing. Marco and Addy kept firing, and the necklace of baby arms burned, but the hybrid only grinned, the electrical bolts bouncing off her skin.

"Ring around the rosie," the hybrid sang, stepping over corpses, moving closer. "A pocket full of posies ..." Mockery dripped from her voice. "Ashes, ashes!" Her song became louder, high-pitched like steam, and her eyes blazed with delight. "They all fall down!"

She raised her arms, and energy blasted out from the palms. Shock waves slammed into Marco and Addy, tossing them across the room. They slammed into the wall and slumped down.

The hybrid laughed, voice impossibly loud and shrill.

"I know who you are." She stepped closer, crushing the heads of dead babies beneath her feet. "Marco Emery. Addy Linden." She sneered. "My grandmother, the Goddess Nefitis, will be happy to see you."

Marco managed to rise to his knees. It felt as if every bone inside him had shattered. He raised his gun again, aimed at an eye. The hybrid pointed at him, and another shock wave blasted out, knocking him back. Marco screamed as his arm dislocated. His gun clattered onto the floor.

Addy screamed and leaped toward the hybrid, only for a blast to toss her back, to shatter what remained of her armor. She fell to the floor, moaning. When Addy tried to rise again, the hybrid swung her arm. A pillar tore free and crashed onto Addy, pinning her down.

Marco tried to crawl toward Addy. But the hybrid grinned, curled her fingers inward, and an invisible force raised Marco from the floor. He hovered, kicking, a foot above the floor. The hybrid held him in an astral grip. She stepped closer, curled her fingers tighter, and invisible fingers seemed to tighten around Marco's neck. He gasped for air. The tendons in his neck creaked. He clawed at the ghostly fingers, feeling nothing. He kicked wildly, trying to break the spell, but hung in the air.

The hybrid tilted her head.

"So frail," she whispered. "So … small. I imagined a great warrior. The famous Marco Emery, alien killer. I see only a child."

She stepped closer. She placed one hand around his throat, keeping him elevated, and stroked his hair with her other hand. Her claws scraped his scalp. Marco tried to speak, could not. No air reached his lungs.

"What's that? You want to speak?" The hybrid pouted. "I like you silent. At least until it's time for you to scream. I think I will make you my mate." She licked Marco's cheek, her bristly tongue rising from his chin to his forehead. She purred. "You are delicious. I will enjoy you. You ruined my necklace. The arms of our children will form a new one."

A *thud* sounded behind. The room shook. The hybrid spun around, dropping Marco to the floor. He gasped for air.

"Linden!" the hybrid screeched.

Addy had pushed off the pillar, cracking it on the floor. She limped toward the hybrid, bloodied.

"Hands off him, you hybrid bitch," Addy said. "He's mine!"

As the hybrid screamed and raced toward her, Addy reached into her backpack. She pulled out something pale and wet, unfurled it like a napkin, and tossed it.

A slimy sheet wrapped around the hybrid's head, covering her face.

No—not a sheet! One of the fish from Taolin Shi! The same one that had wrapped around Addy!

George, Marco remembered. *Its name is George.*

He rose to his feet, coughing, swaying. Stars hovered before his vision. The hybrid queen shrieked, spinning around, desperate to rip off the fish. Marco ran toward her. He grabbed an electrical gun from the floor. He fired a bolt at the aquatic alien.

The creature burst into flame.

The hybrid shrieked.

The flat fish clung to her, wrapped around her head, blazing. The fire spread. Howling, the hybrid finally tore it off.

Her skin ripped off with it. Her head was burning. She screamed. Her flesh was melting.

Addy fired her own gun. Marco fired too. Their bolts slammed into the hybrid's ravaged skull, stoking the fire. The inferno spread across the rest of the hybrid, melting skin and muscle, revealing the bones. Yet still the creature stood, cackling.

"You cannot stop her!" rose a demonic voice from the blaze. "You cannot stop Nefitis!" The voice became so high-pitched that Marco covered his ears, but still the sound pierced him. "She is coming for you! Nefitis is coming with all her hosts! How you will scream!"

Marco and Addy fired again, hitting what remained of the hybrid's head. Her skull shattered, and finally the creature fell down dead.

For a moment Marco and Addy just breathed. Every breath sawed at Marco's throat, and every breath was wonderful.

Finally he looked up at Addy. "You smuggled George out of Taolin Shi."

"I couldn't just leave him behind." Addy looked at the burnt fish. "And now you burned him into a Filet-O-Fish. Poor, poor George."

Marco sighed. He swayed. Addy limped toward him, and they embraced.

"You all right, Addy?" he whispered.

She nodded, holding him. "Bruised as fuck, but I'm fine. Had worse in hockey fights. You?"

He nodded. "Bruised as fuck." He touched her cheek. "You saved my life, Ads. Again."

She wiped away her tears and grinned. "I had to. That bitch was going to steal you from me. I couldn't allow that. You're my cute little poet."

He kissed her cheek. "I love you so fucking much, Addy. You know that, right?"

Her smile widened. "I know. Because I keep saving your ass. It belongs to me, after all." She looked back at George. "I just wish we could have saved my pet too." She sniffed. "You know, he kind of smells like fried fish. You hungry?"

"Addy!" Marco stepped away from her. "You're not suggesting we eat George, your beloved pet!"

"But I'm hungry!"

He groaned. "There's food back at the mecha."

"But that's far! I'm hungry *now*."

Marco rolled his eyes. "Addy."

She sighed. "Fine!"

No more grays lived in the colony. Marco and Addy moved room by room, finding more atrocities. Women with their legs sawed off, bellies swelling. The corpses of men, mutilated. Hybrid babies, hissing, revealing needlelike teeth. They collected the survivors. They burned the dead.

Marco knew that Earth still stood; he had picked up signals from the planet on his way into the solar system. Here was a taste of Earth's fate should the grays conquer it. Here was what humanity would become should the grays win—tortured, mutilated, the men murdered, the women used for breeding.

We will not let this happen to Earth, he vowed. *With Kaiyo and Kaji, we will defend our world.*

They loaded their mechas with survivors, filling the lounge areas, the corridors, the storerooms, even the elevator. Dented and charred from the battle, Kaiyo and Kaji flew again. They left Titan behind. They flew onward to Earth.

As Marco piloted his mecha, as Earth grew ahead, the hybrid's warning kept echoing in his mind.

Nefitis is coming! How you will scream!

CHAPTER TWO

The *Lodestar* flew into the depths of space, exploring darkness that no human ship had ever lit.

Captain Einav Ben-Ari stood on the bridge, clad in the navy-blue uniform of HOPE, gazing at the stars. HOPE—the Human Outreach Program of Exploration—was Earth's premier scientific and diplomatic agency, and the *Lodestar* was its flagship. The bridge was shaped like a planetarium, its dome covered with screens, affording a view of the stars all around them, along with holographic stats and diagrams. Even the floor was covered with viewports, showing the stars beneath the ship. The bridge was actually deep inside the starship, protected behind thick bulkheads, and the views came from cameras mounted on the hull. But standing here, Ben-Ari felt as if she and her crew floated in space.

We are traveling to new stars, she thought. *To seek the great Galactic Alliance of Civilizations. To seek help. To seek hope. To light the darkness.*

"We were wanderers from the beginning," Ben-Ari whispered, gazing at the stars. "The open road still softly calls, like a nearly forgotten song of childhood."

Professor Noah Isaac approached her. He smiled softly. "Carl Sagan. *Pale Blue Dot*, 1994."

Ben-Ari nodded. "You know your Sagan, Professor."

The professor gazed at the stars and spoke softly. "I am tormented with an everlasting itch for things remote. I love to sail forbidden seas ..."

Ben-Ari smiled. "Herman Melville. *Moby Dick*, 1871."

"1851," the professor corrected her.

Ben-Ari's smile widened. "I must have been thinking of the sequel."

My dear professor, she thought. He made this darkness, this loneliness bearable. He was forty-six, fifteen years her senior, and when she had first come aboard this ship, feeling so overwhelmed to command it, he had been a father figure— guiding, teaching, comforting her. Yet over the past year aboard the *Lodestar*, the professor had become something different to her. Something even more meaningful. As she smiled at him, she remembered how they had embraced, how they had shared a kiss. And the budding feelings of love warmed her.

I've never loved a man, she thought. She had always been too busy with the tragedies of life. She had grown up a military brat, the daughter of a famous colonel, the granddaughter of a general, moving from base to base, rebelling, running away again and again, a girl with no mother and no friends other than gruff sergeants and stray dogs. She had been only a teenager when she joined Officer Candidate School, graduating as an officer at twenty. And since then?

Eleven years of war. Of leading troops in battle. Of facing death every day, of seeing terrors that still haunted her most nights.

I fought the scum in their tunnels, she thought. *I faced the horror of the marauders in the depth of space. I fought the grays upon the burning fields of Earth. Romance? Who the hell had time?*

And so she had grown from rebellious daughter to military officer and now this—the captain of a ship, only thirty-one, a woman with the fate of humanity on her shoulders. A heroine. Her face famous across the world—the legendary Einav Ben-Ari who had led the platoon that killed the scum emperor and the lord of marauders. A woman tasked with saving humanity a third time. A woman who was scared, who found the burden nearly unbearable.

And a woman in love. A woman who had found a man she could finally open her heart to.

"My dear professor." She took his warm hand in hers. "Still you teach me things."

He gazed at her softly. He did not recoil at her touch. Only one of her hands was real, of course. The other was cold metal. She had lost that hand, along with the arm, while battling the grays in Mongolia. Her new prosthetic was slick and silvery and loaded with tricks: it could project a holographic monitor, connect to the internet, and hide objects in a hidden chamber. Some of the crew members would furtively glance at it. Sometimes Ben-Ari felt self-conscious, no longer fully human, some cyborg warrior. But the professor never stared at her prosthetic, never saw her as anything less or more. She loved him for it.

"Well, don't you two dags have dinkum banter." Fish came strolling toward them, his grin as toothy as his crocodile-tooth necklace. "Seeing you two crack onto each other makes me happy as a dingo in a nursery. Just don't pash here on the bridge."

Ben-Ari could still barely understand what the Australian exobiologist, the famous Richie "Fish" Fishburne, was saying half the time. She stared at his khaki shorts in distaste.

"I told you to put on your uniform, Fish," she said. "This is the flagship of Earth, tasked with representing humanity to the Galactic Alliance of Civilizations, not the set of *Alien Hunter*."

Fish's eyes widened in his tanned face. "You say that like *Alien Hunter* was shonky chunder! I'll have you know it was true blue telly, top of the ratings three years in a row." He gestured down at his khaki shorts and shirt. "And I wore this every episode, even the ones where I wrestled Orionite slime-devils."

Out of morbid curiosity, Ben-Ari had streamed an *Alien Hunter* episode on her prosthetic arm's monitor. She had seen Fish trekking across alien planets, finding exotic alien animals, and wrestling them into submission. The man was supposedly a scientist, but he was more of a celebrity.

Just the sort of man who could convince the taxpayer to fund the *Lodestar*. Just the sort of man who made Ben-Ari's job all the more difficult.

She pointed at the elevator. "Go. Off my bridge. Come back with a uniform. And damn it, cut that ridiculous long hair of yours."

His eyes widened. "These beautiful golden locks? Sheila, these locks are what will impress the aliens and let us join their alliance!"

She kept pointing. "Go!"

Muttering that his captain had a few kangaroos loose in the paddock, Fish trudged off the bridge.

Ben-Ari turned toward the professor and sighed. "*That* was the man in charge of introducing us to aliens."

"Fish isn't that bad," the professor said.

"Noah, when we encounter the elders of the Galactic Alliance, Fish is likely to leap onto them and wrestle them."

The professor patted her hand. "Don't worry, Einav. I'll keep an eye on Fish and make sure he behaves. And it'll be you who introduces us to the elders."

Ben-Ari winced. "That's not comforting. I tend to stumble around my tongue. Fish wrestling them to submission might be more diplomatic."

The professor raised his eyebrows. "Stumble around your tongue? You're an eloquent speaker, Einav."

She smiled wearily. "I know how to deliver speeches to soldiers before a battle. I know how to quote old literature.

What do I know of diplomacy? My father was the diplomat. I'm just a soldier."

"You are far more than just a soldier, Einav." Holding her hand, the professor turned to gaze at the stars. "You are an explorer. You are an envoy of humanity. You are—we all are on this ship, perhaps more than anything—dreamers. You are wise, Einav Ben-Ari, and you are strong, and you are eloquent, and mostly you are kind. I can think of no one better to represent our species."

"You," she said.

Isaac smiled at her. "And I'm with you. Always."

She inhaled deeply. He comforted her, yes, but still the fear lingered deep within her. The fate of humanity rested on her shoulders. They had to fly through uncharted space, a darkness full of danger. They had to reach the headquarters of the Galactic Alliance, an organization uniting many of the Milky Way galaxy's mightiest civilizations. She had to convince them that Earth—humble Earth, a lone planet with only a handful of ships and a smattering of colonies—was worthy of membership. If Earth could join the Galactic Alliance, humanity would fall under its umbrella of protection. The Alliance's fleets would defend Earth from the grays.

Yet what chance do we have? Ben-Ari thought, gazing at the distant stars. *The civilizations of the Galactic Alliance are mighty. Some of them span hundreds of star systems. They command great fleets. They possess technology humans cannot even comprehend. They would see us as savages, mere apes taking our first steps into the cosmic ocean.*

She sighed. Yet it was Earth's only hope. The scum, then the marauders, then the grays had destroyed humanity's fleets. Only a handful of human starships remained. They needed the protection of the Alliance … or the next time the grays attacked, they would crush humanity.

"You've taken two shifts on the bridge," the professor said. "Would you like to rest, Einav? I'd be happy to take a command shift."

"I'm tired," she confessed. "But I'd like to remain on the bridge for a while. To reflect. To gaze at the stars. I find it soothing here."

The professor smiled. "You find captaining a starship at wartime soothing?"

She raised an eyebrow. "You're the one who relaxes by reading scientific papers."

"Touche."

And so she remained on the bridge. She gazed out at the stars. An explorer. A leader. A woman with a billion humans behind her, with the hopes of humanity ahead.

No human ship has ever flown this far, she thought, gazing at the distant lights. *What will I find here? Aid or death?*

As she gazed into the distance, she frowned. She tilted her head. A few of the stars were vanishing, reappearing, flickering away. A bad pixel on the monitor? No. A shape. Something …

Ben-Ari reached out, activating the holographic interface for one of the displays. She zoomed in.

Her frown deepened.

An object was floating ahead. Square. Black.

She zoomed in closer.

"Professor, are you seeing this?"

He stared with her. "Hmm." He scratched his chin.

"Hmm indeed," said Ben-Ari. "It looks like …"

"Like a wall," said the professor.

Ben-Ari turned toward Lieutenant Connor Smith, one of her bridge officers, a young man with a brown beard and a bionic eye. Sometimes he joked that he and Ben-Ari should become pirates—after all, he was missing an eye, she was missing an arm, and they already had a ship. His twin brother served on the bridge too, sporting the same beard. The only way Ben-Ari could tell the Smith Bros apart was by the bionic eye.

"Connor," she said to him. She always referred to the twins by their first names to avoid confusion. "What are the dimensions of this object?"

The one-eyed lieutenant manipulated holographic displays. He looked at her. "Half a kilometer wide, half a kilometer tall, according to my estimates. I'd have to send out a probe to estimate the width."

She shook her head. "No. Save our probes."

She kept staring. A wall in space. Just floating ahead. Facing them. Was it an alien starship? It wasn't moving. She saw no portholes, no exhaust pipes. Just a smooth dark facade.

"The object is emitting no signals," said the professor, working at the science station. "It seems to be made of stone."

"Stone?" Ben-Ari said. "Not metal?"

"Stone, Captain," the professor said. "It's bizarre. But we seem to be facing a stone wall in space. And it's directly ahead of us, blocking our present course."

They kept flying closer. Soon Ben-Ari wouldn't need to use the zoom function to see the wall.

She turned toward Aurora, the ship's pilot. "Aurora, adjust our course. Give us a wide berth around the wall. Whatever it is, let's not disturb it."

Aurora nodded—at least as much as a mollusk could nod. The Menorian slumped in her seat, boneless and blobby. Her skin turned deep purple, then flashed with swirls of gold and blue. A camera attached to her seat picked up the patterns—her species' language—and translated them into English.

"Yes, mistress of dark waters," the translator intoned in a calm, feminine voice. "We shall swim around the jagged boulder like a lone podling seeking not to wake a jaw-snapper of the depths."

Ben-Ari nodded. "Thank you, Aurora."

The mollusk gave another nod, then reached out her eight tentacles. The digits manipulated eight holographic interfaces that hovered around the pilot. The *Lodestar* changed course, thrumming as it turned left, steering clear of the wall in space.

As they kept flying forward, the wall moved to block their passage.

Ben-Ari frowned.

Once again, they were on direct course to meet the wall.

"Aurora, fly around it!" Ben-Ari said.

The pilot hit more controls. The *Lodestar* thrummed unhappily and swerved, this time moving to the right.

Once more the wall moved, again blocking their course.

"Mistress, we're about to hit!" Aurora said.

"Full stop," Ben-Ari said.

With the hum of brakes and thrusters, the *Lodestar* came to a halt. The wall hovered before them, smooth and dark, just large enough to block their passage. Ben-Ari stared. She saw no bricks, no bolts, no mortar—just a wall of polished stone.

"Are we detecting anything?" she asked the professor. "Any radiation? Signals? Something?"

The professor looked up from his controls. "No, Captain. It's very curious. We seem to have discovered something completely unique."

"Wonderful," Ben-Ari muttered. She turned toward her communications officer, a young woman with a mop of red curls under her cap. "Lieutenant Hirsi, send out a message. Say hello. See if anyone answers."

The officer nodded. "Yes, Captain. Sending standard Earth greeting in two hundred languages." She hit a few buttons, then waited. "No response, ma'am."

"Feels like we're talking to the wall," Fish said, stepping back onto the bridge. Finally he had put on his uniform, though he still wore his shark-tooth necklace.

"Hilarious." Ben-Ari turned back toward Aurora. "Back up. Just a short distance. Then fly as fast as you can over the wall."

Aurora flashed yellow and green. "Yes, mistress of the dark seas."

The *Lodestar* reversed. The wall stood ahead, still, and Ben-Ari had the uncanny feeling that this black square was staring at them. For long moments they kept backing up, and the wall grew smaller and smaller.

They came to a halt. For a moment they hovered in place.

Then the engines roared.

The *Lodestar* charged forward and upward at top speed.

The wall shot up to meet them.

"Stop!" Ben-Ari shouted.

Aurora hit the brakes. The *Lodestar* rumbled to a halt. The bridge rattled. Alarms flashed. Crew members fell. Ben-Ari had to grab her seat, and the floor trembled beneath her feet.

They came to a stop only meters away from the wall. It hovered before them, impassive, silent, still.

Ben-Ari sneered.

"Aurora, fly upward in a direct path."

"Yes, mistress."

The *Lodestar* changed course. They began soaring. The wall followed. It curved above them, blocking their ascent. Once more, they screeched to a halt. The wall stood before them.

"Some kind of ancient guardian, I assume," the professor said, staring at the wall. "Protecting this sector of space. We should study it. Whatever civilization built this wall must possess astounding technology."

Ben-Ari sighed. "We have no time for games nor investigations. A guardian protecting its territory? Fine. We'll take a detour. Aurora, do a U-turn. Fly us a hundred million kilometers back from where we came. We'll take a detour, giving the wall a nice astronomical unit as a berth—too far to possibly disturb it. It'll add a few hours to our journey, but we can tolerate that."

As the starship was turning around, the professor's gaze followed the floating wall. He sighed.

"I hope to someday return and study this artifact," he said. "I hope that someday, when war ends, we humans can resume our true purpose: exploration and noble understanding."

Has that ever been our true purpose? Ben-Ari wondered. Throughout history, it seemed to her, humanity had fought wars, had struggled, had faced evil, sometimes falling to darkness, sometimes rising from ashes with new fire. To the professor, perhaps, humanity found nobility in understanding. Ben-Ari often felt that she understood too much—about the nature of evil, about darkness and despair. To her, human nobility was found in struggle, in shining light in darkness.

Yet perhaps that was exactly what the professor was doing too, what all science did. It lit the darkness. A single candle in the night.

Perhaps we soldiers and scientists aren't that different.

They began to fly away, leaving the wall and its mysteries behind.

And the wall followed.

It shot overhead, so fast it appeared as a blur, and descended ahead of them, blocking their retreat.

Ben-Ari cursed as Aurora hit the brakes. The *Lodestar* again slammed to a halt, rattling the ship. Again crew members fell, and alarms blared. They stopped only meters away from crashing into the wall.

"Aurora, do whatever you can to get past that thing!" Ben-Ari said.

The pilot nodded. She flew upward, downward, side to side. Wherever they moved, the wall followed. No matter how fast Aurora flew, the wall was faster. Ben-Ari felt like the ball in a game of Pong.

"Full stop," Ben-Ari said. They came to a halt, the wall once more ahead of them. "I've had enough of this. Lieutenant Hirsi, open another communication channel. Connect it to my mic."

The young officer nodded. "Yes, Captain. Connecting … You're on."

Ben-Ari walked toward the edge of the bridge. In the circular room, with its viewports covering every surface, it felt like standing face-to-face with the artifact.

"Alien vessel!" she said. "I am Einav Ben-Ari, Captain of the ESS *Lodestar*. You are preventing passage of a diplomatic vessel through neutral space! If you do not move aside, we will be forced to destroy you."

No reply came.

Ben-Ari turned toward her crew.

"Suggestions?"

They stared at her. Professor Noah Isaac, her chief science officer and second in command. Richie "Fish" Fishburne, her exobiologist. Aurora, her pilot. Half a dozen junior officers. They were all silent, out of ideas.

It was Lieutenant Commander Niilo Virtanen, her new security officer, who stepped toward her.

Last year, her old security officer—the famous martial artist Mario Marino—had betrayed her. She had killed him herself. Niilo had joined them only weeks ago, replacing the traitor. He was a towering, burly man, hailing from the hinterlands of Finland, and liked to boast of his Viking blood. His hair was long and platinum, so pale it was almost white, and hung down to his waist. His beard was just as blond and forked into two braids. A medallion shaped like a drinking horn hung around his neck. He wore a HOPE uniform—navy blue with brass buttons—but Ben-Ari imagined that he'd be more comfortable in furs and leather, rowing a raiding boat, an axe instead of a gun hanging from his side.

"I say we blast it apart, Captain," the Viking said, voice rumbling. "Our cannons will make short work of it."

The professor gasped. "This is a valuable, perhaps ancient piece of technology. We cannot simply blast it away. We are explorers. Not vandals."

"Wrong." Ben-Ari turned toward the professor. Her voice was hard. "We are soldiers."

The professor stared at her. She saw the feeling of betrayal in his eyes. It pained her to publicly contradict him. She loved him. But she had to make him understand.

"I am no soldier," the professor said softly.

"We all are." Ben-Ari's voice softened too. "Every man, woman, and child. Every human healthy or ill, strong or weak, young or old. We are all soldiers now. Our entire species is an army. Our entire species is at war. There will be time for exploration, for wisdom, for the beauty of understanding. Right now it is time for war. We need to reach the Galactic Alliance. We need to join their union, to seek their fleet. And that wall is in our way. And we will let nothing stand in our way." She turned toward Niilo. "Blast it away."

The towering Fin nodded. "Gladly, Captain."

The warrior returned to his control panel. Engines thrummed deep within the *Lodestar*. They watched as shells flew out.

The shells slammed into the wall and exploded.

Shrapnel flew through space.

When the dust settled, they all stared at the wall. Stains appeared there—the remains of the shells.

The wall itself was undamaged.

"Plasma blasts!" Ben-Ari said. "Melt that thing!"

They fired bolt after bolt of plasma. These weapons could melt through hulls of warships. They could liquefy asteroids. The inferno kept blazing, washing across the wall. When the fire finally died, the wall still stood, showing no sign of harm. They tried other weapons. Lasers. Even conventional bullets. They tried everything other than the *Lodestar*'s nuclear weapons, which Ben-Ari didn't want to risk at such close range. Nothing so much as scratched the wall.

"Curious," the professor said, tapping his chin. "I called the wall stone, but surely it's made of a different material, artificially created by brilliant chemists. I would love to fly out with a mobile lab and run some tests."

"Professor, the fate of humanity!" Ben-Ari said, letting her exasperation sound. "Remember?"

He nodded. "I do indeed, Captain. The first step in solving a problem is understanding the problem. We do not understand this wall."

"We don't have time for research," she said. "But I have an idea. We have two shuttles on this ship. We send one shuttle flying below the wall. Presumably, the wall will move down to block it. Then we fly over the wall. So far, even as it chased us among the stars, the wall has shown us only one facade. Why does it keep only one side facing us? It's possible that the other side of the wall is undefended, that we can destroy it from there."

"And if we can't?" the professor said. "Would we abandon the shuttle—and its pilot—behind?"

Ben-Ari shook her head. "We'll continue confusing the wall. Flying at it from two directions. If it's a simple algorithm, it'll follow whatever vessel approaches first, allowing the other vessel to pass through. We'll get our shuttle back."

Niilo, the towering security guard, stepped forth. The two golden braids of his forked beard swayed. He puffed out his massive chest.

"Allow me to fly the shuttle, Captain. I volunteer."

She shook her head. "No. I need you aboard." She turned toward Lieutenant Jordan Smith, one of the twins. "Jordan, you're a quick pilot. You'll man the shuttle. Don't worry. We won't leave you behind."

The young man smiled. "I'm Connor, Captain. That's Jordan." He pointed at his twin. "I'm the smart one. He's the good pilot."

The real Jordan bristled. "I'm smart!"

Ben-Ari cursed inwardly. She always got the twins confused. Only one of them had a bionic eye, but the damn thing was so lifelike.

"Jordan, come." She snapped her fingers. "Connor, you stay and keep helping Aurora."

Jordan rose and nodded. "Yes, Captain. It would be my honor."

Ben-Ari waited on the bridge as Jordan made his way to the shuttle bay. The wait seemed intolerably long. The wall kept hovering ahead, and she couldn't shake off the feeling of consciousness, of that black surface staring at her like the black eyes of the grays. Of something there mocking, calculating, and cruel.

Finally the shuttle emerged from the *Lodestar*. Ben-Ari saw it flying beneath her feet, heading toward the wall. It descended deeper and blasted forth, ready for an attempt to fly under the obstacle.

As expected, the mysterious wall began flying lower, prepared to block the shuttle.

"Fly over it!" Ben-Ari shouted. "Now!"

The *Lodestar* blasted forth.

Everything happened at once.

The shuttle kept flying. At the last moment, the wall seemed to notice the *Lodestar* attempting to fly over it. The wall changed course. It shot upward, flying to block the *Lodestar*, leaving the shuttle unmolested.

The *Lodestar* had to slam to a halt.

The shuttle almost made it under the wall.

And from the bottom of the wall, a beam of searing, blinding laser emerged.

The beam slammed into the shuttle. The small vessel exploded.

The *Lodestar* hovered before the wall. Below them, the shuttle was mere shards. Lieutenant Jordan Smith was gone.

Connor, his twin brother, stared with huge eyes. He let out a hoarse cry.

"Jordan," he whispered. "Jordan ..."

Ben-Ari stared at the wall.

She took a deep breath.

"Fire every goddamn weapon we have!" she shouted.

They fired. They fired everything. Plasma, shells, bullets, lasers. They pounded the wall with a force that could topple civilizations.

And the wall moved—toward them.

"Reverse, reverse!" Ben-Ari shouted, and Aurora grabbed controls, and the *Lodestar* began to move back, but the wall was too fast, and—

Viewports shattered.

The bridge shook so madly control boards ripped free from the floor.

Crew members shouted and fell, and klaxons blared. Robotic voices sounded across the bridge.

Front hull cracked. Front hull cracked.

Deck 17C breached!

Sealing off corridors 17I to 17K.

Ben-Ari reeled. She rose to her feet, stumbled toward a fallen control panel, and summoned a holographic diagram of the ship. The *Lodestar* was shaped like an old sailing vessel sans the masts. Now their prow had crumbled. Their figurehead—Eos, the Greek goddess of travel—hung loosely. Cracks ran across the front of the ship.

"Casualty report!" she barked.

A robotic voice answered. "Eight crew members no longer show signs of life. Number of wounded—unknown."

Reports came in from the medical bays. Already the paramedics were rushing into the breached bays, wearing helmets, trying to rescue whoever they could. Ben-Ari knew that when the dust settled, the casualty count would climb.

Kneeling, Ben-Ari looked up. Through strands of loose hair, she stared at one of the monitors that still functioned.

She stared at the floating wall in space.

She rose to her feet.

She opened a communication channel and spoke in a cold, hard voice. "Who are you?"

Ahead of them, the wall changed.

Its surface bloated, bubbling outward in a thousand black boils. The dark tumors took form, becoming a twisted, leering face.

Across the bridge, officers gasped.

With hard eyes, Ben-Ari stared at the face on the wall.

It was a massive face, as tall as the *Lodestar*. The eyes were black pits, the mouth wide and filled with black teeth. There was no color, just that black stone, twisting, staring.

And the face on the wall spoke.

"I ... am ... Beleth."

Ben-Ari squared her shoulders. "I am Captain Einav Ben-Ari of Earth. Beleth, you have carried out an attack on a starship of Earth. Move aside now, and resist us no further, or we will consider your hostility a declaration of war."

Beleth laughed. The deep, grumbling sound emerged from every speaker on the *Lodestar*, reverberating through the ship.

"Humans … So violent. So aggressive. So quick to declare war. Such barbarous, pathetic apes."

"You are the one who greeted us with aggression!" Ben-Ari said. "You destroyed one of our shuttles! You rammed into our hull!"

Beleth sneered. His deep voice rumbled. "Your little vessel almost fled me. I could not allow that, Captain. You are my toy-things. You are my slaves. Rebel against me again, and more of you shall die."

The face melted back into the wall.

Ben-Ari stood for a moment, staring.

Then she spun around and began walking toward the elevator.

"Fish!" she barked. "Niilo! With me." She paused, then turned toward Lieutenant Connor Smith. "You too, Connor. Come with us."

The young officer nodded, eyes still damp. His twin brother had died only moments ago, but he joined them, chin held high, back straight.

"Yes, ma'am!" the young officer said, voice trembling yet determined.

Before they could reach the elevator, the professor rushed toward them.

"Einav, what are you planning?" the professor said.

"I'm going out there," Ben-Ari said. "In a spacesuit. I'm going to land on that damn wall and climb over it. Fish, Niilo, and Connor are coming with me."

The professor's eyes widened. "The wall will shoot you when you approach. You saw what it did to our shuttle."

"That's why you'll blind it," Ben-Ari said. "When I give the signal, blast out lights. Crank up those lights as bright as you can. Blind the son of a bitch."

The professor still blocked her passage to the elevator, himself like a wall.

"Even if you can make it over the wall," he said, "what do you expect to find?"

Ben-Ari smiled thinly. "The unknown." On a whim, she kissed the professor's cheek. "Your favorite thing. You have command of the bridge, Noah."

She left the bridge. She walked down a corridor past running engineers and technicians, under flashing lights, over shattered glass. Two medics raced by, carrying a wounded man on a litter. With Fish, Niilo, and Connor, she made her way to the armory.

They pulled on armored spacesuits with jetpacks. Niilo was so large they had made him a custom suit when he had joined the ship. They grabbed rifles and climbing gear—suction cups that attached to their boots and gloves, able to pump out air to work in vacuum. They headed toward the airlock.

Ben-Ari spoke into the communicator built into her prosthetic arm.

"Professor?"

Isaac's voice emerged from the speakers. "Here, Captain."

"We're ready to fly out. Ready to turn on the lights?"

The professor paused. "Captain, I've done the math. I can reroute energy from other systems to produce an intense beam. Enough to burn your eyes."

"We won't look directly at the light."

"That won't be enough, Captain. You'll have to set your visors to maximum radiation. And keep your eyes closed. I also recommend covering your eyes with cloth inside your helmet. I'm not kidding. Stuff your helmets with towels."

"Understood," Ben-Ari said.

She had an ensign run to fetch towels, and they covered their eyes, then placed on their helmets and set the visors to black. No light would reach their eyes. She walked blindly toward the edge of the airlock. The four of them stood together. Ben-Ari. Fish. Niilo. Young Connor. All four of them—blind, communicating with the microphones built into their helmets.

Fish grumbled. "We're like blind bats trying to catch a black wombat under a new moon."

Niilo laughed. "Simply fly straight, little man. A big wall is hard to miss."

Fish scoffed. "Little man? I'm over six feet tall, you know, and weigh two hundred pounds."

The hulking security officer snorted. "As I said. Little man."

"Enough," Ben-Ari said. "Your helmet can still provide audio coordinates. Rely on your hearing. And stay inside the professor's beam. So long as we fly in the beam, Beleth won't see us. Understood?"

"Understood," said her crew, speaking together.

"Good," Ben-Ari said, then spoke into her communicator. "Professor, are we ready?"

His voice emerged from her communicator. "Ready. Godspeed, Captain."

She nodded and blindly hit the airlock controls.

The air whooshed out of the ship.

Ben-Ari leaped into space.

An instant later, the lights turned on.

She had her eyes closed, wrapped in a towel, hidden behind a black visor. And she still *saw* that light. She *felt* that light. It blazed over her, searing hot. It thrummed in her ears. She screwed her eyes tighter, grimacing, and kept flying. Her helmet read out her coordinates. She hit her jetpack's thruster, flying faster. She could hear Niilo and Fish breathing through her communicator.

"Almost there, boys!" she said. "Hold on!"

"Captain!" It was Connor's voice. "Captain, where are you? I'm not sure where I'm flying!"

"Stay cool, Connor," Ben-Ari said. "Follow your helmet's instructions."

"Captain, I can't see!" Connor was panicking now. "I have to take the visor off! I'm flying too far. I—"

"Connor, calm yourself!" Ben-Ari said.

"I can't feel the beam anymore!" Conner shouted. "I'm out of the light! Captain, I'm spinning, I—"

Searing heat flared nearby.

Connor screamed.

Then his voice went silent.

A grumbling laughter rose—Beleth's laughter.

Ben-Ari gritted her teeth and kept flying.

Her helmet spoke in her ears. *Impact in ten, nine, eight* ...

Ben-Ari slowed down. She braced for impact. She hit the wall. An instant later, she heard two more thuds—Niilo and Fish hitting the wall with her.

"Climb!" she said.

They climbed up the wall, using their vacuum-enabled, air-pumping suction cups. HOPE loved its gadgets, and Ben-Ari was grateful.

And as she was climbing, she felt the wall change.

Its smooth form grew tumorous bulbs. She struggled to cling on. They climbed faster. She felt features form. The wall was growing a face again—a face the size of a house. She heard a rumbling voice.

"Turn off the light!" Beleth roared, voice twisted with fury. "Do you think you can defeat me with simple lights, humans?" The creature's voice rose even louder. "Turn them off!"

"Captain?" The professor's voice emerged from her communicator.

"Give me ten more seconds!" she said.

She kept climbing, faster now. Niilo and Fish were with her; she heard them breathing.

"Turn off the light!" Beleth rumbled. "Turn it off now! Turn it off or you shall die!"

The searing beam from the *Lodestar* shut off.

Ben-Ari shook her head wildly, letting the towel drop off her eyes, and saw the top of the wall. With a burst from her jetpack, she reached the top and dived overboard. Fish and Niilo dived with her.

They plunged down.

They had made it over the wall.

They stared at the far side, and Ben-Ari gasped.

"It's not a wall," she whispered. "It's not a wall at all. It's a starship."

On this side, instead of a smooth surface, she saw many features. Exhaust pipes. Domes. Vents. Lights. It was a massive machine.

And she saw an airlock.

She glanced at her companions. Fish and Niilo too had shaken off the towels from their eyes. She pointed at the airlock. They nodded. Rifles held before them, the three walked across the hull, their suction cups holding them in place. The alien ship was rumbling as, on the opposite side, the face spoke. Its voice trembled up Ben-Ari's boots.

"If you turn on that beam again, humans, I will destroy you! I am Beleth! I am a god, and you are my slaves! You will behave, or I shall smite you!"

Good. Beleth was too furious with the *Lodestar* to notice the three humans walking across his inner side. Ben-Ari had no idea what Beleth was. A lifeform inside this ship, projecting its face onto the hull? An AI system? The name of this entire flat starship?

We're about to find out.

She reached the airlock and yanked the door open. She stepped into the vessel, and Fish and Niilo followed.

The airlock was small, dark, and dusty. It seemed like nobody had been here in years. Cobwebs covered the controls, and tiny creatures—they looked like spiders with a hundred legs—scurried over the webs. She cleared away cobwebs and found an inner door. It jammed, and it took Niilo to shove it open. The crew entered a low, narrow hallway. They had to walk stooped over. All the while, the ship shook, and they heard Beleth rumbling.

"Foolish humans! Do not try to escape me! I am Beleth! Your starship is my toy. You must do what I say. Disobey me again and suffer!"

Yet as they kept walking down the corridor, passing through dust and cobwebs, they heard another voice. A high-pitched voice. Female. A voice that sounded less cruel and more … cranky.

It's a little girl's voice, Ben-Ari thought.

"You are my toys!" The voice grew louder, whinier. "You must do what I say! You must or I'll punish you."

As the girlish voice whined, Beleth's deep, booming voice spoke in unison.

Ben-Ari looked at her companions. They stared back and shrugged. They kept walking through the alien starship, following the voice.

They reached a round chamber. Dozens of iron braziers hovered, filled with luminous orange orbs. Pipes covered the ceiling and floor, pulsing with yellow liquid. A round monitor hung from one wall, rimmed with iron, displaying a view of the *Lodestar*.

The high-pitched voice filled the chamber.

"Good. Good, humans. Now you're behaving!"

Ben-Ari froze and reached for her gun, then realized the voice was referring to the *Lodestar*.

"Don't move again! Don't shine any more lights! I, Beleth, am a wrathful god. I will not tolerate disobedient slaves."

Ben-Ari frowned. Both voices were speaking in unison. The deep voice was distant now. The high-pitched, whiny voice was closer. It came from an iron cauldron in the center of the chamber.

Ben-Ari stepped closer. Fish and Niilo walked at her sides, guns raised. They reached the cauldron, leaned over the rim, and stared inside.

Ben-Ari's eyes widened.

Dear lord, she thought.

"Cute little bugger!" Fish said. "Like a bald little wallaby."

Niilo grumbled. "Ugly critter."

An alien lay inside the cauldron. She was small, no larger than a toddler. Her body was blobby, lined with several limbs that could manipulate control panels inside the cauldron. She had no head, but a face grew on her body. She stared up with large blue eyes. A small mouth opened, lined with sharp teeth.

"I'm not ugly!" Her eyes dampened. "You're mean! You're a bully! I hate you!"

The alien burst into tears.

"My God," Ben-Ari whispered. "She's a child."

"I'm not a child!" the alien blurted. "I'm three hundred and four. I'm big! Go away!"

Ben-Ari frowned and accessed the interface built into her prosthetic arm. When she patched into the *Lodestar*'s cameras, she saw that Beleth—the face on the wall—was mimicking this little alien's facial expressions and repeating her words. Inside the cauldron, she saw what looked like a camera. Ben-Ari covered the camera with her towel, the one she had used on her eyes. At once, the face of Beleth vanished off the alien ship's flat hull.

Just an illusion, she thought. *Just this little girl's alter ego.*

"All right," Ben-Ari said softly. "You're a big girl." She reached into the cauldron and stroked the alien. Her skin was clammy and rubbery. "I'm sorry that we frightened you."

"I'm not scared of anything," the alien said. "You didn't scare me." She pointed at the monitor that showed the *Lodestar.* "That's my toy. It's mine!"

"What's your name?" she said. "Your real name?"

"Call me Beleth," the alien said.

Ben-Ari shook her head. "I won't. That's the name of a demon from Earth mythology. You chose that name to frighten us. You obviously know something about us. Tell me something about yourself. Tell me your true name."

The alien scoffed. "You would not be able to pronounce it."

"I say we call her Wilma," said Fish. "Aww, isn't Wilma a beautiful little bludger?" He reached down and lifted the alien. "Little cutie."

Ben-Ari glared at her exobiologist. "This little cutie killed ten of my crew members."

Fish had the grace to look ashamed. "You're right, Captain. I get excited when I meet aliens."

He leaned down, about to return the alien to the cauldron. But the small creature clung to him.

"Don't put me down," the alien said. "Carry me. It's been so long. So long since somebody held me."

Niilo stepped forward, fists clenched. The burly warrior turned red beneath his yellow beard. "I don't care how adorable you think that little monster is, Fish. It murdered our crewmates. It dies now." He raised a fist. "I will kill it myself."

The alien whimpered and cowered. "No. Don't let him hurt me! I'm sorry. I'm sorry!" Tears flowed from her eyes. "I was lonely. I just wanted a toy. I don't know where my parents are." She trembled, weeping. "They left me out here. They said I was a bad girl. That was years ago. I'm scared. I'm so alone. Don't hurt me! I just wanted to play."

Fish looked at Ben-Ari. "Can we take her with us, Captain? She's scared."

Niilo growled. "We must kill it. We must avenge our crew."

Ben-Ari thought for a moment. Take this alien with them? An alien who had already killed ten humans? No. She would not place this creature on their ship. It was too dangerous. Kill her? Perhaps she should. Yet it felt wrong to kill what was obviously a child—even if Beleth was centuries old.

I know something of being a scared, angry little girl, Ben-Ari thought, thinking back to her own lonely childhood.

"Put her back down, Fish," she said softly. "Back into her bowl."

The exobiologist's eyes widened, but he nodded. He placed the alien back into the cauldron.

"Good," said Niilo. "We kill it. I will make it painless. Mostly."

Ben-Ari shook her head. "No."

Niilo inhaled sharply. "You will let this creature live? Let it remain in its starship? After it killed our crew?"

She gazed at the alien. Beleth—or whatever her true name was—lay there, a blob with many limbs and damp eyes.

She's barely even a child, she thought. *She's a toddler who doesn't know her own strength.*

"Fish," Ben-Ari said, "do you still have those Orionite hound-beetles in the Lodestar's biolab?"

"Yes, Captain," he said. "Marvelous little creatures. As lovable as dogs, as durable as tardigrades. Just had a litter of cubs."

"Good." She nodded. "Fly out. Choose one of the cubs. And bring it back here."

Fish's mouth hung open, but then his eyes softened. He nodded. "Aye, Captain."

He left the alien bridge, and in the monitor, Ben-Ari could see Fish flying toward the *Lodestar*. He soon returned, carrying a juvenile hound-beetle. It was a fluffy, purple critter the size of a house cat, a smooth black shell topping its back. Fish placed the cub inside the cauldron. Beleth caressed it, and the animal purred.

"Would you let us pass by, Beleth?" Ben-Ari said. "In exchange for this gift? Isn't this better than an old starship?"

Beleth patted the hound-beetle. The cub nuzzled her.

"His fur is soft," Beleth said. "And his shell is hard and smooth. Is he smart?"

"As smart as dogs on Earth," Ben-Ari said. "He'll be a good companion."

Beleth hugged her pet. She looked at Ben-Ari with damp eyes. "I'm sorry. I'm sorry for being bad. You may pass. If you're not angry at me."

Even Niilo's rage seemed to subside. The giant loosened his fists.

"You are a special woman, Captain Ben-Ari," the burly Viking said. "And a damn fine soldier. A true shieldmaiden."

Ben-Ari smiled and placed her hand on his broad chest. The top of her head didn't even reach his shoulders. "Thank you, Niilo. I'm sorry you didn't get to crush anyone to death with your bare hands on this mission. Maybe next time."

They flew back to the *Lodestar*. When they stepped back onto the bridge, they saw the alien wall descending until it vanished in the darkness.

Ben-Ari cleared her throat. "Aurora, continue on our course to the Galactic Alliance headquarters. Full speed ahead."

The mollusk flashed gold and blue. "Yes, mistress."

Aurora hit a few buttons, and the *Lodestar* thrummed and flew—dented, battered, and still exploring the darkness.

The professor came to stand beside Ben-Ari. He looked at her, one eyebrow raised.

"What did you find behind that wall, Einav?"

She turned and gazed back into space. In the distance behind the *Lodestar*, she could see a glint—the starlight reflecting on the alien starship.

"A girl," she said softly. "A girl who needed a puppy."

The professor's second eyebrow rose. He opened his mouth, ready to ask another question, but then shut it, perhaps seeing sadness in Ben-Ari's eyes. He nodded.

"Quite curious," he mumbled under his breath and returned to his workstation.

The *Lodestar* flew onward, delving deeper into the unknown.

CHAPTER THREE

As the mechas approached Earth, Marco's heart sank.

"We're too late," he whispered. "Oh God. We're too late."

Even from here, he could see the devastation. The husks of dead warships guarded Earth like ghosts. The satellites were gone. Debris hovered in space—shattered cockpits, burnt chunks of metal, and corpses. A dead Firebird lost its orbit and plunged down to Earth, burning up in the atmosphere. Down on the surface, things seemed dire too. When Marco zoomed in, he could see smoldering battlefields. Thousands of charred tanks. Mass graves. Burnt cities.

Among them all lay shattered saucers.

"The grays were here," Marco said. "Thousands of them."

"The grays lost!" Addy said. "Look, Marco. All those saucers? They're burned up. We won this battle! And thanks to these mechas, we'll win the next one too."

He was flying inside Kaiyo, the male mecha. He used the giant's hammer to knock aside debris. Addy flew beside him inside Kaji, the female mecha. When a burnt saucer hovered toward her, she sliced it with her sword.

"Earth's fleet is gone," Marco whispered, staring at the floating wreckage of a massive warship. Thousands of soldiers must have once served aboard it. Now holes filled its hull. The insides were burned out. A crack gaped open like a screaming mouth, revealing a charred engine room.

"No," Addy said. "*We* are Earth's fleet."

Communication signals began coming in from the planet, voices warning that missiles were aiming at the mechas, were ready to blast them apart. Marco grabbed his communicator.

"This is Lieutenant Marco Emery!" After so long as an enlisted man, it still felt strange to refer to himself as an officer. President Petty had given him a battle commission two years ago, but the rank still felt like the wrong pair of shoes. "Lieutenant Addy Linden is here too. We're a bit late to the battle, sadly."

"But we brought cookies!" Addy said.

For a few moments, silence.

Then President Petty's voice emerged from the speakers.

"Emery. Linden. Thank goodness you're here. What the hell are those things you're flying?"

"The cavalry," Addy said.

The general-turned-president grunted. "Land them at the coordinates I'm feeding you. We've got a lot to discuss."

"Yes, sir," Marco said. "I would request that medics await us. We bring the survivors of Titan with us. They need help."

"The medics will be there," Petty said.

Marco fed the coordinates into his navigation system. He was surprised to see the destination—Jerusalem.

He knew of Jerusalem, of course. It was among Earth's most ancient cities, the birthplace of Abrahamic religions, a city conquered and destroyed and rebuilt time and time again. The scum had destroyed Jerusalem during the Cataclysm, killing half a million of its residents—nearly the entire city. Only a few had fled from the devastation.

The history was impressive, but Marco had a personal connection to the city. Einav Ben-Ari, his commanding officer and dear friend, was from Jerusalem. Or at least her family was; her father had been born in Jerusalem before the scum had destroyed it. The city had lain in ruins since. Its refugees had found new homes in the military, had never rebuilt their city. But Marco knew that Einav Ben-Ari, though raised as a military brat, still considered Jerusalem her hometown.

Why there? Marco wondered. *Why are we to land among ancient ruins?*

Kaiyo and Kaji entered the atmosphere and flew toward the Middle East. Marco gazed at the deserts sprawling below him. He saw tan mountains, rolling dunes, the land that had birthed Judaism, Christianity, Islam, and many other faiths. A mountain rose from the desert, and upon it he saw the ancient city.

Jerusalem. At a staggering five thousand years old, it was among the oldest cities on Earth. Throughout most of that time, humans had fought over it. The Israelites, the Ottomans, the Crusaders—century after century, nation after nation had tried to conquer the holy city. It had been attacked, conquered, and destroyed dozens of times. Today it lay in ruins. Ancient walls and gateways. Domes. Houses of worship, some dating back thousands of years. All lay crumbling, abandoned, filled with ghosts.

It was here that King David had reigned. Here that King Solomon had built the Temple. Here that Jesus had preached and died. Here that the scum had first struck.

And now another great event will occur here, Marco thought. *Now Earth musters among these ruins.*

The city's inhabitants had perhaps perished or fled. But new life now filled these ruins.

The Human Defense Force.

Their bases sprawled across the mountaintop between ancient domes and minarets. Tanks rumbled along cobbled streets. Soldiers in olive-green fatigues manned ancient walls where soldiers had fought thousands of years ago.

The coordinates led the mechas to a sandy hill. They landed with clouds of smoke and dust. It was here that the ancient Hebrew priests had reigned, here that Jesus had been crucified, here that so much of history had played out—was still playing out.

The dust settled, and the medics rushed forth. The survivors of Titan—along with their hybrid children—were taken to infirmaries. The mothers would need prosthetic feet, nourishment, and counseling. Marco knew that shell shock could be worse than physical wounds; he had suffered enough of both in his life. He could not imagine what life awaited the hybrid babies, no more than he knew why the grays had created them.

Petty met them among the sandy ruins. The gruff old soldier still looked uncomfortable in his suit; Marco had always imagined him as the sort of soldier who slept in full uniform. Marco and Addy both saluted. They were only in the reserves now, and Petty was no longer a general, but saluting felt right. Petty greeted them with a grunt, raised his head, and gazed at the mechas. The two machines stood in the dust, towering over Jerusalem, two skyscrapers here in these biblical desert ruins.

"The cavalry, huh?" he said.

Addy nodded. "Did the job on Titan, sir. Will do the job if those sneaky gray fucks attack Earth again. I'm sorry we missed the first round. Can't fucking wait for the second."

Marco nearly fainted. He glared at her. "Addy! You can't curse around the president!"

She looked at him. "Why the fuck not?"

Marco wanted the ground to swallow him. "Addy! He's the president of the Alliance of Nations!"

Addy scoffed. "I bow to no one. No dogs, no hamsters."

Marco rolled his eyes. "The saying is: No gods, no masters."

"Ah!" Addy nodded. "You know, that makes a lot more sense. And explains some weird looks I got when returning sandwiches at the deli."

Petty stepped closer to them. Sand filled his grizzled hair. He furrowed his heavy brow over his dark eyes. He bared his teeth and glowered at Addy.

"Lieutenant Linden," he growled, "you are a goddamn fucking pain in the ass. But I'm glad to see you."

And to Marco's shock, the president pulled Addy into a crushing hug and lifted her off her feet. He then gripped Marco's hand, squeezed nearly strong enough to break it, and slapped Marco on the back.

"I'm glad to see both of you. Now come with me. There's a special visitor waiting to see you. Somebody you haven't seen in a very long time."

Addy's eyes widened. "Is it the Pillowman?"

Marco groaned. "Addy, shut up."

They followed the general through the ruins, passing between palm trees, under crumbling archways, and around fallen columns. Soldiers bustled around them, and Humvees roared along sandy roads.

"Is it a pigman?" Addy said, hopping after the general. "I once saw a pigman at High Park, you know."

Marco rolled his eyes. "It's not a pigman, Addy."

"How do you know? It could be! Pigmen are very secretive, you know, and this is a secret military outpost. Maybe he's used to sniff our land mines." She gasped. "Wait a minute. Is it Lil' Pupper, that three-legged dog I once found when I was a drill sergeant?"

The general only grunted and kept walking through the ruins. They followed, passed under an orphaned archway, and stepped across a cobbled courtyard where a stray camel brayed. A handful of soldiers stood here, helmets sandy, rifles in hand, guarding an ancient church.

Churches back in Canada were sometimes two or three centuries old. In Europe they dated back to medieval times. *This* building looked *thousands* of years old. Its bricks were tan and craggy, and weeds grew between them. A robed monk prayed in the courtyard.

We're walking where Christ walked, Marco thought, *where King David fought a thousand years before Christ. Every brick beneath my feet saw millennia of history.*

He had seen many wonders in space, many ruins older than these. But here was so much human history that his head spun.

The guards stepped aside, and they entered the church.

Soldiers bustled through the nave. Control panels and workstations filled the place. A shaft had been carved into the floor, and they climbed down to a network of modern bunkers. More soldiers rushed back and forth here underground, and doorways led to chambers filled with computers, monitors, and maps. Many of the officers here were high ranking, stars or even phoenixes on their shoulders. Here were generals.

It's the command center of the HDF, Marco thought, feeling woozy. *The hidden heart of the military.*

"When do we get to meet this person from our past?" Addy was bouncing with excitement. "I can't wait!"

Petty led them down a corridor, opened a doorway, and gestured at a room.

Marco and Addy stepped inside.

It was a small lounge, the size of a bedroom, with two couches and soft drinks on a table. Tail wagging, a Doberman stood under a poster of an old starfighter. Lailani rose from one of the couches and waved.

"Oh." Addy's chest deflated. "It's just de la Rosa."

"Hey!" Lailani said.

"Sorry, Tiny," Addy said. "But I thought you were a pigman."

Lailani tilted her head. She looked at Marco questioningly.

"Forget it, Lailani," Marco said. "It's Addy." He stepped toward Lailani and embraced her. "Glad to see you again. I missed you."

She smiled and squeezed him in her arms. "Good to see you too, Marco."

Addy joined the embrace, nearly crushing them. "Aww, I love ya, Lailani. You know that, right? I love ya to bits. It's just that Petty told me somebody from my past is here. I know I haven't seen you in a few months, but I thought Petty meant somebody from way back."

Lailani pulled away from the embrace. She bit her lip and twisted her fingers. "Actually … Petty was right." She turned toward a doorway that led to a kitchen. "Come say hi."

A young soldier stepped into the lounge. He was thin, and he wore dusty battle fatigues stitched with the insignia of a private. His face was sharp, his sideburns long. He gave them a shy wave, followed by a karate chop.

"Hey there, hound dogs."

Marco nearly fainted.

Addy gasped.

They stared, silent, shocked.

Before them, back from the dead, stood Benny "Elvis" Ray.

* * * * *

Lailani sat quietly on the couch, gazing at the boisterous reunion.

"I cannot believe this!" Addy roared. "I *cannot* believe this!" She grabbed Elvis, crushed him in an embrace, and lifted him right off the floor. "You goddamn little fucker! We should call you Marty McFly, not Elvis."

Marco kept rubbing his eyes, staring at his old friend. "You … She …" He looked at Lailani. "You traveled back in time? And brought him here? I …" He rubbed his eyes again. "I can't believe this!" Then he shed tears, and he embraced Elvis again. "I can't believe you're back!"

The three spent long moments laughing, crying, embracing, speaking of Lailani's daring rescue through time. Epimetheus was one of the gang, wagging his tail and jumping on everyone.

All the while, Lailani sat quietly, watching from the corner.

I did this, she thought. *I changed time. And it feels so wrong.* She thought back to the tear in the universe. That gaping pit she had created. *And I'm scared.*

She had saved Elvis. But she had failed to save Sofia.

Don't let Sofia drop! she had cried to her younger self.

But it hadn't worked. She had returned to the present day, to the year 2155. And Sofia was nowhere to be found. And Lailani still remembered her lover falling into the fire. Remembered trying to grab her. Remembered watching Sofia die.

I changed the past. But I could not save her. I need to go back again. I need to save her. But I broke spacetime. I left a hole in the universe. And now—

Sudden pain flashed across her.

Visions danced.

Time. Time flowed and crashed and branched off.

She saw herself as a child, huddling in a shantytown, her body that of a rotten centipede.

She saw herself as an old woman, hunched over, and a hooded figure leaned over her, placing claws on her chest.

She saw her friends dying upon ankhs.

She saw a ring of crystals, hovering like a Ferris wheel, and in the middle hung a bloated, deformed creature with skin sewn over his eye sockets. His jaw was long and lined with teeth, drooling, and a hundred arms grew from his body. He raised his wrinkled head toward Lailani and smiled.

She screamed.

"Lailani!" Marco rushed toward her. "Lailani, are you all right?"

She gasped for air. The visions cleared. Epimetheus leaped up beside her, licking, calming her.

"I'm fine," Lailani whispered. "I … I'm fine. Just …" She touched the back of her head. "The new chip. It acts up sometimes."

They were all staring at her, silent, concern in their eyes.

Lailani forced herself to smile shakily.

"So hey, remember that time at boot camp, how Elvis started singing 'Suspicious Minds' in the showers, and the entire squad joined in?"

"I remember like it was yesterday," Elvis said.

"It *was* yesterday for you," Addy said. "God, those fucking communal showers. I remember how Marco use to try to sneak peeks at de la Rosa's tits."

Marco flushed deep crimson. "Addy! I did not." He glanced at Lailani, turning even redder. "I did not, Lailani."

"I believe you." She patted her chest and sighed. "You'd need a microscope."

They kept reminiscing, retelling the old stories. How during high alert, confined to their tent for hours, they had peed into milk cartons and juice bottles, only for Sergeant Singh to trip on them. They imitated the gruff mess hall cook who exploded with fury if you asked for a second slice of Spam, and they remembered how Sheriff had fried up—and smuggled out—pancakes during his kitchen duty. They reenacted the old propaganda reels, chanting together, "This is why we fight!" And they laughed. And by God, it was like the old days again.

"It's so strange," Elvis said softly after a lull in the conversation. "This all just happened a few weeks ago for me. I'm still eighteen. For you it's been eleven years. You guys are almost thirty now." He shook his head in wonder. "I mean, de la Rosa still looks like a kid. She's barely aged. But you, Marco. Look at you! You're an adult now. And you, Addy—"

"What?" Addy grew red in the face. She grabbed Elvis's collar and twisted it. "Don't you *dare* mention how I gained weight! Don't you *dare* say I have crow's feet! I might be older, and my ass might be bigger, but I'm still stronger than you, and—"

"Actually, Addy," Elvis said, "I was going to say that you look more beautiful than ever."

She loosened her grip on his collar. "Aww. Such a smoothie." She mussed his hair. "And you still look like Elvis's scrawny kid brother."

"And I just cannot believe that you and Poet are now a couple." Elvis looked at Marco, then back at Addy. "I mean, aren't you two brother and sister or something?"

"No!" they both blurted out together.

"Eww, don't say that," Addy said and shuddered.

"She only lived in my house for a few years," Marco said.

"Not even!" Addy said. "And I barely even saw him there. Eww."

Marco sat beside Lailani on the couch. "So you can time travel now. You still have the hourglass?"

Lailani nodded. "Yes. And yes. At least I can time travel once or twice more. Until the hourglass runs out of sand. Every time you use it, more sand burns up."

Marco glanced at the others, then at Lailani. "Have you decided how else to use the hourglass? There are so many people we lost. Family. Friends."

They were all silent for a moment. Marco, Addy, and Elvis all lowered their heads. Lailani knew they were thinking of their fallen loved ones.

Lailani wanted to tell them. About the tear in the universe. About the visions of twisting, shattering time. About what HOBBS had told her, how time travel could create paradoxes, could destroy the galaxy.

Instead Lailani said, "I can't go back again. President Petty won't let me. We only have enough sand for another round-trip. He wants to go to the future, Marco. A million years to the future. To where the grays have their empire. He wants to hit them on their own turf."

Marco's eyes widened. "A million years in the future …" He looked back at Addy. "So we were right. The grays are evolved humans."

Lailani nodded. "Yes. They're humans from a million AD. Highly evolved. To them, we're just cavemen. And sooner or later, Petty said, they'll strike us again. It could be any day now. Ben-Ari flew out into space to seek allies, but we can't just count on her. What if she fails? Petty said we need to destroy the grays before they destroy us. And now we can." She opened her pack, pulled out the hourglass, and showed it to them. "With this. We open a portal to the future. We fly a million years ahead. And we kill those fucking creatures."

Addy leaped off the couch. "Fuck yeah! I'm going!" She gave a wild kick. "Time to kick some gray asses!" She punched the air. "I'm gonna punch them right in their giant, fucking gray heads!" She grabbed Marco. "And you're coming with me, Poet."

Marco turned ashen. "Maybe we should let somebody else go. Does it have to always be us who save the world?"

Addy nodded. "Yep. We're the best at it. And besides, we love it! We love killing aliens!"

Marco now turned green. "I don't love it."

She wrapped her arm around his neck and mussed his hair. "Sure you do!"

He shoved her away. "Get off, you lunatic. I never wanted to kill aliens, just to read books."

She shoved a book at him. "Here. Read some *Freaks of the Galaxy*. Just be careful with it. It's my favorite book."

"It's your *only* book," Marco said.

"Not true!" Addy said. "I also own that art book."

"Addy, that's a children's coloring book. And you made all the drawings indecent."

She nodded. "I'm a misunderstood artist."

"You're a misunderstood freak," Marco muttered. "You should be in *Freaks of the Galaxy*."

Addy gasped. "I'd be honored! Aww, Poet, that's the sweetest thing you've ever said to me." She kissed his cheek.

He sighed. "You know that I've said that you're beautiful, brave, and amazing, and that I love you, right?"

Addy nodded. "I know. But I'd rather be a freak."

The door opened. President Petty stood there with several guards. The friends all rose and stood at attention.

"De la Rosa," the president said. "We need you."

Lailani nodded and approached him, thankful for the distraction. She had become uncomfortable in this room. The old banter, the old friendships, the old memories—it all felt too wrong, too confusing, the past and present mixing together. She couldn't stop seeing that tear in space. Couldn't stop feeling only half here, slipping from reality.

How many miles to Babylon?

The song echoed in her mind.

I don't know. I don't know. I have no more candlelight.

She joined General Petty, and they left her friends behind in the lounge. They walked down a bustling corridor here beneath Jerusalem, the new headquarters of the HDF. Once more she wore an HDF uniform—olive-green trousers, a buttoned shirt, leather boots, a black beret. They had promoted her—along with Marco and Addy—to captain. Three stars now shone on each of her shoulders. She was a higher rank now than Ben-Ari had been during the Scum War. It was strange to contemplate.

What would that young girl at boot camp, a scared Filipina with a shaved head and scarred wrists, think of me now, a captain and war heroine? I still remember thinking that Ensign Ben-Ari, who was just twenty back then, was a goddess. Now twenty seems so young.

"Mister President," Lailani said, "where are we going?"

Petty walked at her side, stiff, staring ahead. His graying hair had gone completely white at the temples, and he still kept it buzzed like a soldier.

"To find answers," he said.

He led her to a steel blast door. Three guards stood here, armored and carrying assault rifles. They saluted, turned a winch, and unlocked the massively thick door. Petty and Lailani walked down a tunnel, and more guards stood here, clad in full riot gear, rifles in hand. They passed through a second blast door, entering yet another tunnel full of guards.

"What have you got hidden in here?" Lailani said. "The leaked script to *Space Galaxy XIV*?"

Petty paused outside a third metal door. He turned to face her. He leaned down, almost crouching, to bring himself to eye level with her.

"Lailani," he said, and his voice was surprisingly soft.

"Mister President?"

It seemed to her that this hard, gruff man, this warrior who had been fighting for decades, softened before her, that his eyes were filled with ... It was hard to believe, but there it was. With compassion.

"Lailani, I know how much you fought. How much you suffered. I know how much we put you through."

She felt a lump in her throat. Her voice was a hoarse whisper. "It's all right, sir. I ..." She glanced down at her wrists. At the tattoos of flowers that hid her scars. She looked back up into the president's eyes. "I'm all right now, sir. I have Epi, my dog. I have HOBBS. I have my friends."

And amazingly—impossibly—it seemed like the president, this legendary general, was almost about to cry. But no. She must have imagined it. His eyes remained dry. His face hardened again.

"Yet all these things might be lost if the grays return," he said. "They are planning another assault. An invasion to make the last one seem like a mere sortie. We have no fleet. We have barely an army. We have barely any hope. We must know their plans. We must know more about their world. We must know their weakness. If there is hope, we must destroy them before they can destroy us. We must know how." He placed a hand on her shoulder. "And you must find out."

She tilted her head. "Me, sir? I'm just a technician in the reserves."

Petty straightened. "You are Captain Lailani de la Rosa, the soldier who led the famous Spearhead Platoon to the scum emperor, who faced Lord Malphas in battle, who retrieved a time machine at our hour of need. You have greater power than any human on Earth. For you are not fully human. You have inside you the might of an ancient alien civilization. When you turn on that power, you are stronger, faster, deadlier than any soldier in my army. But you can do even more." He leaned closer to her. His eyes lit up. "You can read minds."

Lailani took a step back. She hit the wall. "Read minds, sir? No. No! I ... I can detect some brain waves. Patterns. Visions. But I'm no mind reader."

"Today you must be," Petty said. "Or humanity falls."

He opened the third and final blast door. He gestured for her to step through.

Lailani entered a chamber.

The blast door slammed shut behind her.

She stared ahead.

Oh hell no.

Lailani spun around and banged on the door.

"Let me out of here, damn it! Petty! Let me out!"

The door remained closed. From behind her, in the chamber, she heard the creature cackle.

Sneering, Lailani spun back toward him. The gray sat on a chair, bound in chains. Blood trickled from his mouth. He grinned at her and licked his bloody teeth.

"Hello, Lailani," the gray hissed, voice like footsteps on shattered glass. "I know you. I have seen your future. I have seen your ... deformation."

She stared at the creature, her fists clenched. The army had stripped him naked, had roughed him up, but still the gray's oval eyes glimmered with amusement. Large eyes, the size of her fists. Pure black—no white to them, no irises, just pure darkness that gazed into Lailani's soul, that stripped back her uniform and skin, that carved her insides. She knew nothing about this gray, not even his name, but she could tell he was high ranking. Ritualistic scarring covered his torso and ropy limbs, depicting ankhs, eyes, and coiling hieroglyphs. Three iron disks were nailed into his skull, perhaps denoting his rank.

His eyes were cutting her. But Lailani refused to look away. She stared right back.

"I see your future too," she said softly. "In about ten seconds, unless you play nice, I'm about to gouge out those freakish eyes of yours."

Fury exploded in those black eyes.

The gray leaped forth.

Lailani stood her ground, refusing to even flinch.

The chains tightened, pulling the gray to a halt mere centimeters away from Lailani. The creature howled, snapping his teeth at her, spraying her with saliva. His voice emerged, high-pitched, raspy, and demonic.

"You fucking little whore!" The gray yanked at his chains, desperate to reach her. "I'm going to fuck you raw before I rip out your heart! I'm going to feed you your own entrails! I am Orobas, General of Sanctified!" He cackled madly, screaming, twisting. "You will beg me to die!"

Lailani stood still, staring at him. "Are you done?"

Orobas sneered at her, eyes narrowed. Slowly a grin spread across his face, and he eased back into his chair. The cuts had widened on his mouth. His blood dripped onto his chest.

"I will tell you nothing," he said.

"Oh, you already told me a few things during your tantrum," Lailani said. "Your name and rank were a good start. You're going to tell me more. Much more. You're going to tell me everything."

Orobas sneered. "And why is that? Do you think you can torture me?" He laughed. "Upon joining our holy hosts, every Sanctified Son is tortured beyond what any human can envision. You cannot hurt me. I know no pain."

Lailani stared at him.

"I do," she said softly. "I know pain. I know the pain of loss. I know the pain of despair. I know the pain of love, perhaps the most painful emotion of all. I hurt and I hurt because I am human. I fought and I fought because this is my home. I fought the centipedes and I fought the spiders. I fought the demon inside me. I fought all my life for this world. And I will not let you have it. I will not let my pain have been in vain."

She inhaled deeply.

She raised her chin and closed her eyes.

Nightwish.

As she shut off her chip, the cosmos expanded.

She was aware of the entire bunker, tunnels and shafts and chambers spreading below Jerusalem. She could sense the ruins above, the crumbling temples and domes and archways. She could see ancient prophets shuffling above, hear clerics blow ram horns, witness the rise of Rome and the fall of antiquity. She could see her friends, the people she loved most in the world.

And she could see the gray ahead of her.

Not just the bruised, bleeding wretch. She could see a great lord in armor. A charred skeleton enveloped in reeking flesh. Crowns of glory and rust. Thoughts. Fear. His mind—black and coiled up like serpents inside his skull.

She reached into his mind.

And Orobas fought her.

He thrashed in his chair, shrieking. He built walls around his mind. Walls of hatred. Of fury. Of bloodlust.

Lailani leaned forward, staring into his eyes, forcing her mind against his, carving, digging, trying to shatter his defenses.

The gray general laughed, head tossed back, jaws snapping, saliva dripping. His claws dug into his seat. He spoke in her mind.

You cannot break through.

She thrust her consciousness with all her strength. She hit his dark walls of malice.

I will break through!

You cannot. You are weak. You are frail. You are human.

My humanity makes me strong.

You are barely even human. You are a hybrid. Diseased. Impure.

I am more human that you will ever be.

She thrust again, trying to enter his mind. She caught glimpses of what lurked within—of twisting, scuttling thoughts. His walls thickened. With all his cruelty, he blocked her access. The gray general cackled.

You ... are ... alien.

I am human!

You are weak. You know nothing of true strength. Of true glory. Of ambition, desire, strength. You seek to break me, yet I am so much stronger. You seek to fight us, yet you are so meek. You cannot comprehend our cruelty.

And Lailani saw it. She saw this cruelty. She saw the bodies nailed into the ankhs, their organs removed yet still living, lives extended for centuries. She saw Nefitis and her lieutenants tear open the wombs of pregnant women, feast upon the living fetuses as the mothers screamed. She saw world after world enslaved, mere stepping-stones to the true prize. To Earth. To humanity broken and reformed into wretches.

Yes. She saw cruelty. Distilled. Pure. Evil at its truest form.

But she did not see strength.

"You are weak," she whispered.

Orobas sneered. "After all that I showed you, you call us weak?"

Tears streamed down her cheeks. "You are so sad. So broken."

He laughed. "You will learn what it means to be broken."

"I have already learned," Lailani whispered. "I lost Sofia, a woman I love. I lost so many friends. I lost my mother. I forgot how many miles there are to Babylon. I lost my candle in the darkness. But I've always known love. I've always known kindness. I've always known joy, even at my darkest hours. That is what makes me strong, Orobas. That is what makes humanity strong. Stronger than you'll ever know. You are us, Orobas. You are what we would become if we abandoned our kindness. And you are so broken." She smiled through her tears. "You lie at the end of a dark path. You are a warning about what we might become. You are a failed branch of evolution. And I'm sorry. I'm so sorry for what we created. We made you. And I pity you so much."

And there—Lailani saw it.

A chink in his armor.

A glimpse inside.

A child. Inside his memories, a cowering child, begging as his father struck him. A child forced to slay his younger brother, to consume his flesh, even as he wept. A young man, broken, shattered, rebuilt again and again, turned into a demon, but inside still so afraid. Still cowering.

"You're still human," she whispered. "Somewhere deep inside you, you're still afraid."

Orobas screamed in fury. And in fear.

Lailani pushed harder and shattered the armor around his mind.

She drove in.

The chasm of Orobas's mind spread around her, rife with rot. She saw that cowering child in the corner, begging as his father beat him again and again, shattering his bones. She moved deeper. She saw a youth, forced to become a soldier, fly from world to world, destroy civilization after civilization, but always dreaming of Earth, of the promised land.

And she saw a world. A black, charred planet, ash covering the ground, smoke hiding the sky. A wasteland of howling winds and scattered fires, a desolation where mutated animals shrieked and hunted and perished of hunger. It was a world where no life should exist. And yet an empire rose there.

Their city spread across the wasteland. Gehenna. She saw its name. A city where millions fought and hungered and dreamed of old Green Earth. A city of obelisks and vicious gods, of bodies tortured on ankhs, a city hidden beneath a sky of saucers. A city prepared for war.

Orobas struggled against her. With all his willpower, he tried to banish her from his mind. Lailani gritted her teeth and dug deeper. How he fought her! He thrashed at her. He hurt her. He hurled all his rage and hatred against her, and as she explored his mind, she fell to her knees, and her ears bled, and her chest felt ready to crack, and the centipedes laughed inside her, and still she dug deeper. To see.

In the center of the city—a pyramid. Black. Towering. Taller than any building on Earth. She knew its name. She whispered it with a mouth full of blood.

"Golgoloth."

Orobas screamed and lashed at her. The pain was terrifying. Claws ripped at her insides. With her chip deactivated, the centipedes were rising inside her, feeding. She kept going, peering deeper. Peering at that pyramid. At the center of their power.

A platform stretched out from the top of the pyramid. There, upon her throne, she sat. Nefitis. Goddess of the Sanctified Sons. Watching over her realm.

"Who are you?" Lailani shouted. "What do you want?"

Nefitis sat hunched over. Her head was bowed. She did not reply.

A deep laughter grumbled.

A voice. A presence. Deeper. Inside the pyramid.

A creature.

Laughing. Mocking. Calling her.

Every bone seemed to shatter in Lailani's body. Her teeth seemed to crumble. But Lailani pushed deeper, thrusting her consciousness into the pyramid.

There, inside, in a dark chasm—a ring of crystals.

In the middle—his jaws. Grinning. Biting.

He had no eyes, but he saw her. He gazed into her soul. He licked his jaws, and with a hundred arms, he reached to her.

She wept. She wept blood.

She knew him.

"The Oracle," she whispered, blood flowing from her eyes to her mouth. "The Crystal Seer. The Tick-Tock King." She trembled. "Nefitis's father."

His body was small and deformed, but his jaws were so large. They opened, and he hissed her name.

Lailani screamed.

She fell.

She fell from the dark world.

She fell from the sky.

She slammed onto the floor in the bunker, thrashing, screaming.

Orobas sat in his chair, laughing. He had ripped off his own hands to flee the chains. He still sat, stumps bleeding, cackling madly.

"Now you see!" Orobas laughed as his stumps spurted. "Now you see, now you see!"

Lailani lay on the floor, bleeding from her mouth, from her ears, fading away.

Serenity. Serenity. Serenity.

Yet there could be no more peace. No more hope. She wept.

The door burst open. Petty raced in, along with guards. The soldiers leaped onto Orobas and began kicking and punching, knocking the alien down. Petty lifted Lailani in his arms. He carried her out from the room.

"I saw," Lailani whispered. "I saw!"

"What?" Petty said, staring into her eyes. "What did you see?"

"Death," she whispered. "Terror. Evil." She smiled, blood in her mouth. "And a way to win."

CHAPTER FOUR

They stood on a hilltop in Jerusalem, a small group of survivors, gazing at the dusty ruins. President Petty today wore a leather bomber's jacket instead of a suit. Marco, Addy, and Lailani wore their military fatigues once more, sand clinging to the olive drab, insignia of captains on their shoulders. Elvis— still only eighteen, promoted that morning to corporal—stood with them, looking so young, so confused, a mere child. All had helmets on heads. All held rifles. All waited for war.

Marco stared across a valley. Upon a hillside sprawled an ancient necropolis, its tombstones clustered together, no space for grass between them. The dead there were thousands of years old, ancient prophets and kings. Beyond them rose the Western Wall, the last relic of the biblical Temple, weeds growing between its craggy bricks. All around spread the devastation—archways and fallen temples, palm trees growing between chipped columns, piles of rubble, biblical gateways, and abandoned souks.

Barely any monks and clerics still lived there; only a handful tended to what remained. Thousands of soldiers, however, moved among the ruins. Jets streaked overhead. Jeeps and tanks rumbled. This city had known many wars, perhaps more than any city in history. Now it prepared for the final war.

Marco turned back toward his companions. A gust of wind rustled their uniforms and scattered sand.

"So we have to travel a million years into the future," he said, "find this forbidden city, enter this pyramid, and kill the creature inside."

Addy yawned. "Piece of cake. We'll be back by lunch."

Marco was not so sure. He turned toward Lailani. She looked up at him, eyes haunted. Strands of her dark hair hung out from her helmet, fluttering in the wind. She looked so small, so frail, like a child in her father's uniform. He wanted to pull her into his arms, to protect her. Instead he merely stood facing her, and he spoke softly.

"Lailani, can you tell us more? About that creature you saw in the pyramid?" He held her hand. "I know it's hard. I know it hurts. But you must tell us everything. Every last detail."

Lailani nodded. After interrogating the captive gray general, she had passed out, had lain unconscious for a day. She was still pale.

"We don't have long," she said softly. "I saw a sky full of saucers. A million gray soldiers. They can't invade so close to their last assault. They can't risk rupturing spacetime so near their last invasion. But soon. Maybe in a few weeks. Maybe in just days. They will attack again with all their might." She trembled. "*He* will send them. *He* commands them." Her voice dropped to a whisper. "The one in the pyramid!"

She was shaking so violently Marco was worried she would fall. But her Doberman rushed up toward her, ever loyal, and Lailani patted him until she calmed.

"Who is he?" Marco said. "Can you tell me?"

The others were all watching. Marco knew that President Petty had already tried getting more details from Lailani, but that she had been too terrified to speak.

But she'll speak to you, Petty had told Marco that morning. *And we need answers.*

"I don't know his name," Lailani whispered, keeping her hand on her dog's head. "There are some who call him the Oracle, others the Time Seer. He calls himself the Tick-Tock King." She shivered, struggling to whisper the words. "He rules them all."

Marco frowned. "I thought Nefitis rules the grays."

"No." Lailani shook her head. "She is powerful. She rules the city. She rules the armies. But she pales in power to the Tick-Tock King. He is her father. He is the eyes, the claws, the vision of the Sanctified. That is what the grays call themselves. He sends them through time."

"So he controls time travel?" Marco said.

Lailani nodded. "Within the pyramid I saw many azoth crystals. Each was huge, the size of my head, larger than any azoth crystal humans have ever found. The crystals form a vertical ring like a Ferris wheel. The Tick-Tock King hangs

among them, held up by cables and hooks that pierce his skin.
His head and jaws are large, but his body is small, deformed,
wrinkled. He has no legs, but he has seventy-three arms,
spreading out around like a Hindu god. He has no eyes on his
head. The skin has been stitched over the empty sockets. But on
each hand, he has an eye, and he gazes into the crystals. In the
crystals, he sees time. With his claws, he can grab, twist,
manipulate, and bend time around him."

Marco shuddered to imagine such a creature. "So using
those crystals, he can open and close time portals for the
saucer? Like your hourglass?"

"He can do more," Lailani said. "Much more. He is
more powerful than the hourglass by far. Any azoth crystal can
tear a portal through time. But the Tick-Tock King *understands*
time. He can predict paradoxes. And he can fix them."

"Paradoxes?" Addy said, stepping toward them. "Like
how Marco landed a beautiful babe like me?"

"More like how somebody with a head so big can have
absolutely no brain," Marco muttered.

"Aww, your head isn't *that* big!" Addy said. "Let me
check for brains." She began knuckling his head.

"Enough!" Petty barked. "Linden, go take a walk.
Emery, keep speaking to de la Rosa."

As Addy wandered off, Marco looked back at Lailani.
"We were talking about paradoxes."

Lailani nodded. "Yes. HOBBS taught me about them. If
you change the past, you can create a paradox in the present.

That could have devastating effects, ripping holes through spacetime. A small paradox can destroy a planet. A big one can destroy a galaxy. When I went back to save Elvis, I had to fake his death. I couldn't tamper too much with the timeline."

Marco frowned. "But I still remember him dying, remember his chest torn open ..." He shuddered.

"Ouch!" said Elvis, touching his chest. "Let's not remember that."

Lailani nodded. "Because when saving him, I faked his death. I had to make sure the timeline remained intact. And that was just one small sortie into the past that changed one tiny thing."

"I am not tiny!" Elvis said.

"Actually, you are a bit scrawny," Lailani said, smiling for the first time that day. "But you're still much bigger than me, so just hang nearby and you'll always seem tall."

Elvis slung an arm around her. "Happy to comply."

Lailani leaned against him. Some color returned to her cheeks, and her voice was more steady. "Now imagine thousands of grays traveling back in time. That has the potential to create massive, destructive paradoxes. The Tick-Tock King can detect any potential paradoxes before they happen. He can then prevent them—calling back a certain saucer, maybe retreating a certain infantry company. And if a paradox does happen, he can alert his guys. He can have them fix it. Like I fixed the paradox by faking Elvis's death. The Tick-Tock King has all this power. Without him, the grays cannot time travel."

Addy popped up from behind a fallen column. "No problem! So we use Lailani's hourglass. We fly with the mechas to the future. We smash their pyramid and kill that Tic-Tac-Toe guy."

They all turned to gaze at the mechas. Kaiyo and Kaji stood nearby, towering over the desert.

"It won't be that easy," Lailani said. "Many saucers defend Gehenna, city of the grays. Many grays fill Golgoloth, the pyramid in the city center. This is an enemy beyond any we have faced. The grays are smarter and stronger than the scum and marauders. Their cruelty ..." She grimaced and doubled over. "It still burns me. I can still see it, feel it inside me. Pure evil. They are formed of pure evil."

Marco knelt beside Lailani and held her close.

"We've always been good at defeating evil," he said, embracing her.

"Especially me," said Addy. "I'll fly Kaji, and Marco will fly Kaiyo, and we'll get the job done."

"And I'm going with you," Elvis said, raising his chin. "Hell, I missed most of the Scum War and the entire damn Marauder War. I ain't missing this."

"I'll go too," Lailani said.

Epimetheus barked as if he too volunteered.

They all turned to look at Petty. The president stared at them, one by one. His eyes were hard, his face stony, but Marco thought he saw something beyond that armor. Something sad. Weary.

"I do not like sending young men and women to battle," the president said. "Every soldier who has died under my command is a burden on my shoulders. Yet again we face a great threat. This time it is not an alien threat. It is ourselves. This is a battle against our own future, our own souls. The enemy plans to strike us on our turf. So we must strike him on his. Captain Marco Emery and Captain Addy Linden will lead the mechas to strike at Gehenna, capital city of the grays. Each of you will command a company of elite infantry, which I will send with you—one inside each mecha. You will travel to the future. With the mechas, you will break through the grays' aerial defenses. And with your infantry, you will break in to the pyramid and slay the Oracle."

Marco inhaled deeply. He looked at the ruins around him. At a city that had fallen again and again, suffering conquest after conquest, witness to genocide after genocide— yet always rising like the phoenix. He looked at the phoenix banners that waved over the city, emblems of the Human Defense Force. He looked at his comrades. At Petty, his president, his leader, a solid pillar in a crumbling world. At Lailani, a woman he still loved with all his heart. At Elvis, back from the dead, himself like a phoenix. Finally he looked at Addy—his oldest, his best friend, the love of his life.

"I never wanted to fight," Marco said softly. "I wanted to be a writer. Yet the scum attacked. I wanted to find some peace after my military service. Yet the marauders invaded our world. I moved to an island, and I got married, and I wanted to forget about war. Yet now the grays have come. Perhaps it's my lot to always fight. To be a soldier. I love this world. Earth expelled me after the Scum War, but this is still my home. This is still where my heart beats. These are the people I love. So I will do this. One final time, I will fly to war. Because I would never run from a fight. Not when Earth is on the line."

Addy placed an arm around him, mussed his hair, and kissed his cheek. "I'm with you every step of the way, Poet. Always."

Elvis and Lailani glanced at each other, then at Petty. "What about us?"

Petty stepped closer to them. "Captain de la Rosa, Corporal Ray, you two stay here. With me."

Lailani and Elvis began to object at once, speaking about how they'd never abandon Marco and Addy. Epimetheus barked along with them.

"Enough!" Petty said. "It's too dangerous to send you two. I've already confirmed that with my physicists. Both of you, de la Rosa and Ray, have already time traveled, already messed up your timelines. It's too risky to send you on another journey through time. Not without risking paradoxes. You two stay here." The president smiled wryly. "If Emery and Linden fail, you'll have plenty of fighting on your hands."

Lailani looked at Marco. He met her eyes.

Ten years ago, she'd have howled in protest, Marco thought, *insisting that she wants to go kill the damn grays. Now her eyes are haunted.*

Lailani stepped toward him. She embraced him.

"Be careful, Marco," she whispered. "He's dangerous. He's smart. He sees so much."

Addy raised her hand and flipped off the heavens. "Then see this, Tic-Tac-Toe. We're coming to kick your—" She paused and looked at Lailani. "Does he have an ass? Or are we back to thoraxes?"

"Get some sleep tonight, Emery and Linden," Petty said. "You leave tomorrow morning."

Addy's eyes widened. "So soon? Can't we at least spend a week here, getting drunk and eating chicken fingers? We do have a time machine, you know."

"Not if the grays destroy our world," said Petty. "And they might strike any day now. Go rest. That's an order. You fly out at dawn."

* * * * *

They spent their last evening together among the ruins, having a campfire.

Marco. Addy. Lailani. Elvis. Four last soldiers of the Dragons Platoon of Fort Djemila.

"Four friends left," Marco said softly. "Most of the others are gone."

"Well, aren't you a ray of sunshine," Addy said, but she quickly grew solemn too. They all stared into the fire.

"I still can't believe you guys are captains now," Elvis said, breaking the silence. "I mean, you guys outrank Ben-Ari!"

Marco smiled thinly. "Last I heard, she's a major in the reserves, and she ranks even higher in HOPE. She still outranks us. But she's busy commanding the flagship of humanity, seeking allies, leaving us here in the trenches."

Elvis whistled softly. "Fuck. You guys have been busy during the past eleven years. *Earth* has been busy."

Lailani leaned against him. "We missed you. A lot."

"Aww, they're in love!" Addy said. "Look!"

"Sorry, babe," Elvis said, "you missed your ride on the old love boat." He pointed at himself with both thumbs.

"Damn," Addy said. "I'm heartbroken. I'm going to drown my troubles in food." She stepped aside, leaned behind a pile of fallen bricks, and returned with a rake. "Look what I got, bitches!"

"Oh God," Marco said.

Addy grinned. "You knew this was coming."

She skewered hot dogs on the rake's prongs and roasted them over the campfire. They feasted. Elvis sang a tune, and they joined in. They reminisced. They laughed. They stared silently into the fire, afraid of tomorrow.

Addy left the campfire, then returned again with a six-pack of beers.

"Where do you keep finding these things?" Marco said.

"I have a nose for it," Addy said. "You remember how I always found us food and drink at boot camp." She handed out cans of beer. "Let's drink. For victory. And for lost friends."

Marco raised a can. "For lost friends."

Lailani stood up and raised her beer. "For lost friends."

Elvis rose too. His eyes were damp. His pain was fresher. For him, most of the platoon had only died weeks ago.

"For lost friends," he said, voice choked.

They drank. They sat in silence, gazing at the fire. Addy curled up by Marco, and they wrapped a blanket around themselves. Lailani leaned against Elvis, and he placed his arms around her. They remained outside for a long time, not wanting to sleep, not wanting dawn to come.

Finally Lailani fell asleep, nestled against Elvis, and Epimetheus slept beside them. Yet Marco found no rest. He rose and left the campfire. Addy joined him, and they walked through the moonlit ruins of Jerusalem. She slipped her hand into his. The night was surprisingly cold. They found their way into a little garden of palm trees, and they paused and gazed up at the moon.

"Hey, Poet," Addy finally said. "We'll be all right. Right?"

He nodded. "Of course. We're always all right."

She lowered her head. "Most of our platoon is gone. Even Kemi is gone. Poet, I don't want to be next." She turned toward him, held his hands, and looked into his eyes. "I love you so much. I'm happy with you. Finally, for the first time in my life, I'm truly happy. I don't want to lose this."

"We'll survive this," Marco said.

"How do you know?" she whispered.

"Because the Leafs haven't won the World Cup yet," Marco said. "And you need to be alive to see that."

"The *Stanley* Cup, silly. And they *did* win. Back in 1967." A tear streamed down her cheek. "We'll see them win next year. Once we come back. Once there's peace. We'll go to that hockey game. We'll see it live. We'll eat hot dogs and drink beer, and Lailani and Elvis will come with us. And we'll forget about everything. About the wars. About what happened in Haven. And we'll live happily ever after. You and me." She pulled him into an embrace. "You're the love of my life, Marco."

He kissed her. "And you are mine."

She laughed through her tears. "You're the poet, and that's the best line you can come up with?"

He mussed her hair. "Oh, shush. I write novels. I haven't written a poem in years. Tonight, I'd rather kiss you."

He kissed her for a long time under the moonlight. They lay down between the palm trees, and they made love in the shadows—slow, gentle, growing faster and more desperate until their passion flared, and he looked into her eyes and whispered, "I love you."

She lay afterward in his arms, her head against his chest.

"I want to stay like this forever," she whispered. "Here in your arms. I feel safe and loved. Never let me go."

He kissed her cheek, and they slept.

Dawn rose golden and cold over Jerusalem. A few camels chewed their cud under an old archway. Doves pecked for seeds outside an ancient church. Fighter jets shrieked overhead, and tanks rumbled over ruins. As the sun emerged over the desert, the soldiers of the HDF marched toward the alien mechas. One company, under the command of Captain Addy Linden, entered Kaji, the female goddess. The second company, following Captain Marco Emery, entered Kaiyo.

With roaring fury and blazing fire, with smoke and dust that blew over the city, the two mechas rose. They soared, engines thrumming, bending the palm trees below, scattering bricks across the ruins.

They flew into deep space. They flew until Earth was but a blue marble in the distance. They kept flying, leaving the heliosphere, for they would not rip spacetime within the solar system. They flew into the deep darkness.

The *Ryujin* flew with them, a small starship, barely visible by the mighty mechas. When they reached interstellar space, they slowed to a halt.

Inside the *Ryujin*'s cockpit, Lailani pulled out her hourglass and gave it to HOBBS. The robot tilted it. The sand spilled. Ahead in space, a ring of blue lights shimmered. Spacetime tore open. The portal appeared, reaching forward a million years.

Kaji flew into the portal first, vanishing at once.

Kaiyo followed.

Behind them, the portal closed.

* * * * *

Lailani sat in the cockpit, gazing at the hourglass.

The last grains of sand fell and burned away.

The hourglass dimmed.

It rested in HOBBS's hands, empty.

Lailani looked up at HOBBS. "The sand is gone."

HOBBS lowered his head. "Yes, mistress."

She looked back out at space. The mechas had been gone for only a few seconds. She watched the portal fade away, leaving Marco and Addy a million years in the future. Stranded.

She looked at HOBBS again.

"Why didn't you tell me?" she whispered.

HOBBS would not raise his head. "I am sorry, mistress. President Petty forbade it. He programmed me to keep the knowledge from you. Sending Marco and Addy to the future used up all the azoth sand. We cannot reopen the portal. We cannot bring them back home. Petty said that if you knew, you would never agree to send Marco and Addy to the future."

She gazed out into space. She couldn't speak louder than a whisper. "I told them I'd reopen the portal for them. That I'd

give them a week, then reopen it. HOBBS. We've sent them to
their deaths."

The robot nodded. "To save humanity, yes. We
sacrificed the few to save the many." He placed a hand on her
shoulder. "I am sorry, mistress. I wish I could have told you."

Lailani stared out at space. The portal was gone. Marco
was gone. Addy was gone.

Her tears fell. Her chest felt empty.

I'm sorry. I'm sorry. I'm so sorry.

She lowered her head, covered her face, and sat silently
in her starship, alone in the vast darkness.

CHAPTER FIVE

The *Lodestar* flew toward it—the largest structure Ben-Ari had ever seen. She stood on the bridge, gazing at the megastructure, her eyes damp.

"A Dyson sphere," she whispered. "An entire solar system enclosed within a metal shell." She couldn't help it; she laughed in awe. "It's amazing. It's the most amazing thing I've seen."

It floated ahead, a metal ball in space, dotted with lights. The structure itself was simple enough, an unexciting sphere. If she hadn't known its diameter, Ben-Ari would have shrugged, perhaps thinking it a mere satellite. But the *size*. The *size* of the damn thing. It spun her head. The sphere ahead was larger than a planet. Larger than a star.

It enclosed an entire star system.

Here was the fabled Lemuria, home of the Galactic Alliance. If the stories were true, the Alliance headquarters were inside this sphere.

The professor stood beside Ben-Ari, so giddy he was positively hopping.

"A Dyson sphere! An actual Dyson sphere!" His eyes were like saucers. "Incredible! Did you know, Einav, that science fiction authors as far back as the 1930s theorized that Dyson spheres might exist?"

"I did not," she said.

The professor nodded vigorously. "It's true. You see, even back then, scientists understood that advanced alien civilizations would require massive amounts of energy. The best place to find such energy? Their stars! At first, civilizations would place solar panels upon their planets. That way, they could begin to collect some of their star's energy. But very soon, as the civilization would advance, their energy needs would grow. They would begin to place solar panels in space, to let them orbit their star. Over time, more and more solar panels would be raised. Eventually the most advanced civilizations—truly technological empires—would want to harness every last drop of energy their star provides. The solution? A Dyson sphere. It's a shell that encompasses the entire star. On the outside, it's dark and cold. But the inside! Ah, the inside is coated with solar panels, letting no photon escape into interstellar space. The entire energy of the star— contained within the sphere, powering the civilization within. The sphere before us has the diameter of Earth's orbit around the sun. Astounding!"

Ben-Ari stared at the massive sphere as they flew closer, though massive seemed an understatement.

"I can barely comprehend building something so big," she said. "Earth would be invisibly small against this sphere, like a grain of sand on a beach ball. How does one build anything so large? Where do you get all the material?" She blew out her breath. "The Galactic Alliance must truly be astoundingly powerful. We'd seem to them like apes."

The professor nodded excitedly. "Like worms! Have you heard of the Kardashev scale?"

Ben-Ari nodded. "Yes. I've been studying it as part of my classes." She had been spending many evenings studying electronic courses from Galactica University, working toward her undergraduate degree. "On the Kardashev scale, there are three types of civilizations. A Type I civilization can collect all the solar energy reaching its planet. A Type II civilization can harness the total energy of its star."

The professor nodded. "Very good, Captain. What we see here is a Type II civilization. The Galactic Alliance has managed to build a Dyson sphere, to collect the entire energy of its star. Thus, they are comfortably a Type II civilization."

Ben-Ari winced. "And Earth isn't even a Type I civilization yet. To qualify for Type I, you need to harness the entire solar energy reaching your planet. Earth only collects a small portion of its solar energy, letting most go to waste. We still burn fuel half the time."

"We were on our path toward becoming a Type I civilization before the scum attacked," the professor said. "Sadly, they set us back a century."

"I just hope the Galactic Alliance is forgiving. I'm not too excited about showing up, waving, and saying we're a Type

Zero." She frowned and turned toward the professor. "Is there a Type III civilization?"

"In the books, yes," said the professor. "A Type III civilization can harness the entire solar power of its *galaxy*. No such civilization exists in the Milky Way. As far as we know, none exists in the cosmos. At least none that we've detected."

"And I hope we never run into one," Ben-Ari said, "or the worms will make us seem advanced."

As they flew closer, details on the Dyson sphere emerged. The lights on the sphere were dim, but the *Lodestar*'s monitors painted a picture using the sphere's infrared radiation. There were several gateways on the sphere, and many starships were flying in and out of the megastructure.

"There, that one." Ben-Ari pointed toward a round gateway. Dozens of starships were flying through the passageway. "Aurora, take us there."

"Yes, mistress!" Aurora said.

The Dyson sphere now encompassed their entire field of view, hiding the stars. It felt like flying toward a metal planet— except this planet could swallow stars. Many alien starships flew around the *Lodestar*. Here were ships of many civilizations, each vessel unique. Some ships were swirling balls of energy, solid cores barely visible in their centers. Others were massive cubes, bristly with pylons and pipes. Some starships were shaped like giant crabs, large enough to crush the *Lodestar* in their claws. Other starships were no larger than shoe boxes, perhaps containing aliens the size of ants. Ben-Ari saw faery ships that extended lavender sails. Other ships looked more like warty toads. Here was the nexus of the Orion Arm, the spiral arm of the Milky Way where Earth resided. If this galactic neighborhood had a capital, it was here.

"The ancient world had Rome," she said softly. "The new world had New York City. We have Lemuria, home of the Galactic Alliance."

As they approached the gateway, several starships flew toward them. They were shaped like starfish, each about half the *Lodestar*'s size, and lights shone on their arms like suction cups on tentacles. Rings of cannons thrust out from their centers like teeth. They hailed the *Lodestar*, and metallic voices filled the bridge, speaking in a foreign language.

Ben-Ari frowned.

They're speaking Mandarin, she realized. She tapped a few buttons, setting the *Lodestar*'s computer to translate the words.

"Earth ship!" spoke the starfish vessels. "We have identified your star of origin, and we have adapted our translators to speak your homeworld's most common language. Speak your purpose."

Ben-Ari could speak fluent English and Hebrew, both far less common on Earth than Mandarin. She replied in English, hoping the alien ships could interpret that language too. "This is Captain Einav Ben-Ari of the ESS *Lodestar*. I come as a representative of humanity to introduce our species to the Galactic Alliance and apply for membership."

A moment of silence. Ten of the starfish ships now surrounded them. Finally another message came through.

"You may enter Lemuria, but be warned, Earth ship. You are here representing your species. Any act of aggression will be interpreted as a declaration of war and thus met with the immediate destruction of your homeworld." The starfish ships pulled back, allowing passage to the gateway. "Welcome to Lemuria."

"Lovely welcome," Fish said. "The Walmart greeters could learn a thing or two from them. Welcome to our store! You broke it, you bought it, and we'll exterminate your entire species."

Ben-Ari ignored the Australian. She turned toward her pilot.

"Aurora, fly us in."

The *Lodestar* flew through the gateway, entering the Dyson sphere.

Ben-Ari stared ahead, barely able to breathe. The professor had tears in his eyes. For long moments everyone on the bridge was silent, just gazing with awe at the wonders ahead.

"Explore," Ben-Ari whispered, tears on her cheeks. "Do not grow old, no matter how long you live. Never cease to stand like curious children before the Great Mystery into which we were born."

"Sagan?" the professor asked.

"Einstein," she whispered. "He understood."

A star shone in the center of the Dyson sphere, illuminating the star system. But it felt wrong to think of this place as a star system. It was so much more. When seeing it from the outside, Ben-Ari had imagined the inside of the sphere coated with solar panels—an amazing yet ultimately uniform inner surface. She had been wrong. The inside of the sphere was ... a world. An artificial world. Its surface area must have been millions of times the size of Earth. She saw forests, rivers, oceans larger than Saturn, soaring mountains, sparkling cities drenched in eternal light. Yes, there were solar panels here— great shimmering surfaces of them, so many solar panels they could cover a million Earths. But there was also wilderness. Life. So much life.

"If you flattened Earth," the professor whispered, "and placed it onto the inner surface of this sphere like a sticker, you wouldn't even see it. It would be as tiny as a pinprick on a tablecloth."

"I'm not feeling like an ape compared to this civilization," Ben-Ari said. "Not even a worm. I feel like an amoeba."

"No one civilization built this place, mistress," said Aurora, glancing over from her controls. "My people, the Menorians, are junior members of the Galactic Alliance. A thousand sentient civilizations cooperated to build this great shell in the cosmic ocean, and it took thousands of years. We Menorians helped fly the construction ships."

Several planets were orbiting the star, their orbits contained within the sphere. Each planet was fully urbanized, coated with cities. Countless starships were flying everywhere, moving between the planets and the inner sphere. Space stations floated everywhere. Earth would have disappeared here.

And Ben-Ari also saw military might.

Starfish-shaped fighters flitted back and forth. Great warships, larger than any Earth had ever built, lumbered across space and docked at floating ports. Silvery ships shaped like spiders, their legs as long as highways, moved back and forth, red and blue lights flashing across them, slender cannons thrusting out from their hulls.

Here is the might we need, Ben-Ari thought. *Warships that can defend Earth. That can help us fight the grays. I must join this alliance. I must earn its protection. I must bring back aid to Earth.*

"Aurora, do you know where the Galactic Alliance headquarters is?" Ben-Ari asked.

"There are many Alliance ports inside Lemuria, Captain," the mollusk said. "Military bases, universities, administration buildings—all scattered across the sphere like coral reefs in a warm sea."

"What about an admission center?" Ben-Ari asked. "For new applicants. Do you remember when your own species applied for membership?"

"Yes, mistress," said the pilot. "I will take us there."

They flew between thousands of starships and space stations, heading deeper into the sphere. Ben-Ari had never seen such a variety of ships and species. There were giant floating platforms topped with terrariums. Spinning rings like ancient orreries. Ships round, triangular, elongated. Ships the size of moons and ships the size of marbles. Some ships were clouds of luminous gas. Some aliens flew in swarms of tiny drones. A few aliens were riding starwhales.

The *Lodestar* kept flying, heading toward the sphere's inner surface. Forests rolled below them, and mountains soared over verdant valleys. Rivers coiled between towns, and waves washed over golden beaches. Ben-Ari could hardly imagine a world so large; trillions of aliens could live here comfortably and never feel crowded.

"The surface area inside the sphere must be millions of times Earth's surface area," she said in wonder.

"*Hundreds* of millions," the professor said. "Astounding."

Aurora took them toward a mountainous island that rose from a tranquil sea. A temple crowned the mountaintop, shaped as a white lotus. Its marble petals rose toward the sky, snowy white and shimmering. Gardens draped the mountainsides, large enough that Ben-Ari imagined she could spend months exploring them. It was a serene place, and the white lotus building, with its simple elegance, seemed as wondrous as this entire sphere.

Several round vessels rose from the temple to greet the *Lodestar*. They looked like giant pearls, but when they flew closer, Ben-Ari saw that their shimmering surface was translucent. Lights shone inside the orbs, and she could just make out the forms of aliens inside.

"Welcome, ESS *Lodestar*." The voice emerged from the bridge's speakers, deep and melodious. "The Galactic Alliance has heard of your coming. We have never met an Earthling, and we much desire to learn more about you. In seven of your hours, we will welcome two humans of your choice—one male and one female—into our blessed Lotus Temple, where they will be honored guests. We will send a shuttle to fetch the pair. Do not bring your mothership closer to the Holy Lotus. Any hint of aggression will be interpreted as an act of war, resulting in the immediate destruction of your homeworld."

With that, the pearly ships descended back toward the temple. The *Lodestar* remained flying above.

Niilo, the *Lodestar*'s hulking security chief, grumbled, and his face reddened beneath his forked blond beard.

"If I chose to be aggressive, I would smash this whole temple down." The Fin clenched his fists, each the size of a roast ham. "I would need only my fists."

Ben-Ari smiled wryly. "I'm sure you would, my dear Viking warrior. But we've come here as diplomats, not as soldiers. The time for smashing will come—once we return to Earth with a fleet and meet the grays." She turned toward the professor. "In seven hours, join me. They want one female, one male. You and I will go meet them."

Niilo stepped forth, his long platinum hair swaying. "Captain, let *me* go with you! You need a strong defender."

"I'm perfectly capable of defending myself, Niilo," Ben-Ari said. "I might be small compared to you, but I've trained for years in Krav Maga, and I've fought in many battles." She placed her hand on Niilo's broad chest. "I need you here. To defend the ship."

The Fin loosened his fists. He placed one hand on his heart. "I will always defend the homestead, Captain. I will defend the *Lodestar* as a Viking defends his dragonship."

She nodded. "Good. You have the bridge."

She took the elevator to her quarters. She needed to sleep. To shower. To eat. To rehearse her speech to the Galactic Alliance. Yet she found herself restless, too nervous to sleep or eat. She washed quickly and donned a fresh service uniform. The blue fabric was stiff, too formal, uncomfortable. Often she missed the loose, casual fatigues of the battlefield. She had always felt more comfortable in them than this formal uniform.

She looked at herself in the mirror.

I'm finally showing my age, she thought. She was almost thirty-two, and she no longer looked like a kid. Her blue eyes seemed sunken to her. Too weary. Eyes that seemed too old, that had seen too much. Her blond hair was pulled into a ponytail, and her cap rested on her head. Her cheeks were pale. She pinched them in an attempt to restore some color.

Her doorbell rang. She checked her clock; there were still two hours to go.

"Come in."

It was Professor Isaac. He too wore his formal uniform, complete with his cap. He held a picnic basket.

"Have you eaten?" he said. "I made my famous roast venison and mustard sandwiches. Of course, the artificial venison we grow in the ship's lab isn't as good as real meat. But I think all things considered, quite tasty."

She smiled. "My stomach is too knotted to eat. But if these are your famous sandwiches …"

They sat at her table, and they ate while gazing out the porthole at the rolling landscape below.

"It's so vast," she said. "So much wilderness—forests, fields, and plains. Millions of Earths could fit here. We would be safe inside the sphere. Out there, in the open galaxy, it's so dangerous. There is so much evil, so many predators roaming the darkness. In here is safety. Imagine if they let us have a new home here! All of humanity, all the billions of us, would barely take up any space. They wouldn't even notice us, no more than you'd notice a single ant in a castle."

The professor nodded. "True. Of course, there would be the problem of transporting billions of people across the galaxy. We only have a handful of ships left."

She swallowed her bite of sandwich. The venison, though artificial, was good. "And as beautiful as this place is, it's not Earth. Not our home. Not the place we fought for, bled for, that so many of us died for."

"Many new spacefaring civilizations go through this period," the professor said. "We wake up. We take a step into the cosmic ocean. The water seems inviting, so we take another step. And a third until soon we're knee-deep. And then we meet the sharks."

She smiled wryly. "I've met enough sharks for a lifetime."

"Many, perhaps most species never make it farther," the professor said. "They meet an alien predator like the scum or the marauders. Perhaps they are confronted by their own demons, as we are with the grays. They fall back into obscurity. Another light snuffed out. There are ten thousand spacefaring civilizations in the Milky Way in this era alone. Millions have come before us, most of them gone now. Countless more civilizations rise and fall in other galaxies. We humans are not unique. We have, perhaps, survived our infancy. We are now going through a dangerous adolescence."

She looked out the porthole. "And out there—the species who live inside this sphere—are the adults."

The professor nodded. "And we'll soon know if they'll let us sit at the adults' table."

"Let's review my speech one more time," she said. "Pretend to be a judgmental alien."

She spent the next hour rehearsing with him, pitching humanity, tweaking and perfecting her speech. But it was one thing to deliver the speech to the professor, a kind and gentle man. Quite another to a roomful of highly advanced aliens with technology that made the *Lodestar* seem like a wheelbarrow.

"So did I make us sound somewhat noble?" she asked.

"You will amaze them, Einav, as you amaze me," Isaac said. "And I'll be there with you. Always."

She looked out the porthole. A pearl shuttle was rising to meet them.

"Our ride is here."

The alien shuttle came to hover outside their airlock. Ben-Ari and the professor stepped into the circular vessel.

Inside, a tall and slender alien greeted them. Her body was vaguely humanoid and coated with blond fur, and her face reminded Ben-Ari of a deer. She wore flowing white robes, and silvery antlers grew from her head. Her arms too were like antlers. They branched out at the elbows, splitting into several forearms, each ending with a slender hand with many fingers.

She looks like a cross between Bambi and a mutant elf, Ben-Ari thought.

"Welcome," the alien said, voice soft and melodious. "I am Nala, servant of the Galactic Alliance. Would you care for some refreshments?" She held out a bowl of grass.

"We've already eaten," Ben-Ari said. "Thank you, Nala."

She decided not to reveal that she had eaten venison.

"You are welcome," Nala said. "Come, I will take you to see the elders. They much desire to learn more about humanity."

The round shuttle descended toward the surface. The mountain soared below them, rising from the sea. The Lotus Temple rose on its crest, shimmering in the sunlight. The shuttle landed in the gardens, and they stepped outside. It was pleasant. The air was crisp and scented of flowers, grass, and the sea. A breeze rustled Ben-Ari's uniform. It could have been a lovely spring day on Earth. Several aliens, similar in appearance to Nala, were ambling through the gardens outside the temple.

Oddly, of all possible emotions, envy filled Ben-Ari.

Back on Earth, we suffer, we fight, we die, we hunger. Our world lies in ruins, and the grays seek to destroy all that we have left. And here is paradise!

It seemed so unfair, and standing here, seeing this beauty, the suffering of her people weighed more heavily than ever upon her.

She looked around her at the gardens. Flower beds. Pebbly paths. Singing butterfly-like aliens. Marble statues and streams. Peace.

She forced a deep breath.

Let this be a place of hope and inspiration, not envy, she thought. *This is what we humans can aspire to. This is a paradise we too can build. Maybe not in my lifetime. Maybe not for many generations. But let this be an inspiration, a vision of what humanity can become. Not the grays. Not creatures of evil living in desolation. Let this be the path we choose. In a million years, let this be our destination.*

Two paths. Two possible futures for humanity. Down one path—the grays, creatures twisted and evil. Down the other path—utopia.

The grays warn us. This place—let it inspire and guide us.

"Come, Earthlings," Nala said. "The elders will see you now."

She led them toward the Lotus Temple. Its marble petals were so tall Ben-Ari could barely see their tips. An archway rose ahead, its keystone engraved with suns and planets. They stepped into the temple.

They found themselves in a vast hall, a chamber so large cathedrals could fit inside. Murals spread across the ceiling. They reminded Ben-Ari of the Sistine Chapel, but here were scenes of science. One mural seemed to depict the Big Bang. Another showed an early universe, its planets swirling balls of magma. Other paintings depicted evolution, showing the progression from simple molecules into cells and finally into animals. Some paintings seemed to represent the elements, depicting various atoms, while other paintings showed galaxies. A few murals depicted themes she could not understand; here was science beyond what humanity had discovered.

It's a hall of science and knowledge, she realized, eyes damp. *And it's beautiful.*

Furtively, Ben-Ari instructed her bionic arm to snap a photograph of the ceiling. It was, without a doubt, the most astounding work of art she had ever seen.

She forced herself to look down. Beneath the ceiling too was wonder.

A horseshoe-shaped table stood on the floor. At the table sat a hundred aliens or more, each of a different species. Ben-Ari had never seen such variety of life. Most of the aliens were organic—tall and furry, slender and scaly, a few feathered, some slimy, others coated with naked skin not unlike humans. Other aliens were more bizarre. One alien looked like a giant crystal with light shimmering inside. Another alien was liquid; it swirled inside a globe of water. A few aliens were gaseous, hovering as clouds. One alien seemed to simply be a hovering metal ball. The smallest aliens were no larger than insects, most were roughly human-sized, while a handful could dwarf elephants. The largest alien, a rocky creature with lava gurgling inside its mouth, nearly reached the ceiling.

Ben-Ari and Professor Isaac stepped forward. All eyes, tentacles, whiskers, and sniffing snouts followed them. They came to stand in the center of the horseshoe table.

Ben-Ari waited for somebody to speak. Nobody did.

She took a deep breath.

"Greetings!" she said, perhaps too loudly. Her voice echoed. "I am Captain Einav Ben-Ari, a human from Earth, and with me is—"

"We know who you are," rasped an alien. He seemed ancient, covered with long white hair, complete with a shaggy beard. His skin—whatever was visible—was pink and wrinkly. Sharp teeth filled his mouth, and he blinked at her with four blue eyes. "We care not about your rank or name, only about your species."

Ben-Ari stiffened.

Very well, she thought. *I've been chewed out by worse than cranky Ewoks.*

"We are a young species, but a curious one," she said. "We have only just taken our first steps into space. We know we are young. We know we have much to learn. We are eager to grow, to—"

"Spare us your platitudes." The shaggy alien harrumphed. His voice made gravel sound soft. "Every damn species that comes in here, it's the same damn story. We are young. We are curious. We want to learn. Bah!" He spat into a bowl. "All of you are savages. All you care about is war. You all come here with the same ulterior motive—to use our fleets in your battles. Well, you can't have 'em." He barked a laugh. "How's that, missus?"

Oh, be quiet, you sentient hairball, Ben-Ari thought, daring not voice the words.

The professor stepped forward. "Dear council! I assure you, while it's true that our species has struggled with aggression, we've made great strides in science, in art, in humanitarian pursuits, and—"

"*Human*itarian pursuits?" The furry alien scoffed. "Still you are ethnocentric! Caring only about your own species, nothing about the galaxy." He turned toward his fellow aliens. "These humans are savages. Let's cast them out. Toss 'em out with the trash, I say! If you ask me, we should destroy their entire planet and be done with."

Another alien spoke. She was a shimmering creature with glassy skin. On the inside, she was all flowing light.

She looks like a living lava lamp, Ben-Ari thought.

"Now now, Grumstaf," said the glowing alien. "Let's not be so quick to dismiss them. Yes, they are savages. But I see potential in them. They gazed upon our ceiling in awe for long moments. These are beings who love art and science."

"Their brains are too small," said the shaggy Grumstaf. "Bah! Look at them. Their skulls are tiny. Did you see their ship? Primitive! My granddaughter could build it, and she hasn't even hatched yet."

Another alien hovered up from his seat. He looked like a shrew with dragonfly wings. "Do you judge me by the size of my head, Grumstaf?" the tiny alien said. "Are my people not renowned as masters of science and art?"

The furry old alien harrumphed again. "Your achievements speak for themselves, Shmet. Yet these humans. What have they achieved? We've all looked at the records on their ship. A barbaric world! War. Violence. Hatred." He scoffed. "They burn fuel and pollute their world, even two centuries after discovering solar power. They slay one another over imaginary gods or the color of their skin. What science have they achieved?"

Ben-Ari turned from alien to alien. "We've achieved so much! In the past century alone, a single human lifespan, we've built warp engines. We've developed wormholes. We've built robots with true artificial intelligence and consciousness. We've colonized our solar system and even solar systems beyond ours. All this in a century! As for wars? In the past, yes, we fought one another based on race or religion. But the past few wars were forced upon us. Cruel aliens attacked us. We had to defend ourselves! We—"

"Do you not still fight amongst one another?" said the shaggy alien. "We know of your world. We downloaded the history records from your ship. Even in the ruins following your latest war, your species fights amongst itself. Those you call fascists, communists, anarchists, theocrats—all still battle for scraps of your pathetic little world." Grumstaf leaned forward in his seat, eyes blazing. "Even your new war is simply a war against your own species. Those you call grays are human too, only slightly less barbaric. You have nothing to give us, yet you want to take so much. The Galactic Alliance exists to promote civilization. Not barbarism." He snorted. "Maybe we should accept the grays instead. At least their heads are large enough."

Ben-Ari turned away from him. She looked at the other aliens. Scaled, feathered, large, small, aliens of stone and light and gas.

"Will nobody else speak for us?" she said. "We are more than what Grumstaf says. We humans love science too. We love art. We love beauty. We love literature and poetry and music and—"

A melodious chord sounded at her side. Ben-Ari turned toward the sound. One of the aliens had spoken. This alien was tall and the color of maple. Many strings stretched across her body. With long fingers, the alien plucked her strings, emitting another chord.

"I don't understand," Ben-Ari said.

A slimy alien peeked out from a spiky shell. "She speaks with music. She asks you to sing for her. She wants to judge your song."

Ben-Ari blinked. Sing?

She turned toward Isaac.

"I'm not much of a singer," the professor whispered.

Ben-Ari winced. Neither was she. She enjoyed listening to opera, but she had not sung a song since childhood. She had always felt too shy to sing.

"Well?" said Grumstaf, leaning forward in his seat. "Do you disobey a request of the council?"

Ben-Ari sighed. Cheeks burning, she began to sing the only song she had ever sung before. She would sing it with her father on Passover, a holiday lament about the trials of the ancient Israelites fleeing slavery in Egypt. She felt ridiculous singing this old keen. She wouldn't have minded if the Lotus Temple collapsed onto her, burying her for all eternity. The aliens all listened. She sang her song. A song from her childhood. A song of memory.

And as she sang, those memories flowed back into her. Memories of her father. Of candles and light. Of her mother.

She missed them. She missed her parents. She missed her home. She had almost forgotten this song. She had almost forgotten her mother's face.

She ended her song and lowered her head.

For a long moment, silence filled the hall. The professor held her hand.

Grumstaf sniffed, peering at her. "What is that salty discharge from your eyes? Are you expelling waste, here in our temple?"

"She is weeping, Grumstaf!" said the luminous alien. "She is overcome with memory. I see it around her, glowing softly. It is beautiful. Sad yet filled with such light."

The musical alien, the one with strings on her body, plucked a bittersweet D minor.

"It's a song of my home," Ben-Ari said softly. "I used to sing it with my father." She lowered her head. "He died only weeks ago. This song is all he left me."

Grumstaf grunted. "It sounds like a religious song to me." He spat again into his bowl. "Do you still worship deities?" He turned toward the others. "You see? Primitive! Barbarians! The humans insult me with their very stench. Cast them out!" He turned back toward Ben-Ari, his eyes narrowed, and he bared his teeth. "You are unwanted."

Around the table, other aliens nodded their agreements. A few began to leave the room. The shaggy Grumstaf began limping away, leaning on his cane. He looked surprisingly small outside of his seat, barely four feet tall and hunched over.

Isaac sighed. He placed a hand on Ben-Ari's shoulder.

"We tried, Einav," he said softly. "I'm sorry it didn't work out."

She barely heard him.

That last word kept echoing in her mind, over and over. *Unwanted. Unwanted.*

Yes. She had always been unwanted. A motherless child neglected by her father. A child without a home. A warrior for a species lost in darkness, fighting alone. Unwanted.

"Shame on you," she said softly.

The shaggy alien looked over his shoulder at her. "What are you still blathering about?"

Ben-Ari inhaled sharply. She clenched her fists.

"Shame on you!" she shouted. Her voice echoed through the chamber.

The aliens all turned toward her. A few scoffed. Others shook their heads sadly.

Ben-Ari plowed on, her fury blazing. "I did not cross hundreds of light-years to be insulted. I did not pass through fire and rain to be dismissed like an errant child. I did not defeat alien invasions and rebuild my civilization to be called barbaric. You call yourselves enlightened? You call yourselves advanced? How quick you are to dismiss us at a glance! You hear a snippet of song, you steal a scrap of records from my ship, and you think you can judge us? You know nothing of humanity!"

The aliens were all staring at her, somber.

"Watch yourself, child—" began Grumstaf.

"Silence!" Ben-Ari barked at him. "I've heard enough of your talk. Stick your slithering tongue back into your jaws. I came here, and I saw great wonder. I saw a sphere that engulfs a star. I saw marvels of technology that amaze me. But now I see your true heart, and it is rotten. You meet a species struggling to rise, to achieve nobility, a species that seeks wisdom and knowledge—and you cast us back into the mud! You would leave us to die because you judge us impure! You condemn us humans for fighting amongst one another. But we humans know compassion! We help the weak! We elevate those who climb! We would never turn away from a species seeking survival, never look down upon them for their simplicity, never deem them barbaric merely because they are weaker. That is what you've done here. You have shown me your true colors. You have shown me a civilization that is great in technology and poor in spirit. And I judge humanity superior! Good day to you all."

She turned and began marching away.

She was at the doorway when the voice rose behind her.

"Human! Wait."

She paused at the doorway. She turned back.

One of the aliens hobbled toward her. He had huge flat feet with toenails the size of coasters. His body was bulky and coated with white fur, and he wore a blue robe embroidered with stars. His conical snout drooped over a white beard that flowed to the floor. He reminded Ben-Ari of a wizard from an old fantasy novel—at least if wizards had feet to shame elephants and snouts the size of baguettes.

"Wait," the old alien said again, voice hoarse. "We had to test you, human. We had to present you with some adversity. To see how you defended yourself. You have performed …" He shuffled another step closer, robes rustling. " …wonderfully."

Ben-Ari exhaled in relief.

"Thank you," she said.

"I am Eredel," said the old wizard, "head of the Admissions Council. I find you most fascinating." He looked at the professor. "According to the records we have studied, it is this human—Professor Noah Isaac—who figured out how to build a wormhole. Is that correct?"

"I had help from many talented scientists," Isaac said. "I cannot claim all the credit. We humans are good team players."

Eredel seemed to smile, though it was hard to tell with his massive beard and drooping mustache.

"You are a young species, indeed," the alien said. "Mere babes taking your first steps. You have not yet learned to fulfill your energy needs with solar power, criteria we normally demand from members. And yet you have shown remarkable ingenuity, developing spacefaring technology within only two of your centuries. So young you are. You have so far to go. Therefore, while I am most impressed with your potential, I cannot yet grant you membership in the Galactic Alliance. Return here in a thousand years, and we will reconsider your request." He smiled. "I have a feeling that by then, you will be ready."

Ben-Ari gasped. Her heart sank. "But … after all those compliments, you would still reject us? I …"

Her head spun. It seemed impossible that she would be turned away. Earth needed this! She could not fail! Her mind raced.

"I'm sorry, child," old Eredel said.

Ben-Ari thought furiously. There was something on the edge of her mind, the tip of her tongue …

"Junior membership!" she blurted out, remembering. "My pilot is a Menorian. Her species is a junior member of the Galactic Alliance. If we humans cannot become full-fledged members, grant us junior membership."

The wizard-like alien seemed to consider. His mustache fluttered as he breathed. "Would your Menorian pilot vouch for you?"

Ben-Ari nodded. "I'm sure she would."

Shaggy old Grumstaf limped forward and pointed his cane at the wizard. "You know our laws! To become even junior members, young species require a full ten sponsors, all from different sentient species. This girl's pet Menorian would not be enough."

"And if I find twenty sponsors?" Ben-Ari said. "You would grant Earth membership?"

"*Junior* membership," said Grumstaf. He snorted.

"Then I won't return in a thousand years," Ben-Ari said. "I'll return in weeks. Give me this time, and I promise you: I will find ten sponsors." She raised her chin. "And I will do more. I will prove humanity's worth."

The *Lodestar* flew out into space, leaving Lemuria behind.

They flew as fast as they could.

They did not have a lot of time. And they had a lot of distance to cross.

* * * * *

"Captain," the professor said as they flew in the darkness, "where are we going?"

Ben-Ari stood on the bridge, gazing at the stars, a small smile on her lips.

"Twelve years ago, humanity had a hundred thousand starships," she said. "We flew them five hundred light-years into the scum empire, liberating besieged planets, uniting species against a common enemy. I think it's time to call in a favor."

They flew to the ocean world of the Gurami, a species of intelligent fish that flew in starships full of water. Twelve years ago, Ben-Ari had found a world under scum siege, most of its cities gone. A handful of Gurami starships had joined the human fleet then, had helped defeat the centipedes.

Today the Guramis would fly with her again.

"Years ago, you gave us hope, Captain Ben-Ari," said the lord of the Guramis, an indigo fish with flowing purple fins. "We will vouch for you. We are forever in your debt."

One of the Gurami ships, an elongated tube of water with delicate solar sails, rose to fly with the *Lodestar*.

They flew onward. They reached the forested world of the Silvans, furry aliens with many arms that lived among their towering trees. A Silvan ship, made of wood and crystal, rose to fly with them.

"We still tell tales of your courage, Captain Ben-Ari," the furry creatures told her. "Without you, we would still be living under the threat of the centipedes. You are forever a heroine in our world. We will fly with you. We will tell the Galactic Alliance that you are noble."

World by world, they flew, their fleet growing. They flew to Altair, and they visited a world of tall, green humanoids with eight eyes. Ben-Ari had rescued their prince from the scum hives on Abaddon. Today he rose to fly with her. She flew to Alpha Pavonis, where a Klurian ambassador—a blobby, semiaquatic alien—joined her on the *Lodestar*, for the Klurians had still not developed ships of their own. They flew to Nandaka, the planet where her father had hidden away, and one of the natives—small aliens with four arms, mouths on their hands—joined her on the *Lodestar*. He was a relative of

Keemaji, he said, the Nandaki who had helped Ben-Ari find the Ghost Fleet; he would be honored to serve humanity.

For years, Ben-Ari had explored the galaxy, helping species weaker than humanity. For decades, her father had done the same.

Today they rose to fly with her. Not the minimum ten but a full twenty-one alien civilizations. None were members of the Galactic Alliance. Some had only simple starships with no warp drives; they had to fly within the *Lodestar*'s warp bubble. Others had no starships at all and hitched rides on the *Lodestar*.

All would vouch for her.

They flew through space, heading back toward Lemuria, a flotilla of united species.

She and Professor Isaac stood in the *Lodestar*'s lounge, gazing out at the ships flying with them. Round ships filled with water. Ships of crystal and light. Clunky cogs and elegant, spinning ships like dandelion seeds.

"In a galaxy that has suffered so much evil, here is unity," the professor said. "Here is nobility."

Ben-Ari smiled thinly. "A part of me is cynical. A part of me thinks they simply want an ally in the Galactic Alliance so that we can vouch for them in the future. A vote from a member species is worth a lot."

Isaac smiled too. "I've always been more of an optimist than a cynic." But his smile faded. "Optimism is often a luxury. I grew up in a loving home. When I was very young, my parents shielded me from the nightmarish war against the scum.

I used to climb onto my roof as a child, to gaze up at the stars, to wonder. My parents taught me that the stars were filled with life, with adventure, with beauty. So yes, I'm an optimist. I have that luxury, a luxury most do not. I did not see battle as you did. I did not see evil face-to-face. I've always chosen, even in the darkness, to seek light."

She leaned against him. "That's why I love you, Noah. You're purer than I am. I'm broken. I struggle to see light."

He wrapped his arms around her. "No, Einav. You've gone through shadow and still seek the light. That is purity of courage. That is why I admire you."

"I don't want you to admire me," she whispered, looking up into his eyes. "I want you to love me. Like I love you."

She immediately regretted those words. She was not used to exposing her feelings this way. She had always hidden behind armor. She had always been the stern leader, daring to show no weakness or emotion to her troops. Yet Professor Noah Isaac had never felt like somebody under her command. He had always felt more like a mentor. A guiding light. A pillar of optimism. Yes, perhaps that was why she had fallen in love with him. Not merely because he was intelligent, kind, and wise. But because he showed her optimism. Her life had always been in shadows; he showed her light.

And so she took him into her bed. It had been so long since she had made love. She had almost forgotten what it felt like—to feel desirable, to feel warm and safe, to feel loved. She was shy at first, worried that he would not like her body, or that her prosthetic arm would disgust him. But he held her and called her beautiful. And he told her that he loved her. And afterward, they lay in bed together, telling silly jokes and laughing, then talking for hours about many topics.

If I ever retire, she thought, *I want to spend my time like this. Delving into deep conversations. Laughing. With him.*

And yet a fear had begun to grow in her. A fear that she would not survive this war.

The grays were planning a massive invasion. She had already repelled one assault, merely the first wave. She had lost her fleet, thousands of troops, and her arm. Even if she could come home with an Alliance fleet, the grays had all the time in the world. They could rebuild their army over and over, send wave after wave.

Was this a war humanity could not win?

She was still lying in bed with Isaac when the alarms blared.

"Captain!" Niilo said, speaking through a communicator. "Ten enemy saucers approaching. It's the grays."

She ran to the bridge.

When she got there, the battle was already raging.

The saucers fired their lasers. Blasts slammed into the *Lodestar*, shaking the shields. One of the two Gurami vessels— a tube of water with slender wings—shattered and spilled its contents into space. A Taelian starship, a modified asteroid with engines attached, split in two.

And then they fought back.

The *Lodestar* fired her cannons. Her companion ships were smaller and weaker, but they too fought with a fury, blasting the saucers with all their weapons. Humans and aliens—they fought side by side, shattering the saucers, routing the enemy. When the last saucer turned to flee, they chased and tore it apart.

It had only been a small sortie of grays, perhaps a group of scouts or spies. But to Ben-Ari, this victory was hope. It was unity. In the darkness, there was light.

They flew onward, leaving the wreckage of the saucers, until they reached Lemuria again.

"We vouch for her!" said the Gurami ambassador, floating inside a mobile globe of water.

"We vouch for humanity!" said the Silvan, his furry, disk-shaped torso balanced on several legs.

"Humanity is noble," said the Nandaki, already aging even after the short flight, for his species only lived for several months. "They are heroes in our realm."

One by one, the species spoke up for Ben-Ari. For humanity. She stood before the Galactic Council, eyes damp, chin raised. Proud.

Eredel, head of the Admissions Council, listened carefully, stroking his white beard and nodding his long snout. At his side, the shaggy Grumstaf huffed, snorted, swung his cane, but said nothing.

Finally the last alien had given his testimony.

Ben-Ari stood facing the council, silent, waiting.

Eredel walked toward her, his wide feet shuffling across the marble floor. A kindly smile spread below his mustache.

"I am proud to announce that humanity is now a member—"

"A junior member!" Grumstaf cut in.

Eredel shot his companion a glare, then looked back at Ben-Ari, and his smile returned.

"You are now a *junior* member of the Galactic Alliance." He clasped both her hands, the real and the prosthetic, and shook them. "Welcome, my friend. Welcome."

Tears in her eyes, Ben-Ari breathed a sigh of relief. On a whim, she hugged the bearded old Eredel. Farther back, Grumstaf scoffed. She ignored him.

"Thank you," she whispered, dampening Eredel's beard with her tears. "Thank you."

Light in darkness.

Hope in despair.

We can win.

CHAPTER SIX

A million years in the future, space was remarkably unchanged.

Marco stood inside Kaiyo's sensor suit, flying the mecha. The giant robot felt like his own body. It felt like swimming through a sea of stars.

"A million years seems so long to us humans," he said, speaking to Addy through his communicator. "But it's barely a lazy afternoon for the universe."

She flew beside him inside Kaji, the female mecha. She nodded.

"It took me longer to read your last book." She yawned. "We need some music as we fly."

She patched him into her audio feed. "Ripple" by the Grateful Dead began to play. For a moment they flew without speaking, listening to old music from a million years ago. It felt good to listen to music. To something familiar. Something human.

This is what we're fighting for, Marco thought. *Music. Art. Beauty. The nobility of humanity. The grays make no art. Humanity can be cruel, petty, hateful, violent. But it can make beautiful music. It's worth fighting for.*

They flew in silence, listening.

"Hey, Addy?" he finally said.

"Yeah?"

"I've been reading the news and catching up on the past million years. Guess what? The Maple Leafs *still* haven't won the Stanley Cup."

"I owe you an elbow to the ribs as soon as we reach Isfet," she said.

Isfet. It still lay light-years away. A desert planet, searing hot, a hellish world. It was there that the Nefitian monks had built their pyramid, had conducted their experiments. It was there that Ben-Ari had marooned them, smashing their starships, computers, and their time machine prototype. It was there that the monks had evolved, eventually becoming the grays, eventually perfecting time travel. It was there Marco and Addy now flew.

When Lailani had read the gray general's mind, she had seen a barren, desolate world. A pyramid rising to the glory of Nefitis. Ben-Ari, afflicted with visions after battling the grays, had seen the same place. It could only be Isfet. The desert world had become, over a million years, even more wretched, dark and desolate, filled with rust and death.

The mechas now flew toward that distant world. To face the grays on their own turf. To face the goddess. To face the terror that lurked within the pyramid. To destroy humanity's evil and restore their species to the path of light.

It seemed an impossible task.

What am I doing here? Marco thought. *I never wanted to be more than a librarian.*

He sighed. Life was not what he had expected.

"Think about it, Addy," Marco said. "We're a million years in the future. I can barely wrap my mind around it. According to everything we learned from the grays, Earth is gone. It's surreal."

"What's surreal?" Addy said.

"This!" Marco said. "Flying inside giant alien robots. Carrying four hundred marines inside our metal bodies. Being a million years in the future. Earth gone. Going on a quest to kill the Tick-Tock King, a monster inside a pyramid."

Addy's mecha tilted her head. "No, I mean—what does the word *surreal* mean?"

"It means this is fucked-up," said Marco.

Addy nodded. "Ayep. Shit's fucked-up all right. But we'll unfuck it, little dude. We're good at that. Unfucking things is our specialty."

Marco rolled his eyes. "Your specialty is poking me in the ribs. Wait. Addy! Stop! Stop poking me in the mecha!"

Kaji's colossal elbow drove into him. "Poke, poke!"

His mecha jolted. "Addy, my belly is full of marines, stop!"

They kept flying, moving at many times the speed of light. The Taolians, builders of the mechas, had been brilliant scientists; these ships could fly faster than any human vessel. The stars streamed at their sides.

Even at this remarkable speed, it would take days to reach Isfet. The mechas could be set on autopilot, allowing Marco to eat and sleep. But he spent most of his time in the mecha's head, strapped into the sensor suit. In here, Marco didn't feel like a passenger. He felt like Kaiyo himself, flying freely through space. It was a meditative experience—at least when Addy wasn't poking him and streaming her playlist into his cockpit.

Finally they saw it ahead: a small yellow star. The same star Ben-Ari had flown by a million years ago, picking up a distress signal. The same star around which she had found Yarrow, a planet of missing children, and Isfet, a planet of cruel monks. A planet with a pyramid. A planet where an evil empire had risen. The two mechas flew side by side, the marines within them, heading toward the star.

It begins, Marco thought, trying to suppress his fear. The great battle for Isfet. Two mechas against an army.

"You ready to kick some ass, Poet?" Addy said, speaking through his comm.

His palms were sweaty. His heart was pounding. Even Deep Being could not calm him now. This seemed different than any other battle he had faced. In other wars, he had flown with fleets. Now it was just him, Addy, and two companies of soldiers. True, he had the mechas. And true, they were mighty machines. But surely the grays had hundreds of thousands of ships. Could he and Addy even get near Isfet, let alone reach the pyramid and kill the Tick-Tock King?

It was likely, Marco knew, that they were flying to their deaths. A foolhardy mission. A desperate attempt to stave off extermination.

But he only nodded.

"Yeah, Addy. Let's kick some ass."

They flew closer.

They flew in silence.

They glided through space.

"Weird," Addy said. "Aren't the grays guarding their star system?" She swung her sword and raised her voice. "Come on! Where are you fuckers? I wanna fight!"

"They must be deeper into the system, guarding their planet," Marco said.

"Where *is* that planet?" Addy groaned. "I can't see anything past that asteroid field."

Marco frowned as they flew closer. Countless asteroids flew ahead, most just the size of boulders, some the size of mountains.

"This asteroid belt wasn't here a million years ago," Marco said. "We studied the holograms."

"Poet, things change over a million years," Addy said. "Think about it! A million years before our day, dinosaurs roamed the Earth."

"Actually, a million years before our time, there were already early humans on Earth," Marco said.

Addy nodded. "Exactly! And they rode dinosaurs. I saw it on *The Flintstones*."

"You don't actually think—" Marco groaned. "Never mind. Fly with me between these asteroids. Let's find Isfet. At least the asteroids might hide our approach."

They flew between the asteroids. Addy sliced a few of the smaller rocks with her sword. Marco had to nudge one asteroid aside with his hammer. He kept working the mecha's scanners, seeking a planet-sized object. The scanners should have been able to detect a gravitational field of that size.

And yet, nothing.

"I think dinosaurs ate the planet," Addy said.

Marco looked around at the asteroids. He spoke carefully. "I think this *is* the planet."

Addy whipped her head from side to side. She looked at him. "You mean, these asteroids …?"

Marco nodded. "Pieces of Isfet. The planet was destroyed."

With her mecha's giant fist, Addy grabbed one of the rocks. She jostled it. "Fuck, Poet. My holographic scanners are showing me the chemical composition of this rock. It matches Isfet." She hurled the asteroid away. "Somebody got here before us! Somebody else destroyed the grays. Fuck. I wanted to do it!" She sighed. "Well, at least those fuckers got blown to bits."

Marco's heart sank. "Addy, this is the right year. The era when the grays have their empire. Nobody else defeated them." His head spun. "I don't think the grays come from Isfet."

"What?" She scoffed. "Of course they do! Ben-Ari visited here a million years ago, remember? Back when she marooned the monks. She saw a pyramid. That's where the monks lived. And when Lailani interrogated the gray, when she saw a vision of his homeworld? She saw a pyramid! The same pyramid."

"What if there are two pyramids?" Marco said. "Hear me out. Ben-Ari marooned the Nefitian monks on Isfet a million years ago, right? They evolved into the grays. They built saucers. If they had space travel, why stay on Isfet, a desert world? They must have moved to another planet—and built a new pyramid there." He looked around him at the asteroids. "This is all that's left of their old world. Hell, could be the grays themselves destroyed it. Maybe this place had bad memories."

Addy groaned. "Great. So they moved! How the fuck are we going to find them now? Does one of these asteroids have a forwarding address on it?" She grabbed an asteroid the size of a house and shook it. "Hey, any grays inside here?" She hurled the rock, slamming it into another asteroid. "Fuck!"

The two asteroids cracked.

Marco stared, frowning.

Inside that asteroid, had he seen …?

"Goddamn fucking stones!" Addy grabbed another asteroid and tossed it, then another, then a third. "How the fuck are we going to find the grays now? Out of all the planets in the galaxy!" She groaned and sliced an asteroid with her sword. "We'll never find them! We—"

"Addy!" Marco shouted. "Stop! The asteroids!"

"I know, they're fucking everywhere!" Addy said. "Getting in my way, and—"

"Addy, look!"

Finally she fell silent and stared.

"What the—?" she said.

Things were moving inside the shattered asteroids. Black-and-red tentacles reached out from them. Jaws emerged. The asteroids crumbled, hatching hideous creatures.

They looked like krakens. Their tentacles were black and lined with claws, large enough to crush warships. Their red eyes blazed with hatred, and their jaws opened in silent screams, revealing teeth the size of buses. They must have curled up inside the asteroids, living there like serpents under rocks. Their sleep disturbed, they roared in fury, tentacles lashing. More asteroids shattered across the belt, and more of the krakens emerged.

The beasts were massive. Their tentacles were as long as the mechas were tall. The creatures spurted ink, propelling themselves forward in space. They charged toward the mechas.

Marco and Addy stared ahead.

From the arms of Kaiyo and Kaji, the cannons emerged. They fired.

Rounds shot forth and slammed into the krakens.

The creatures bellowed silently, no sound carrying in space. Holes blasted open in their flesh. Blood flew in a mist. One shell severed a tentacle.

And the beasts kept flying.

They reached the mechas, and their tentacles lashed out.

Addy swung her sword, severing one tentacle. Ten others grabbed her mecha, enveloping her. Claws lined the tentacles, cutting into Kaji's armor, punching holes through the metal. Inside the mecha, Addy screamed. She lashed at the creatures, struggling to free herself.

A kraken leaped toward Marco, tentacles flailing. Marco swung his hammer. A tentacle wrapped around the weapon and yanked, nearly ripping it from Marco's grip. More tentacles reached out to grab him. He fired his cannons, tearing through the beast. Gore sprayed him. Through the red mist emerged two more krakens. Their tentacles wrapped around Kaiyo, and jaws tore through the mecha's belly.

Screams rose from deep inside Kaiyo.

The tentacles were slicing the marines inside the mecha.

Controlling the machine from its head, Marco grabbed the tentacles with Kaiyo's metal hands. He strained to rip them off. With every tentacle he removed, another lashed against him. He spun through space. He fired again. He hit a kraken. He swung his hammer, crushing one of the beasts, only for tentacles to grab the weapon and yank it free.

Another tentacle slammed into his belly, punched the hull, and tore out a patch of armor.

Marines spilled into space, silently screaming, failing, freezing in the vacuum.

Marco fired cannons from both his arms. He hit kraken after kraken, pulverizing the creatures. A kraken leaped on him from behind, and teeth dug into his shoulder. Alarms blared. Smoke filled the mecha. Through the cracks in his body, marines in spacesuits were firing rifles at the krakens, but their bullets could not harm the massive aliens.

At his side, he was vaguely aware of Addy struggling too, slicing at tentacles with her sword. Holes gaped open on her mecha. She too had lost some of her marines, maybe all.

"Addy, we got to get out of here!" Marco shouted.

"I retreat from no fight!" she shouted back.

"This is not our fight!" Marco said. "We have to find the grays. This is not our hill to die on."

She ripped off a tentacle, only for another to grab her mecha's leg, to squeeze. More tentacles pulled the limb. A dozen krakens were now working together, pulling at Kaji's limbs. Addy screamed.

"Addy!"

Marco flew closer. He fired at the krakens, trying to rip them off Addy. More of the monsters grabbed his arms, tugging them back.

A gargantuan kraken, as large as the mechas, flapped toward them. Ink filled space, hiding the battle. The creature gazed with red eyes. Its tentacles reached out, grabbed Kaji's torso, and pulled. The smaller krakens yanked at her legs.

With bursts of fire and shattering steel, Kaji's left leg tore off.

Inside the mecha, Addy screamed.

Marco's hammer was gone. His cannons were barely making a dent in the horde. More asteroids kept cracking open, spilling out more krakens. Across the asteroid field, they kept hatching. Soon hundreds of the monsters were swarming.

But the smaller asteroids, Marco noticed, remained intact.

Some krakens seemed to fly around those small asteroids, to ... protect them.

Addy was still screaming, one of her mecha's legs missing. The krakens were still tugging her limbs. With a shower of sparks, her right arm tore off too. She yowled.

Marco turned to fly away.

"Poet!" she shouted. "Poet, damn it, help! Poet!"

Her cries tore at his heart. But he ignored her. He charged in the opposite direction, moving away from Addy, knocking his way through the swarm of krakens.

He reached one of the small asteroids. It was no larger than a sedan, small enough to fit into his mecha's hands.

He grabbed the asteroid, spun toward the horde, and shouted, "Let her go!"

The krakens spun toward him.

They opened their jaws and shrieked silently. There was no sound in space. They could not hear each other. But he saw the terror in their eyes.

"Let her go!" he shouted again, raising the small asteroid with one hand. He pointed at Addy.

The krakens growled and kept tugging on Addy's mecha. She had only two limbs left, and the krakens seemed determined to tear those off too.

Marco sneered and crushed the small asteroid in his hands.

A kraken hatchling—no larger than a man—died in Kaiyo's metal hands, staining them with blood.

The krakens roared.

They charged toward him, and Marco grabbed another small asteroid. No—not an asteroid. These were eggs.

"Let Addy go!" he cried, knowing they couldn't hear, hoping they still understood the message. He began flying toward Addy, the new asteroid held between his hands.

And the sea of krakens pulled back.

All around him, they snorted. They drooled. Their tentacles flailed. But they retreated from his advance.

He reached Addy. He waved the stone egg around. The krakens holding Addy released her, sneering, glaring at Marco with unadulterated hatred.

Her mecha was a mess. One leg and one arm were gone. A hole gaped open in her torso, revealing shattered decks and dead marines.

"Addy, you still with me?" he said.

She growled and hurled herself back toward the krakens, shouting and waving her remaining arm. Marco had to grab her and pull her back.

"Addy, no!"

She roared. "Those fuckers killed the marines inside me! They killed them!"

She howled wordlessly and attempted to leap back into battle. Marco gripped her with one hand, holding the asteroid with the other hand.

"Addy, these krakens nearly destroyed us," he said. "We have to fight the grays. That is our battle. Fall back with me now."

She stared at the creatures. The krakens loomed ahead, hundreds of them, maybe thousands. Their clouds of ink hid the stars. Marco couldn't believe how massive they were.

What the hell are these creatures? he wondered. He had studied alien species that lived in this sector of the galaxy, looking at thousands of photos on Wikipedia Galactica. He had never seen creatures this huge, this hideous. Obviously, they were a new species—at least, no older than a million years. What other terrors would Marco find here in the future?

The mechas began retreating. When they were far enough, Marco rolled the asteroid—and the baby kraken inside it—back toward the horde. The krakens protectively wrapped their tentacles around it. And it seemed to Marco that they were gentle. Loving. That they were scared.

Some things don't change even in a million years, Marco thought. *Even here, parents love their young.*

The two mechas flew away, leaving the asteroid belt. Marco looked back once, and he saw the krakens collect their dead. Their movements were gentle, and when they gathered the juvenile kraken Marco had killed, they seemed to weep.

"They were just trying to protect their young," Marco said softly.

Missing two limbs, punched with holes, Kaji looked at him.

"So are we, Marco," Addy said softly. "You did good. You saved me."

Yet as they flew onward, the dread kept growing in Marco.

They were a million years in the future. The galaxy had changed. Planets were gone. New terrors roamed the darkness. Their mechas were damaged, and they had lost two hundred marines. They had to find the Tick-Tock King inside his pyramid, yet they didn't even know where to look.

Perhaps the odds of success had always been small. But now they seemed nearly impossible.

"Addy, where the hell do we go now?" he said.

Addy was silent, an event as rare as an eclipse. They flew on through the darkness.

CHAPTER SEVEN

"Step forth, Einav Ben-Ari, daughter of Earth!"

She took a deep breath and approached the tree stump. The tree must have once been larger than a redwood; one could have built a house atop this stump. A stairway was carved into its side, and Ben-Ari climbed. She stood atop the stump and looked around at the council.

Before, back at the Lotus Temple, she had met the Admissions Council. Here was a different group—the Galactic Alliance Security Council. A couple hundred aliens had come, each of a different species, representing the foremost military powers of the Galactic Alliance. Here were the superpowers of the Orion Arm, the neighborhood of the Milky Way where the Alliance reigned.

This was, Ben-Ari thought, the last place she would expect generals to meet. The scenery seemed plucked from the pages of *Winnie the Pooh*. The grass swayed in the breeze. Flowers filled the valley. A pond shimmered nearby, and white mountains soared in the distance. This place was inside the Lemuria Dyson sphere, but it seemed more like a page from a storybook. A beautiful place. A piece of paradise.

And it was filled with killers.

Ben-Ari looked at these aliens, these ambassadors from warlike empires. A cyborg glared at her, a monstrosity of pink flesh and steel blades and saws. A crab was snapping its claws, its eight eyes moving on armored stalks. A towering bird, larger than an elephant, clacked its beak and clawed the earth. Inside the pond, a fish with teeth like swords stuck its head out from the water, gazing at Ben-Ari with a dozen eyes on barbels. One alien, standing on the grass, looked like a cute, petite little girl, but when she grinned, that grin extended from ear to ear, filled with fangs. She gave Ben-Ari a maniacal wink.

That must be why they meet in a peaceful, storybook valley, Ben-Ari thought. *Without this serenity, they'd butcher one another.*

She cleared her throat.

"Ladies and gentle—" She swallowed, cursing herself. "Fellow ambassadors! I am honored to stand here today, the first human to address the Security Council of the Galactic Alliance. I—"

"She looks weak," grumbled a creature that looked like an armored warthog the size of a brontosaurus.

"Hush, Balas!" said a towering, lanky humanoid with white skin, a bald head, and yellow eyes. Blades hung across his body. "Let her speak. You'll have your time to grumble later."

A little warrior trundled toward them. He looked like a psychotic dwarf, his orange beard wild. "Let the lad grumble!

I'll gladly cut the tongue from his mouth. And cut the wee willy between his legs."

For some reason Ben-Ari's translator gave the dwarf a Scottish accent.

The massive, armored warthog lifted a foot over the dwarf. "I would gladly crush you if I weren't concerned with getting shit on my foot."

Ben-Ari watched them for a while in amazement. Soon dozens of species were arguing.

Just like the old United Nations back home, she thought. Perhaps she shouldn't be surprised.

"Ambassadors, please!" she said. "Will you rest from your quarrels and listen to me?"

They looked back at her, grunting, snorting, hissing. One alien, a python clad in armor, kept hissing at her. She didn't like the look in its eyes.

These are not my enemies, she reminded herself. *These aren't the scum or marauders. These are the good guys.*

Yet it seemed that to get far in the cosmos, one needed a vicious streak. If so, she supposed that boded well for humans.

"I am Einav Ben-Ari, a human of Earth," she said. "We humans are proud to be new junior members of the Galactic Alliance. Our planet shows much potential. We have colonized our solar system and several neighboring star systems. We know the secrets of warp speed and wormholes. We are making great advances in solar power, and—"

"Spare us!" hissed a reptilian humanoid. "You are like an ape that boasts it can lick ants off a stick."

Apes have also been known to rip people's faces off, she thought, glaring at the reptilian.

She took a deep breath, calming herself.

"We show remarkable potential, yet we are in danger," Ben-Ari said. "An enemy threatens our world. An attack on one member of the Galactic Alliance is an attack on us all. I've come here to request military aid."

The aliens burst into laughter.

"An attack on a junior member?" A wrinkled, twisted creature with many eyes snorted. "Is that what you convened the council for? I must return to my wart bath."

A creature that looked like a living tree turned to leave. "Waste of time. Even for one with a lifespan like mine."

In the water, a pair of eels spat at Ben-Ari, then turned and swam away. A few insects—they were so small Ben-Ari had not noticed them until now—buzzed off in disdain.

"Wait!" Ben-Ari cried. "I read it in the charter. If one Galactic Alliance member is attacked, you have a pact to defend it! You—"

"You are a *junior* member," said a tall, female humanoid. Her skin was glimmering blue, her eyes indigo and mysterious, and lustrous white hair flowed down to her hips. "None of us are sworn to defend junior members." She laughed—a trilling sound. "If we were, we'd spend all our time fighting meaningless wars. Junior members are constantly bickering."

"We only care for the great wars," rumbled a living metal cube with legs. "Not petty skirmishes at the edge of the galaxy."

"I've heard enough from this wee lass." The red-bearded dwarf spat. "Never trust an alien with no beard!"

Ben-Ari looked around in dismay at the remaining members.

"Will no one help?" she cried. "The Galactic Alliance has massive fleets! Earth has much to give, to contribute, to learn and grow! Don't abandon us now."

Yet the aliens only snorted and turned away. She heard somebody muttering something about how junior members were a dime a dozen, and if they couldn't fight their own battles, what good were they? Ben-Ari stood on the stump, dejected.

A buzzing sounded beside her. She turned to see two metal balls—they were about the size of oranges—hovering and spinning around each other. Ben-Ari's hair crackled. The metal buttons on her uniform began pulling toward the balls; they were exerting a powerful magnetic field. The balls began to vibrate. A humming emerged from them, forming words.

"As a junior member, you do not qualify for protection from fellow civilizations," said the metal balls. "Yet you can purchase weapons from the Galactic Alliance Arms Dealers."

That was something at least.

"I would need more than weapons," Ben-Ari said to the floating balls. "I need ships."

The spinning balls bobbed in the air. "The Galactic Alliance Arms Dealers offer a wide variety of starships for sale. If you need them, they also sell robotic pilots, as well as infantry bots. Many species do not wish to risk the lives of their own soldiers, and they choose to purchase robotic warriors along with their ships. I am a member of the Arms Dealers Guild. I would be happy to negotiate a price with you."

Finally—hope.

"I would be most interested to—" she began, but an obese, orange alien stepped onto the tree stump, interrupting her.

"Off, off!" the orange alien said, shooing her away with flippers. "It is our turn to speak."

"Off, off!" said the alien's second head.

"Come, human," said the floating balls. "We will speak in another setting."

She followed the floating metal orbs through meadow and forest. This wilderness spread across the inner shell of Lemuria's Dyson sphere. The professor had told her that there was more mass in this sphere than the entire solar system back home, a fact that still spun her head. Thankfully, they didn't need to travel for millions of kilometers. The orbs took her to an elevator that rose from the surface, moving along cables wider than her body.

They traveled in the elevator for an hour, and the lands below—the inner surface of the Dyson sphere—became a patchwork of green, blue, and gold. In the distance, millions of kilometers away, Ben-Ari could just make out a haze—the opposite side of the Dyson sphere, as distant as Venus from Earth. In the center of this gargantuan megastructure floated the system's star, filling the sphere with heat and light, its energy powering the Galactic Alliance and all her might.

She wondered if any other Dyson spheres existed in the galaxy. The Milky Way was a large place, and the Galactic Alliance only controlled one of its spiral arms. And what of other galaxies? There were billions of other galaxies out there, far beyond the reach of even the fastest warp engine. The entire Milky Way, so vast humanity had barely begun to explore it, was just a tiny speck in the universe. And what of parallel universes? There were such wonders in the cosmos, and Ben-Ari's head spun to imagine what else was out there.

When I was a young cadet in Fort Djemila, I never imagined that someday I'd be here, seeing such marvels.

As they traveled in the elevator, the two floating magnetic balls spoke to her, vibrating to produce the words. The being's name was Kal Talek, and he came from a highly magnetized planet. Billions of years ago, Kal Talek explained, flecks of metal had begun to clump together on their world, to take form, to replicate their structures. Most life in the galaxy was organic; theirs was metallic. They had eventually evolved into their present form—the Kalatians. Each Kalatian was formed of two metal spheres, both filled with complex molecules able to manipulate electromagnetic radiation. Each Kalatian was both male and female, one sphere representing each gender, though they shared a single consciousness.

"We cannot see light, nor can we hear sound," Kal Talek said, his two spheres lazily orbiting each other. "We see the cosmos through electromagnetic energy, which is completely invisible to you humans."

"Fascinating!" Ben-Ari said.

The cosmos was filled with electromagnetic radiation, she knew. Everywhere she went, the air was rife with it. Yet it was a world completely invisible to her. What would it be like to actually sense this world? As a child, Ben-Ari had heard that dogs had a sense of smell a thousand times stronger than a human. She had tried—and failed—to imagine what it was like to "see" with your nose, to perceive a rich, wonderful world she could only sniff bits of. She couldn't even imagine what it was like to sense magnetism.

That is why we have science, she thought. *To detect the cosmos that is invisible to us humans. Dark matter. Electromagnetic radiation. Ultraviolet light. So much our bodies cannot sense! Truly, we are still biological apes.*

Kal Talek seemed to sigh. "How wonderful it must be to see the world! To hear sounds! To smell a flower! I cannot imagine experiencing the world in such a way. Truly you humans are blessed, and we Kalatians live in darkness!"

Ben-Ari smiled thinly. "The grass is always greener on the other side."

"I would not know," Kal Talek said. "Would that I could see the green of grass! Ah, but here we are. I can sense it in the magnetic fields. Behold, Einav Ben-Ari the human! The armory of the Galactic Alliance."

She gazed out the elevator and gasped.

Metal rings spread out around them, hundreds of them, rings within rings. The largest could have encircled a planet. Countless ships docked at these rings. Ben-Ari saw small starfighters, just large enough for a single pilot, along with warships the size of towns. Barracks rose atop the metal rings, and she glimpsed armored vehicles, formations of robotic fighters, cannons, tanks, mechas, and all variety of weapons, some she couldn't even understand.

She had never imagined an armory this large. Every weapon Earth had ever built, from the first stone-tipped spear to the great starfighter carriers of the twenty-second century, would have vanished here, drowning in this sea of weaponry. Here were enough weapons to conquer a galaxy.

By God, she thought, not sure if she was awed, horrified, or both.

The elevator detached from the vertical cable. It connected to a rail and began moving along one of the inner rings. Warships docked alongside the ring, while cannons, armored vehicles, and a host of other weapons rose atop the ring's flat surface.

Kal Talek spoke as they flew by. "Aren't they beautiful? We have Hunter-class starfighters, see them there? Top-of-the-line technology, each ship built with its own warp drive, fully equipped with plasma rifles, smart missiles, and laser blasters, and the cockpit comes with its own AI. No human pilot required! Ah, and look here!" They zoomed on by. "See those cannons? Those are Stinger-class hell-blasters, their shells built with drills that can penetrate even the thickest hulls. Simply fire-and-forget. Ah, and here! Up here!" The elevator zipped up to another layer of rings. "See there? Robo-troops. We sell them by the thousand. Each machine has the strength of fifty biological fighters. They will never tire, never disobey, and will assure your victory in the field. Yes, ma'am! We sell graviton-grenades, nuclear bunker-busters, electromagnetic disrupters, sonic rifles, and railgun tanks. Whatever you need, we sell it! Want to use your own biological soldiers? Not a problem! Here, see these mechas! See these transporters! If you need it, we sell it. With our weapons, you will win. Guaranteed every time."

Ben-Ari listened to the spiel. She had to admit: At first she had thought Kal Talek would be offering her weapons for free. A perk of junior membership. But this was a sales pitch. As a junior member, she couldn't borrow weapons. She could simply step into the store.

And she was broke.

Was there even any point to becoming a junior member?

"And we have whizzer-stars," Kal Talek was saying as the elevator zoomed by the weapons. "Cast out a thousand and watch them rip through an enemy fleet! And if you're looking to carpet-bomb a hostile world, nothing beats these older bomber-orbitals. And if you *really* mean business, we can sell you antimatter grenades under the table. Each one can destroy a small moon. Technically they don't exist, but for the right price, we—"

"Kal Talek," she said, interrupting the spinning balls, "I don't have much money."

He fell silent at once. The elevator screeched to a halt between a row of tanks and a spiky warship. The two spinning orbs seemed to stare right at her.

"How much do you have?" he asked carefully.

"None," she confessed.

Kal Talek hovered before her, silent.

"That does make things somewhat more complicated," he said. "But not impossible." He bobbed upward. "We do, you see, also offer loans."

Ben-Ari nodded. "Tell me about these loans."

He took her into an office, where Ben-Ari spent a while looking at graphs, then stepped out a few moments later, with Earth deep in debt.

I'm sorry, Earth, she thought. *It'll take you a century to pay this back. But without an army, you won't last a year.*

With every breath, she could feel the interest ticking up. With every heartbeat, Earth sank a little deeper into debt. Her grandchildren, most likely, would be cursing her name. But at least they would be around to curse.

Her pocket heavy with borrowed credits, she went shopping.

A few hours later, the *Lodestar* flew out of Lemuria, heading back to Earth.

Behind her flew ten thousand warships.

Most were U-Wing starfighters, small and fast and deadly. They were shaped like horseshoes, their heels mounted with cannons. An independent AI computer flew each one. On Earth, she would swap the AI with human pilots, for she trusted human instincts more than algorithms. Behind the starfighters flew warships, each the size of the legendary *Minotaur* that had fallen in the Marauder War. Thick shields coated the warships, and their cannons could devastate cities. Within each warship flew an entire brigade, five thousand strong, of robotic infantry. Each robot stood seven feet tall, coated with graphene armor, and wielded the firepower of a small army.

They were weapons of the Galactic Alliance. Weapons that could turn the tide for Earth. Machines of war built with the best technology the galaxy had to offer.

And with these terrors flew other ships.

Elongated tubes of water spun lazily, their sails as delicate and shimmering as dragonfly wings, looking from a distance like plankton. Inside them flew the Guramis, their fins like indigo banners. There were crystal ships, able to fire laser beams, and inside them flew the furry Silvans. There were rectangular warships lined with lights, piloted by the tall and green Taelians. There were Menorian ships too, shaped like spiral shells, and inside them flew Aurora's comrades—intelligent mollusks, the best pilots in the galaxy.

Ben-Ari gazed at this army from the bridge of the *Lodestar*. Her chest puffed out with pride.

"We have allies," she said. "We have friends."

The professor smiled at her. "For a moment there, you almost sounded like an optimist."

"All soldiers are optimists deep down inside. It's why we keep fighting. And I will never stop fighting for Earth."

Sadness filled the professor's eyes. "I hope that someday you can stop. That you can rest. That we can find peace."

"Peace?" Ben-Ari said. "I visited the Galactic Alliance, the headquarters of the most advanced species in our galaxy. And I saw machines of war. I saw armories that could devastate civilizations. I saw quarreling, warlike ambassadors itching for a fight. I wonder if peace is but a pipe dream, if every war we win leads to but a brief moment in the sun before the storm strikes again. Is that all we're doing? Surviving for brief moments of sunlight between eras of darkness?"

The professor held her hand. They gazed out at the stars together. "The most advanced species in our galaxy? No, Einav. We humans are adolescents, perhaps only toddlers, taking our first steps in the galaxy. The species we met are far more advanced than we. Yet they are, by and large, still biological, even if their biology is vastly different than ours. They are still governed by their animal instincts. Still quarrelsome. They are much like us humans, simply with better technology. They have formed societies. They maintain law and order. They have become Type II civilizations on the Kardashev scale, a goal humanity might not realize for thousands of years. But they are not the most advanced species in the galaxy."

She looked at him. "So who are?"

"We cannot see them," the professor said. "They have long ago abandoned their biological bodies. Some, perhaps, have uploaded their consciousness into machines. Many have abandoned the physical world altogether. They live as gods now, formless in the ether. Some perhaps are mere observers. Others perhaps still invisibly nudge galactic events like deities of ancient mythologies. Some might have forgotten the physical universe exists. There are levels beyond what the Kardashev scale describes."

"Is seems so far away," Ben-Ari said. "So difficult to comprehend. Do you think humans can ever reach that level?"

"No," he said. "For we would no longer be humans. But perhaps our descendants, a million years from now, will ascend above the petty quarrels of biological species. We would then become beings of pure consciousness and thought. The grays are not our only possible future. Perhaps instead of demons we can become angels."

"I'm not sure I would like that," Ben-Ari said.

Professor Isaac raised an eyebrow. "Oh?"

"Because without a physical body, I wouldn't be able to do this." She pulled him into her arms and kissed him.

"Hmm." He nodded. "You do make an excellent point."

As she stood with her professor, she never wanted this to end. Never wanted to reach Earth. With all her heart, she wished she could just keep flying, to find a peaceful world, to hide away. There were countless habitable worlds out there, places she and the professor could disappear, live an idyllic life in a forest or glen. She could send the *Lodestar* onward with another captain, perhaps Niilo or Fish or Aurora. Hadn't she earned this rest? She had fought so much, bled so much, killed so much for Earth. Did she not deserve some peace at last?

She sighed.

That is what my father did, she thought. *He hid away. He abandoned Earth at its hour of need. I never will.* She tightened her lips and squared her shoulders. *So I return to war. To blood. To killing. And maybe I fly to my death. I fly to Earth, a world that perhaps will never know peace. A world that I love, that I would die for. Because that is what soldiers do. We bleed in shadows so that others might stand upon our shoulders and glimpse the light.*

They flew on through the darkness, thousands of starships. They flew to war.

CHAPTER EIGHT

Kaiyo and Kaji hovered in space, lost in darkness, a million years in the future.

For hours they floated, marooned.

Finally—Addy's voice emerged from Marco's speakers. "Poet?"

He blinked. He had fallen asleep in his sensor suit. He turned his head, and Kaiyo turned his massive head in tandem. The mecha creaked with the movement. It had suffered serious damage while fighting the krakens. Several holes filled its hull. A platoon of marines had died in the assault; their blood still stained the cracks. He still carried three platoons. The marines huddled in the lower decks now, many of them wounded. The mighty Kaiyo, legendary mecha of Taolin Shi, now limped through space like a broken toy.

Marco looked at Kaji, Addy's mecha. It looked worse. It was missing a leg and arm. All but fifty of its marines had died in the battle, and holes the size of houses pierced its chest and belly. Scratches covered its feline face, deforming its beauty. Kaji looked like she had flown through Hell and back. Repeatedly.

"What's up, Ads?" he said, speaking into his mic.

"Wanna switch mechas?" she said.

"No."

"Come on! Be a friend."

"No, Addy."

She sulked. "You suck."

They flew in silence.

After long moments, Addy spoke again.

"Poet?"

"Yeah?"

"Wanna wrestle?"

"No Addy."

She groaned. "But I'm bored!"

"I'm trying to think, Ads. And you're disturbing me."

She flew closer to him. "What are you thinking about? Freaks?"

"What? No!"

"Um … neither was I," Addy said, sounding sheepish. "I wasn't at all imagining what the son of the Pillowman and Lobster Girl would look like." She thought for a moment. "Probably just like the Pillowman since you need limbs to have lobster hands. Hey, Poet, do you think that if the Elephant Man had a baby with the Bearded Lady, that it would become a Mammoth Boy, or—"

"Addy! For Chrissake! Firstly, you're being offensive and shouldn't call people freaks. Secondly, I'm trying to think of where the grays are. Where that pyramid is. And I have an idea." He sighed. "Not an idea I like to contemplate."

"Tell me," Addy said, sounding more serious. When she looked at him, he could only see her mecha's scarred face, but somehow he could see Addy's gaze in the robotic eyes. And he knew that all her jokes—about freaks, about hot dogs, about wrestling—were her way of coping with the horror. Back on Earth, as children, they would often run into bomb shelters as the scum rained death from the sky. At those times, Addy would laugh, would boast about slaying the aliens, would pretend Marco was an alien and wrestle him. She would act the clown. That's how he would know she was terrified.

She is the woman who raised Earth's survivors in rebellion against the marauders, he thought. *She is among the strongest, wisest, bravest women I know. She jokes now because she's scared. Because she's lost. Because she knows how dire things are but dares not confess it.*

"I'm thinking that we should go to Earth," Marco said.

Addy stared at him. "What? Poet, remember what the grays said? Earth is destroyed! We're a million years in the future now. Earth is gone. That's why the grays want to come back to our time. To conquer Earth."

"I know," Marco said. "But …" He sighed. "It's just a thought. A guess. A hypothesis. I have to see."

Addy shrugged. "All right, Poet, we can fly there. But we'll just find Earth smashed into chunks." Her eyes lit up. "Hey, there might be more crackers there!"

Marco frowned. "Crackers? Addy, stop thinking about food."

"I'm not! You know, crackers! With long tentacles, squirt ink, live inside asteroids …"

"You mean krakens!" Marco rolled his eyes.

"Yeah, whatever. Those assholes with the long tentacles. I've got a debt to pay." She clenched her one remaining fist. "I'm going to smash a few of those tentacled fuckers."

They engaged their engines.

They soared through space at warp speed.

For long hours they flew. Hours turned into days. They slept and ate in their mechas. They kept flying.

They charged forward, finally passing by Alpha Centauri, and saw Sol in the distance. Their home star. From this distance, it looked like any other star. But it was *their* star. It was the sun. And it looked the same as ever.

"Home," Marco whispered as they flew past the heliosphere, leaving interstellar space behind and entering the solar system.

They saw familiar sights. Pluto was there. Neptune shone ahead, shimmering blue. A few hours later, they passed by Jupiter. Its red storm was gone now, and the swirling patterns of orange, yellow, and red were different, but it was the same old planet, otherwise unchanged. It was the same old solar system.

When they flew past Mars, they were close enough to zoom in on Earth.

They expected to find chunks of asteroids, the planet gone, as the grays had described it.

They saw, instead, a new planet.

Addy and Marco gasped, staring through their telescopic eyes.

Where Earth had once been, a blue and white planet, they saw a black, desolate world.

"What the fuck?" Addy muttered, staring with him. "Who swapped Earth with that lump of coal?"

Marco sighed and lowered his head. "It's as I suspected. That is Earth."

"Bullshit!" Addy spat. "Earth is blue and green and white. It's beautiful. Almost as beautiful as me. That's just a black piece of shit in space!"

They zoomed in as much as they could. The black planet seemed lifeless. No blue oceans. No green forests. A haze of dark clouds cloaked it. Smog filled its atmosphere. It seemed inhospitable to life, crueler than Titan or Haven had ever been. A wasteland.

But it was Earth all right. The moon still orbited it. And when the smog parted, they could just make out the shape of the continents. The landforms had moved over the past million years, and the oceans had blackened, but there was no mistaking the general shape.

"It's Earth," Marco said. "Black Earth. An Earth polluted, ruined. An Earth destroyed." He switched off his telescopic lens and looked at Addy. "When the grays spoke of Earth's destruction, they didn't mean it was destroyed into pieces like Isfet. They meant this. An Earth turned into a wasteland."

"Poet, look!" She pointed back at Earth. "I see …" She gasped. "There's lights there! A city! Look!"

Marco looked back at Earth. As it rotated, the Middle East—at least what had once been the Middle East—came into view. Right around where Jerusalem had once been, they saw lights. It was a city. Marco zoomed in closer. Closer. As far as his zoom would go.

It was hard to be sure. From this distance, the image was still blurry.

But there, in the center of that dark city on the dark planet, rose a pyramid.

He switched off the telescope. He had seen enough.

"It's there," Marco nodded. "That's where Nefitis rules. That's where the gray army musters for war. On Earth."

"But … But …" Addy stared at the distant planet, then back at Marco. "But it's Earth! Fuck, Poet. The grays … I always thought …"

Marco sighed. "The grays were always saying they want to conquer Earth, right?"

Addy nodded. "Right."

"They said that in the future—in the time we're flying now—Earth was destroyed. Right?"

Addy nodded. "Right."

"Well, we always assumed that meant Earth was completely gone. Just chunks of rock floating through space.

We were wrong. They meant *this*. They *did* conquer Earth already. They conquered it in their own timeline, leaving the ruins of Isfet behind. They conquered *this* version of Earth—a ravaged world, polluted, disgusting."

Addy frowned. "The grays were always boasting about how they wanted to conquer Earth. Now you're telling me they already did conquer Earth?"

Marco nodded. "They want to conquer *our* Earth. A planet that's still green—mostly green, at least. A paradise compared to this place. Look. Lailani and Ben-Ari both saw the same vision. A dark, desolate world of ash. On that world, they saw a decaying city, a pyramid in its center. We always just assumed that's a futuristic Isfet, because that's where Ben-Ari marooned the monks, and that's where she saw a pyramid. We were wrong. The grays had built *another* pyramid. And it's right ahead of us."

Addy stared at him. Her mecha's face was expressionless, but he could practically hear her frowning.

"Fuck," she finally said.

Marco nodded. "Fuck indeed."

"So there's Black Earth, the ruin in front us, where the grays live. And there's Green Earth, the world we came from, which the grays want."

Marco nodded. "And remember, the grays can't go back in time to the really early days of Earth. They can't conquer Earth during the Stone Age, say. If they did, they'd stop Ben-

Ari from ever being born, from ever marooning the monks, from ever giving rise to their species. A paradox."

Addy sneered. "So it's a battle for Earth—here too. Our planet is ruined now, but it's still our planet. And the grays are infesting it. I say we exterminate them all."

"We can't," Marco said. "We only have these two mechas, and they're badly damaged. And we only have two hundred marines inside us. But we can try to reach the pyramid. We can try to break in. And we can kill the Tick-Tock King. Remember, he lives inside the pyramid. Nefitis's father. The creature that controls time travel. If we kill him, the grays can't time travel anymore. And our Earth—Green Earth—will be safe."

Addy clenched her fist. "Sounds good to me. Let's kill that Tic-Tac-Toe Fucker."

"Tick-Tock King," Marco corrected her. "Not Tic-Tac-Toe."

"Yeah, yeah, whatever. Hey, Poet, I bet that king would make an excellent freak. I'll photograph him before we kill him. I'll submit him for the next *Freaks of the Galaxy* edition. Fuck, I should have taken a photo of those tentacled crackers too! Can we fly back real quick and snap a photo?"

"No, Addy." Marco fired up his engines. He kept flying closer to Earth. "Come on. Let's go home."

They roared through space, streaming toward Black Earth, a planet once beautiful, a planet now desolate. A planet that maybe they could still save.

* * * * *

The mechas stood on the dark side of the moon. Hiding. Waiting. Planning.

Four marine platoons had survived the battle with the krakens. The soldiers now gathered on the lunar surface, wearing black spacesuits, railguns in hand. The company sergeant was speaking to them, preparing them for the war ahead. Above the marines loomed the two mechas, empty now, two dark sentinels.

Marco and Addy left the soldiers in the valley. They crawled up a hillside, scattering pebbles and dust. It was a long, steep climb.

"Poet, carry me!" Addy said.

"Addy, no."

She climbed onto his back. "But I'm tired!"

He groaned, clinging to the hillside. He struggled to shove her off. "God, Addy, you weigh as much as a tank."

"But we're on the moon now!" she said. "I only weight half as much here."

"As I said. As much as a tank." He finally managed to shove her off. "Climb nicely."

"But I'm not nice."

"Pretend for today," Marco said.

They kept climbing. Finally they reached the hilltop. From here they could see it on the horizon. Earth. A dark, wretched ruin. For a moment they could only stare in silence. Their sight of their beloved home, blackened and desolate, weighed upon them.

"Desolation, desolation, I owe so much to desolation," Marco quoted softly. "Jack Kerouac."

"Hot dogs, hot dogs, I owe so much to hot dogs," Addy said. "They're why I weigh as much as two tanks. Addy Linden."

Marco pulled out his binoculars. He focused them on Earth. His heart sank at the sight. He would never get used to seeing his homeworld like this. A black miasma hung over Earth. The oceans had turned black with filth. There were no more forests, maybe no more plants at all. The only sign of life was that city that rose upon Jerusalem's ruins.

And orbiting Earth—saucers. Thousands of saucers. *Hundreds* of thousands. He increased the zoom, trying to find the pyramid.

"Let me look!" Addy grabbed his binoculars.

"Hands off!" He shoved her back. "Where are your binoculars?"

"I, um ..." She twisted her fingers. "I tried to build a death ray with them."

"You *what*?"

She groaned. "A death ray, all right? I thought that if I took the lenses and added a flashlight, and— Oh forget it. Give me your binoculars!" She grabbed them and stared at Earth. "Fuck me. There are about a million saucers there, did you know?"

"I had an inkling." Marco sighed. "Maybe if our mechas were in top form, we could have broken through. Made it to the pyramid. But Kaji is missing two limbs. Kaiyo is full of holes, and one of its cannons is dead. We'll have a tough time taking on the gray fleet."

"I can take 'em all with one arm," Addy said.

"No," Marco said. "We need to be smarter. We need to do what we did back in the Marauder War."

Addy tilted her head. "You plan to abandon me to captivity, then go gallivanting across the galaxy with your friends?"

"No. Never again, Addy." He held her hand and looked into her eyes. "I will never abandon you again."

"And I will never say 'gallivanting' again. That literally hurt my tongue."

Marco smiled thinly. "Back in the Marauder War, we commandeered one of the marauders' ships. While we were gallivanting, we were able to pass as marauders for a while. So here's my plan. We attack with the mechas. Full force. But that'll only be a distraction. During the assault, you and I will commandeer a saucer. Then, while the mechas are still fighting, we'll make our way down to the pyramid."

Her eyes widened. "We'll have to find somebody else to fly the mechas."

Marco nodded. "Yes. We'll choose two marines as pilots. You and I should be the ones who fly down to Earth, who face the Tick-Tock King. That'll be the hardest part of this plan, and we're the two most experienced soldiers here. We're the soldiers who found and killed the scum emperor. You're the soldier who raised Earth in rebellion, and I helped find the Ghost Fleet—"

"While gallivanting," Addy said.

He nodded. "While gallivanting. The bottom line is: facing the Tick-Tock King is our task. So we'll hand the mechas over to two other pilots. We'll grab a saucer. We'll go down there. We'll get inside the pyramid and find the Tick-Tock King. And we kill the fucker."

Addy nodded. "That last part is my favorite."

They returned to the lunar valley.

They stood before their marines in the shadows of the mechas. Before them mustered the best warriors from Earth— from Green Earth, the Earth that had been. Each man and woman here had fought many battles. Many were veterans of the Scum War. All had fought the marauders. They were humanity's best.

It's so strange that we lead them, Marco thought.

He remembered himself and Addy a decade ago, mere corporals, joining Lieutenant Ben-Ari's elite platoon, the force tasked with finding and killing the scum emperor. Back then, Marco and Addy had been the most inexperienced soldiers in the group, two teenagers, terrified to be among such vicious killers, among the military's most decorated warriors.

Today he and Addy were captains—higher ranking than Ben-Ari had been that day years ago. Today they were war heroes, the famous soldiers who had slain the scum emperor, who had defeated the marauders, who would now lead the charge against the grays.

Deep down inside, Marco still felt like that young, scared boy. It was hard to believe he would be turning thirty next month. That he was divorced. That he had lost two children. That his body was covered with the scars of many battles. That now he commanded—not just stood among, but led—Earth's elite task force.

He looked at Addy. She stood there, wearing the same spacesuit as he did, black and coated with graphene armor. Behind her visor, her face was stern, proud, framed with blond hair. She was every inch the warrior, tall and strong and noble. With her shoulders squared and chin raised, she looked like the famous Addy Linden who had raised Earth in rebellion against the marauders, who had inspired millions to fight.

But Marco knew a different woman. He knew the Addy who cuddled with him at night when the nightmares haunted them. The Addy who joked about hot dogs and freaks because silence was too horrible, too filled with fear and memories. The Addy he had met at a planetarium twenty years ago. The Addy he had grown up with. Who was his best friend. His lover. His other half. The Addy who was the love of his life.

When my world collapsed, you were there for me, Addy, he thought. *You were always there. We'll never be apart again.*

And now the fear grew stronger than ever. Because Marco had already lost so many. His friends, Beast and Caveman. His commanders and mentors, Corporal Diaz and Sergeant Singh. Women he loved—Manisha, Kemi. He knew death was so common in this cosmos of war. He knew that their lives were so fragile. Even his. Even Addy's. And he could not bear the thought of losing her today.

Perhaps more than he feared for himself, even for Earth, he feared for Addy.

If she should die, I would lose all meaning to my life, he thought. *Love in war is fear distilled.*

He spoke to their marines.

"We came here to save Earth. We came here, and we saw what Earth could become. We came here to find a dystopia: our planet desolate, our species deformed into cruel beasts, all the hopes and dreams of humanity turned into nightmares. This all happened. But this can still be changed! Today, a million years past our time, we will face this dark future, and *we will change it.*"

The marines all stared at him, eyes somber, ready to fight. He saw their fear but also their determination, their courage.

Marco continued speaking.

"On Black Earth, there is a city of grays—the creatures who call themselves the Sanctified Sons, the mutated spawn of humanity. In the center of that city is a pyramid. Inside the pyramid is the creature some call the Oracle, others the Time Seer, and some call the Tick-Tock King. We will kill him today. And once we kill him, the grays will lose their ability to time travel. Our Earth—Green Earth—will be saved. Between us and that pyramid wait thousands of saucers."

One of the soldiers, a sergeant with long red curls and green eyes, spoke up. "Sir, how can we get past thousands? We could barely defeat those krakens."

"The mechas will no longer be our primary invasion force," Marco said. "We have perhaps overestimated their power. They are badly damaged now. Relying on them to reach the pyramids is too risky. But they can create a distraction. We will engage the saucers head-on. In the chaos, we will commandeer a saucer. Captain Linden, myself, and fifteen volunteers will board the saucer and attempt to reach Earth. The rest will remain in the mechas, attempting to break past the defenses using sheer force. If one of our groups fails, the other will continue with the mission."

"So we split up," said the redheaded sergeant. "One group attacks with brute force. The other group sneaks in."

Marco nodded. "Exactly."

"Sir?" the marine said. "I'd like to volunteer for the sneak assault. Sounds like more fun, sir."

They divided into groups. Marco, Addy, and fifteen marines joined the squad tasked with commandeering a saucer and sneaking down to the pyramid. The other marines, numbering a hundred and eighty, would remain to fight in the mechas. Two among that latter group volunteered to pilot the mechas instead of Marco and Addy; both had years of experience fighting in Earth's smaller mech-suits.

Before they entered the mechas, Marco addressed the marines again—final words before the battle.

"We've all fought aliens before. We fought scum. We fought marauders. We showed humanity's strength. Yet now we fight an enemy more terrifying. Now we fight ourselves. Here is not only a warning of what Earth might become—but of what *humanity* might become. Today we face two paths. One path leads humanity to the stars, to hope, to civilization, to light. Another path leads here—to evil, to desolation, to despair, to a cruel and twisted mutation of humanity festering on a ravaged world. Today we choose the right path! Today we choose hope! Today you are all soldiers of light!"

Addy stepped forward and raised her fist. "And today you fuck grays up the ass! Kill those fucking assholes! No soldier retreats! No soldier surrenders! If any one of you sons of bitches hesitates for a *second* in battle, I will personally ram my fist down your throat and yank out your goddamn fucking balls. We will show the enemy no mercy. We will win!"

"We will win!" they cried.

"Kill those fucking gray cocksuckers!" Addy shouted. "For Earth!"

"For Earth!" the marines cried back.

As they entered the mechas, Marco leaned toward Addy.

"I have to admit," he whispered. "Your speech was crude, but it did a better job of riling them up."

Addy patted his cheek. "That's why I raised Earth in rebellion against the marauders, while you were busy gallivanting." She kissed him. "My sweet little gallivanting poet."

Inside the mecha, they suited up for war. They grabbed railguns, the latest in HDF tech. These assault rifles fired regular bullets, but they were powered by electromagnetic force instead of gunpowder, allowing the bullets to travel much faster with far more energy. If a regular assault rifle could fire through a brick wall, railguns could fire through a tank. These weapons made their old T57 assault rifles, the guns that had won the Scum War, look like peashooters. They strapped on tactical vests filled with magazines and grenades. They wore graphene body armor, the material harder than diamonds. They slung jetpacks across their backs. Finally they grabbed laser blades for slicing through the hulls of enemy ships.

When they were ready, Marco and Addy stared at each other.

"Do I look like a killer?" Addy said.

Marco nodded. "Always."

She grabbed his head with both hands and gave him a deep kiss, ignoring the cheers from the marines around them.

"Let's go kick ass, everyone!" Addy shouted.

They all cheered louder.

The engines rumbled.

The two mechas took flight, soaring off the lunar surface.

They charged toward Earth. Toward thousands of saucers. Toward near-certain death and a sliver of hope in the dark.

CHAPTER NINE

Kaiyo and Kaji, two ancient mechas, were five hundred years old. They were rusty. They were cracked and filled with holes. Kaji was missing two limbs, while Kaiyo had lost his hammer. Centuries ago, they had been among the greatest weapons in the galaxy. Today they were relics.

Today they charged to new glory.

They stormed toward Earth headfirst, cannons firing. They had come from a million years ago. They had come to kill. They were humanity's last hope.

Earth grew closer ahead. The blue marble, cradle of humanity, had become a lump of coal. Its oceans were black with filth, and islands of plastic floated on its oily surface. Soot covered the continents. All plant life had perished. The polar caps had melted. All that remained was a blackened, charred sphere, dead but for a single city.

It was desolation. It was despair. It was the most precious planet in the cosmos.

And from that planet they flew.

They came charging toward the mechas. Thousands of them. Tens of thousands. The saucers.

Addy, Marco, and their squad of marines flew inside Kaiyo, the male mecha. They stood inside the giant robot's head, staring through a viewport at the battle.

Beside Marco, a sergeant stood inside the sensor suit, connected to the mecha's massive body. However the sergeant moved, the mecha moved. Nearby flew Kaji; another marine was piloting the female mecha.

Ahead swarmed the saucers. Closer. Closer. A thousand kilometers away. Five hundred. A hundred.

"Remember, we move quietly, in darkness," Marco said to the squad. "We grab a saucer in the chaos. We blast open the airlock. We do it quick and easy."

Addy sneered. "Show them no mercy. Give them nothing but death. You are soldiers of Earth!"

The mechas opened fire.

Kaiyo thrummed as his cannons blasted. The shells slammed into the charging gray fleet. Several saucers exploded. Myriads kept flying toward them.

The saucers flew closer. Fifty kilometers away. Ten. Five.

Space exploded.

The mecha jerked so violently Marco fell, and Addy fell onto him.

"Get off!" He shoved her. "You weigh a ton."

They struggled to their feet. The battle raged everywhere. The saucers were firing all their guns. Blast after blast hit the mechas. Hole after hole pierced the giant machine.

Fire blazed. The saucers streamed like schools of fish, swarming up and down, surrounding the two mechas, blasting their guns. Everywhere was fire and light and shattering metal.

"Fire!" Addy shouted. "Cut through them! Kill those sons of bitches!"

The mechas fired their cannons. Each blast tore through the lines of saucers, taking out dozens, maybe hundreds of the starships. Hundreds more replaced the fallen. It was like two humans running through a swarm of hornets, firing handguns, stung every step. A chip of armor fell off Kaiyo. Kaji lost her second arm. Blasts rocked the machines.

"Get us closer!" Addy shouted hoarsely. "Charge, charge! Tear through them!"

Marco grabbed her. "Addy, we have to deploy!"

She was sneering, staring out the viewport, waving her fists as if she were still flying a mecha. "Break through! To Earth!"

He could barely hear her. The battle was deafening. Explosion after explosion rocked the mecha. The machine jolted so madly they fell again. Kaiyo's leg tore free and tumbled through space, plowing into saucers. The pilot screamed. Earth was barely visible past the swarm of saucers.

Nearby, Kaji had lost her cannons. The female mecha was reduced to fighting by swinging her one arm, knocking saucers aside like a woman swatting at flies. Countless saucers kept firing their lasers, peppering the mecha.

Kaiyo rocked again. Explosions blasted against them. The mecha was burning. Kaiyo swung his own arms, tearing through saucers, but the enemy seemed endless. The mighty mechas were falling apart.

"Addy!" Marco grabbed her and shouted into her ear. "We have to deploy! Now!"

She nodded.

They ran.

Their squad of marines ran behind them.

The mecha jolted. Blasts shook the machine. Fires raged everywhere, and cracks raced across the hull.

The squad reached the airlock at the back of the mecha's head. The marines closed the visors on their helmets.

Marco stood on the edge for a second, staring, eyes hard.

The battle blazed before him, thousands of saucers flying everywhere, firing, shattering, an inferno above Earth.

He leaped out into Hell.

Behind him, Addy and fifteen other soldiers followed.

Their jetpacks roared, and they flew through the storming, furious, blazing battle.

Marco could barely make up from down, left from right. The formations of saucers flew everywhere. Laser beams flashed all around. Explosion after explosion lit space. Behind him, the two mechas were struggling to charge forth, to break through the swarm, to reach Earth with the marines inside. Another explosion rocked Kaiyo, and the massive mecha nearly split in two. Holes gaped open in its chest, revealing marines inside—screaming, burning, dying.

Marco kept flying.

Addy flew at his side. Their marines flew with them. Their jetpacks left trails of fire behind.

"See that enemy formation?" Marco said. "Fly to the saucer at the back."

"Why that one?" Addy said.

"It's small. Less grays aboard. Come on!"

They flew.

Above them streamed a squad of saucers, blasting out lasers. Fire lit space. Marco glanced behind him to see Kaiyo split in half, showering sparks.

Fuck.

"Forward!" he shouted.

Kaiyo's top half, head and arms and flaming torso, came falling toward them.

"Forward, forward!" Marco cried.

The squad streamed forth, blasting their jetpacks. Marco and Addy flew at the lead. Behind them flew the fifteen marines. The top half of Kaiyo was burning, a hellish monument the size of a starfighter carrier. It came crashing down toward them.

"Forward!" Marco shouted at the top of his lungs.

They blasted forth as the ravaged mecha fell.

Kaiyo's flaming head took out the back of their squad.

Marines screamed and were gone.

The remains of Kaiyo fell below them, burning up as they crashed toward Earth. Addy and Marco kept flying. With them flew only eight marines.

"Make it to the saucer!" Marco said. "Hurry!"

Kaji was still fighting, keeping the saucers occupied. But the female mecha was crumbling, burning, losing more and more chunks of metal. Her remaining leg crumbled.

Marco focused on reaching the saucer.

He flew closer. He was only moments away.

And the enemy saw them.

Three saucers streamed toward the marines.

Lasers blasted.

The beams took out one marine. A second. A third.

"Kaji, we need help!" Marco shouted into his communicator.

The saucers flew around them. More lasers fired. A fourth marine died. A fifth. The squad was now down to just Marco, Addy, and three others.

The saucers flew upward, then prepared to swoop and slay them all.

"Kaji!" Marco shouted.

And through the battle, Kaji flew.

The female mecha was just a torso, a head, and one arm. Burning. Scattering parts. But still Kaji fought. She swung one flaming arm, an arm the size of an office tower, and sent saucers flying.

If any more saucers had intended to attack Marco and his marines, they were now charging at Kaji.

Explosions rocked the mecha.

Her torso shattered open, spilling out marines.

They gave their lives to save us, Marco thought. *To save Earth.*

He kept flying.

He saw his destination—the small saucer ahead. Slower, smaller than the others. He gritted his teeth and slammed into the hull with a thud and terrifying pain.

Addy thumped into the hull a second later.

Three more marines hit the hull with them.

They crawled toward the airlock. They got to work at once. Their laser blades made short work of the lock, and the door swung open.

The marines leaped inside, railguns firing.

The grays were waiting for them.

The lanky, wrinkled creatures stared with their black eyes. They raised guns and fired. Electrical bolts slammed into the marines. One man fell from the airlock, chest burned open, only for another saucer to slice him in two. Marco took a blow to the shoulder. It hurt like a son of a bitch, but he stood his ground. He fired his railgun.

His bullet ripped through a gray. Addy fired with him, shouting hoarsely. Their last marines—only two men—fired their guns in a fury. Grays fell. Lasers and bullets flew back and forth. A blast tore the arm off one marine, but the man stayed standing and howled, firing his railgun with one hand, tearing down more grays.

Finally the battle ended. They stood over the corpses of grays—Marco, Addy, and two marines, one with a missing arm.

"Come on, charge!" Addy shouted, racing deeper into the saucer.

They ran.

As they raced down the corridor, more grays burst out ahead of them. The soldiers fired their guns. Blasts tore through the creatures. Marco took a bolt to the thigh, screamed, and limped onward, firing his railgun, tearing through the enemy. The grays were everywhere. They scuttled along the walls. They leaped down from the ceiling. Their mouths opened to howl, revealing teeth like needles. One gray leaped onto Addy and bit, tearing through her shoulder, and Marco ripped the creature off and riddled it with bullets.

They ran onward, plowing through the enemy until they reached the saucer's bridge.

Two grays stood in the round, dark chamber, working at control panels. A screen revealed a view of the battle outside. Kaji was burning, flailing her last arm. Saucers had attached to the mecha like leeches, and grays were already boarding her.

One of the gray pilots turned away from his control panel. He leaped toward the invaders.

Marco put a bullet through the creature's head.

The second gray froze, hands hovering over his control panel. He hissed, hatred twisting his face.

"I … surrender …"

Addy raised her gun.

"Wait." Marco pulled her gun down. "We need him alive. If he behaves, at least." He walked toward the gray and pressed the barrel of his gun against the creature's bulbous head. "You'll behave. Take us down to Earth. Now! One wrong move and I spray your brains over the controls."

At the doorway, a marine collapsed, bleeding profusely from the stump of his missing arm. His friend began applying a tourniquet. Addy stood by Marco, bleeding from her shoulder, panting, her eyes still hard, showing no pain. Outside, the battle still raged.

"Now!" Marco shouted, jabbing the gray's head with his barrel.

The creature sneered and began to fly the saucer.

They left their formation of saucers and headed through the swarm toward Earth. The other saucers parted to let them pass.

Behind them, a massive explosion tore through space.

Shrapnel flew.

Fire raged.

Chunks of metal rained down toward Earth. One was Kaji's head.

The great mecha was gone.

Marco stared in horror.

Of two mechas and four hundred marines, they were all that remained: him, Addy, and two other soldiers in a commandeered saucer, one of them gravely wounded.

They were the last hope of humanity.

"What else is new," Marco muttered to himself.

With the mechas destroyed, the battle was dying down. Through the viewport, Marco saw roaming squads of saucers seek out surviving marines. A handful of human soldiers still floated through space in their suits. Marco watched, grimacing, as the lasers took them out. Each death stabbed him. Each death was to give him life.

You will not have died in vain, he swore.

At his side, Addy clenched her fists. Her eyes hardened. Her jaw tightened. She was watching them die.

Some saucers remained around the wreckage of the mechas—at least the parts that had not yet crashed to the planet. But most of the saucers were now flying back to Earth.

"Keep us flying nice and steady, buddy," Marco said, keeping his muzzle on the gray's head. "You're going to take us straight to the pyramid. You just breathe wrong and I blow out your brains. Capiche?"

The gray glared at him, silent.

Addy added her muzzle too, poking the creature's bloated, wrinkled head. "Got it, you ball sack with eyes?"

The gray sneered. A deep, grumbling laughter bubbled up from him.

"So much pain awaits you ... The Oracle knows you're coming." He coughed a laugh. "I will gladly take you to him. To your eternal misery."

"Less talking, more flying," Marco said. "Go on. Fly!"

They headed down toward Earth, flying among thousands of other saucers. They left behind the wreckage: a few chunks of mechas, hundreds of shattered saucers, and the corpses of marines. On the floor of the commandeered saucer, the marine with the missing arm had passed out. His comrade was still kneeling above him.

Four soldiers against an empire, Marco thought. *One of us dying.*

Addy placed her hand on his shoulder and squeezed.

"We've faced worse odds," she said with a crooked smile.

He nodded.

We did. And we still won. And I lost nearly all my friends. He looked at Addy. She smiled at him. *I can't lose you too.*

He returned his gaze to the viewport, watching Earth grow nearer. Soon the dark planet encompassed his entire field of vision. Africa and Europe were closer now, squeezing a canal of polluted water. With the oceans black with soot, Marco could barely distinguish water from land. The smog covered everything. It was a world painted in charcoal and burnt browns. A dead world. A blackened Earth.

And there, in the Middle East—a patch of lights.

A city.

The homeland of the grays.

In its center—the pyramid.

We're close, Marco thought. *We're so close. He's down there. The Oracle. The Seer. The Tick-Tock King.*

He stared at the city below.

An image flashed through his mind.

A hideous creature, hanging by cables within a ring of crystals. A creature with skin sewn over its empty eye sockets. With a leering, drooling jaw full of fangs. With a hundred claws, reaching out. A creature cackling. Waiting. Whispering.

Marco ... I see you ...

He grimaced.

He fell to his knees.

"Poet!" Addy knelt by him and helped him up. "Poet, what's wrong?"

He stood, wobbling, and rubbed his eyes. "Nothing. I … I'm fine."

The gray pilot laughed.

Addy spun back toward the gray and jabbed his temple with her barrel. "Shut the fuck up, baldy, and keep flying. Laugh one more time and bullets meet brain."

They flew closer. They dipped into the atmosphere with a rattle and fountain of fire. Dark clouds filled the air. No, not clouds. This was smog. A veil of smoke and foul gasses enveloped Earth. It was like flying over a coal refinery. There was no blue to the sky, no green to the land below. Everywhere was gray and black and rusty brown.

As they were flying down to the city, a monitor on the bridge crackled to life.

Addy and Marco ducked, hiding under a metal slab.

From his hiding place, Marco could see a hideous visage appear on the screen. It was a gray, skin wrinkly and splotchy. A scar ran across the creature's face, digging across one empty eye socket. The gray barked a few words in a guttural language. The saucer's pilot answered, then looked back. He grinned down at Marco and Addy.

"He wants to know why I've left my squadron," the gray hissed. His grin widened, and saliva dripped from his fangs.

"Your squadron was destroyed in the battle," Marco whispered. "You request to land in the city starport."

The gray hissed at Marco, a sound halfway between disdainful sneer and mocking snort. He looked back at the gray on the monitor. He spoke a few words in his harsh tongue. The scarred gray on the monitor answered, voice growing louder, lips peeling back to reveal his teeth.

The pilot turned back toward the crouching Marco and Addy.

"He wants to know why I have a pair of humans visible on my security camera."

Addy fired her railgun.

The bullet tore through the pilot's head and shattered the monitor. The scarred gray vanished in a fountain of shards.

"Shit pilot anyway," Addy said. "He didn't offer us peanuts."

Marco cursed and leaped forward. The saucer tilted, then began to plunge downward. Marco shoved the dead pilot out of his seat and grabbed the controls.

Below them, several saucers were soaring toward them, lights flashing.

"Addy, the cannons!" he shouted.

"Where?" she cried.

He pointed. "There! Those controls!"

Addy leaped into a seat and hit buttons. Laser blasts flew out from the saucer's cannons, slamming into the ships ahead.

The ships fired back.

Blasts hit their saucer.

They swerved, careened, and tumbled down through the air.

"Poet, damn it, fly straight!" Addy shouted.

"I'm trying! Keep firing!"

They spun madly through the sky. The other saucers circled around them, vanishing and reappearing through the smog. Sirens blared. More blasts hit them. They jolted, and cracks raced across the bridge. Fire burned in the corridor behind them.

"Poet!"

He yanked the yoke with all his strength. He managed to steady their flight. He could no longer see the city below. They shot forth. He didn't know which direction they were moving. The smog obscured everything.

An enemy saucer appeared out of the smog. Addy fired, scoring a direct hit. The shuttle exploded, and they shot through the shrapnel. But more saucers were still chasing them. Another blast hit them. They tumbled downward. Marco yanked on the controls. He managed to steady their flight. They dipped out from smog and saw mountains dangerously close below.

"Poet, there are still five saucers behind us!" Addy shouted.

"Keep fir—"

Blasts hit them.

They dipped.

They stormed toward a mountaintop, spewing smoke. Addy screamed. Marco pulled the controls, and they veered to the left. They skimmed the mountainside. Stones cascaded. The side of their saucer tore open, and foul air streamed into the ship. They coughed.

"Poet, fly us higher! Fly! Into the smog!"

She was firing madly. She took out another saucer. More kept pursuing.

Marco stared ahead, sneering, struggling to gain altitude. He managed to rise, to reach toward the smoggy clouds.

Two saucers emerged from the smoke.

Lasers blasted.

The bridge shattered. Fires blazed. The ceiling tore open, and smoke filled the commandeered saucer.

They dived down, wreathed in smoke.

Marco and Addy screamed.

They glanced off one saucer, careened, and hit a mountainside. They tumbled downward. Their engines blazed.

"Addy, down!"

He grabbed her. They stormed toward a valley. They flattened themselves on the floor, shut the visors on their helmets, and covered their heads. Marco had a sudden vision of them as children, huddling in a bomb shelter, gas masks on.

They hit the ground.

The cosmos itself seemed to shatter.

Every shard of Marco's being screamed with pain.

Fire washed over him.

Metal beams crashed onto him.

In the devastation, he reached out and gripped Addy's hand.

He was a child in the snow, his mother dead.

He was a youth growing up in the war, hiding in bomb shelters.

He was soldier, huddling in a tent, a helmet wobbling on his head, a rifle slung across his back, just a kid, his uniform too large, the war too big.

He was languishing in Haven, rotting away in his cell.

He lay in devastation. Maybe dying. Maybe already dead.

But she was with him.

As always—through all his despair, through darkness and light, through fire and rain, she was there. Addy.

And in the ruin of this saucer in a nightmarish future, her hand tightened around his.

Addy. She was alive.

Marco grimaced and pushed against the rubble trapping him. It weighed him down. He groaned and shoved with all his might, knocking back a beam and section of bulkhead. His spacesuit was armored, built to withstand bullets. Without it, he would have been a red smear on the floor.

He pulled wreckage off Addy. She lay on the floor, moaning.

"Ugh, Poet, I feel like an elephant fell on me."

"Now you know how I always feel when you sit on my lap," Marco said.

He helped her to her feet. They stood inside the saucer's smashed bridge. Electrical cables sputtered. Scattered fires burned. Through the shattered roof they could see the smoggy sky.

They checked on the two marines. Both lay dead. The marine with the missing arm had died from blood loss, it seemed. His friend lay with a metal rod piercing his visor and skull.

"Fallen warriors," Addy said and lowered her head. "Heroes."

Marco lowered his head too. For a moment they both stood in silence.

Guttural voices interrupted their silence.

Marco spun around, then ducked and pulled Addy down.

Through the cracked hull, they could see them. Grays were walking across the landscape toward them.

Marco gestured silently. He and Addy crept toward the dead marines, stripped them of ammo and grenades, then pulled the dead bodies toward the saucer's smashed controls. The grays were speaking louder now, moving closer.

Marco and Addy slunk out of the smashed cockpit. They walked at a crouch. The land was dark, and they wore black, and they had trained for years to move in silence. They made their way across a rocky landscape. They still wore their visors down, breathing through their oxygen tanks, not daring to breathe this smoky air.

They found a boulder in the shadows. They knelt behind it and gazed back at the crashed saucer.

Marco was shocked by the damage. There was barely anything left, just a pile of debris. His and Addy's graphene spacesuits were wonders of technology.

A group of grays reached the smashed saucer. Even in the darkness, they needed no flashlights. With their large eyes, even these shadows probably seemed as bright as day to them.

The grays spent a while in the wreckage, lifting chunks of metal, poking, prodding. When they found the two dead marines, they cackled and spoke gruffly in their language. One gray tore the leg off a soldier. The others leaned in, ripped into the marines' torsos, and pulled out the organs. And they began to feed.

"Sick fucks," Addy whispered. She raised her railgun.

Marco hushed her and pulled her gun down. They crouched lower behind the boulder, hiding. But they could still hear the grays eating—crunching, chewing, slurping.

"They're cannibals," Addy whispered.

Marco shook his head. "We're just animals to them. Keep quiet."

They waited behind the boulder until the sounds of feasting ended. Thankfully the ground here was solid stone; they had left no footprints. When Marco glanced around the boulder again, he saw the grays departing.

"They'll be back soon with a salvage crew, I reckon," Marco whispered. "We better get far from this wreck."

"How far are we from the city, do you reckon?" She poked him in the ribs. "Cowboy."

He gazed back at the wreckage. He sighed. "We were flying fast. And we were high in the atmosphere, on the edge of space, when they chased us off course. Addy, we could be hundreds of kilometers away from the pyramid."

Her mouth dropped open. "Fuck me. *Hundreds* of kilometers off course?" She looked around her. "Are you telling me we have to walk hundreds of kilometers? With no food or water? That could take …"

"In this terrain?" Marco sighed. "Weeks."

She clutched her head with both hands. "This is fucked, Poet. This is fucked! We'll die of dehydration or hunger before we reach the pyramid. And God knows how many grays are in our way."

Marco shrugged. "Probably not many. After all, it's hundreds of kilometers of desolate wasteland, bereft of all sustenance or hope, where none could expect to survive. We're lucky."

"You're lucky I don't pound you in the face," Addy muttered. "All right! Fuck it. Come on. Let's walk. When I get hungry, if I can't find a Hot Dog Shack, I'm eating *you*."

It seemed hopeless. It seemed like a slow death. Perhaps it would be more merciful to place their guns to their heads and pull the triggers.

But they had always lived on the edge of hopelessness. They had always lived in despair.

They walked across the badlands under a sky of smog, leaving the wreckage behind. Ahead, the desolation spread to the horizon.

CHAPTER TEN

Lailani stood in the ruins of an ancient church, shaving her head.

Other soldiers filled the church, this shell of old bricks in Jerusalem. They cleaned their guns, climbed crumbling stairs to the belfry, slept in corners, ate battle rations, prepared to kill, waited to die. Lailani wore secondhand battle fatigues, the olive-green fabric frayed at the hems. She stood in front of a dented bronze mirror. She ran the electric razor over her head, and her black locks fell around her boots.

When finally her work was done, she spent a moment gazing at herself in the mirror. She was going to turn thirty in only a few days, but she still looked like a teenager. She looked like the old Lailani. The girl who had joined the Human Defense Force at eighteen, scars on her wrists. That little girl, four foot ten and full of piss and vinegar, eager to slay the scum. Ahead in the mirror, that girl stared back. War paint on her cheeks. Her almond-shaped eyes hard. Her hair buzzed down to stubble. Among the smallest soldiers in the army, not even a hundred pounds, but fierce. Always fierce.

And yet … No.

She was not the same girl.

Tattoos of her favorite flowers now covered her scars, softening her. She wore new insignia: three brass circles on each shoulder, denoting her a captain, a leader, no longer a mere private.

And her eyes—yes, they were different too. Still hard. Still fierce. But there was new wisdom to them. New ghosts.

And new softness.

Here was no longer the suicidal girl who had known nothing but the shantytown. Here was a woman who had loved and lost. Who had made dear friends. Who loved so much. At eighteen, she had wanted to die in battle, a glorious suicide. She had hated life. Now, nearly thirty, she loved life and loved humanity so much her heart felt full to bursting.

"Mistress, why are you crying?"

HOBBS moved through the church toward her. His footsteps thundered, and his metal body clanked. The robot stood over seven feet tall, dwarfing even the mightiest human soldier. The others moved back before him, gazing up and muttering about the metal beast. Following the robot loped Epimetheus, Lailani's loyal Doberman. The dog too was imposing; he was larger than Lailani, and his muscles rippled, and his jaws looked like they could rip off a man's arm. Yet Lailani knew that both HOBBS and Epimetheus were gentle giants—gentle, at least, among those they loved.

She wiped her eyes.

"I was just remembering old friends," she said.

HOBBS halted before her. He placed a metal hand on her shoulder. His hand was so large it engulfed most of her upper arm. Epimetheus nestled her.

"You have new friends, mistress," HOBBS said. "Friends who love you."

Lailani embraced him. She laid her cheek against his wide, cold chest.

"Thank you, HOBBS." She smiled up at him. "And I told you—you don't have to call me mistress. Just Lailani or Captain if you must."

HOBBS nodded. "Yes, Captain Lailani."

She snorted out a laugh. "That works too."

Epimetheus sniffed at her fallen locks of hair, then jumped up, placed his paws on Lailani's chest, and began licking the stubble on her head. She laughed and mussed his droopy ears.

She was about to seek out some battle rations when the rumbles came from outside, and the church trembled.

Lailani inhaled sharply and grabbed her rifle.

"The grays," she whispered.

She ran across the church nave. The other soldiers ran with her. They burst outside into the searing sunlight.

The ancient city of Jerusalem spread around them—at least what was left of it. It was here that the scum had first struck Earth sixty-two years ago. It was here that the first great alien battles had been fought. Every last soul in Jerusalem had perished or fled that day. Yet destruction was nothing new to

Jerusalem; the city had been sacked by the Crusaders, the Romans, the Babylonians, by many others going back thousands of years. Like a phoenix, it had risen again and again from the ashes. Here was a microcosm for Earth.

All around her, the city spread across the mountaintop. Orphaned archways of craggy bricks, the walls around them long fallen. A few scattered palm trees growing from rubble. A handful of stray camels snorting and chewing their cud by wells. Old domes and minarets. The remains of ancient churches, synagogues, and mosques, some of them thousands of years old. Every brick was the same limestone, craggy and large, the stone's color either white, beige, or gold depending on how the light hit it. Beyond the city walls spread the desert— dry hills rolling toward dunes and a hazy horizon.

A city in ruins. But there was new life here now.

Thousands of soldiers filled the ruins. They watched from guard towers. Their tanks stood at the city gates. Their cannons lined the walls. Beneath the city, thousands of other soldiers worked in bunkers. Here was the great central command of the war. Here they were set up to await the grays.

The grays would attack again. They all knew that. They were all waiting for a doomed battle.

The rumbles sounded again.

The city shook. Bricks rolled. Pebbles danced. An archway cracked. The sky seemed to open, and the vessels emerged.

Lailani sneered and raised her gun, for an instant sure
the grays were attacking. But no. Those were not saucers that
emerged from the sky, engines rumbling. They were round,
boxy shuttles, each the size of a bus. They were alien, had to be
alien; Lailani had never seen shuttles of such a design, boxes
that could fly with no wings. Yet the phoenixes of the Human
Defense Force were painted on their sides.

The shuttles landed in the city with thuds. One shuttle
landed only meters away from Lailani.

She kept her rifle in her hands, staring.

A hatch opened on the shuttle before her. Across the
city, soldiers stared at other shuttles, guns pointed and loaded.

A ramp extended from the shuttle, and out stepped Ben-
Ari.

Lailani gasped.

Ben-Ari wore the uniform of HOPE rather than the
HDF—it was navy blue with brass buttons. Her ranks shone on
her shoulders, denoting her a captain of HOPE, humanity's
premier space agency. In the military, a captain was only a
junior officer; it was the rank Lailani herself now had. But in
HOPE, a captain was a senior rank, equivalent to an HDF
colonel. Einav Ben-Ari had come a long way from the young
ensign Lailani had met over a decade ago; she was now among
Earth's greatest leaders.

Lailani knew she should salute. She knew she should
show deference and respect to her commanding officer, to her
heroine.

Instead she ran up the ramp, leaped onto Ben-Ari, wrapped all four limbs around her, and squeezed her in a crushing embrace.

"Captain!" Lailani said. "I mean—Major! I mean—Ben-Ari, you're back!"

Lailani was probably breaking every rule of decorum in the book. Another officer might have court-martialed her. But Ben-Ari only smiled, hugged her back, and kissed her cheek.

"Hello, Lailani."

From inside the shuttle, she heard metal clanking. And they began to emerge.

Robots. Hundreds of robots. Ben-Ari and Lailani rushed down the ramp, and the robots marched out after them. More robots were emerging from shuttles across the city. Each one looked even deadlier than HOBBS. They were like humanoid tanks. Guns were mounted onto their forearms and shoulders, and their feet shook the earth. They took formation across the ruins.

More shuttles kept landing. More robots kept emerging. Thousands soon covered the ruins.

"Wha—?" Lailani blinked, rubbed her eyes, and stared around her. "How—?"

"I went shopping," Ben-Ari said.

President Petty marched up toward them, surrounded by security. He had finally removed his business suit and wore a leather bomber jacket and a helmet. Ben-Ari and Lailani stood at attention and saluted.

Petty stared at the robotic troops, then back at Ben-Ari. He returned the salute.

"God bless you, Einav Ben-Ari," he said.

Ben-Ari spent a while describing her ordeal, how she had found the Galactic Alliance headquarters, how she had secured junior membership, how she had purchased weapons on credit. The scum, the marauders, and the grays had destroyed humanity's fleet. But now, Ben-Ari said, ten thousand new warships were orbiting Earth. Now the world was defended. Now they were ready to face the grays.

As they stood in the dusty ruins, Lailani listened carefully to all this. And as she listened, dread grew in her.

Petty was saying how his scientists had detected irregularities in spacetime, how the attack was near. Ben-Ari recommended troop placements. The gray invasion was only days, maybe only hours away, they were saying. The great, final battle of this war. The battle in which Nefitis unleashed all her fury upon Earth. The battle in which Earth stood or forever fell.

And as she listened, Lailani remembered the hourglass, the sand trickling out and burning away, leaving an empty bulb.

"Mister President?" Lailani said. "Major Ben-Ari?"

They turned toward her.

She wanted to look down at her feet. To clasp her hands behind her back. Instead she met the president's gaze, then stared into Ben-Ari's eyes.

"All this talk of war against the grays. Of a great invasion coming. Of a doomsday battle. This is all just a backup plan, right? Only in case, for whatever reason, Addy and Marco fail? Because if they kill the Tick-Tock King, the grays can't reach us. Right? So all this …" She swept her arm across the ruins. "It's just precautions. Because Addy and Marco are going to make it, right?"

Ben-Ari and Petty shared a quick glance.

Ben-Ari looked back at Lailani. She held her hand.

"Lailani, you understand that the chance of Addy and Marco succeeding is small."

Lailani stared up into her commander's eyes. "But they still have a chance."

"A small chance," Ben-Ari said, voice soft. "Maybe a fool's chance. But yes, a chance. And we all hope and pray for them."

Lailani pulled her hand back.

"You're lying!" she said. She pointed at Petty, her finger shaking. "You sent them there to die! You—"

"Lailani!" Ben-Ari said.

"Don't you silence me!" Lailani said. "Do you know what he did, Ben-Ari? What Petty did? He calculated how much sand was left in the hourglass. He knew there was only enough for a one-way trip. That we could send Marco and Addy to the future, but not open a portal to bring them back home. He knew!" She pointed at the president again, her eyes wet. Her voice shook. "You sent my friends to die."

Petty stared at her. His eyes were hard. His face was stone. Ben-Ari stared at them both, shock filling her blue eyes.

Finally Petty spoke.

"Yes." His voice was a low grumble. "Yes. I sent them to die."

Tears ran down Lailani's cheeks. "Why?" she whispered.

"Why?" Petty rumbled. "*Why*? For the same reason I sent tens of thousands to die in the scum and marauder wars. *Hundreds* of thousands." His voice rose. "So that others may live! I sacrificed Emery and Linden, knowing they can never come back, knowing that if they can infiltrate that pyramid and slay the terror within, we can all live. The billions of us still left on Earth. And I would send them again. I would kill them with my own bare hands if that could save the world. And you would too."

Lailani stood, trembling. She turned toward Ben-Ari, expecting some aid, some hope.

"But we can still save them, right, ma'am?" Lailani said. "We can build a time machine, or create more sand for the hourglass, or …"

But she saw the answer in Ben-Ari's eyes.

"Lailani—" she began, reaching out to her.

Lailani took a step back. "How could you?" she whispered. "You knew too. Addy and Marco. Our friends. You knew. You sent them to die."

Lailani was sobbing now. She turned. She ran.

Epimetheus met her at the foothills. She embraced him, crying into his fur.

She had lost her friends.

"Lailani?" A concerned voice sounded ahead. "Lailani! What's wrong?"

She looked up. Through her tears she saw Elvis approach. She stepped toward him and all but fell into his arms. He held her. They stood together among the ruins, holding each other, as the troops marched around them, as the warships rumbled above, as this ancient city and young planet waited for war.

CHAPTER ELEVEN

They trudged through the ashes of a dead world.

The desolation of Black Earth spread around Marco and Addy. Soot covered the rocky fields, swirling around their boots. Canyons carved up the land, scarred pits filled with tar. Mountains rose in the distance, jagged, pitiless, burning with scattered fires where bitumen seeped out. A stream flowed across the land, but the water had gone black with filth, and no life could survive within it. Marco walked with his helmet on, breathing from his oxygen tank. His air would run out by tomorrow; he was not looking forward to breathing this foul miasma.

They had been marching for a full day now. Marco was exhausted. His feet were blistering. His legs ached. His lower back cried out in protest. He had taken long marches before, especially during boot camp. But he had been eighteen then. Now, a month shy of thirty, he was starting to slow down. And this landscape was harsher than Earth's deserts by far. If only he could have seen a patch of blue sky or a star, it would have lifted his spirits. But there was no sky over Black Earth, just a veil of smog.

"Poet," Addy said, panting at his side.

He groaned. It hurt to talk. "What?"

"Can you carry me?"

"No, Addy."

She pouted. "But I'm tired!" She jumped onto his back. "Give me a piggyback ride."

"Addy, for Chrissake!" He shoved her off. "You're the famous Addison Linden, the legendary warrior who raised Earth in rebellion against the marauders. You don't need piggyback rides."

She groaned. "I don't want to be a heroine with you. You're Poet. You're my best friend. I want to be myself."

"Yourself is bloody annoying!" Marco said.

She crossed her arms and stuck her tongue out at him. "Well, if you can't carry me, you're just a weakling."

He sighed. "Fine, Addy. Let's rest if you're so weak and tired that you can't walk anymore."

There was no use seeking a comfortable place to rest. They ended up camping on a rocky hillside. Their spacesuits perhaps were hardened, able to resist bullets, but they could still feel the sharp rocks beneath them. Marco had neglected to take any battle rations when boarding the enemy saucer, but Addy always thought with her belly. She had stuffed her backpack with food packets. They were just powders, meant to mix with water into a fluffy paste, and a couple of boxes of granola bars. It would do.

To eat they had to open their visors. The instant he breathed in the air, Marco nearly gagged.

"Ugh! It's like wrapping your mouth around a car's exhaust pipe." He coughed.

Addy sniffed and grimaced. "Gross! It smells like a dead, rotting skunk that fell into the sewer outside an ashtray factory."

Marco inhaled again and nearly fainted. "It smells like an army latrine after a scum used it."

"Let's eat quickly, then visors down."

Addy tore open one pouch of powder. When mixed with water, it supposedly turned into meat loaf. They had no water. Addy spilled the powder into her mouth, swallowed, and shuddered. Marco tossed down powdered chicken casserole. It tasted like sand. With relief, they closed their visors and breathed from their oxygen tanks for a while.

"Great," Addy said. "The stink is inside my helmet now."

"That's just your breath," Marco said.

"Ha ha, very funny." She punched him. "Any more wise talk from you, I'll smash your visor and you'll have to breathe this air constantly."

He sighed. "Soon enough, we'll both run out of oxygen. Then it'll be this lovely aroma for both of us." He rose to his feet. "Come on, let's keep walking."

They kept trudging across the barren wilderness. Marco kept checking his compass. At least he hadn't forgotten to bring that. In their commandeered saucer, Marco had fled the pursuers west. He wasn't sure how far he had traveled, but he figured that if they walked straight eastward, they'd arrive in Gehenna, the city of the grays. Geographically, it rose over the ruins of Jerusalem.

It was strange, he thought, that Jerusalem should be a nexus of such great events in human history—the birthplace of Abrahamic religions, the center of so many human wars, the place where the scum had first struck Earth, and now the lair of the grays. Perhaps the location had some cosmic importance, a spring of energy science had not yet detected. Perhaps the grays had realized its significance. Perhaps it was merely a coincidence.

Jerusalem is now called Gehenna, Marco thought. *The ancient Hebrew word for Hell. The holy city has become cursed.*

He had told Addy that they might be a thousand kilometers off course. He hoped he was wrong. With the saucer crashing through the atmosphere, falling apart in midair, who's to say how far they were from Gehenna? Maybe they were a hundred kilometers away, could be at Gehenna within two or three days. He let a little optimism fill him.

"Poet, it's getting darker," Addy said. "I think the sun is setting."

They couldn't see the sun through the smog, but Addy was right. Black Earth was always dark, but now the darkness was deepening fast. One side of the sky turned pitch-black, the other pale gray as the sun set beyond the veil.

"Let's keep walking until it's totally dark," Marco said. "Then we'll rest again."

They took a few steps, pebbles crunching beneath their boots.

Add frowned. "Hey, Poet?"

"Yeah?"

"Did you know that in the future the sun sets in the east?"

He froze. He stared.

"Fuck."

Addy groaned. "Poet! You don't mean …"

He had to sit down. "Oh fuck." He stared at the direction they had been walking all day. At the setting sun. "We've been walking west all this time."

Addy yowled. "Poet! But you said Gehenna is in the east!"

"It is!" Marco said. "And my compass pointed us east!" He raised his compass. "Look, Addy! Look. The needle's pointing east, and—" He blinked. "Of course. Oh shit, of course. It's a million years in the future. Earth's magnetic pole must have shifted."

Addy tilted her head. "Earth's what now?"

"Earth is a giant magnet," Marco said. "Back in our time, the north pole is, well, in the north. But every few hundred thousand years, the pole flips. Suddenly north is south, south is north, east is west, west is—"

"I get it, Poet. So your compass is fucked-up."

"Well, my compass is just built for the twenty-second century. Over here, it works in reverse. We have to travel west now, not east." He sighed. "We wasted a day. A day of air. A day of food. A day of energy. I'm sorry, Ads."

"Aww, it's not your fault." She patted his helmet. "Your compass was broken."

"Actually, I just forgot that—" He bit down on his words. "Yep. You're right, Addy. Compass is broken. But we'll go the right way from now on. Let's rest until dawn. There are too many canyons and holes in this landscape to be walking in darkness."

They were just about to lie down when it began to storm.

Gray, acidic rain sizzled across their spacesuits, melting the phoenix logos printed on them. Wind gusted, thick with black sand and pebbles. They could, perhaps, have slept through even this, but then the lightning began. Bolts slammed down onto boulders around them. One blast cracked a boulder in half.

"We need to find shelter!" Marco shouted.

"Save me, Captain Obvious!" Addy cried back.

They trudged through the storm. The sun vanished but bursts of lightning kept illuminating the world. Cliffs loomed ahead. They struggled toward them, hoping to find shelter between walls of stone. Lightning slammed into a boulder ahead. The wind gusted, shrieking, deafening, so powerful it lifted Marco and Addy off their feet. They flew and hit the ground, struggling for purchase, and pulled themselves up. The rain kept lashing them, each drop like a bullet. Mud tugged their feet like the claws of buried demons.

A shadow lurched ahead.

Marco started.

"Addy, I saw something! A shadow."

She grabbed his hand and pulled him along. "This whole planet is a fucking shadow. Come on."

They kept struggling toward the cliff. Lightning flashed every second. Thunder boomed. Every step was a war. And there! Marco saw it again. A shadow loping in the rain. Lightning flashed. White eyes glared, and a jaw hissed. The darkness fell, and when lightning flashed again, the creature was gone.

"Poet, move your ass!"

Addy pulled him. They ran at a crouch. Stones flew in the wind, buffeting them. Finally they reached the cliff. The wind kept lashing them, even here. Stones fell from above. A rock the size of a brick slammed into Marco's shoulder, and he bellowed. Stone buffeted their helmets.

"It's even worse here!" Marco shouted.

Addy pointed. "Look! A cave."

They slogged through the mud, the cliff to one side, the storm to the other. Stones kept hitting them. Their armored spacesuits held, but within those suits, Marco felt like a slab of tenderized meat. Bruises would cover him tomorrow.

A distant sound rose—a howl. An organic creature, crying out.

"Addy, did you hear that?" he shouted.

"Just the wind. Come on! Into the cave."

More rocks kept falling. They ran. Finally they reached the cave in the cliff. The opening was just a crack, maybe two feet tall and ten feet wide. They had to squeeze through on their hands and knees, wriggling like snakes.

On the inside, the cave was thankfully larger. The storm could not reach them here, and they both sighed in relief. They could even stand up, though their helmets brushed the ceiling.

"Good thing you're short, Poet," Addy said.

"We're the same height!" he said.

She nodded. "But I'm a girl. I'm tall and lovely with long legs." She poked his chest. "You're a hobbit."

He groaned. "Can we focus on surviving now?" He looked around him. "Let's make sure this cave is empty."

"What do you think is in here? The boogeyman?" She gasped. "Maybe the Pigman! Poet, let's look for the Pigman! I need a photo to send *Freaks of the Galaxy*."

"There's no such thing as pigmen!" he shouted.

Instantly he regretted his raised voice.

From deep within the cave, a growl rose.

They both stared into the shadows, seeing nothing.

"Pigmen," Addy whispered, clutching his hand.

"Shut up," he whispered and reached for his flashlight.

Addy grabbed her flashlight too, and they shone twin beams into the darkness. Something wriggled and grumbled ahead. They advanced slowly, flashlights in their left hands, rifles in the right. The cave sloped down into a hollow bowl. Their lights fell upon the burrow.

"Aww, they're adorable!" Addy said.

Marco gulped. "What *are* they?"

"Puppies!" Addy said. "Can I adopt one?"

Marco grimaced. "Those aren't puppies, Ads. Some kind of canine maybe. But I don't think you want one as a pet."

The cubs were hairless, their skin wrinkly, gray, and warty. Their eyes were small and pink, and whiskers stretched out from their pointed, quivering snouts. Those snouts sniffed, and their jaws opened, revealing sharp teeth. Perhaps they had evolved from wolves or dogs, though it was hard to tell.

Addy sighed. "Well, they're no pigmen. But I'd adopt one of these cuties." She knelt to pat them. "Hi, cuties! Hi— ow!" She pulled her hand back. "Fuckers bit me!" She aimed her rifle. "I'm going to kill those sons of bitches!"

A deep growl sounded behind Marco and Addy, echoing in the chamber.

They spun back toward the cave opening.

Marco gulped. "You shouldn't have insulted their mother, Addy."

A shadow blocked the cave entrance. A creature loped toward them. It was massive. It was the size of a horse. Its claws scratched the floor, long and sharp as daggers. Wrinkly white skin coated the canine, and its lips peeled back, revealing fangs.

"Uh, nice puppy," Addy said, taking a step back. "Good puppy ..." She pulled out a packet and waved it. "Want some powdered meatloaf?"

The creature leaped at them.

Marco and Addy fired their rifles.

Bullets tore into the monster, but it didn't slow down. The beast slammed into them, knocking Marco and Addy down. The claws lashed at their suits, thankfully unable to pierce the armor. Marco tried to fire again, but the creature pinned down his rifle. Addy managed to release a bullet but couldn't aim, and the bullet slammed into the cave wall and shattered. Marco's ears rang.

He struggled to rise, but the monster pinned him down. Its jaws bloomed open, revealing rows of teeth that flowed down the gullet. Marco managed to free his rifle, to swing the barrel, but the canine knocked it aside. The creature grabbed his helmet. The animal had more than mere paws; its fingers were long, jointed, and tipped with curving claws. The monster slammed Marco's head against the floor again and again. He screamed.

"Let go of him!" Addy shouted. She lifted one of the pups. "Back off, or I kill your kid!"

But if the trick had worked on the krakens, it failed here. The enraged mother leaped toward Addy, spraying saliva. The

massive beast slammed into Addy, knocking her down. The
claws shattered her visor.

"Marco!" she cried.

Marco managed to rise. His helmet was dented. His
head spun. His visor was cracked, and he could barely see
through it. He pulled his helmet off, aimed his rifle, and fired.

His bullets slammed into the creature. The canine arched
its back, roaring. Marco couldn't believe how much punishment
it could take. He kept firing, and bullet after bullet drove
through the animal, but it didn't bleed. It seemed made of solid,
raw muscle. The beast leaped toward him again, and Marco
ducked, barely dodging the claws.

Addy screamed and fired her own gun. Bullets drove
into the monster's head, ripping off wrinkled skin, exposing the
bone. Marco loaded another magazine and added his bullets to
hers. With his helmet off, each bullet was like a punch to his
ears.

The creature's head was nearly gone by the time it
finally crashed down. Even then the beast twitched.

Marco fell to his knees, breathing raggedly. His ears
rang. God, it hurt. More than the monster banging his head
against the floor, the sound had hurt him, the roar of so many
bullets in this enclosed space. He had already lost some hearing
during the Scum War, especially in his right ear. He hoped that
if he ever made it home, it would not be as a deaf man.

Addy kicked the dead creature. "Not so tough without a
head, are ya?"

The cubs mewled. They crawled toward their dead mother and began to nurse from the corpse. Marco watched with a mixture of disgust and pity.

"Poor little buggers will die in this cave," he said.

"Does that mean we can adopt them?" Addy said.

Marco glared at her. "It means I feel like shit. This was their home. We killed their mother and doomed the pups to death."

Addy scowled. "Spare me, Poet. They're fucking monsters. I care about Earth. *Our* Earth. I care about humans. *Our* species. Fuck these little dog-assed fuckers. I'll put them out of their misery now if that makes you feel better."

She aimed her rifle at the pups.

"Addy!" He pulled her barrel aside.

"What, Marco?" Her face turned red. "What the fuck do you want? You prefer them to starve to death? Why are you so worried about cubs? Even back in the Scum War, you were worried about killing fucking maggots. For God's sake, Emery. We're at war. We're soldiers. We kill. That's what we do. So stop being so fucking ..." She let out an enraged groan. "So fucking empathetic."

He sighed and nodded. "You're right, Ads. You're right. I've never been good at killing anything. I wasn't made for this. Despite all the wars I fought, I hate killing. I guess I'm not a very good soldier."

Addy's face softened. She caressed his cheek. "That's what makes you a good soldier. The best soldiers hate killing.

The best soldiers cherish life. They raise weapons to defend life, not to take it needlessly. I was just being an asshole. I wouldn't love you if you were just a mindless killer. You're intelligent. You're wise. And most importantly, you're decent."

"You forgot devastatingly handsome," he said.

She kissed him. "Devastatingly handsome too."

"*And* humble," he said. "And an excellent cook. And—"

"Don't push your luck, hobbit."

He groaned. "We're the *same height*!"

He missed Lailani. At least he seemed tall with her around.

They dragged out the stinking corpse, then returned to the cave. They lay down to spend the night. The cubs kept whimpering, but Addy and Marco were so tired they fell asleep with ease, whimpering cubs and booming thunder and rocky floor and all.

* * * * *

The dawn rose gray, cold, and foul. After swallowing more packets of powder, they set out again. Their helmets were both smashed, but they were nearly out of oxygen anyway. There was no avoiding the rancid air now. Addy was kind enough to volunteer her bra; they used the cups as makeshift dust masks. Marco felt utterly ridiculous, but at least it provided some protection from the smog.

They walked across the desolation. The rocky plains spread into the horizons. They saw no greenery, not even moss. The ash glided through the sky like snow, burning when it touched bare skin. A few animals lived here. Beetles crunched underfoot. A snake hissed from behind a rock. At one point, something that looked like a bat glided overhead, but it seemed the size of an eagle. They still had found no clean water, and thirst began to bother Marco more than his aching muscles or ringing ears.

"What the hell happened to Earth?" Addy said. "A million years isn't even that long for a planet. It's like an afternoon."

"*We* happened," Marco said. "Look."

He pointed. It was barely visible in the distance, but as they moved closer, it came into view.

It was a factory. It was ancient, falling apart. There was barely anything left aside from two cracked, crumbling cooling towers. Soot and soil buried most of the shorter buildings.

"A power plant?" Addy said.

Marco nodded. "We polluted the fuck out of Earth back in our era."

"Fuel, Baby, Fuel," Addy said. "There's a Wolf Legion song with that title. My favorite off *Wolf it Down*, their second album."

"Fuel, baby, fuel," Marco agreed. "And the world goes to shit. And here we are. A million years later."

Addy looked around her. "It's definitely gone to shit. Fuck you, Wolf Legion."

"Not their fault," Marco said. "Cars. Factories. Goddamn cows belching up methane in factory farms. Deforestation—not enough trees left to breathe in the CO_2 and convert it to oxygen." He sighed. "We got addicted to burning. We burned too much. Now the whole world is toast."

Addy licked her lips. "I could go for some toast now. Poet, the instant we get back home, we're making delicious toast. With baked beans on top. And eggs. And sausages."

"And bacon," Marco said. "And lots of coffee. With extra cream and sugar."

"Now you're talkin'." Addy's eyes dampened. "Poet, how the fuck are we going to get home? Lailani is supposed to open a portal for us to get back. But she thinks we're at Isfet, light-years away from here. And she's only supposed to give us a week. How are we going to get back there?"

Marco held her hand. "Let's focus on our mission first. After we kill the Oracle, we can steal a saucer. Like we did before. We can make it back in time to Lailani's portal. I promise."

Yet the odds of that were small, he knew. Maybe nonexistent. To make it to the pyramid, to find the Tick-Tock King, to steal a saucer, to fly all the way back to Isfet—all within a week?

It was impossible.

"Poet," Addy whispered, "have we come here to die?"

Marco wrapped his arms around her. "I don't know, Addy."

Her tears flowed. She nodded. "All right. If we die here, we die together. But not before we kill that fucking Tic-Tac-Toe piece of shit scumbag. Deal?"

"Deal," he said. "But let's still try to make it back home. We have all that toast to make."

Addy nodded, tears on her cheeks. "And lots more things. To be together. To play hockey. To write books. To be in love. To grow old together. I want to do all those things with you, Poet. We saved Earth already. Now we have to save it again. And after all this work, I want to finally enjoy the damn planet." She wiped her eyes. "And if we can't, if we die, then we'll save Earth for others. For Ben-Ari. For Lailani. For Elvis. For everyone else."

He kissed her cheek. "I love you, Addy."

She hugged him close. "I love you too, Marco."

They kept walking. They walked for hours through the rain. A single ray of sunlight, a single blade of grass, a single bird's song would have lifted Marco's spirits. They found none. Just the barren land. The acid rain. The deformed, shrieking animals. Marco had been to harsh planets before—the deserts of Abaddon, the inferno of Haven, the hell of Titan. But this was worse. Because this was home. This was Earth. This was the planet he had been fighting for since joining the army nearly a dozen years ago. This was the planet they had failed.

We're not just here to stop the grays, Marco realized. *We're here to see what we humans have done. What we can still undo.*

After walking all day, they reached a beach. The water was gray and tipped with sickly yellow foam. It spread to the horizon, churning, malodorous. Marco's head spun to smell it. Strange creatures moved within the water, sometimes breaching the surface to snap and growl, then sinking again. Spiky brown seashells littered the shore, and oozing creatures lived within.

"Um, Poet?" Addy said. "Should there be a giant sea in our way?"

He winced. "Let me check that compass again."

"Poet!" Addy tugged her hair. "For fuck's sake. Are we lost again?"

Marco wanted the ground to bury him. "The pole flipped, but it might have also shifted a few degrees." He looked up at the sky. "We might have to wait for the sun to set to know which way is west exactly, then adjust the compass, and—"

"Marco!" Addy grabbed his shoulders and shook him. "We have a week. A week! And it's already been almost a week."

"I know, I know! Look, Addy, I'm sorry. I thought we were going the right way. I—"

"We could be anywhere!" Addy shouted. "We could be in Africa. We could be in Europe. We could be in fucking Madagascar for all we know. We're lost! We're fucking lost on a giant ruined planet, no spaceship, no map, and a compass that's fucking worthless! Poet, this isn't just about you and me. It's about everyone! If we can't do this, everyone dies."

"I know!" he shouted. "Addy, I fucking know! What do you want me to do?"

"To stop getting lost!"

"I'm trying!"

"Give me." She snatched the compass from him. "I'm leading the way from now on. You're fucking useless."

He wanted to argue back. Fury rose in Marco. He bit down on his tongue. He tried to enter Deep Being, but he couldn't focus on his breath. Every breath in this damn world burned his lungs and tasted like fumes. He let the rage boil inside him. They were both terrified. He knew this. He would let Addy rail against him.

"We just have to keep going," he said softly. "We'll find a way. For toast, Addy. For bacon and hot dogs and—"

"Enough." She began to walk away. "I don't want to hear that stupid joke anymore. Just come on." She pointed at the sky. "See? Look at the bright smudge in the clouds. The sun's already past its zenith." She pointed ahead. "That's east. Now come on. Keep up."

"I'll try to keep up with my hobbit legs," he said, hoping to lighten the mood, but Addy didn't look back at him. She marched as fast as she could. He struggled to keep up.

They kept moving across the plains, traveling in a new direction. Rocky hills rose into mountains. They climbed. Sweat filled their suits. All around them, strange animals howled and yipped and hissed. They spent two hours following an animal's prints through the dust, finally coming across a stream of brackish, gray water.

They had no choice. They needed to drink. They filtered the water through some cloth. They shot the mutated animal, burned its body for fuel, and boiled the water in one of their helmets. They took a leap of faith and drank. The water burned their mouths and throats and roiled their bellies. They lost whatever lunch they had eaten. They trudged on.

They slept in the hills, taking turns guarding. Throughout the night, the strange wolves howled around them. Twice the animals approached, and Marco fired his gun, scaring them off. He began to worry about their ammunition. They needed to conserve bullets if they hoped to slay the Tick-Tock King.

"No more wasting bullets," he announced at dawn. "If we need to fight along the way, we use our knives."

Addy nodded. "Knives, stones, fists, teeth, nails. Got it. Saving bullets for Tic-Tac-Toe."

Suddenly she grimaced, ran behind a boulder, and threw up. When she returned, her skin was ashen. Her eyes were sunken. Sweat dampened her brow. Marco himself felt sick. It was the damn water. But they had to drink, so they drank it again.

They both felt weaker that day. Their pace was slower. At least they seemed to be heading in the right direction, finally adjusting their compass to the movement of the sun. In the afternoon, they reached a canyon, one Marco thought he remembered seeing from the saucer. There was no way around it. They spent long hours climbing down the canyon, finally reaching the bottom at sundown. They lay down for another long, cold, miserable night.

Scorpions the size of cats kept assaulting them throughout the night. Marco crushed them with stones and burned their corpses, creating a ring of fire around their camp. Addy and him dared drink no more of the gray water. They caught a snake and drank its blood.

In the morning, they climbed onto the opposite side of the canyon, limbs shaking and heads spinning. By the time they reached the top, both felt half-dead. They collapsed, feverish, shivering. They allowed themselves a luxury—they ate a few of the granola bars, but they couldn't keep them down. Their stomachs expelled anything that entered. The vomit came out gray with ash. Their lungs, Marco imagined, looked the same. He'd have given up all the granola bars in history for a new helmet visor and oxygen tank.

They trudged across rolling badlands. Giant bats kept circling above, shrieking. Ashy rain began to fall again, and demons of smog swirled ahead. Still they saw no sign of the city.

"We should sing as we walk," Addy said. "To lift our spirits. Remember how we sang during marches in the army?"

She tried it. Marco even tried to join her. But they kept coughing. Their voices grew too hoarse. They had to continue walking in silence. The physical pain was bad—his aching muscles, the hunger, the thirst. The rancid water still churned his belly and brought sweat to his forehead. But worse was the cloud that had begun to claim their spirits. Their commanders in the army used to speak of morale, and Marco would scoff at the idea; what did morale matter when you were digging trenches, or marching across the desert, or firing a gun? Now he understood. A shadow seemed to fill him, a despair like a demon in his chest. More than fresh air he now desired sunlight, even just a single ray in the distance. He would have given the world to see a flower, to hear a bird's song. This landscape was depression personified.

There had been beauty even in Haven, he remembered. There had been beauty to the clouds, to the shining towers in the city core. Here there was nothing but ugliness. Nothing but despair. Kilometer after kilometer of it: black stones, filthy water, wafting smog, desolate hills, hissing snakes. The world had ended. Here was its corpse.

Addy pointed. "Poet, look!"

They stared across the landscape. On a distant hill burned several fires.

"Campfires," Addy said.

Marco shook his head. "Just more oil pits. We've been seeing them all over."

"I see a wall. No, a fence." She pulled out her binoculars and stared. "A village, Poet! Maybe they'll have clean water. We can storm the place, kill the grays, take their water."

Marco took the binoculars from her. He stared. A rusty fence. A handful of fires. He saw no more.

"We'll check it out," he said. "But no wasting bullets. Knives only unless our lives depend on it."

They began walking toward the village. It was desperation that drove them. They dared not drink the foul water anymore. They needed fresh water, needed food, needed more weapons if they could find them. Hopefully a map too. They walked, knives drawn.

Atop the hill, they realized their error. It was not a fence they had seen but a palisade of rusty metal poles. Skulls topped the poles—the huge skulls of grays, the eye sockets massive, the jaws lined with teeth like needles. One skull was still draped with rotting flesh.

Marco and Addy glanced at each other. Knives drawn, they stepped between two poles.

They counted five campfires. There was little else here. No huts, no wells, not even a tent. Four of the campfires were unattended. A group of pale, naked humanoids hunched around the fifth campfire, roasting a large animal. Their backs were turned to Marco and Addy. The creatures had prominent spine ridges, wrinkly white skin, and heads coated with scraggly gray hair. Their ribs were massive, flaring out to twice a human's width, but their limbs were rail thin, their bellies gaunt, their necks gangly.

The creatures took the animal off the fire and began tearing into it, ripping off shreds of pale meat. Then Marco realized what they were eating: it was one of their own.

"Cannibals!" Addy whispered.

The creatures froze. Their ears cocked. They spun toward Marco and Addy.

Their faces were hideously deformed. Boils covered them. White hairs filled their nostrils, acting as natural filters against the smog. Their jaws opened wide, revealing fangs. Their eyes blazed, white and cruel.

They were not grays. And yet they were humanoid. Not alien. Too similar to humans to be aliens.

"They're—" Marco began.

He could not finish his sentence. The creatures grabbed spears and charged toward them.

"Fuck knives!" Addy grabbed one of the poles, yanked it from the ground, and shook off the skull.

The creatures reached them.

Spears lashed.

Marco cried out and leaped back. One of the creatures' spears scraped his side, denting his armored spacesuit. These things were *strong*. He lashed his knife, hit the creature's skin, but it was like trying to cut hard plastic. The creature leaped onto him, screeching, eyes wide and bloodshot. It knocked Marco down, then raised his spear.

Marco rolled. The spear slammed into the earth beside him, cracking stones. Marco leaped up and jabbed his knife upward, hitting the creature under the chin. He drove his blade deep, piercing the beast's mouth, then pulled back, yanking the jawbone clean off. Blood gushed.

Marco had no time to finish the kill. Two more creatures leaped onto him. Addy was busy fighting three others. Marco lashed his knife and took a spear to the leg. He yowled. He tossed his blade, hit a creature's throat, then knelt and grabbed a fallen spear.

Fuck knives indeed.

He leaped forward, thrusting his spear. He had never fought with a spear before, but Ben-Ari had drilled them relentlessly with bayonets. Marco used the same moves here. He thrust the blade into a creature's stomach, making it double over. Then he swung the spear's shaft upward, knocking the shaft into his enemy's chin. The creature's head whipped backward, neck snapping.

The rest of the creatures fell quickly. They were wretched, sickly things, physically strong but unhealthy. They were easier to kill than grays. Soon Marco and Addy stood over their corpses.

Addy spat and wiped her hands on her pants. "What the fuck are those things? Not grays. Their heads are too small."

Marco stared down at the corpses. He spoke softly. "They're human."

Addy raised an eyebrow. "The fuck they are. They look like Gollum."

They gazed at the wide ribs, the nostrils filled with thick hair, the long and thin limbs, the claws.

"The grays used to be human too," Marco said. "They spent a million years on Isfet, evolving there into the grays, finally returning to Earth. When they came here, they found a ruined world. But not a lifeless world. A few humans had survived the apocalypse, had evolved to survive in a polluted world. Look at them, Addy. Their nostrils and lungs are designed for the bad air. Their claws are made for climbing and digging. The rest of them is human. Like us. They're just another branch in human evolution."

Addy shuddered. "I don't want us turning into these creatures."

"We won't," Marco said. "Not if we can save Earth. If we can get back home and warn people, if we can stop the pollution that ravaged this place, that derailed these creatures' evolution."

Addy shuddered. "Fuck that shit. Not our job, Poet. Our job is to kill Tic-Tac-Toe. Our friends back home will have to figure out how to save the baby whales. Lailani and Ben-Ari both saw visions of this place. Even if we don't make it back, they'll know what to do. Our mission is to find that pyramid and kill the sicko inside."

They spent a few moments exploring the campsite. They found a tunnel that led underground. They entered, knifes held before them, and found a burrow where the creatures must have lived. There were no guns, no advanced technology at all, but they found crude blades, pots, and pans. There was lots of rancid, maggoty meat—nothing they dared eat. There was water in urns, but it was the same gray filth. They boiled the water in a pot, strained it through cloth, boiled it again, and finally drank. It tasted like slow death.

"Not a sausage to be found," Addy said on their last sweep of the camp. She glanced at one of the pale corpses and shuddered. "Fuck, I preferred this world when no humans lived on it. This makes things even worse."

"I agree," Marco said. "But hey, look here. Something useful."

It was clutched in a corpse's clawed hand—a scroll made of skin. Marco wasn't sure if the skin was from an animal or humanoid. He didn't want to know. A map was drawn onto the parchment.

Addy's eyes widened. "A map to Gehenna!"

"So it would seem," Marco said.

The map showed hills, mountains, rivers, and a dotted line leading toward a city. In the center of the city, the mapmaker had drawn a pyramid with an eye on its crest.

Addy tapped the pyramid. "Tick. Tack. Toe."

They hated the idea of sleeping in this camp. But the creatures had dug a dry burrow, and it was storming again, and wolves howled in the wind. They tossed the maggoty meat outside—the smell was too awful to tolerate. Finally they huddled up in a dry corner of the burrow, a warm and safe place for the night. For the first time in days, they peeled off their spacesuits. Their bodies were bruised and pale. Marco felt as if he were already evolving into one of those twisted creatures.

"You look like shit, Poet," Addy said, concern in her eyes. "You're too pale and too thin."

Marco looked at her. He touched her hair. She too was pale. Her eyes were sunken.

"And you're beautiful," he whispered.

Tears filled her eyes. She hugged him. She cried softly.

"It's horrible," she whispered. "This place. This world. What became of Earth. Of humans. Of us. I'm scared, Marco. I'm scared we'll fail. That we'll die here. That we can't stop this."

He stroked her hair. "I'm scared too. But we're still breathing. We're still fighting. So long as we have each other, we have hope."

She nodded and wiped her eyes. She laughed softly. "I got snot on your shoulder."

He grimaced. "Eww! Addy, gross!"

She laughed and wiped her nose. "I'm sorry!"

Her laughter grew louder. She doubled over, laughing and crying, and soon Marco was laughing too, tears in his eyes.

When their laughter faded, they lay down in the corner, holding each other close, face-to-face.

"We survived the scum," Marco said, looking into her eyes. "We were only kids, and we survived them together. We survived the marauders. And we'll survive this. That's what we do. We're survivors."

She nodded. "Survivors," she whispered. "Addy and Marco, heroes of the universe."

He caressed her hair as thunder boomed and wind shrieked outside, as creatures yowled and roared.

"Pretend we're back at the cove," Marco whispered.

"Shipwreck Cove," Addy whispered, holding him close.

"Our secret place," Marco said. "Imagine that we're there. That we can hear the water whispering over the sand. That the moonlight is shining on the seashells, the sea, the white cliffs."

"The shipwreck full of treasure," Addy whispered. "I can imagine it. It's so beautiful, Marco. I never forgot that place." A tear flowed down her cheek. "Maybe we'll never see it again. But I still remember. It's our place. We're there now. Not in this burrow. We're there at Shipwreck Cove."

She closed her eyes. The wolves howled louder outside. The thunder boomed and the burrow shook. They slept fitfully until dawn, holding each other the whole night through.

In the cold, wet, rainy morning, they stepped outside. The campfires had died. The corpse of the cooked humanoid had fallen off the spit; it lay on the ground, rotten, filled with worms. Addy and Marco hefted their weapons and packs and headed out, following the map. Ahead of them, the desolation still spread into the horizon, leading past mountains, canyons, and poisonous rivers toward the pyramid. Toward the Oracle. Toward the faintest hope in a world of despair.

CHAPTER TWELVE

Ben-Ari stood on the observation deck of the *Lodestar*, gazing at Earth.

She was orbiting five hundred kilometers above the surface. From up here, the damage from the long galactic wars was barely noticeable. It still looked like good old Earth, the home that she loved. Forests rolled across the northern wilderness. Deserts sprawled across the Middle East. Lakes and rivers shimmered. When she passed into night, the cities lit the darkness, fragile and beautiful.

Ben-Ari had no single hometown. As a child, her father had fled the destruction of Jerusalem. She had been born in exile. She had grown up on military bases, never staying long in one place. She had only one home: Earth, the entire planet.

As an officer, she had traveled across the galaxy, visited many worlds, flown by countless stars, yet there was no planet in the cosmos so precious, so beautiful. Earth, she knew, was but a speck of dust in the infinite emptiness, barely visible in the galaxy. Yet here, on this fragile marble, was all that Ben-Ari loved.

She raised her eyes, and she gazed at the fleet orbiting the planet with her.

Ten thousand starships flew around Earth.

Most were U-wings, small starfighters shaped like horseshoes. Ben-Ari had disabled the AI systems they had come with, installed by the Galactic Alliance. Instead, human pilots now flew the starfighters. Ten heavy warships flew here too, each larger than the *Lodestar*. They were long and rectangular, built of silvery steel coated with graphene, and cannons lined their sides. Turrets rose atop them. If the *Lodestar* was shaped like a sailing vessel of Old Earth, these alien warships reminded her of the great aircraft carriers of the twentieth century. Aboard them now flew a mix of robotic technicians—they had come with the ships—and human commanders.

This army had cost a fortune. It cost so much that every human on Earth would spend their rest of their lives paying for it. But if this army could save the precious blue marble, it would be worth it.

Yet can we truly save the world? Ben-Ari thought.

Their scientists reported massive ripples in spacetime. Something big was coming. An army that could dwarf the last invasion of the grays, the one in which she had fought Abyzou. She remembered the visions Lailani had reported: a host of saucers covering the sky, an army of countless grays, a host to destroy worlds.

Earth had ten thousand ships. It had fifty thousand robotic troops. It had what remained of the HDF's ground forces. It was a sizable force, and these ships were state-of-the-art, more advanced than anything human engineers had ever built. Against the scum and marauders, it might have been enough. Yet when the grays swarmed, when hundreds of thousands of saucers filled the sky, when millions of gray soldiers stormed the world—how long could Earth resist?

Ben-Ari gazed out across the stars.

"Be strong, Marco and Addy," she whispered. "I need you to be stronger than ever." She lowered her head. "I'm sorry. I'm sorry we sent you there. To die so far from home."

Footsteps sounded behind her. Petty came to stand by her at the viewport. They gazed out at space together. For a long time, they were silent.

Finally the grizzled president spoke.

"You could have told her." His voice was raspier than ever. "You could have told Captain de la Rosa that I kept you in the dark too. That you were as shocked as she was."

"And what good would that have done?" Ben-Ari said. "She is a captain in the Human Defense Force, a junior officer. You and I are leaders of humanity. As far as Lailani is concerned, we are united in our knowledge, our decisions, our moral convictions. Let her believe that. Let her believe it had to be done."

Petty turned to look at her. His face was like a slab of rock—it had always been stony—but there was new weariness there, new wrinkles, new white hairs.

"And do you believe that, Einav?" he said.

She gazed into his dark eyes. She spoke carefully. "I believe that Marco and Addy are my friends. My best friends.

That I love them deeply. That my heart is broken. That I am filled with more pain than you can imagine. I am in mourning. I cannot comprehend a world that is saved without them here." She raised her chin. "And I believe that they will find a way home. I don't know how. But I know them, James. If there's a way back, Marco and Addy will find it."

"But only if they first succeed at their mission," Petty said. "If they can kill that goddamn monstrosity inside the pyramid." He looked back out into space. "God, the horrors out there ... The monsters we find in the shadows ..."

"These are the monsters inside us," Ben-Ari said softly. "Perhaps they were always there."

And perhaps there are monsters inside Petty, she thought. *Inside me. We sent our friends to death.*

She had learned as an officer to sacrifice the few to save the many. Every commander at war had to learn this bitter lesson. And during her fourteen years in the military, she had sacrificed soldiers. Friends. Had watched too many die. Her dear Sergeant Singh, a mentor to her. Most of her platoon in the mines of Corpus. Dozens of her soldiers in the hives of Abaddon. Yes, many times she had sacrificed the few to save the many. But it had never hurt so much.

And she knew why Petty had lied to her. Why he hadn't told her the hourglass had only enough sand for a one-way trip, that their engineers didn't know how to manufacture more of the sand, that Addy and Marco could never come home.

Because he knew, she thought. *He knew that I would have said no. That I would have sent other soldiers—soldiers not as qualified, not as experienced. He knew that I would have jeopardized the mission. And he's right. Not even for the world could I have done it.*

"I'm heading back to the surface," Petty said. "I'll be commanding the hosts from the bunkers beneath Jerusalem. I want you to spend the next day resting."

"Mister President, we have more war games to play. More drills to run. More—"

"When's the last time you slept, Einav?" When she couldn't answer, he nodded. "Rest."

She nodded. "Yes, sir."

He turned to leave, then turned back.

"Einav," he said softly. "If anyone can lead this fleet to victory, it's you. You are my finest soldier. I'm proud of you."

She nodded, smiling thinly, not sure if her smile was proud or bitter.

"I am not your finest soldier," she said softly. "Marco and Addy are. For that, I'm grateful."

Petty nodded. He left. Only moments later, she saw his shuttle depart from the *Lodestar* and glide down to Earth.

She walked through the starship's corridors. The *Lodestar* had been refitted for war. The science labs had been converted into munition bays. Most of the scientists were down on the surface, working for military R&D. Gunners and security troops had replaced them on the *Lodestar*. Holes had been drilled into the hull, and cannons now thrust out into space. Thicker shields had been added. This had once been a ship of exploration, of discovery. It was now a battleship. And though Ben-Ari had spent her life in the military, this saddened her.

It was still a HOPE ship. She still wore her HOPE uniform. She still fought for HOPE, not the Human Defense Force. Yet today HOPE was a military force. Today all of Earth was an army. Today every factory, every mom-and-pop shop, every kid with a nickel to donate, every old veteran with one more fight in him—they all joined the war effort. They all fought for Earth.

May the Lodestar *someday become a ship of science again,* she thought. *May someday I be an emissary of peace rather than an angel of war.*

She returned to her quarters. She showered. She considered putting on her bathrobe—she was off duty for the night—but decided instead to don her uniform again. The war was so close. The alarms might blare at any moment. She needed to be ready.

She looked at her prosthetic arm, slick and silvery. She opened the hidden compartment on her forearm. Her derringer lay within. She took out the small pistol. Her grandfather had given her this gun on her twelfth birthday—her first gun. It was her only memento from the old general. It was, perhaps, the most precious object she owned. It was her only connection to her past.

I was always a soldier, she thought. *Ever since I was a girl. Even now I carry my first gun with me. Even now, a captain of HOPE, I wear my HDF dog tags under my uniform.*

She returned the pistol to the compartment on her forearm, then closed the hatch, sealing it within. She kept the derringer loaded. It was not just a family heirloom. It was insurance.

She lay on her made bed atop the blankets. She picked up a book from her beside. *Love in the Time of Cholera.* But the words blurred. Her mind was a storm. Finally she placed the book aside, shut off the lights, and lay in darkness.

She had dared not show Lailani weakness. She would not even show that weakness to herself in a lit room. But in the darkness, Ben-Ari wept. For Earth. For Marco and Addy. And for what she had become.

CHAPTER THIRTEEN

They must have crossed hundreds of kilometers before Addy fell.

It happened in a dusty valley under dark clouds. She and Marco had been walking for many hours straight, limping, sweating, trembling. Their food was gone. Their water was gone. For the past day, they had been eating whatever bugs they could catch, rarely holding down the meal.

They had a map. They were moving in the right direction. But Gehenna was still so far.

In the valley of shadows and swirling ash, Addy fell. Too weary to continue. Barely able to breathe. She gasped for air and gazed up at Marco with glassy eyes.

"Addy!"

He knelt by her. He held her in his arms. She smiled up at him weakly.

"I slipped," she whispered.

She was lying, he knew. She hadn't slipped but collapsed. Her cheeks were pale and sunken. Her hair was damp with sweat. She had become gaunt, felt bony in his arms. Her skin burned with fever.

He himself looked no better, Marco knew. His limbs were thin, rattling inside his spacesuit like twigs in a bottle. Sweat kept dripping into his eyes. He had no mirror, but he imagined that he looked like Addy—weary, pale, a dying wretch.

He pulled out his canteen. He poured some of the water into Addy's mouth. She tried to swallow, coughed.

"I know it's still dirty water," Marco said. "We'll find clean water in the city."

She blinked, struggling to maintain her smile. "It's just over the horizon, right?"

He nodded and clasped her hand. "That's right, Addy. Just over the horizon."

She struggled to rise but fell back down. She spoke in a hoarse, weak voice. "You just need to rest for a few minutes. Just to catch your breath, Poet."

He nodded and lay down beside her. They lay on their backs, gazing up at the swirling smog, and held hands.

"Just to catch my breath," he agreed.

A few of the giant bats were circling above, vanishing and reappearing in the smog, perhaps waiting for Marco and Addy to die, waiting to scavenge two pale, thin corpses.

"Hey, Addy," he whispered, feeling too weak to speak any louder.

"Yeah, Poet?"

"Remember when we were kids, how we used to make bullet necklaces?"

Her smile grew a shade. "I do."

"There used to be so many bullets around Toronto," Marco said. "Thousands of soldiers everywhere. Scum attacks every day or two. We used to walk outside after the battles and find fallen bullets, the casings still on." He gave a weak laugh. "Funny how soldiers keep losing bullets. Remember the little factory we had at home?"

Addy nodded. "I do. I would use the plier to take the casings off the bullets. And I'd drain out the gunpowder, then reassemble the bullet. You'd use a drill to make a hole in each bullet. We'd then sling them on strings, making necklaces."

"We sold a bunch of them!" Marco said. "Some money for books and candy."

"I wonder what ever happened to the necklaces we made for ourselves," Addy said.

"God knows," Marco said. "Probably buried under the rubble of the library. You know, Ads, on the face of it, it seems almost gruesome. Two kids collecting bullets after battles, using them as toys. But we had fun, didn't we? Even though we grew up in a war, we had fun."

"We had fun," she whispered. "Because we were together." She looked at him. "You're the only thing that saved my childhood, Poet. I was fucking miserable until I met you. My dad—always in and out of jail. My mom—always drunk or high on the couch, beating my ass whenever she managed to stand up. My teachers hated me, stuck me in the remedial class. I was nothing but a stupid juvenile delinquent when we met. I was addicted to cigarettes by eleven. The school shrink thought I was half-retarded. They all told me I'd end up in prison like my old man." Tears were now flowing down her cheeks. "You saved me, Poet. You saved my life. Once I moved in with you, I was different. I was happy."

He wrapped his arms around her. "We've been through some shit together. I know it. I feel like I can't catch my breath. Like we leap from disaster to disaster. From the war in our childhood. To the army. To the scum. To poverty on Haven. To the marauders. To Tomiko losing her pregnancies, then us losing our house. Now to here. I don't know why we're so cursed, Addy. I don't know why this all happens to us, again and again. I just want … a few months. Just a few months to catch my breath. To rest before the next tragedy. We never even get that. But I'm glad, Addy, that through all this shit, we're together. And we'll always fight together. We'll always turn bullets into necklaces."

Now she grinned, showing her teeth. "When life gives you bullets, make necklaces. I like that saying."

"When life gives you hot dogs, get a rake," Marco said.

"When life gives you tits, turn your bra into dust masks," Addy said.

Marco thought for a moment. "When life gives you a crazy hockey player who keeps poking you in the ribs, make her your girlfriend."

Addy beamed. "When life gives you freaks, write a book about 'em!"

"That's offensive, Addy. They're people, not freaks."

"Freaks are people too!" Addy said. "Like me. I'm a freak now. I have scars on my body. I still have some shrapnel stuck in my ass. Maybe I should be in *Freaks of the Galaxy*."

"Addy, you are *not* a freak," Marco said. "I don't care if you have scars. You are beautiful. You are perfect."

She kissed his cheek. "Such a poet." She hugged him. "We'll keep going. We'll get this over with. So we can go home. So we can finally catch our breath. So we can finally be happy."

He nodded, eyes damp. "Finally be happy."

They rose together. Hand in hand, they limped onward through the valley of death. The smog surrounded them, and endless shadows still lay ahead.

* * * * *

By the end, they were crawling.

Marco wasn't sure how many days had passed since they had crashed their saucer. Perhaps it had been only a couple of weeks. Perhaps it had been years. Time had lost all meaning. He could barely remember his life before these badlands. The past had vanished. Shadows shrouded the future. All there was, all there had ever been, all there could ever be lay around him. Dust. Shadows. Hissing serpents and scuttling insects. Pitiless mountains and dark pits. Stones that cut him. Water that twisted his insides. Fever. Pain. Smoke in his lungs. Him and Addy, two pale, shivering creatures, crawling. They had no more strength to walk.

We are like the humanoids we found around the campfire, he thought. *We are dying.*

It felt like they had crossed continents. Sometimes getting lost. Sometimes falling, needing long hours of rest. Often Marco thought they could never rise again, that the illness, dehydration, and hunger would slay them. His piss was deep orange and grainy. His head always spun. His lungs, he imagined, must look like the rest of this land.

And yet they crawled on.

Meter by meter. They grabbed stones. They pulled themselves onward, over hills, across desolate fields. They ate worms when they could catch them. They used one bullet to slay a bat, and they ate its raw flesh, drank its blood, vomited and lost the meal.

They crawled onward.

They would die crawling.

They would die fighting.

They would die on Earth.

On a hilltop, they collapsed, too weak to even crawl downhill. They lay on their stomachs, wheezing, gagging, coughing. Ashy rain fell on them. It seeped through the cracks in their spacesuits. It burned them. It left raw wounds on their skin. The wind gusted and the smog filled their lungs.

"Another kilometer," Marco whispered.

"I can't," Addy whispered.

"Another meter," Marco said.

Addy nodded. "Another meter."

They crawled another meter. They fell again. Below the hill, smog filled the valley, so thick they couldn't see the ground. They would have to pass through it. Marco knew they didn't have the strength to emerge from that soup onto the next hill.

In that valley, their death awaited.

They lay in the black rain, exposed to the wind. Lightning flashed in the distance. The desolation was never ending. They were lost. They were alone.

"Is this it?" Addy whispered. "Marco, hold me. If this is it, hold me."

He held her. They shivered, cheek to cheek, as the ash burned them, as they lay slowly dying.

As always, together. Like they did all things.

The rain washed them.

And from above, some light.

Just a glowing haze like a watercolor stain. A golden shimmer in the clouds. Marco raised his eyes.

"Look, Addy," he whispered, voice hoarse, weak, cracking. "The sun is rising. Behind the clouds. You can almost see its shape."

They watched it together. A faded yellow patch beyond the smog. A mere smudge above the veil. It was up there. The sun. *Their* sun. The cosmos. And when Marco's head fell again, and he gazed ahead, he saw it in the dawn.

The walls of a distant city.

On the horizon, so distant, so small he could barely see it—a black triangle.

A pyramid.

He clutched Addy's hand. "Look, Addy!" He wept. "Look! It's Gehenna. We're almost there! We can make it. We can crawl. Another meter, Addy. Another meter. Together. Come on."

She saw the pyramid too. The rain returned. The haze thickened. The smog hid the pyramid again, but they knew it was there. They knew it was real. They crawled another meter.

And a second meter.

And a third.

Tears on their cheeks, coughing, trembling, burning in the acid rain, they kept crawling.

In the valley, they rose to their feet. Leaning on each other, they trudged through the smoke. A step. Another step. The smog hid everything. It was like walking through the underworld, through a sea of pollution.

They kept walking.

They emerged from the sea of smog.

They rose from death.

And before them, it was closer now, rising in the darkness, flashing when the lightning hit it. The pyramid.

Around it—the city. Above it—the saucers. Inside it—the
creature they must kill.

"We're almost there," Marco whispered. "We're almost
done. We can do this."

Addy nodded. "We can do this."

They dragged their feet across a barren plain,
approaching the walls of Gehenna, city of the grays. It was still
several kilometers away, but they could see Golgoloth clearly
now, the pyramid in the heart of the city. It dwarfed the
pyramids in ancient Egypt. The black monument seemed to
stare at them from the distance. Marco could imagine her there.
Nefitis. Goddess. Sharpening her claws. Waiting. Planning his
torture.

"We can't just walk up to the city gates," Marco said.

"We'll kill the guards." Addy gripped her rifle. "We
have railguns, and these pups can fire bullets through a tank.
We've saved ammo. We have grenades. We'll storm our way
through the city, killing all in our path, an army of two."

"Ads, I feel so weak I don't think I could defeat a
hamster." Marco nearly fell again. "We need a plan. A way to
sneak inside. A disguise."

They walked in silence for a while.

"Helmets," Addy finally said. "We need gray helmets.
Remember when the grays attacked Earth? We missed the
battle, but I saw some of the gray helmets our soldiers captured
as trophies. We need to disguise ourselves as gray warriors."

"Well, your head is big enough already," Marco said.

Daniel Arenson

"Ha ha, very funny." Addy pointed. "Poet, look. A building outside the city walls. A factory maybe? I see smoke. Let's go check it out. Maybe we'll find helmets there." She winked and gave Marco a weary smile. "Hopefully we don't find hamsters."

He returned her smile. "Like the old saying: No dogs, no hamsters."

They trudged toward the factory outside the city. Marco couldn't feel his legs. A pain pounded behind his eyes, as if dwarves lived inside his head, hammering at his eyeballs, determined to knock them out of his skull. Yet the sight of Golgoloth drove them onward.

Closer to the factory, they lay low and crawled, finally stopping between a few boulders.

Addy pulled out the binoculars and gazed at the factory in the valley. She gasped. "Oh no! Hamsters!"

"Give me that." He snatched the binoculars and stared. "Jesus."

The distant building was all black stone and jagged, rusty iron. Three chimneys pumped out smoke. Piles of corpses lay in a courtyard, stripped naked. Corpses of grays. A handful of figures moved around the corpses, clad in black robes and hoods. Large eyes shone within those hoods, and beaks thrust out, curved and cruel. Those strange hooded birds were loading corpses into wagons, wheeling them across the yard, then dumping the dead into ovens. Smoke belched out with every corpse burned.

"It's a goddamn crematorium," Marco said. "Fuck. Who are those beaked creatures? Some mutant birds?"

"Undertakers, I reckon," Addy said.

"Cowgirl." He poked her ribs.

She gasped. "You did *not* just poke me!"

"I reckon I did, little lady." He tilted an imaginary cowboy hat.

Addy grabbed the binoculars and stared. "Dude. Those aren't birds. Those aren't real beaks. Those are masks. Look."

He stared through the binoculars. She was right. One of the creatures turned to load a corpse onto a wagon, and Marco caught a glimpse into its hood. The undertaker was wearing a gas mask. The filter was beak-shaped rather than circular.

"They look like medieval plague doctors," Marco said. "Those beaks are gas masks. They probably don't want to smell the corpses. Addison, my dear, to hell with helmets. I shall require a beaked gas mask."

"Capital idea, old chap," she said. "By the way, why are we British now? What happened to cowboys?"

They loaded magazines into their rifles, deeming this raid worthy of a few bullets. They crawled forward—partly from exhaustion, partly to conceal themselves. After so long in the wilderness, they were covered in filth. From a distance, they would look like two miserable boulders.

Once they were closer, they paused and looked through the binoculars again. The plague doctors were tossing the last few corpses into the ovens. Then the creatures turned and entered the rusty tower. A single plague doctor remained in the yard, watching the ovens work.

Marco glanced at Addy. "Can you run?"

"I think so. I'll pretend an evil hamster is biting my ass."

This was good, Marco thought. A plan. A hope. Some banter. They needed these things as much as water, food, and fresh air. It was amazing, he thought, how hope could give such strength.

"Let's go," he said. "On my mark, we charge."

They crawled closer, then rose and ran.

The plague doctor in the yard saw them. A bullet from Marco's gun tore through his head, shattering both gas mask and skull.

They kept running. More plague doctors burst out from their building. Marco and Addy fired their railguns. Bullets slammed into these twisted plague doctors. Blood sprayed.

They ran onward, adrenaline pumping, using their last drops of strength.

Another plague doctor emerged, this one firing an electrical gun. The bolts hit the ground around Marco and Addy, raising clouds of dust. In this state, Marco didn't think he would withstand a single blow, not even with his armored spacesuit. He fired, taking down the plague doctor.

They raced across the courtyard, passed by the ovens where corpses were smoldering, and burst into the building, guns blazing. Several more plague doctors were here. Bullets tore through them. The creatures fell, their beaked gas masks clattering against the floor.

Marco looked at Addy.

"Let's scan the area," he said. "See if there are more."

She nodded. Both were exhausted. Both were moving on shaking legs. They forced themselves to search, every step a struggle.

The building was tall but narrow. Shelves lined the walls of the ground floor, brimming with oddities. There were statues of hybrids, shrunken heads, dried severed hands, fetuses in jars, and many other curiosities. Ladders led a loft, perhaps a living area, where Marco and Addy found candles, cloaks, and parchments with lurid drawings of deformed, naked grays.

"Ooh, gray porn!" Addy perked up.

Marco shook his head. "Medical texts. The creatures we killed were some kind of doctors. Well, morticians, at least."

Addy raised an eyebrow. "Not very good ones. They looked pretty ugly to me."

"*Mor*ticians, not beau—" He sighed. "Never mind. Let's check the basement."

They climbed down from the loft. Between the lurid curiosities, they found a trapdoor on the floor. Addy aimed her rifle, and Marco opened the door, wondering what horror might leap out. He peered down into the shadows.

He froze.

Tears filled his eyes.

He fell to his knees.

"Addy," he whispered. "Oh God, Addy, are you seeing this too?"

She knelt beside him. Tears flowed down her cheeks. "Marco. Yes. Oh God, Marco." She leaped into the basement. "Hot dogs, Poet! Hot dogs!"

Marco leaped down after her. It was a pantry. Strings of sausages hung from rafters. Hundreds of sausages. There were also jars of mushrooms, crates full of roasted bat wings, and bottles of umber liquid. Marco opened one bottle and sniffed.

"It's some kind of alcoholic drink," he said. "It smells almost like beer."

Addy grabbed it and began drinking. Tears still flowed down her cheeks. "It *is* beer! It tastes like a boozy pig's piss, but it's beer!"

Marco grabbed another bottle. He drank. It was wonderful. By all the stars above, it was wonderful.

Fingers trembling, they snatched the smoked sausages and began to feast. Marco didn't know what meat they were made from. He didn't want to know. He didn't care. It was food. It was real food. He devoured it. They struggled with shaky hands to open the jars, couldn't manage it, and instead shattered the jars onto the floor. Mushrooms spilled out. They gorged themselves.

They were being foolish, he knew. They should take the food to hiding, at least take guard shifts. Yet they were so consumed with hunger and thirst that they threw caution to the wind. They ate and drank with abandon, weeping and laughing.

"Hey, Poet," Addy said between mouthfuls. "See any rakes around here?"

He bit into another sausage. "I just hope this meat isn't made out of gray balls."

"Still not as bad as what's in hot dogs back home." Addy grabbed another.

When they were full to bursting, they stuffed their pouches with more mushrooms and sausages and filled their canteens with beer.

"This ain't so bad, Poet," Addy said. "We got some dogs. We got some beer. We got some gray porn. We can go fuck up Tic-Tac-Toe while drunk. Ain't no thang. Things are lookin' up."

And suddenly she was weeping. And Marco held her in his arms. He knew they should leave. That this place was dangerous. That more grays could arrive any moment. But they were too weary. They slept right there in the crematorium.

When they woke, it was dark outside. They ate and drank again, and they climbed back to the main floor. They approached the dead plague doctors. The creatures had begun to rot. They pulled off two of the beaked gas masks—hideous devices of metal and glass, shaped like the heads of vultures. They took the robes off two grays too. Soon Marco and Addy wore the outfits: black robes, the hems burnt and frayed; gloves with attached metal talons that reminded Marco of Freddy Kruger; and beaked gas masks with thick lenses.

"How do I look?" Addy asked, her voice muffled behind her beak. She raised her steel talons.

"Like a psychotic parakeet," Marco said.

"Cheep cheep, motherfucker." She hid her rifle under her robes. "Ready to enter the city?"

He nodded. "Ready as I'll ever be."

They pulled the dead grays into the ovens and left the corpses to burn. Dressed as plague doctors, they continued traveling across the field, heading toward the walls of Gehenna.

CHAPTER FOURTEEN

Marco and Addy were only a kilometer from Gehenna, city of the grays, when the saucers rumbled and stormed across the sky.

"They saw us!" Addy said.

The saucers were rising from the city like flies from a disturbed carcass. They were countless. Thousand upon thousand roared forth, the sound pounding the world. Marco and Addy dropped down, covering themselves in their ashy cloaks. They were disguised as plague doctors. They still wore their masks. How had the grays seen them?

Lying facedown, Marco reached under his robe and clutched his rifle. He knew he couldn't face them all. But he could shoot himself. If he had to, could he shoot Addy too? He could not allow them to be captured, to be tortured. The saucers rumbled in a fury. The ground shook. He dared glance above him, and the sky was dark with the round, black machines.

"Poet!" Addy gripped his hand. "Look! What's that?"

She pointed. He stared.

The air was crackling. Blue fire filled the sky. Winds gusted, blowing back the smog and clouds. For the first time since landing on Black Earth, Marco saw the stars. And there, in the blackness, the blue flames coiled into a ring. Light shimmered. A portal opened.

The saucers began flying through the portal, vanishing into the light. Formation by formation. Thousand by thousand. The saucers were draining out from Black Earth and flying through the portal.

"Poet, are they flying to Earth?" Addy whispered. "I mean, to our Earth? Green Earth?"

"I don't know," he said. "And you don't have to whisper. Their engines are almost as loud as your snoring. Almost."

She gasped. "I do not snore!"

"Sure, and you don't kick me in your sleep either."

She snorted. "Be glad I don't drool in my sleep."

"You do! I nearly drowned last night."

They lay for a long while, watching the saucers drain from the city. Finally the portal closed, leaving only a handful of saucers over Gehenna. Marco and Addy stood up again.

"We're too late," Addy said, lowering her head. "We came here to kill the Oracle. To stop him from opening portals. Fuck!" She lifted a rock and hurled it. "Fuck, fuck, *fuck*. We're too late! Just a few hours too late! The city is right goddamn there, and we missed our chance."

She was right, Marco realized. They had come here to kill the Tick-Tock King, the oracle who lived in the pyramid, to stop him from opening the time portals. But now the saucers were flying to Green Earth. The battle must be raging there already—or had, a million years ago.

Despair filled Marco. He fell to his knees.

Too late. We failed. We let Earth fall.

"We're fucked, Poet." Addy grabbed him. "We're fucked! What the hell do we do now?"

He closed his eyes. His mind rumbled like the saucers.

Breathe.

He breathed through his gas mask.

Just be.

He sank into Deep Being.

His thoughts stormed above his consciousness like the eternal clouds of this world. He examined them. Anxieties. Plans forming and collapsing. Memories.

"We might still have a chance," he finally said. He opened his eyes and stared at Addy's beaked gas mask. "Lailani told us that the Tick-Tock King does more than open portals. That's the easy part. He does something far more complicated. He prevents or fixes paradoxes."

"So the fuck what?" Addy said.

"Addy, think about it," Marco said. "The guy just sent thousands of saucers a million years back in time. That's thousands of chances to create paradoxes. Fuck, one of those grays steps on a goddamn butterfly, it can ripple across time and destroy this city. The Tick-Tock King monitors it all, according to Lailani. He views the past through his crystals. If he senses a paradox looming, he nips it in the bud. If the paradox appears, he fixes it."

Addy groaned. "So?"

"So if we kill him, it's Paradox Central," Marco said.

Addy gasped. "You mean—tons of dead butterflies all over the place?"

"Well, something like that. It's dangerous changing the past. Changing the future—sure, no problem, we do that all the time. But change even something small in the past, you can fuck up your own timeline." Marco adjusted his gas mask. "We know that some humans survived this long, evolving into those cannibals we saw. Suppose one of those cannibals changed the course of gray history—say, organized a rebellion, or assassinated a gray prince, or bred with a gray to create—"

"Ooh, gray porn!" Addy's eyes lit up.

Marco rolled his eyes. "Yes, lovely. Anyway, the grays can't go back now and kill that cannibal's human ancestor. Or they'll be fucking up their own history. Paradox."

Addy frowned and scratched her chin. "But Poet. They're going to change their *entire* history. They're going to change *everything*. If the grays conquer Green Earth, they'll just go live there, right? Their *whole history* is rewritten. Their *whole existence* becomes a paradox."

Marco had to consider this. "You're right," he said tentatively. "Maybe if the grays conquer Green Earth, all this— this nightmare we're in—vanishes. Maybe as it crumbles, all the grays who are still here—the civilians—quickly fly through the portal. This world falls apart, sucked into a paradox vortex. And the grays live happily ever after on Green Earth, far from the

destruction. But that's conjecture. I just don't know. Even
Professor Isaac struggled with this stuff."

"My brain hurts," Addy said.

"Mine too," Marco confessed. "Time travel is
complicated and messy. It can tear apart spacetime and mend it
in strange ways. The Tick-Tock King has it all worked out
though. He's pulling the strings. Detecting paradoxes. Fixing
holes in spacetime. Diverting the flow of time to suit his
purposes. All this complicated shit? He controls it. All those
saucers we saw flying back home? If we kill the Oracle, they're
like bees without a queen."

"And if we kill him," Addy said, "maybe we'll create a
paradox so huge it'll destroy not just Black Earth but Green
Earth too. Fuck, it might just destroy the entire galaxy, past and
present."

Marco inhaled deeply. "Maybe. But remember,
Professor Isaac looked at this. He gave us the go-ahead. We're
far enough in the future that even if we create a massive
paradox, something truly astronomical, it'll tear through
spacetime *here*, but Green Earth, a million years ago, will be
okay."

"*We* might not be okay," Addy said softly. "If we create
a paradox that destroys this place, we go down with it."

Marco nodded. He spoke softly. "We go down with it."

Addy sighed. "Well, fuck it. Who wants to grow old
anyway, right? I'll die with a belly full of hot dogs, a head

drunk with beer, and my best buddy by my side. Oh, and we'll go down saving the world. What more can a girl ask for, right?"

Marco nodded. His throat was tight. "If we go down, it's together. I can think of no better way to die." He tightened his lips and blinked rapidly. "Now come on, Ads. Let's get this over with. We've got a monster to kill."

They walked toward the city.

A wall surrounded Gehenna, towering and carved of dark stone. Upon it were engraved ancient curses, the letters the height of men. Guards stood atop the wall—gray soldiers in armor, holding electrical rods. The gatehouse loomed, shaped like the snarling maw of a beast. Grays guarded the gateway, black eyes peering through holes in their massive helmets.

Here goes nothing, Marco thought.

He and Addy walked toward the gatehouse, their gas masks' beaks thrusting out from their shadowy hoods. They were short for grays. But they had constructed platform heels for their boots, and they walked stooped to further mask their height. Their heads were too small too. But inside their hoods, they wore their spacesuit helmets, creating large, fake craniums. When Marco looked at Addy, he could see nothing but a tall, humpbacked figure, a plague doctor with a huge head. He had to peer closely to see the human eyes behind her gas mask lenses.

So long as we don't make eye contact, we're fine, he thought, struggling to control his fear. Trembling would not help.

They approached the gatehouse, shuffling, hunched over. The guards stared at them, blocking their passage. The grays spoke in their harsh language.

Marco gulped. Every instinct screamed to draw his rifle from under his robes, to slay these guards. But that would bring the wrath of the city upon him.

Instead, he coughed.

He shuffled forward, robes swishing, and coughed again.

The guards shouted something and stepped back.

Addy followed his lead. She too straggled forward, moving in lurching, twisting steps like Igor approaching Dr. Frankenstein. She too coughed. She reached up as if she would pull off her gas mask.

The guards were grumbling and muttering. Marco could imagine what they were saying: *Damn morticians infected with rot!*

One guard spoke to his comrades. They stepped aside. Marco and Addy walked between them, gas masks jangling, robes swishing.

Finally, after so many days in the badlands, they entered Gehenna.

We made it, Marco thought, breath rattling inside his beak. *We're actually here. We're so close to the end.*

A boulevard spread before them, paved with dark asphalt. Rows of arches rose along the avenue like ribs. Along the roadsides rose statues of deformed gods: women with a hundred bare breasts and demonic faces; nude men with serpents growing from their loins; pregnant females with opened bellies, revealing anguished fetuses; and leering grays with long tongues, hooves, and massive hearts that actually beat upon their stone chests, dripping blood. Beyond the statues spread the dark city, a hive of factories, towers, temples, and obelisks engraved with glyphs.

And there were grays here. Countless grays.

The creatures walked along the streets, some naked, others wearing armor. They sat in taverns, drinking blood from living snakes. They squealed in brothels. They blew horns in temples and bowed before their idols. As Marco and Addy walked along the boulevard, they gazed around with wide eyes, silent, staring, overwhelmed.

"It's ancient Egypt meets Vegas," Addy whispered. "And they elected Lucifer as mayor."

"That's one way to describe it," Marco whispered back. "Now hush. Let's make a beeline to the pyramid."

They kept walking down the boulevard, mimicking the shuffling gait of the grays. Their beaks and metal claws clanked. Thousands of grays moved around them. One wretched, wrinkled creature was feeding on a baby as he walked down the street, the blood dripping down his chin. Three grays stood in an alleyway, torturing what looked like a mutated cat, stoning the poor animal and laughing. Through the window of one shop, Marco saw an elderly gray, her breasts pendulous, cut into the chest of a living humanoid, pull out the organs, and add them to a pot. Other grays picked at the cauldron, feeding.

Marco's belly rumbled. He definitely didn't want to know where those sausages had come from.

Most of the grays here, however, were soldiers. Thousands of them filled the city, marching and drilling. They held electrical guns and spears. They wore burnished armor, and helmets hid their faces, leaving openings for only the soulless black eyes. Red and blue gems on their breastplates formed ankhs. Some of them rode flaming chariots pulled by mechanical horses. Others operated mechas shaped like scorpions, each machine the size of an elephant.

They haven't even sent everything to Earth yet, Marco thought. *First they're tenderizing Green Earth with their saucers. Then the ground invasion will begin.* He gritted his teeth. *But we will stop them.*

He looked up toward Golgoloth. The pyramid loomed ahead, shadowing the city. Several saucers still hovered above it, guardians of the temple. Marco wondered about the war on Green Earth. Was the battle still raging in some alternate timeline? Would the rest of this city soon board the last saucers and fly back to Green Earth, to enslave humanity, to claim Marco's home?

As Addy and he walked closer, Marco frowned. Two massive guardians stood outside the pyramid, arms raised, hands touching, forming an archway. The guardians stood taller than the obelisks and towers around them, as large as the smashed mechas. At first Marco thought them statues. But now he saw that they were moving, staring from side to side. Both guardians were humanoid, mummified, wrapped in shrouds. The wrappings seemed ancient, tattered, falling loose to reveal dry flesh. Even from here, still a couple of kilometers away, their stench hit Marco, infiltrating his gas mask.

"The fuck?" Addy said. "Giant mummies?"

"So it would seem," said Marco.

Addy cringed. "I was wrong. It's not Lucifer who's the mayor. It's Vincent Fucking Price."

Marco smiled thinly. "Our disguises have worked so far. The mummies might let us pass too."

"Might?" Addy said.

"If they don't, we take them down," Marco said. "We've got grenades and railguns under our robes, and we've fought big dudes before. But I'd rather sneak than fight. Come on, Ads. We're almost there. Let's get this over with."

They kept walking down the boulevard, passing under the archways and between the obelisks and statues, heading closer to the pyramid. On the way, they passed by a large building lined with columns. From inside rose groans and grunts.

Marco peered between the columns. The building was a brothel, its halls exposed to the city, its sins on display. Inside, gray soldiers and monks were copulating with female grays, with squealing humanoids, with twisted animals. Some grays gathered around the brothel to watch. Even Addy, who had joked about the lurid parchments at the crematorium, grimaced and looked away.

"Hurry up, Poet," she whispered. "Let's get the hell past this place."

As they were rushing by the brothel, a scream pierced the air.

A human scream.

Marco paused and turned back toward the brothel.

Several grays were manhandling a human girl. Not one of the pale, mutated humanoids Marco had seen in the wilderness. A real human. A woman from back home. The grays must have kidnapped her like they had kidnapped Steve, had kidnapped so many others from Green Earth.

Marco stood, staring, clenching his fists. Fury rose in him. The grays dragged the human into the brothel, laughing, leering. Their claws tore at her clothes, exposing the nakedness. The woman screamed and wept, struggling to free herself, to cover her breasts. Her back was turned to Marco, but he saw flowing black hair, a slender frame. She was young and fair.

Addy stared, sneering. Then she looked away. She grabbed Marco's hand.

"We can't save her," she whispered. "We have to keep going. To the pyramid. We'll save her by destroying this entire fucking city."

But Marco stood frozen. Was Addy right? The grays were now dragging the human toward a bed. He knew what would happen next. How could he abandon the woman, leave her to be raped and brutalized? When her torment ended, would she be forced to bare a hybrid child, or would she be nailed into an ankh and tortured?

Maybe Addy is right, he thought. *Maybe we have to sacrifice her to save the world. Ben-Ari would tell me that.*

He was about to walk away, shame inside him, when the woman turned her head, and Marco saw her face.

His heart shattered.

His breath died.

He stared, barely comprehending, barely believing.

Still caught in the grays' grip, the woman stared into his eyes.

"Tomiko," Marco whispered.

CHAPTER FIFTEEN

Campfires dotted the ruins of Jerusalem. In the night, distant jackals howled. In the sky, the ten thousand warships lumbered, easily visible even with the naked eye. Thousands of soldiers spread across the ancient city. Deep underground, thousands more worked at monitors, studying the patterns of spacetime, reviewing maps, commanding troops across the world and in space above.

Lailani stood before her own troops. Before the company they had assigned her. Before two hundred young soldiers, not one older than twenty. Some were as young as fifteen. With so many slain in the wars, Earth was down to recruiting children.

We are all an army, Lailani thought.

She placed her hands behind her back. She stared at them. She snorted.

"All right, soldiers, I know what you see when you look at me," Lailani said. "You're thinking that I'm small, shorter than the shortest among you. You think I'm a cute little doll. You think I'd be useless in the fight. Let me tell you something about me. I am Captain Lailani Marita de la Rosa. I fought the scum in the hives of Abaddon, and I killed the centipede emperor. I fought the marauders in Toronto and came face-to-face with their lord. And right now I'm here to lead you against the most vicious assholes we've ever known."

She saw Elvis standing among the troops. He gave her the slightest of nods. The tiniest of smiles tweaked his lips.

"You know what I see when I look at you?" Lailani said, pacing before the troops. "I see boys and girls. Young. Inexperienced. You came to me from across the world, brought here to form just another cog in the machine. But you know what else I see?" She raised her voice to a shout. "I see killers! I see warriors! I see heroes who are going to tear through the grays until they reach Nefitis herself and cut out her rotten heart!"

The soldiers cheered.

"I want every last one of you to kill at least ten grays!" Lailani shouted. "Those bastards are on their way. Our scientists tell us they're only days, maybe only hours, maybe only minutes from Earth. Once their portal opens, and once those creatures spill onto Earth, you will show them human strength! You will show them no mercy! You will kill every last fucking one of them, and it will be this company—my company—that kills their queen bitch! Is that understood?"

"Yes, ma'am!" they shouted.

Her voice softened. "It's likely that here, above our central command, the grays will hit us hardest. It's likely that some of you won't make it home. I know you're afraid. I know that some of you have seen friends die in the wars. I know that you never asked for this. But you will still do your duty. Because back home, you have families and friends. Across the Earth, there are billions of people who are depending on you. To them you are heroes. To *me* you are heroes. To history and all future generations—*you are heroes*." Her eyes dampened, and she repeated the words Ben-Ari had spoken to her platoon so often. "I am proud of every one of you."

She turned and left the company.

She walked through the darkness, hiding her tears in the shadows.

She remembered being like them. Just a kid. A private waiting for battle. So afraid. She remembered drawing so much strength from Ben-Ari.

May I offer my soldiers some strength today, she thought. *So many of them will not go home. And those who do will forever be broken.*

Lailani returned to her tent. Normally she shared it with her lieutenants and NCOs, but they were now drilling their platoons, arranging them in position across the ruins. The tent was empty.

Lailani stood still, head lowered, fists clenched.

"Yes, you gave me strength, Ben-Ari," she whispered. "I loved you. I made love to you in the *Marilyn* on a faraway planet. You were my officer, my heroine, my lover. And you betrayed me. You sent Marco and Addy to die."

The grief overwhelmed Lailani. She felt so alone. She had lost her friends. She had lost her mentor and guiding light.

"Be strong, Marco and Addy," she whispered. "I pray for you. Be strong."

A soft voice spoke behind her. "They're strong. They're the strongest bastards I know."

She turned to see Elvis at the tent door.

She frowned at him.

"Salute and announce yourself, private," she said. "This is still the military."

He slammed his heels together and saluted. "Private Benny Ray reporting, ma'am!"

She returned the salute. They stared at each other for a moment in silence. Then they both burst out laughing. Yes, Lailani laughed even as she wept, even as her heart trembled.

Elvis stepped into the tent. "Still feels weird, don't it? That you're twelve years older than me. And a captain. Only a few months ago, you were a pissant private like me."

"It's been years for me," she said softly. "Which makes it even weirder. Yet sometimes boot camp still seems like yesterday. Sometimes I still miss it." She sighed. "All the time."

Elvis nodded. "It was a good time." He pulled something out of his pocket. "And look what I have. I had it on me when you saved my ass."

Her eyes widened. "Spam!" She snatched the can from him. "You know, the HDF stopped making these after too many soldiers got sick. They now just give you tuna in the battle rations." She made a gagging noise. "Tuna!"

"I saw!" Elvis said. "What the fuck has the world come to while I was away?"

"Let's feast," Lailani said. "For old time's sake. Well, old for me."

She opened the can. She had learned in the army to always carry a spoon everywhere, and she took her trusty spoon out of her pack. She dug it into the gooey pink slime and scooped out a quivering ball.

"Look how it jiggles," she said.

"Look at all the pig snouts!" Elvis said. "I think I see some pig lips too."

Lailani swallowed the meat and shuddered. "Oh God. It's just as bad as I remember." She laughed. "Truly horrible stuff. A test of endurance, isn't it?"

"Not for Addy," Elvis said. "God, she used to love eating this stuff. Remember?"

Lailani nodded. "She switched to hot dogs on a rake."

"That chick is crazy," Elvis said. "Still can't believe she's banging Poet. I always figured she'd find some hulking hockey player to shack up with."

Lailani sighed. "They've both been through a lot together over the past decade. They've seen some horrible things." She shook her head sadly. "I miss them so much. I'm so worried. I hope they're all right. God, I wish I could be there with them."

Elvis nodded, head lowered. "Me too. They're my best friends." He wiped his eyes. "Fuck. Look at this shit. Got me cryin'. Give me that can." He grabbed the Spam from her, took a bite, and shuddered. "God damn it's awful. At least in boot camp they fried up the stuff. Why is it all slimy?"

"All that good pig juice," Lailani said. "You know, I realized that I actually don't hate tuna."

They tossed the Spam aside. They didn't have any tuna, but Elvis had procured a bag of lemon candy. They feasted on Lemony Bursts instead.

"Remember that time I handed out candies while we were cleaning our rifles at boot camp, and Corporal Diaz asked Caveman a question, but he couldn't answer because he had a mouth full of Gooey Busters?"

Lailani lowered her head. "No. I've forgotten so much."

"It was hilarious," Elvis said. "Caveman kept trying to talk and kept drooling, and Diaz tried to be angry and shout, but we all saw him hiding his smile. Finally Diaz had to march off in fake anger before he could burst out laughing. Caveman even got some of the candy in his rifle!"

Lailani gasped. "Yes! I remember that!" She laughed. "And his gun jammed at the firing range, and when he opened it up"—they spoke the next words together—"out spilled Gooey Busters!"

They laughed.

They sat in silence for a moment.

"I like your hair this way," Elvis said. "Buzzed off. Like you had at boot camp. It was weird seeing you with longer hair."

She touched her stubbly head. "I dunno. Poet used to say I look androgynous this way."

Elvis tilted his head. "Like a robot?"

"That's what I thought too!" Lailani laughed. "It means I look like a boy."

"I don't think you look like a boy," Elvis said. "I think you look pretty." He touched her hair, then pulled his hand back, and his cheeks flushed. "I mean, for a robot. I mean, you're not a robot. I mean …" He groaned. "Fuck, you're pretty, all right? And I'm glad you buzzed your hair short. And I'm glad you remembered the candy story."

She smiled and touched his hand. "And I'm glad you're here with me, Private Benny Ray." Suddenly her eyes were damp again. "I carried the weight of your death for so many years. That guilt haunted me. And finally now, after so long, you're here again. Come, I want to show you something." She went to her pack and pulled out her framed photograph. "Look. It's us from boot camp."

They looked at the photograph together—the famous photograph Lailani had carried around for years. Ben-Ari stood at the front, just an ensign, so young but still so serious, even then. Marco was trying to look tough, unaware that Addy was holding up two fingers behind his head. Lailani was making her silly face, cheeks puffed out, eyes crossed, and Elvis had his arm around her.

"I remember that photo being taken," Elvis said softly. "It was just a few weeks ago for me."

She wiped her eyes. "I've been carrying it around for years. I never forgot the gang. Not any one of us. I just wish I could bring them all back. Caveman. Beast. Singh." Her voice broke. "Addy. Marco."

"Hey now." Elvis wrapped his arms around her. "Addy and Marco are still alive. Those bastards are tough to kill. They'll find a way home."

"Promise?" Lailani whispered.

He nodded. "Solemn promise. Cross my heart. Hope to—"

She silenced him with a kiss.

"No," she whispered.

He gazed into her eyes silently. He stroked her cheek. And he kissed her—a longer, deeper kiss this time.

Any moment now the grays would invade. Any moment now they all might die. And so Lailani took him into her bed. And she made love to him. And she slept in his arms, protocol be damned. She had killed him. She had saved him. She was healed. In his arms, she felt whole.

She woke once, just before dawn, and nestled closer to him. Elvis was still asleep, and she stroked his hair.

I don't ever want to lose you again, she thought. *I don't want to lose any more friends. I don't want the dawn to come. I'm afraid.*

Yet she knew that dawn would rise. She knew that war would come. She knew that so many would fall. And the pain seemed too great to bear.

"Be strong, Marco and Addy," she whispered. "Find the Oracle. Stop this war. Earth needs you. I need you."

Dawn rose with a siren.

Lailani and Elvis jolted up.

They ran outside the tent into the ruins.

The sirens blared. Soldiers ran. Jets screamed overhead.

The grays, Lailani knew, were here.

CHAPTER SIXTEEN

The portal opened above Earth, shimmering blue, and the wrath of Nefitis emerged.

Ben-Ari stood on the bridge of the *Lodestar*, staring at the horror spilling forth.

Humanity's fleet was orbiting Earth twenty thousand kilometers from the surface. Her own ship. Ten thousand others purchased from the Galactic Alliance, refitted, and manned by human pilots. Below them on the planet, tens of thousands of robotic soldiers, along with millions of human warriors, waited to fight.

It was but a drop compared to the surging ocean of grays.

Thousands of saucers were spilling out from the portal like hornets from a hive. Most were small and red—the starfighters of the enemy. They were like whirring tops, ringed in blades, able to blast lasers to sear through the thickest hull. Other saucers were lumbering motherships, some the size of football stadiums, others the size of towns. The gray fleet kept emerging, seeming to never end. Ben-Ari had never seen so many ships in one place.

For an instant—just one instant—she stared in hopeless, paralyzed horror.

Then the instant ended. And she took command.

"Hit them at the portal!" she cried, voice carrying across the fleet, transmitted to every cockpit and bridge. "Meet them head-on!" She spun toward her pilot. "Aurora, fly!"

The mollusk shoved down the throttle.

The *Lodestar*'s engines roared. They led the charge, and ten thousand other warships followed.

"Fire all cannons!" Ben-Ari cried.

A storm of hellfire flew from the human fleet.

The saucers charged toward them, guns pounding.

Earth's orbit blazed with fire.

Humanity's fleet stormed forth. They were ten thousand strong. They were like a single falling star blazing into a sky of fire.

The bridge of the *Lodestar* was dome-shaped. Viewports covered its every surface, even the floor. Standing here, Ben-Ari had a full view of space all around her, above her, and below her feet. But she could no longer see space. No longer see the stars or Earth. There was only this battle. Only the endless saucers. The fire. Ships shattering around her.

"Destroy that portal!" she cried. "Forward! Through them! Fire!"

The *Lodestar* charged through the saucers, firing all her cannons. But the enemy was everywhere. Blasts hit the *Lodestar*, exploding across her shields. Saucers slammed into the ship, knocking her back. Alarms blared as the hull breached, as a deck shattered. A nearby warship tore open, spilling out soldiers. The U-wings, the horseshoe-shaped starfighters Ben-Ari had bought to replace their lost Firebirds, streamed above and below them, slamming into the saucers. Another warship exploded below Ben-Ari's feet, peppering the bottom of the *Lodestar* with shrapnel and corpses.

"Mistress, we cannot break through them!" Aurora cried.

"We must hit that portal! Forward!"

The *Lodestar* kept charging through space, ramming into saucers, firing their guns. Another deck burst open. Klaxons wailed. Fire filled the ship. All around them battled the multitudes. Saucers and warships collapsed. Shrapnel filled space and rained down to Earth.

"Mistress, we're falling apart!" shouted Aurora.

Ben-Ari pointed ahead. The portal was there. More saucers kept spilling out.

"Destroy that portal!" Ben-Ari cried. "All ships, keep flying!" She turned toward her gunner. "Niilo, fire the nuclear cannons!"

Her towering security chief stood at the cannons, his long blond hair loose, his beard forked into two braids. He nodded, and a grin spread across his wide face.

"For the glory for Earth! For Valhalla!"

He unleashed their nuclear arsenal.

Ben-Ari winced.

The missiles flew forth, carving a path through the saucers, traveling at many times the speed of sound, ripping through the fleet.

The missiles made it halfway to the portal before enemy fire shattered them.

The nuclear warheads exploded.

Light bathed the *Lodestar*'s bridge.

The ship tilted and spun. Radiation baked them, flowing across their shields. Saucers melted around them. U-wings burned. The light shone like a star.

When the blasts faded, thousands of saucers were gone.

The portal loomed ahead, glittering blue, ringed with the shrapnel of shattered saucers.

Ben-Ari rose to her feet, realizing she had knelt and covered her head.

And from the portal, thousands more saucers emerged.

The red, spinning fighters stormed into the human warships, slamming into the hulls, shattering the larger vessels. The gray motherships fired their lasers, picking out the human ships.

Ben-Ari stared with horror.

By God. Even nukes can't stop them.

"Block the portal!" she cried. "All warships, block the portal. Plug it up! Don't let them out!"

The ten largest human ships rose, forming a wall ahead of the portal. But it was like trying to stop a river with pebbles. The saucers tore through them. Another warship shattered. A few U-wings reached the portal, only to fall through it, burning. And the saucers kept emerging, pounding the human fleet.

The floodgates were open.

The saucers were tearing through humanity's defenses like a tank through light infantry.

And they were reaching Earth.

Ben-Ari inhaled sharply through a clenched jaw.

Hundreds of saucers had made it around the human fleet. They were flying toward Earth. The planet was responding with artillery fire. The surface cannons were taking out many saucers. But more joined the assault every moment.

Another warship shattered.

More saucers emerged, plowing through what remained of the human fleet.

The dam had collapsed. And the torrent of saucers spilled forth.

Every instant, another human ship tore apart. U-ships burned. A warship exploded, taking down several ships around it. Down on Earth, countless saucers were mobbing the planet, streaming through the atmosphere, and the artillery couldn't hold them all back.

We can't stop them, she thought. *We can't win this.*

Blasts rocked the *Lodestar*. Holes tore through the hull. An engine shattered and blazed, and the ship tilted. All around them, the human fleet was crumbling. Every second, another warship winked out with a blast of light, falling dark, gone.

Blast after blast. Ship after ship—vanishing. Earth's hope—burning.

She turned toward Aurora.

"Get us closer to Earth! We must protect her skies."

The mollusk grabbed the controls. "Yes, mistress, we—"

A gargantuan saucer emerged from the portal, many times the *Lodestar*'s size, hiding the sun. It was forged of black metal, and a golden ankh was engraved upon it. It was the largest saucer Ben-Ari had ever seen; it could have buried Central Park. She had spent hours studying the grays' language before the battle, and she could read the glyphs engraved upon the hull, the letters larger than houses.

Claw of Nefitis.

Ben-Ari gasped.

Was this the goddess's flagship? Was Nefitis herself aboard?

The mothership came charging toward them, cannons firing.

"All power to forward shields!" Ben-Ari cried. "Return f—"

Hell erupted across the *Lodestar*.

The enemy saucer's wrath hit them like the hammer of a god. The front of the *Lodestar* shattered, and the figurehead tore free and tumbled through space. Blasts ripped the shields open. Viewports shattered across the bridge and fell, revealing the bulkhead behind them. The bridge shook madly, and cracks raced across the walls.

"Fire!" Ben-Ari cried, but Niilo was down, buried under a pillar.

She ran to the gunner's station. She fired everything in the ship. Lasers, photon cannons, railguns. She fired a nuclear weapon, and the blaze washed across space. But the *Claw of Nefitis* kept flying, and her cannons pounded the *Lodestar*, and they were spinning, falling, careening madly, tearing apart. Chunks of the hull tore free and flew through space. The engine room caught fire.

Above, Ben-Ari saw the *Claw of Nefitis* hovering, eclipsing the sun. In its shadow, the *Lodestar* fell.

Earth's gravity grabbed them. They tumbled toward the atmosphere.

"Aurora, keep us flying!"

But the mollusk lay under fallen debris. She wasn't moving.

Ben-Ari stumbled across the bridge. The *Lodestar* spun, gaining speed, crashing down toward Earth. The artificial gravity on the ship died. Ben-Ari swam through the air toward the helm. She grabbed the controls.

Aurora had eight arms, Ben-Ari only two—and even one of those was a prosthetic. She grabbed what controls she could. She hit the thruster, but only one engine was still operating. It sputtered. She slowed their spin. She tried to raise their prow, but there was no prow left, only a gaping hole. The *Lodestar* careened down into the sky.

She switched off the cannons, diverting energy to the engine, and shoved down the thruster.

The *Lodestar* rose from the atmosphere, charging back toward the battle.

Ahead, the *Claw of Nefitis* fired her cannons.

The blasts hit the *Lodestar*, shoving the starship down into Earth's atmosphere.

They plunged through the sky.

I have time, Ben-Ari thought. *I can run to the shuttle bay. I can fly out in a shuttle. If the shuttles are gone, I can find a spacesuit and jetpack and jump.*

She prepared to run, to abandon ship.

But Niilo moaned at her side. The security chief was still alive. One of Aurora's tentacles twitched. On this ship, hundreds were dead, but hundreds still lived.

I will not abandon ship. Not so long as a single member of my crew needs me.

As the *Lodestar* streamed down through the sky, Ben-Ari reached back to the controls, determined to fly her ship.

She could barely see through the viewports. Wind roared through holes in the ship. The sky spun around them.

She pulled the controls.

She adjusted the sputtering engine.

She raised the ship's shattered nose.

A single viewport was still operational on the floor, connected to a camera on the ship's exterior. She could see the ocean below. A blur of land. A peninsula shaped like a boot. She knew where she was.

She was still falling fast. There were still fifty kilometers or more between her and the surface. Flames blazed around them. Shards of the hull tore free. They were burning up, falling apart.

The *Lodestar* was not meant to fly in the atmosphere. She had been built in space. She had been built to fly *only* in space. In the air, with no wings, she was like an anvil with a jetpack attached to the back. Bits and pieces kept tearing free, burning up. The ship was crumbling.

But Ben-Ari refused to crash.

She diverted more power to the shields.

They slipped, their last engine coughing.

They plunged down several kilometers, and her belly roiled and she passed out for a moment, woke up on the floor, grabbed the controls again.

She kept flying, diverting more power to the engines now. The sea blurred below.

And ahead she could see them—thousands of saucers descending through the atmosphere. Thousands of contrails plunging down to Earth's major cities. The ground invasion had begun.

I must reach Petty, Ben-Ari thought. *I must reach Jerusalem. That is where the greatest battle rages.*

Three saucers flew toward them. Ben-Ari fired her cannons, taking them out. The *Lodestar* kept flying, only ten kilometers above ground now and losing altitude fast. Their navigation systems were fried. The computers were dead. She recognized the Nile to her south. She flew with eye and hand.

She saw it ahead. The ruins of Jerusalem.

She flew lower. She was only a kilometer aboveground now. She flew over the desert, roaring toward the ruins. She could see the mountaintop city ahead.

And from the sky, thousands of saucers descended.

The ships charged toward her, lasers blasting.

Explosions rocked the *Lodestar*. Ben-Ari screamed.

She fired her guns. But there were too many saucers. The enemy ships mobbed her. Their blasts ripped more holes through the hull. Fire gusted into the bridge. Ben-Ari stared ahead, desperate to land, to reach the human army, to save those still alive aboard the *Lodestar*. To rejoin the fight. She flew lower. She was almost there. Grays below saw the ship, raised guns, opened fire. Ben-Ari was just a hundred meters over the ground now. She—

A blast hit her last engine.

It burst into flames and shattered.

The *Lodestar* streaked downward and slammed into the ground.

The mighty ship plowed through the earth, uprooting olive trees, shattering stones, burning up.

Ben-Ari grimaced and hit the brakes, desperate to stop the ship. The thrusters screeched. Sparks flew. Smoke filled the bridge. Monitors shattered. The ancient wall of Jerusalem rose ahead, and Ben-Ari screamed as the ship slammed into it.

They tore through the wall with a shower of bricks, screeched across the ancient cobbled streets, and came to a halt among the ruins of Jerusalem.

Ben-Ari lay on the floor, breathing.

I'm alive.

She could barely believe it, but it was true.

I survived.

The bridge of the *Lodestar* was located deep within the ship, protected with additional shielding. She was alive, but was the rest of the crew as lucky? She shoved herself up, limped toward Niilo, and tugged off the beam burying him. The beefy man moaned, bleeding from a gash on his head, unconscious. Ben-Ari turned toward Aurora. The mollusk was struggling to free herself from an overturned workstation. Ben-Ari strained, lifting off the heavy controls, and the alien slithered free.

"Mistress ..." Aurora's translation device was cracked, the voice staticky. "You ... flew ... wonderfully. Like ... a true ... Menorian."

Outside the ship, Ben-Ari heard it. Gunfire. Booming cannons. Roaring engines. The battle for Earth was raging.

She ripped the HOPE insignia off her shoulders.

"Right now I am no longer the captain of the *Lodestar*," Ben-Ari said. "Right now I am Major Einav Ben-Ari, a soldier of the Human Defense Force."

She stepped off the bridge. She moved through the ravaged ship, passing by racing medics and engineers. She paused by the armory, grabbed a plasma rifle and grenades, then made her way to a hole in the hull.

She climbed out into the world. Into war. Into the final battle for Earth.

CHAPTER SEVENTEEN

"Tomiko!" Marco took a step toward the brothel, reaching out toward her. "Tomi—"

Addy grabbed him. She yanked him away from the brothel. They stood on the shadowy roadside, the jagged towers of Gehenna rising around them. They still wore the plague doctor disguises, but thousands of grays crowded the roads here, and eyes were turning toward them.

Addy thrust her beaked gas mask near Marco and sneered.

"What the fuck are you doing, Poet?" she hissed. "You'll blow our cover."

Marco's heart raced. His head spun. He looked toward Tomiko, but the grays were dragging her between their brothel's columns. Marco could barely breathe.

"Addy, it's—"

She gripped him tighter. Her clawed gloves nearly cut his forearms. "I know who it is." Addy's eyes narrowed with fury. "If you go in there to save her, we're fucked. Our cover is blown."

Marco looked from side to side, desperate. The dark city spun around him, the towers leaned in, and the obsidian idols along the roadside seemed to mock him. Addy was right, he knew. If he ran into the brothel to save Tomiko, he might never make it to the pyramid. He'd jeopardize the mission. He had to carry on. And yet how could he abandon Tomiko here to rape, to torture?

"Poet." Addy spoke softly. "Poet, she dumped you. She cheated on you. She treated you like shit."

He shook his head, eyes damp. "No, Ads. I'm the one who treated her like shit. I drove her to leave me. I can't abandon her now. I can't." He touched her shoulder. "Go on without me. Get the job done. Kill the Oracle. I'm going in after Tomiko."

"Like hell I'm going on without you!" Addy said. "Fuck that shit. We do things together. We do *everything* together. Weren't you just telling me that yesterday?"

From inside the brothel—screams. Tomiko's screams.

"Addy, I have to," he whispered.

She sighed and rolled her eyes. "All right. All right! We'll save Tomiko. Fuck it. Why not complicate things? It's tradition." She gripped his hand and pulled him toward the brothel. "So come on, Poet. Let's save the bitch."

In their plague doctor outfits, they stepped between two columns, entering the brothel.

Grays lay around them, copulating on the floor. Others hung from cages, engaged in deviancy for all to see. Across the hall, the grays were dragging Tomiko onto an altar. Chains awaited.

Addy marched across the hall and doffed her robe, exposing her rifle, grenades, and blades.

"Listen up, bitches!" she shouted, boots clattering. "We're here to eat sausages and kick ass, and we're all out of sausages!" She glanced at Marco. "Seriously, we are. I ate the last one on the way here." She looked back ahead and shouted again. "Hand over the human and I might let you live!"

Marco too doffed his cloak, exposing his weapons. He raised his rifle and yanked back on the cocking handle. "Tomiko, I'm here!"

From the back of the temple, she looked at him.

Marco ripped off his gas mask and met her eyes.

God. It was real. It was impossible, yet there she was. She was really here.

Tomiko. The girl he had fallen in love with. The girl who had come into his life with smiles and tears, with kisses and shouts, with fire and water, a tornado of emotions and shattering and rebuilding. A woman he had given his heart to. A woman he had betrayed. A woman who had betrayed him. A woman he hated and still loved with all his heart.

I was broken when I met you, he thought. *I was hurt, so I hurt you and you hurt me, and we created a dance of pain. But I'm here now. And I'll save you.*

"Marco!" Tomiko cried.

The grays spun toward them. They shrieked. Several leaped back. Others laughed. A few copulated with more vigor.

But many leaped toward Marco and Addy, claws lashing.

Marco and Addy fired their railguns. The bullets shrieked out, pounding into the grays, knocking them back. More grays kept leaping toward them. Marco and Addy walked down the hall, boots thumping, firing bullet after bullet, blasting back gray after gray. Blood sprayed. Some grays shrieked and fled. More raced forward. A few fired electrical bolts. A blast hit Marco's chest. His armored spacesuit saved his life, but the blow felt like a hammer. Ignoring the pain, he fired his railgun again and again, taking out more grays. Addy took a blow to the side and kept walking, spraying bullets. Blood washed the brothel, grays screamed, and the creatures scurried between the columns, fleeing the building.

Marco and Addy reached the altar.

Several grays lay dead around the altar in pools of blood; the railguns had torn them apart. One gray was still alive, blood staining his indigo robes. The towering, wrinkly creature held Tomiko, his claws on her neck. The gray leered at Marco and Addy. His eyes filled with delight. He let out a long, luxurious hiss.

"This is getting interesting." The gray licked his lips. "Take one more step, and I slay this whore. And I will take you both to be my slaves. I—"

Marco fired his railgun.

His bullet tore through the gray's head.

As chunks of skull and brain flew, Tomiko twisted herself free from the claws and ran toward Marco. He lowered his rifle, and she leaped into his arms.

"Marco!" Tomiko said, weeping, trembling. "Oh, Marco. They came to your house. They were looking for you. For Addy too. They thought I knew where you are. Marco ..." She dissolved into weeping.

"I'm here, Tomiko," he whispered, holding her close. "I'm here. You're safe now."

"Um, Poet?" Addy said. "That sentiment might be a bit premature."

He looked at Addy. She was pale, gun clutched in her hands. Marco looked around and felt the blood drain from his own face.

Hundreds of gray soldiers were advancing toward the brothel.

Several saucers hovered above.

The troops stepped between the columns, guns pointed at Marco and Addy, eyes glittering through the holes in their helmets. Tomiko clung to Marco. Addy winced.

"So, Tomiko," Addy said, "did you remember to bring the entire HDF with you?"

Marco gently moved Tomiko behind his back.

"Stay behind me, Tomi," he whispered.

One of the gray soldiers stepped forward. She was a towering female in gilded armor. A jeweled ankh hung around her neck, formed from finger bones, and rotting bat wings sprouted from her back. She raised a spear, a pulsing heart skewered upon it. The creature nodded at Marco and Addy.

"Welcome, friends," the winged gray said. "We knew you would come." She turned toward her troops. "Take them alive!"

"Yes, Mistress Isis!" the gray warriors cried.

The grays—hundreds of them—swarmed.

Marco and Addy fired their railguns. Bullets slammed into the grays. Dozens of the creatures fell. But dozens more were charging. Thousands filled the city. The creatures shrieked, cackled, scuttled across the ceiling, climbed the columns. Their guns fired.

Electric bolts slammed into Marco. He took three on the chest but kept firing. A fourth bolt drove between his ribs, cracking his armor, knocking the breath out of him. More blasts knocked him onto the floor. Marco screamed, struggling to shield Tomiko under his body. Addy stood above them, firing in automatic, slaying more grays. Blasts slammed into her. She fell to her knees, still firing, still shouting. A bolt slammed into her chest, and she too fell.

"Keep them alive!" screeched Isis, the winged gray. "Bind them!"

Claws grabbed Marco. He fired his gun. Bullets slammed into the gray gripping him, pulverizing its helmet and the flesh within. Another gray grabbed his hot barrel, and the creature's flesh sizzled, but the gray kept his grip tight. God, the beast was strong. The gray ripped the gun from Marco's grasp.

Tomiko screamed. Claws grabbed her, tearing her skin. Marco shouted and leaped onto the grays, drawing his knife. He lashed the blade. It sparked against armor. Addy fought at his side, screaming, blood in her mouth. The grays were everywhere. More electrical blasts flew, hitting them. Marco screamed and fell back down.

They brought out chains.

They slapped Marco, Addy, and Tomiko in irons.

They lifted them overhead, shrieking, cheering, jeering. Claws cut into them. Their blood fell. The guttural voices chanted in triumph.

"We caught the humans!" cried Isis, her rotting wings spread wide. "Take them to pain! The Tarasque shall feed!"

Addy was screaming and cursing. Marco struggled but knew it was hopeless. The grays carried them out of the brothel and along the boulevard. Across the city, grays stared and laughed and licked their teeth.

I'm sorry, Ben-Ari, Marco thought. *I'm sorry, Addy. I'm sorry, Tomiko. I'm sorry, Earth.*

The grays kept carrying them, moving away from the pyramid, and the crowds roared, and the chant echoed.

"To pain! To pain!"

CHAPTER EIGHTEEN

Lailani stood on the hilltop, rifle in hand, helmet on her head. A dozen years ago, as a young private, she had scrawled words on her helmet with a permanent marker: *Life is a bag of dicks with syphilis.* She had been young, been hurt, been afraid, had sought comfort in her anger and twisted humor. Today was her thirtieth birthday. Today she was a captain in the Human Defense Force, commanding a company of two hundred warriors. Today on her helmet she had drawn only two words: *Earth Eternal.*

Her warriors stood behind her, guns in hand, two hundred of Earth's finest. The hill they guarded was the tallest peak of Jerusalem, overlooking the ruins. Elvis stood at her side, smiling thinly.

"Well, they outnumber us about ten thousand to one," he said. "Plenty for us to kill. I feel almost bad for the poor bastards."

He was telling jokes. But his voice trembled. He was pale. His fingers shook around his gun.

Thousands of saucers hovered above the city. Countless gray soldiers were marching across the ruins, surrounding the hill. Across the land, the HDF was fighting the invasion with artillery, tanks, fighter jets, and good old infantry. Saucers were reported over every major city. This battle raged across the world.

They have us in a stranglehold, Lailani thought. She smiled thinly.

"Those bastards don't know what's coming to them." She slapped Elvis on the back. "Ready to fight?"

Elvis took a shuddering breath. "No. But hell, I missed the last war. Might as well have some fun now."

Grays were beginning to climb the hill. Thousands of them.

Lailani turned toward her troops. "Soldiers! Today you will win! For Earth!" She spun toward the enemy and aimed her rifle. "For Earth, fire!"

She opened fire. Across the hill, her company fired their guns. They tore into the grays. Hundreds of the creatures fell, only for others to step over the corpses, to keep climbing the hill.

"Earth!" Lailani shouted, loading and reloading.

"Earth!" her soldiers cried, guns blazing.

The grays returned fire. Soldiers fell. Gray corpses piled up below. A saucer streaked overhead, and lasers tore through her company. They fired skyward, taking the saucer down. It crashed at their side, crushing an archway. The soldiers kept firing. More fell. The dead lay around Lailani's feet. She tore the magazines off their chests and reloaded her rifle. Hot casings piled up around her. She fought on. Elvis was shouting at her side, firing with her, slaying the creatures.

We cannot win, Lailani knew, gazing across the city. There were more grays here than they had bullets. *But we can go down fighting.*

She fought on.

For Earth.

For her friends.

For the scared, angry girl she had been, and for the woman she had become.

For humanity.

For Marco and for Addy.

"So, de la Rosa!" Elvis shouted over the roar of battle. "Next time you find a time machine, take us to a nice, friendly place, will ya? Elvis's 1973 Hawaiian concert would be a good choice."

She nodded. "Next time I find a time machine, you got it."

They kept firing as their friends fell around them. The dead slid down the hill. The grays were marching up toward them. Elvis and Lailani stood side by side, rifles in hand, facing the fall of their world.

CHAPTER NINETEEN

They languished in the dungeon, beaten, chained, waiting for the torture.

"Let us out of here!" Addy pounded on the door. "Let us out, you fucking sons of whores! I'll kill the lot of you! Let us out!" She drove her shoulder into the iron again and again. "Cowards! Fucking cowards!"

Sitting on the cold stone floor, Marco blinked and groaned. "Addy. I'm trying to think here."

She spun toward him, face red. "How can you think at a time like this? We're locked in a dungeon, about to be tortured to death. Less thinking, more fighting!"

Marco sighed. "Yes, because fighting that door is going so well for you."

Addy growled, leaped toward him, and grabbed him by the collar. "Maybe if you helped, you lazy fuck, instead of sitting here thinking, we'd—"

"Lay off him!" Tomiko rose to her feet. "Marco's coming up with a plan. Let him think."

Addy spun toward Tomiko, eyebrows rising. "Coming up with a plan? *Coming up with a plan?* The last time Poet planned something, it was to save your skinny little ass, which landed us all in this place. So go back to sitting in the shadows, toots, and let me beat the shit out of Marco."

Tomiko glared at the taller woman, then sniffed and retreated into the shadows.

"*Toots*?" Marco said to Addy. "I can't believe you actually said the word *toots*. What are you, a 1920s gangster?"

Addy groaned. "Look who's talking, Mister 'I reckon this, I reckon that.'"

Marco rose to his feet. "So, toots, what say you and I blow this joint, head over to the local speakeasy? Bust out of the cooler. Meet some broads. Duck soup!"

Addy rolled her eyes. "Great. He's joking. We're about to be tortured to death, Earth is about to be destroyed, and the poet is joking."

"He's not—" Tomiko began.

"You—shush," Addy said. She returned to the door and resumed slamming herself against it. "Open up, you fucking cowards! I'll kill you all! Fight me, damn it! Cowards!"

Marco sighed and moved closer to Tomiko. The prison cell was small and dusty. A flickering light bulb shone on the ceiling. Marco grimaced. Every movement ached. The grays had stripped off his armored spacesuit, leaving him in his underclothes. Bruises and cuts coated his body, and after so long in the wilderness, he was thin, pale, sickly. Every breath rattled through his lungs.

He sat beside Tomiko. She leaned against him. She placed a hand on his knee.

"Thank you, Marco," she said. "For saving me."

"I'm not sure that I did," Marco said.

Tomiko bit her lip. "I suppose you didn't." She patted his knee. "But you tried." She sighed. "What is this place? Not just this dungeon—this whole terrifying hell. Who are these grays? What's going on?"

Marco spent a while telling her the tale. About how Ben-Ari had marooned a group of nefarious monks on a planet named Isfet, where they evolved over a million years into the grays. How the grays had eventually returned to Earth, found it polluted and destroyed, and rebuilt their pyramid over the ruins of Jerusalem. How the grays were now flying back to Old Earth, the Earth where Marco and Tomiko were from, to conquer and settle it. And he spoke too of his journey with Addy across the badlands, how they had to reach the pyramid, to kill the Oracle inside, the creature that controlled time.

"We came so close," Marco said. "Only a few steps away from the pyramid."

Tomiko lowered her head. "And I ruined it."

"No." Marco shook his head. "It's not your fault. You were a trap. You were meant to pull me off course. I reckon the Tick-Tock King knew we were coming. That he sent his minions to kidnap you. To lure us off track. You were bait."

Tomiko smiled. "Addy is right. You do say 'I reckon' too much."

Marco stared at her. Then he laughed. "I reckon that I do."

Tomiko laughed too, then sighed. She spent a while telling Marco of her own recent life. She had remarried. She had been living with her new husband in the Greek house. But she was unhappy, she claimed. Her new husband was not wealthy like he had claimed. They fought a lot over money.

"I missed you, Marco," she said. "I'm sorry for what I did."

Marco lowered his head. Even here, facing death, the old betrayal stung. Tomiko leaving him for another man. Tomiko lying to him.

"Your real name isn't even Tomiko," he whispered. "You lied to me."

Tears flowed down her cheeks. "I was born Kiko. But I wanted a new name when I fled the ruins of Japan. And I found your books. And Addy told me about your unpublished book, about the heroine named Tomiko. And I wanted to be that sort of heroine. Strong. Brave. So I gave myself that name. It was similar to my name. I thought it was meant to be. When I told you my name is Tomiko, I lied to you. I'm sorry. But in a way, I was also telling you the truth." She gazed at him with damp eyes. "It *was* my real name. The name I gave myself. The name of a new heroine in a new world."

Marco nodded, head lowered. "And I'm sorry too. For neglecting you. For driving you away. After our divorce, I left Earth for a long time. I sought peace on another planet. I studied Deep Being and learned to be a better man. I know I wasn't a good husband."

Daniel Arenson

Tomiko's eyes were damp. "We were cruel to each other. We were so cruel." She touched his cheek. "Before we die, I'm sorry, Marco."

He held her hand. "And I'm sorry, Tomiko."

Addy knelt before them. "And I'm sorry too."

Marco and Tomiko looked at her.

"You are?" Marco said.

Addy lowered her head. "I am." She looked up, voice growing louder with every word. "I'm sorry that you two *lazy pieces of shit* aren't helping me break that door!" She grabbed them and yanked them up. "Come on! Pull your weight, assholes!"

She shoved them toward the heavy iron door.

And the door swung open.

They all stepped back, gasping.

Grays stood at the doorway. The wrinkly creatures stretched their claws toward the humans.

"Get your stinkin' claws off me!" Addy shouted, swatting them aside.

The grays raised batons. Electrical bolts slammed into Addy. She fell, screaming.

"Stop it!" Marco shouted.

He raced toward the grays, only to get hit too. Bolts knocked him down. One bolt hit Tomiko, and she fell with a cry.

The grays grabbed them. Without weapons, the prisoners didn't stand a chance. The grays were taller, stronger, and armed. They manhandled the three humans out of the prison cell. A tunnel awaited them, branching in two.

A female gray stood there, clad in golden armor. Oily wings grew from her back, and an ankh made from finger bones hung around her neck. Marco recognized her. She had commanded the raid on the brothel. He remembered her name—Isis.

Addy screamed and lunged herself toward the winged gray, only for the guards to beat her back.

"Excellent," Isis said, smiling, revealing long fangs. She stepped toward Tomiko and stroked her cheek. The claws drew blood. "The bait worked perfectly. Tomiko drew in the two captains like a worm drawing in the fish."

"This fish is a piranha that'll bite your ass!" Addy shouted, and the grays punched her in the stomach. She doubled over. Marco screamed and tried to run to her, but the grays held him back.

"Good," Isis said, looking down at the fallen Addy. "You are feisty. You will put on a good show for the crowd." She turned toward her guards. She still spoke in English, perhaps intending to terrify her captives. "Take Tomiko back to her own timeline. Her task here is done. Nefitis awaits her on Old Earth. The girl will make a good slave for the goddess."

The gray soldiers bowed. "Yes, Mistress Isis."

They began dragging Tomiko down one of the corridors.

"Tomiko!" Marco shouted, trying to reach her. But the grays tightened their grips. They delivered punches to his stomach, to his face. He cried out, thrashing, reaching out. "Tomiko!"

But the grays pulled her into the shadows. Tomiko gave a last, wordless cry, then vanished into the darkness.

"You fucking bastards!" Marco shouted, turning toward Isis. "Don't you fucking hurt her! It's me you want!"

Isis smiled. She leaned closer and stroked Marco's cheek, cutting him with her claws. Her breath smelled of lilac and blood.

"And we have you, dear human. Put on a good show for me. Scream a lot as you die." She turned toward her guards. "Take them to the Tarasque!"

They dragged Marco and Addy down the second tunnel. Whenever they resisted, the grays electrocuted, punched, or cut them.

Stay strong, Tomiko, Marco thought as the grays manhandled him and Addy forward. *I'm going to find a way to kill that Oracle. I'm going to end this nightmare. I'm going to save you. Stay strong.*

"So, guys, you can just drop us off at the nearest time portal," Addy said, twisting in the grays' grip. "We'd love money for a cab. We're a bit short. Especially Marco."

Marco rolled his eyes. "We're the *same height*!"

As the grays dragged them along the tunnel, Marco heard a low rumble ahead. With every step, it grew louder. Soon the tunnel was vibrating with the sound. At first Marco thought it some great engine, but then he realized: it was a crowd. It was thousands of voices chanting.

They reached a door at the end of the tunnel. The chants were deafening. The ground shook.

"Poet?" Addy said.

"Yes, Addy?"

"Next time, let's go on vacation to Cancun. Black Earth sucks."

"Agreed," he said.

The grays opened the door and shoved Marco and Addy through it.

They stumbled into a sandy arena. Concrete tiers rose around them in rings, a great amphitheater. Countless grays filled the seats, roaring and jeering. Addy had once dragged Marco to a hockey game, and he had suffered silently in the arena among fifty thousand drunken, screaming fans. That place seemed serene in comparison.

Addy spun back toward the tunnel.

"I changed my mind. I want back into the cell."

But the grays slammed the door shut, blocking her path. Marco and Addy remained in the arena, the crowd spinning around them. Marco nearly fainted. He was already weak from his long days in the desolation. His new wounds and the crowd made him sway.

What torture do they have ready for us here? he thought.

Addy's eyes widened.

"Poet, look! Weapons!"

She darted toward the middle of the arena. She lifted a sword from the sand. Marco joined her. There was a second weapon waiting—a war hammer. As he lifted the hammer, the crowd cheered louder. Marco recognized these weapons—miniature versions of the weapons the mechas had carried.

"I'm not sure I want to play their game," Marco said.

"I'm a simple woman," Addy said. "I see a weapon, I take it. They want us to die as gladiators? Better than torture."

Marco looked into her eyes. "What if they want us to fight each other?"

Addy paled. "Fuck." She dropped her sword. "I'm not doing *that*."

Marco nodded. "Me neither." He tossed his hammer down.

The crowd booed. They pelted the arena with filth.

Suddenly trumpets blared. Lights flashed. Floodlights filled the arena, blinding. The ground trembled, and a massive trapdoor slid open, revealing a gaping pit.

From the underground, a creature emerged.

The crowd cheered. "Tarasque! Tarasque!"

The beast was massive, as large as a whale, with eight thick legs, crimson claws, and jaws filled with fangs. Warts covered its gray skin, and spikes sprouted from its body, each one impaling a human head. Those severed heads were still living, crying out silently, faces twisting in anguish.

The Tarasque's own head was bloated and pale, its eyes oval and black. It was the head of a gray but many times larger, deformed. Perhaps this creature was the product of genetic engineering, a gray grown to grotesque size and twisted into a beast. The monster opened a mouth the size of a garage and howled. Its breath slammed against Addy and Marco like a storm, scented of rot. Human limbs were stuck between its back teeth.

"Changed my mind," Addy said. "I want the weapons!"

She grabbed the sword. Marco hurried to reclaim his war hammer.

The Tarasque leaped toward them.

The crowd cheered.

Marco and Addy scattered. The jaws snapped shut between them. Addy screamed and thrust her sword, but her blade bounced off the monster's hard skin. Marco shouted, swung his hammer, and cried as pain reverberated up his arms. It was like trying to crush an anvil.

The Tarasque lunged toward Marco, jaws snapping. He leaped back. The crowd roared. Marco swung his hammer, a useless gesture. The jaws snapped shut again, missing him by centimeters. Marco retreated until his back hit the wall. The lowest tier of seats rose just above his head, and the audience roared, the grays crying out in their guttural language. The monster howled, opening its jaws to swallow Marco.

"For Earth!" Addy cried. She ran, leaped onto the creature, and grabbed the spikes on its body. She pulled herself onto its back, raced onto its head, and drove down her sword.

The Tarasque bellowed.

Marco ran, fleeing the jaws.

Addy slammed her sword down again, and the blade finally cracked the skin, sinking a few centimeters into the flesh.

The creature roared. It shook madly like a wet dog, scattering severed heads. Addy flew off its back and hit the ground.

"Addy!" Marco rushed to help her up. "Addy, together! We flank it and try to hit the eyes."

She nodded. "Let's kill that son of a—"

The monster's tail swung and slammed into them.

Marco and Addy flew.

Addy slammed into the arena wall. Marco landed on the first row of seats, right among the audience. For a terrifying moment the grays were clawing him, biting him, laughing, drooling, before they finally shoved him down onto the sand. He lay in a daze, bleeding, breathing raggedly.

It was all too horrible. A living nightmare. This place so far from home. These creatures around him. Tomiko—led off to torture. How could this be real? How could such terror exist?

The Tarasque's claws slammed down.

Marco rolled aside, and the claws hit the dirt.

He swung his hammer, hitting the leg. He might as well have axed solid iron.

He struggled to his feet. Addy was circling the monster, sword raised.

"Marco, charge!" she shouted.

They ran toward the beast, weapons raised.

Marco took a gamble. He spun like an Olympic discus thrower and tossed his hammer.

It flew into the air toward the Tarasque's eye.

And he missed.

The Tarasque caught the hammer in its mouth, then spat it out, hurling the weapon into the crowd. The hammer caved in a gray's head. The rest of the audience howled with laughter.

Addy screamed and charged. She tried to climb onto the monster again, to reach an eye. The creature shook her off, snapped its jaws, and tore the sword from her hand. As Addy screamed, the beast spat her blade aside, then knocked Addy down.

Marco ran toward her. The beast snarled, spewing smoke. Marco and Addy retreated until they hit the wall. Weaponless, they reached out and held hands.

The Tarasque stepped closer. Its claws dug deep grooves in the earth. It roared, spraying saliva, blowing back Marco and Addy's hair. They stood against the wall, ready to die.

But then Marco noticed something for the first time.

The Tarasque was scarred.

There were manacles around its ankles, the metal rings nailed into the flesh. There were the stripes of electric whips on its back. A shock collar dug into its neck. Perhaps this creature was not inherently cruel. Perhaps others had been cruel to it.

"Addy," Marco whispered. "Loving-kindness meditation. Now."

The monster scratched the earth and opened its jaws wide, ready to feed.

"What the fuck are you talking about, Poet?" Addy whispered, eyes feverish.

"Loving-kindness!" he said. "Like the guru taught us. It's the only meditation we kept failing. Do it! Now!"

The grays chanted all around them, pounding their chests. Marco couldn't understand their language, but he could imagine what they were chanting. *Feed! Feed! Feed!*

"The monster won't even understand us!" Addy said.

"Most communication is nonverbal. Tone. Body language. Now!" He turned toward the roaring monster and raised his open palms. He spoke to the Tarasque, his voice shaky, trying to sound calm and soothing. "May you be safe and free of suffering. May you know peace. May you have ease of being."

Addy stared at Marco as if he were insane. And yet the monster narrowed its eyes, closed its mouth, and sniffed.

"Do it with me, Ads," Marco whispered.

She sighed. She nodded. They faced the monster. They spoke together, palms open in a gesture of peace, voices soothing.

"May you be safe and free of suffering. May you know peace. May you have ease of being."

The Tarasque stared, confused, then roared, exposing a quivering red gullet. Saliva sprayed. The stench nearly made Marco fall. He and Addy kept talking, keeping calm.

"May you be safe and free of suffering."

Marco hesitated, then placed his hand on the monster.

"May you know peace."

Addy added her hand, stroking the beast.

"May you have ease of being."

And the monster calmed. It knelt before them. It placed its chin in the dust. Its head was the size of a car, bloated, pale, and warty. The teeth thrust up from the underbite like spears. The cranium bulged, and the black eyes dampened. There was such pain in those eyes.

Marco stroked the creature.

"I know they hurt you," he whispered. "May you be safe and free from suffering."

Addy had tears in her eyes. "May you know peace," she whispered, patting the beast.

"May you have ease of being," Marco and she said together.

The creature gurgled and purred. Nearby, Marco saw Addy's sword. He could make a break for it, grab it, stab the beast in the eye.

He let it be.

I never wanted to become a soldier. I never wanted to kill. Yet I've become very good at it. Let this be a time for mercy. For freedom from suffering.

The giant beast lay down, whimpering as Marco and Addy patted it. It wept.

"Maybe for the first time in its life, somebody is showing it kindness," Marco said softly, stroking the animal.

Yet the crowd seemed less compassionate. Grays began hurling stones into the arena, hitting the Tarasque. The audience cried in fury, deprived of its show. The Tarasque reared, roaring in pain as the stones landed. Several trainers—grays in armor—raced into the arena. They lashed electrical whips. The crackling thongs were like flexible lightning. When they hit the beast, it roared. Perhaps the sword and hammer had failed to hurt the animal, but the electric whips tore its skin. Blood spilled.

The gray trainers shouted, pointing at Marco and Addy.

Marco could not understand their words. He didn't have to, no more than the animal had needed to understand English.

"Slay the humans!" the grays were saying. "Feed upon them, beast!"

They whipped the Tarasque again. Bellowing, it turned back toward Marco and Addy.

Marco stared into its eyes.

"May you be free of suffering," he whispered. "May you have ease of being."

Shouting, the grays raised their whips again. They pointed at Marco and Addy.

"Feed upon them, beast!"

The whips tore into the Tarasque.

And it roared.

And it wept.

And it charged forth and closed its jaws around the grays, crushing them between its mighty teeth.

The audience cried in terror. A few grays drew guns and fired, hitting the monster. Guards raced into the arena, firing rifles, hitting the beast with electric bolts. The Tarasque's flesh tore. It bled. It cried in agony.

And it charged.

It trampled over the gray soldiers. Bleeding, hit by round after round, it leaped onto the tiers of seats. It charged through the audience, biting, clawing, lashing its tail. Seats crumbled around it. Cracks raced across the arena. Supporting pillars fell. The entire theater was falling apart, and still the beast charged through the audience, tearing into grays, suffering blow after blow and still fighting. Perhaps for the first time in its life, it was free.

Marco ran toward a dead guard and grabbed the gray's electrical rifle. Addy grabbed a rifle from another corpse.

They ran toward the arena gateway. Guards blocked their way. Marco and Addy fired their guns, taking the grays down. The dead guards had metal spheres attached to their belts, topped with buttons, perhaps grenades. Marco grabbed two and tossed one to Addy. They ran out of the arena, firing their guns, taking down more grays.

As they burst out onto the street, the amphitheater shattered.

The Tarasque burst out through the wall, scattering bricks, and stood on the street, roaring, coated with blood and dust.

Chaos erupted across the city.

Gray soldiers ran toward the rampaging beast, firing their guns. The Tarasque howled and charged, trampling them, crashing into buildings. Mechanical horses raced toward the creature, pulling chariots filled with grays. The monster, bleeding, snatched chariots in its jaws and scattered them like toys. Chariots slammed into buildings. Towers crumbled, and dust flew across the city. Thousands of soldiers ran toward the mad beast, firing their guns. Saucers came to hover overhead.

"Come on, Poet!" Addy shouted, grabbing his hand. "Now! On that chariot!"

They reached toward an overturned chariot. They fired their guns, slaying the grays within, and shoved the chariot back upright. They leaped inside. A control panel operated the four mechanical horses attached to the chariot. Marco shoved down on the throttle, and the robotic horses burst into a gallop.

They stormed down the street, moving through the clouds of dust. Scythes were attached to the chariot wheels, spinning madly. Grays leaped off the road. Some were too slow; the blades tore them apart. Behind the chariot, the saucers were firing. Marco glanced over his shoulder to see the laser blasts hit the Tarasque. The monster wailed and fell.

More blasts hit the mighty beast. Its head hit the ground. Its eyes closed.

Goodbye, friend, Marco thought. *May your pain now end.*

He looked back forward.

The pyramid soared ahead from the dust.

They charged toward it. Their horses' metal hooves thundered. Their chariot clattered. All around them, the dust flew and the city trembled.

A phalanx of grays emerged to block the road ahead, raising riot shields.

A cannon was mounted onto the chariot. Marco pulled the trigger. Red crackling shells flew out, tearing into the grays ahead, shattering their shields. Addy fired her rifle, cutting through more grays.

"Hold on!" Addy shouted.

The chariot plowed through the phalanx of grays.

Shields cracked and flew in shards.

The scythes ripped soldiers apart.

The wheels snapped bones beneath them.

The chariot kept charging onward, moving so fast the buildings blurred at their sides.

Golgoloth, the black pyramid, rose ahead. According to the grays who had taken Tomiko away, Nefitis herself was leading the assault on Green Earth. That was one less problem to deal with here. The pyramid's guardians, however, flanked the avenue, two mummies the size of towers, forming an archway with their arms.

The colossal monstrosities turned toward the chariot. Their hands were fused together, flesh molded with flesh; they could not break the archway they formed. Their tattered shrouds hung loose, revealing dry, rancid flesh. Their eyes burned deep umber like cauldrons of melted skin.

"Stand back, children of men!" the guardians rumbled, their voices echoing across the city. "This place is holy ground."

"Well, call me a sinner," Addy said and lobbed a grenade.

Marco tossed his own grenade, then fired the chariot's cannon.

Explosions rocked the mummies. The shrouds burst into flame. The fire spread, raging up the towering guardians. The creatures screamed. Marco and Addy, still charging forth in their chariot, fired their guns, ripping into the burning flesh.

In the inferno, the conjoined twins ripped apart. Blood rained. The two burning mummies shuffled toward the chariots. They reached down flaming fingers. Marco fired the cannon, knocking them back. Addy tugged the controls, and the chariot veered violently, nearly overturning, and charged between the legs of one mummy.

They had done it.

They reached the pyramid.

Behind them, hundreds of grays were running and firing their guns.

"Hold on tight, Poet!" Addy said, shoving down the throttle.

The horses leaped onto a staircase that stretched up the pyramid's facade. They raced up the pyramid, jostling madly. Explosions rocked the stones around them. One blast hit the chariot, nearly shattering it. Another blast took out a horse. The three remaining mechanical horses kept charging.

They reached a platform that thrust out from the pyramid like a tongue. A throne rose here, but it was empty. Nefitis, goddess of this city, was attacking Green Earth. Several of her priests stood here by an altar, feasting upon headless babies. Addy and Marco fired, tearing through the wretched monks. The creatures cackled as they died.

Marco hit the brakes. The horses reared to a halt atop the pyramid, knocking over Nefitis's throne. It fell with a clang and cracked. Behind the throne loomed a dark archway, leading into the pyramid.

Marco spun back toward the city.

Thousands of grays stood below the pyramid. Hundreds of chariots gathered among them. The creatures stared up, still, silent. The mummies had fallen. Those gargantuan guardians were burning lifelessly across the streets.

"Why aren't they chasing us anymore?" Addy whispered.

"The pyramid is holy," Marco said. "They can't."

She scoffed. "Morons."

"Or maybe they are wise," Marco said softly. "Maybe they fear the horror within Golgoloth."

A chill seemed to emanate from the pyramid. Marco and Addy turned to face the archway. They could see nothing but darkness within. Perhaps it was just the wind, but Marco thought he could hear a deep grumble, a laughter from the shadows.

"He's in there," Marco said softly. "The Oracle. The Time Seer."

"Tic-Tac-Toe." Addy nodded. "Let's go kick him right in the tacs. Ready?"

Marco nodded. "Ready."

Addy took a step toward the archway, then paused. She grabbed Marco's head with both hands and kissed him hard on the lips.

"It's almost over, Poet," she whispered. "I love you."

"I love you too." He clasped her hand. "Let's get this over with and go home."

Hand in hand, they stepped through the archway, entering the shadows.

CHAPTER TWENTY

Petty stood in the bunker beneath Jerusalem, turning from monitor to monitor, watching the world fall.

His generals worked around him in a frenzy, barking orders into communicators, sending troops and fleets across the world. From here, this hub beneath the ruins, they commanded Earth's armies. Monitors hung across the war room, showing San Francisco, London, Beijing, Paris, the alpha cities of the world.

And Petty watched them fall.

The saucers fired their lasers, destroying the Golden Gate Bridge, the Petronas Towers, the Taj Mahal. Armies of grays, millions of them, swarmed across the planet, overwhelming the human forces. More portals were opening up around Earth. More saucers were emerging. The last of humanity's warships fell. Millions of human soldiers were fighting around the globe, yet they could not hold back the tide.

We cannot win, Petty realized, standing in the bunker. *Marco and Addy failed. Earth will fall.*

A boom shook the bunker. Dust flew and monitors rattled. The grays were pounding Jerusalem above. The grays were unleashing their largest force against Jerusalem.

They know I'm here, he thought.

More blasts shook the city. The bunker rattled. Monitors cracked. Bomb after bomb hit the ruins, digging into the ground. The bunker was deep, but it would not withstand this assault forever.

"The Pacific Rim has fallen!" a general shouted.

"Grays are swarming over the South American Central Command!"

"The fleet is gone, sir! I repeat, the fleet is gone!"

And thus the world falls, Petty thought. *Not fighting an alien. Fighting ourselves.*

A shadow covered several monitors. Petty looked and saw a massive saucer, nearly as large as the entire city, lower itself to hover over Jerusalem. Golden glyphs were engraved upon its black hull. He had taught himself to read their language.

Claw of Nefitis.

The grays' flagship.

Petty walked across the control room, approaching the exit.

"Mister President?" a general called after him.

"The Command Center is yours," Petty told him.

"Mister President, where are you going?"

He left the room.

"To go down fighting," he muttered.

A blast shook the bunker. Bricks fell. A tunnel cracked and dust rained. Petty stopped by an armory. He removed his suit, this shell that had trapped him for too long. He pulled on battle fatigues. He grabbed a rifle and helmet. He climbed a trembling, crackling shaft and emerged into the ruins.

A gray leaped at him.

Petty fired his gun, and the creature fell, head blasted open.

Petty climbed onto a pile of rubble and gazed around.

He stood on the hilltop, on hallowed ground, this ancient center of the Holy Land. It was here that King Solomon had built his temple, that Jesus had been crucified, that so many religions had risen. It was here, perhaps, that Earth would now fall.

Barely anything remained of Jerusalem now. Nearly all the last buildings, some of them thousands of years old, had fallen. The battle raged across the rubble. Tanks plowed paths between piles of bricks, cannons blasting. Artillery boomed on the hilltops. Fighter jets blazed across the sky, firing missiles. Thousands of infantry warriors were running, firing their rifles. Explosions rocked the ruins. The smell of gunpowder and blood and dust filled the air.

But humanity's might drowned under the assault. The grays were everywhere. They covered the city. They fought from hills and valleys. Their landing vessels kept touching down, spilling out more troops. Their saucers kept circling the city, firing lasers, burning human platoons.

The largest saucer hovered above, its shadow covering the ruins. The *Claw of Nefitis*.

A hatch opened in the mothership. Red light emerged. A beam extended down to the city, illuminating the sand only a few meters away from Petty.

A creature descended in the beam of light, coming to land beside him.

She was a gray but taller than the others, maybe twice Petty's height. She was rail thin, her limbs knobby, her ribs prominent, her naked breasts dripping bloody milk. Her skin was the color of old concrete, wrinkly and liver-spotted. The face was small and pinched, the lips thin, but the cranium was bloated. Jagged iron spikes had been hammered into that head, blood dripping from the nails, forming a rusty crown. The creature unfurled her claws and turned toward Petty. Her eyes, pitiless black ovals, met his. Her lipless mouth opened in a snarl, revealing teeth like infected needles.

"Petty," she hissed. "King of Apes."

Petty knew her. He spat out her name.

"Nefitis."

The goddess leaped toward him, claws extended.

Petty fired his assault rifle on automatic.

His bullets hit the creature's desiccated flesh. They fell to the ground, flattened. An instant later, the goddess slammed into him.

Claws tore into Petty. He fell onto his back, blood spurting. The creature reached down, clutched his throat in her claws, and began to squeeze. She lifted him off the ground. His feet kicked the air.

"Useless maggot." Nefitis leaned her head forward, peering into his eyes. Her tongue emerged to lick her teeth. "This is the king of the apes, the great warrior? How weak is his flesh!"

With her second hand, she thrust her claws.

She pierced his belly.

Petty screamed, dangling in her grip. He fired again. His bullets bounced off her skin. They slammed into Petty, lacerating his chest and arms. He couldn't breathe. Hanging in her claws, he drew a knife. He thrust it, aiming for an eye, but she caught his wrist.

With a grin, she tightened her claws, slicing into his wrist, cutting deeper, snapping the bone, then finally severing his hand.

The hand thumped into the dirt, fingers twitching.

Petty screamed.

"Your world will fall," Nefitis hissed, her breath assailing him. She still held him above the ground by the neck. "The reign of humanity ends. The Sanctified rise."

Petty stared into her eyes, and he saw visions in the black orbs. Humanity enslaved, the men butchered, the women used for breeding. The grays reigning upon Earth. A nightmarish future. All the work of mankind—undone.

"And now, Petty," Nefitis said. "Now you d—"

An explosion burst across her shoulder.

Nefitis screamed.

A projectile flew.

It slammed into her back, and a second explosion rumbled. Nefitis howled, stumbling several feet forward.

The goddess dropped Petty to the ground. He landed with a thud, bleeding, broken, barely alive. His severed hand lay beside him.

He looked ahead, fading, and saw the woman there, walking up the hillside, emerging from the dust.

"Ben-Ari," Petty whispered.

The major wore her battle fatigues, once more a soldier. A helmet topped her head, and armor covered her body. She held a massive .50-cal railgun, a weapon that could blast a hole through a tank. She cocked it, loading another round.

Nefitis spun toward Ben-Ari, shrieking.

"How dare you disturb my meal?" the goddess shrieked. "I came to feast!"

Ben-Ari smiled thinly.

"Eat lead, bitch."

She fired her railgun.

The blast shook the hill.

Dust and blood showered Petty, and he sank into darkness.

CHAPTER TWENTY-ONE

Marco and Addy entered the shadows of Golgoloth, rifles pointed ahead.

A tunnel stretched before them. Candles burned in alcoves, casting dim light. Murals covered the walls, depicting gods devouring men. The light flickered. A cold wind blew through the pyramid. A laughter echoed in the deep.

A shadow stirred.

A monk emerged around the corner, clad in a robe. He led an animal on a leash—a dog with the head of a human girl. When the monk saw them, he froze, oval eyes widening. He reached into his robe for a knife. Addy and Marco opened fire, slaying the monk and his pet. They kept walking, stepping over the corpses.

The tunnel sloped downward, so steep Marco and Addy had to place their hands against the wall for support.

"Add some water, it would make a great slide!" Addy said.

Her words echoed. From deep inside the pyramid, the laughter grew louder. Inhuman laughter. Sinister.

Marco placed a finger on his lips, urging Addy to hush. They hurried onward. The tunnel corkscrewed downward, taking them deep into the pyramid, perhaps deep underground. Marco remembered exploring the hives on Abaddon, plunging deep to find terror. He focused on his breath. He sank into Deep Being. He would not panic. He would do his job.

For Earth. For humanity. For Tomiko and Ben-Ari and Lailani and all his friends back home. He must succeed.

A second archway rose ahead. Through it shone dim lavender light. A deep breathing, snorting, and cackling sounded from beyond.

Marco and Addy paused in the tunnel. They looked at each other. They did not need to speak. Marco saw the determination, courage, and love in Addy's eyes. He could think of nobody else he wanted to fight alongside. She was his best friend. She was his lover. She was his heroine. She was his sister-in-arms. She gave him a small smile and nod. He nodded back. They raised their rifles and stepped through the archway, entering the chamber in the heart of the pyramid.

Marco inhaled sharply.

Addy cursed and tightened her grip on her rifle.

"Fucking hell," she whispered.

Marco could barely breathe, couldn't move, only stare in horror.

The chamber was cavernous and dim. A ring of azoth crystals rose ahead, arranged like a Ferris wheel, perhaps twice a man's height. Marco had seen the small crystals that powered great warships, allowing warp drives to bend spacetime; those precious crystals were the size of erasers. Yet here shone azoth crystals the size of his head, intricately cut. Dozens floated in a ring of light.

Here it was. The control center of the empire. The grays' time machine.

And in the center of the crystal ring hung its operator.

The Time Seer. The Oracle.

"The Tick-Tock King," Marco whispered.

His body was small. No larger than a child's. Metal hooks pierced his gray skin, holding him up on cables. His head was larger than his body, the cranium bloated and embedded with crystal shards. Each shard was like a dagger, piercing the skull, reflecting the brain within. The creature's jaw thrust out, lined with sharp teeth, a jaw like a barracuda's. The Oracle had no eyes. They had been gouged out, the skin stitched over the empty sockets. Only thin scars remained where eyes had once been.

Yet strangest were the creature's arms. Dozens of arms thrust out from his body, arranged like the blades of a windmill. The fingers sprouted claws, and an eye blinked on each palm. There were as many arms as crystals in the ring, Marco realized. As he stood watching, the Oracle kept reaching out different hands, grabbing different crystals, and peering into them.

And inside the crystals, Marco could see visions. He could see Green Earth. He could see a great battle raging, the saucers filling the sky, the human army falling before the grays.

He is peering across time, Marco thought. *The great battle rages here, on this ground, in this city, a million years ago. The Oracle knows. He is the master of time.*

The creature raised his head. He looked at Marco and Addy. He grinned, hissing and drooling.

Marco and Addy shouted and opened fire.

The Oracle laughed. He grabbed several crystals from the ring and held them out. The bolts hit the crystals and shot back. One blast hit Marco's leg, and he screamed and fell, his flesh sizzling. Another blast slammed into Addy's shoulder, knocking her against the wall.

They tried to keep firing. But the Oracle held out two other hands, these ones empty. An invisible force reached out and grabbed the rifles. The guns tore free from Marco and Addy, flew through the air, and ended up in the Oracle's hands. The creature grinned as he crushed the rifles, crumpling the metal. He tossed the ruined rifles aside. With a sweep of one hand, he slammed the door shut from afar, sealing Marco and Addy in the chamber.

"He's some kind of fucking Jedi," Addy whispered, gripping her wounded shoulder.

"Tooth and nail!" Marco shouted, running toward the creature. "Fight!"

Addy screamed wordlessly and joined him. They raced toward the Oracle, determined to slay the beast with their bare hands. They leaped up, reaching for the deformed creature.

The Oracle swung his arms.

One of his fists, hard and cruel as a brick, slammed into Marco's head. He fell. Blood dripped from his temple. Another fist hit Addy's jaw, knocking her to the floor. She bled from her mouth.

They struggled to their feet, wheezing, bleeding, facing the Oracle. The creature hung in the center of the crystal ring, suspended on the cables. He cackled.

"Captain Marco Emery," the Oracle hissed, his voice like wind in a graveyard. "Captain Addy Linden. I smelled your stench from years away. I lured you here. Welcome."

Addy shouted and leaped forward again. Another blow knocked her back. She fell to the floor and spat out a tooth. Marco rushed to her side. They knelt, facing the monstrosity that hung before them. Its dozens of arms spread out their claws, forming a wall of blades. It seemed impossible to reach its body. Marco and Addy had no weapons. They had no way to slay this beast.

We came so close, Marco thought. *Only to fail.*

He rose.

He charged at the Oracle in blind fury.

The claws grabbed him, lifted him from the ground, and tossed him against the wall. Marco fell down hard, banging his tailbone, maybe cracking it. He couldn't breathe. The claws had sliced him. He bled.

"What do you want?" Marco shouted. "Why don't you just kill us?"

The Oracle opened several of his hands. The eyes on the palms stared at him.

"Kill you?" the creature hissed. "No. Death is a mercy to vermin such as you. I want you to live for many decades. To suffer for as long as your pathetic lifespans will allow. Like I made ... *her* suffer."

Addy pushed herself up, mouth bleeding, shoulder burnt. She spat out blood. "Who are you talking about?"

The Oracle laughed, a sickly sound like bones crunching.

"Still you don't know!" the beast said. "Still you have not understood. All this while, you have been fighting Nefitis, goddess of the Sanctified Sons. Do you still not know who Nefitis is?"

Marco struggled to rise. His cuts were deep. They wouldn't stop bleeding.

"Nefitis is your daughter!" he shouted at the Oracle. "We know this. Lailani saw this truth."

The Oracle licked his jaws. His tongue was lined with teeth. "Yes. Nefitis is my daughter. I fathered her many years ago. And do you know who her mother is?" The creature's grin widened. "Do you whose womb I placed the holy seed into?"

"We're not interested in riddles," Marco said.

"Ah, but life is a riddle," said the Oracle. "Space and time are a great riddle. And I am the riddle master. I see all paths. I uncoil all mysteries. I shatter. I mend. I ask. And I answer. This is the greatest of riddles. Who gave birth to

Nefitis? Who grew her seed in the womb, who nursed her at the breast? The mother was not Sanctified. She was a human woman. Yes. She was a human as you are. You see, hybrids are strong. Hybrids are built to survive on Old Earth. I have kept my mate here. Decades later, still she lingers in my den. Still she serves me. Still she pleasures me. Still she suffers. See her! See the mother of Nefitis! See your own future!"

The creature reached behind him and opened a door on the opposite wall. His claws reached into the shadows, grabbed a figure, and pulled it into the light.

Marco and Addy found themselves staring at an elderly woman.

She must have been a hundred years old. Her skin was saggy and splotched with liver marks. Her hair was white and thin. Marco had a flashback to Abaddon, to seeing the old woman the scum emperor had kept captive. For an instant he thought he was gazing at the same woman.

But then he stared closer.

He gazed into this old woman's green eyes.

And there was no more riddle. He knew her.

Tears streamed down Marco's cheeks.

"Ben-Ari," he whispered.

* * * * *

Ben-Ari, a hundred years old, frail and wrinkled and bent, gazed at Marco and Addy. Her eyes flooded with tears.

"Marco," the old woman whispered. "Addy. After so long ... it's really you."

She wept.

"No," Marco whispered. He fell to his knees. "God. No."

Tears flowed down his cheeks. But he knew it was true. That it was her. That he had failed to save her. That Ben-Ari, his heroine, his guiding light—that she had been suffering here for decades. He sobbed.

"You fucking liar!" Addy shouted at the Oracle. "This is fake! Ben-Ari is young! She's young! She's ..."

"She's been here for decades." The Tick-Tock King laughed, clutching Ben-Ari in his claws. "My soldiers captured her not long after you left Earth in your mechas. They brought her to me seventy years ago. I enjoyed the first few years, when she was young and fresh, not yet broken. She gave me many children. Most died, as hybrids often do. I enjoyed consuming their flesh. But one, a daughter, lived. Nefitis lived! Nefitis— strongest among us. In her veins flows the blood of the oracles and the blood of Einav Ben-Ari, strongest of human women. And Nefitis grew mighty. She traveled to ancient Egypt and found humans to worship her. She sent her monks to live on Isfet, to glorify her name. And now, Marco and Addy, now Nefitis is assaulting your world, conquering Old Earth, preparing it for my arrival. Soon we will go there together." He swung on his cables, bringing himself closer to Addy, and sniffed. "This one will make a good mate once Ben-Ari is dead."

Addy sneered. "I'd rather fuck a porcupine's prickly dick."

The Oracle licked his jaws. "Ah, humor. That is one of the things that breaks first. And it will break, Addy. When I torture you, it will break. Like the rest of you. Like Ben-Ari broke."

The Oracle swung one arm, backhanding Ben-Ari.

The elderly woman fell, blood splattering.

"You son of a bitch!" Marco shouted, running forth.

The Oracle cut him. Marco kept running, suffering the wounds. Bleeding, weak, maybe dying, he reached Ben-Ari. He knelt by her. He pulled her into his arms. She gazed up at him, blood trickling from her mouth. Her skin was wrinkled, sagging. One of her eyes had gone blind. Her hair was but wisps.

"I've got you, Einav," Marco whispered. "I've got you. I'm here."

With arthritic fingers, she gripped his hand. She was trying to speak. Her voice was too soft. He leaned down.

"Marco," she whispered into his ear. "Fight him."

Daniel Arenson

CHAPTER TWENTY-TWO

Ben-Ari stood on the pile of rubble, facing the goddess. The ruins of Jerusalem spread around them. She had lost her helmet in the battle, and the sandy wind blew her long blond hair. She was thirty-two years old. She was a major in the military, a captain of HOPE. She was a woman alone, death around her, facing a goddess of evil. With a thin smile, Ben-Ari raised her massive .50-cal railgun.

Nefitis shrieked, jaws opened wide, revealing human flesh in her gullet. The goddess outstretched her claws, bellowing, her stench on the wind. Around her spread the devastation. Fallen archways, cracked minarets, and crumbling domes. Thousands of dead warriors, humans and grays alike. Burning tanks. Shattered saucers and jets. The battle was still raging, but here they stood alone.

Ben-Ari.

Nefitis.

They faced each other upon this biblical mountain. Around them, the world burned.

"You cannot take this world!" Ben-Ari said. "This is not your time, Nefitis. This Earth belongs to us. You must leave this place."

356

Nefitis screamed and leaped toward her, claws lashing. Ben-Ari fired her railgun. A bullet the size of a dagger slammed into Nefitis, knocking her back a step. The goddess roared, blood seeping from her chest.

She can be hurt, Ben-Ari thought. *She is no goddess. She is mortal. She bleeds like the rest of us.*

"Call off your troops!" Ben-Ari said. "Retreat back to your own time! This era is forbidden to you. Retreat now with your hosts, and I will let you live. Stay and I will shatter your bones upon this mountain."

Nefitis advanced toward her. Her foot crushed Petty as she walked over him. The president was unconscious, maybe dead already. Blood seeped from a gash on his belly, and his hand was severed.

"You fool," Nefitis hissed at Ben-Ari. "Do you still not know who I am?"

"You are Nefitis, a wretched creature," Ben-Ari said. "You are no goddess. You are humanity's malice and cowardice distilled. You are the end of a path we will not tread. Leave now! I am Einav Ben-Ari, a captain of HOPE, a soldier of Earth. Leave now! This planet is forbidden to you. I banish you from this world."

The sun set. Shadows fell upon Jerusalem. The battle raged on, explosions lighting the night.

Nefitis stared at Ben-Ari. She tilted her head. And she began to laugh.

"No. You still do not know." Nefitis cackled. "But you will. It is time for our conquest. Time for my reign to begin. And time for truth."

Nefitis leaped forward.

Ben-Ari fired her railgun.

The hypersonic bullet slammed through the creature's chest, shattering ribs, emerging from her back, a blow that could have slain a bull, but Nefitis did not even slow down. She rammed into Ben-Ari with the might of a crashing warship.

Ben-Ari screamed, knocked onto her back.

She fired again. Her bullet plowed through Nefitis's head, taking one eye, bursting out the back with a shower of brains.

Yet still the creature lived.

Her claws—by God, they were so strong—grabbed Ben-Ari's railgun and shattered the barrel. The claws then drove into Ben-Ari's shoulders, piercing deep, and she screamed.

Nefitis straightened, lifting Ben-Ari like a piece of meat on a skewer.

The creature's remaining eye stared at Ben-Ari in amusement, filled with visions of a dying world.

"You cannot kill me," Nefitis hissed, and a cruel grin twisted her thin mouth. "I am your daughter."

Ben-Ari hung in the creature's grip, staring, unable to breathe.

"No," she whispered. "No! You lie!"

Nefitis sneered. "Look. See the truth."

And in that black eye, Ben-Ari saw her future.

She saw herself captured, taken a million years to the future, to a blackened Earth, the era of the grays. Taken to a time seventy years before the grays had launched their invasion.

She saw herself beaten, chained.

She saw a deformed creature with a hundred arms mount her, rape her, impregnate her.

She saw herself giving birth to a twisted babe, a hybrid, created to have her strength, to survive on Old Earth, to fight for her monstrous father.

A babe named Nefitis.

A babe who grew into a goddess, a terror.

The visions faded, and Ben-Ari wept.

"Yes," Nefitis whispered. "Now you see. Finally, Mother, you understand. I will take you to my world now. To a time before my birth. To my father. And he will impregnate you. He will create me in your womb. A circle in time. It has always been. It always will be. You created our race, Einav Ben-Ari. And you created me."

Ben-Ari stared, trembling, bleeding.

No. This can't be real. This is a lie. A deception. This can't be true.

Yet she knew that it was.

She hung her head low.

Around them, the world was falling. Platoon after platoon fell dead. The corpses of humanity piled up. Petty lay on the rubble, bleeding, dying. Ben-Ari looked around her, and she saw the faces of the dead. So many gone. Because of her. Because of her …

Gray soldiers were climbing the Temple Mount, rising toward Nefitis and Ben-Ari.

I am surrounded, Ben-Ari thought. *We have lost this world. We have failed. Humanity will fall. What have I done?*

Still holding her above the ground, Nefitis laughed.

"Do not weep, Mother. You have given birth to a great race. Forever shall we praise your name. You created us. You gave us this world. And now, Mother, now it's time to meet Father. Our story has been cycling throughout eternity. It's time to begin the cycle again."

A portal opened above them, blue and crackling, leading to the future.

Inside the portal, she saw him. Waiting. Licking his lips. He hung from cables in a ring of crystals. The Tick-Tock King. A creature with many arms. A creature ready to mount her, impregnate her, break her.

So I must break them.

Ben-Ari had lost her rifle. No more human troops were here to save her. She was wounded, she was weak. The claws tightened.

"I cannot kill you," Ben-Ari whispered. "But I can break the cycle."

She raised her prosthetic arm and opened the hatch, revealing the hidden compartment.

She pulled out the derringer from within. The pistol her grandfather had given her on her twelfth birthday. Her first gun.

Nefitis's remaining eye widened.

Yet Ben-Ari did not aim the gun at that eye.

She placed the derringer against her own temple.

Nefitis shrieked, terror filling her eye.

"What are you doing, ape?"

"Ending this," Ben-Ari whispered. "Making sure you will never be born. Creating a paradox."

She took a deep breath.

She thought of the rolling hills of Earth, of green fields and golden deserts, of snowcapped mountains and deep blue seas.

She thought of the beauty and nobility of humanity, of symphonies and literature and paintings to make one weep with wonder.

She thought of those she loved. Of Lailani, forever in her heart. Of the professor, the only man she had ever truly loved. Of her lost parents. Of Addy. Of Marco. And her tears fell, and her heart was full.

She thought of a pale blue marble. Of a mote of dust suspended in a sunbeam. Of Earth.

Because Earth is my home, she thought. *Earth is here. Earth is beautiful. Earth is eternal.*

She gazed upon the ruins of Jerusalem. Her father had been born here. This was her home. This was a good place to die. And as she gazed around her, Ben-Ari no longer saw the grays, no longer saw the cruelty of Nefitis, no longer saw the death of thousands.

She saw snow falling in a winter's dawn.

She saw flowers blooming as spring's birds sang.

She saw generations crossing hills and meadows to sing, to pray, to tell stories, to love.

She saw more than just Earth. She saw humanity. And it was good.

It was farewell.

"It's beautiful," she whispered, tears falling. "It's so beautiful."

She smiled and closed her eyes.

She pulled the trigger.

CHAPTER TWENTY-THREE

Hanging from the cables in the heart of his pyramid, the Oracle laughed. He reached out his claws. He grabbed Marco and Addy, digging into their flesh. He lifted them off the floor. They kicked, legs dangling, bodies bleeding. The azoth crystals surrounded them, a vertical ring of light, controlling spacetime. Other crystals thrust out from the Oracle's head, embedded into his skull. In the crystals, they could see Old Earth falling. See humanity perishing. See the grays conquer the world.

We failed, Marco thought. *We lost.*

"Now your torture begins." The Oracle laughed and licked his lips. "First, humans, I will shatter your limbs, then your ribs, then your spines, but I will not let you die. I will heal you. Then shatter you again. Then heal you. Then break you a third time. Over and over, I will break and mend you. Once you are begging for death, I will carve you open. I will remove your organs, but I will keep you alive. I will keep you in pain. I will stitch you up. And then, humans, then the true pain will begin. And it will last for many decades."

They struggled in the creature's grip, desperate to flee, unable to free themselves.

Panic seized Marco. Even Deep Being couldn't help him now. His head spun. Sweat mixed with his blood.

We were fools! Fools to come here! We should have fled.

He wanted to go home.

He wanted to be with Addy back on the beach.

He wanted to forget this place.

As the claws tightened, Marco shed tears.

I'm sorry, Ben-Ari. I'm sorry, Addy. You don't deserve this.

Ben-Ari still lay on the floor, bleeding. Slowly, creaking, the elderly woman rose to her feet.

She stared at the Oracle. At her captor. Her tormentor. The father of her daughter.

She smiled.

The Oracle spun toward the old woman, sneering.

"Why do you smile, wretched ape? I will give you a red smile. I will rip off your lips and leave you with an eternal grin of agony."

Ben-Ari's smile never faltered. "You might be too busy for a while. I created a paradox."

The Oracle backhanded her, knocking her down, spraying blood.

"You are a miserable wretch," he hissed. "You are powerless. You are my slave."

Lying on the floor, blood in her mouth, Ben-Ari laughed. She gazed up at him. "This form of mine is. This form is an old woman, frail, powerless. But the other Einav Ben-Ari. She is young, a great leader, a great warrior. I remember." She rose to her feet, staring at the Oracle. "I remember! And now you are undone. Look, Time Seer. Gaze back and see."

The Oracle spun toward one of the azoth crystals and stared. Marco and Addy stared with him.

Inside the crystal, they saw a vision of the past. Ben-Ari stood there, a woman in her early thirties, a captain of HOPE, a warrior of the HDF. Grays surrounded her. The corpses of dead soldiers lay strewn at her feet. Nefitis loomed above her, wretched and cruel, prepared to grab her, to take her captive, to begin her long torture that would culminate here—with an elderly woman, trapped and beaten and bloody.

"I let myself be captured once," the old Ben-Ari whispered, gazing at the crystal. Tears flowed down her cheeks. "Not this time."

In the crystal, the young Ben-Ari placed a pistol to her head.

She pulled the trigger.

"No!" Marco shouted.

He reached toward the crystal as if he could save his friend. His breath trembled.

No. No! He had lost so many. He couldn't lose her too. He wept.

The Oracle shrieked.

The old Ben-Ari stared at the creature.

"I am fading away already," she said. "I died young, Seer. I killed myself at thirty-two. I died before you could rape me, place your seed in my womb. Before I could give birth to the wretched, twisted monster you call Nefitis. Before Nefitis could lead her hosts in your war. Time is undone. All your empire will be sucked into the paradox. Watch. It already begins."

With every word, she was fading. Her body withered, the flesh cracking, the eyes sinking. Fading. Fading from reality.

And in the crystals, the gray army was fading too.

Back on Green Earth, saucers tilted. Gray warriors fell.

Hanging in the ring of crystals, the Oracle shrieked so loudly Marco had to cover his ears.

Frantically, with dozens of hands, the creature reached toward crystals. He jangled on his chains, grabbing some crystals, releasing others, barking commands.

"Sanctified Sons! Go back in time to grab a younger Ben-Ari!"

In one crystal, a saucer flew into a portal. In another crystal, a vision appeared of a teenage Ben-Ari captured, of the Oracle mounting her, impregnating her, of a creature emerging. A hybrid. But not Nefitis.

"Too different. Too different! The DNA is wrong. Wrong!" The Oracle screeched. He turned toward another crystal. "Soldiers! Find the factory that made her pistol. Sabotage it!"

In another crystal, grays obeyed. In the past, they invaded a weapons factory. They sought the derringer that Ben-Ari would use to kill herself. They tinkered with it.

The factory workers opened fire. One of the grays died. The other grays returned fire, slaying the factory workers.

Hanging in the ring, the Oracle screamed.

"Do not slay those apes! Those apes are fighting us in Jerusalem as old men!"

He spun toward another crystal, showing the same factory workers—dead in the past—fighting in the Battle of Jerusalem. They were twenty years older but still alive, still fighting. In the battlefield, they began to fade, ripping open spacetime around them, sucking in grays.

"Paradox, paradox!" the Oracle cried. "A paradox in our battle! Restore the factory! Sabotage the gun another time!"

The paradoxes spread from crystal to crystal, timeline to timeline. With every change the Oracle made, another paradox appeared. Cracks appeared one after the other. Time began to unravel. Rips tore through space.

The Oracle moved faster and faster, grabbing more and more crystals, frantically fixing paradox after paradox. In his panic, he released Marco and Addy, bringing his claws toward other crystals. Soon all his arms—there were nearly a hundred—were engaged in his task.

With Ben-Ari killed, with Nefitis never born, with the old woman in this very chamber now an impossible reality, the cosmos was fraying.

And the Oracle was desperate to hold it together.

His many hands grabbed and released and tugged. The eyes on his palms peered. His blind, bloated head swung from side to side, mumbling, shrieking, ordering, screaming.

Marco looked at Addy. She lay on the ground, bleeding from many cuts, maybe dying. But she met his gaze, and she rose to her feet. They limped forward together.

"Redo the opening salvo!" the Oracle shrieked. "Use the replacement commander! If Nefitis is not there, fight in the name of the new goddess I've named you!" He whipped toward another crystal. "Return to the man's birth. Make sure he founds the factory! Make sure she gets that faulty pistol!"

Marco and Addy took another step closer. The Oracle dangled ahead on his hooks, not even noticing them, all his hands occupied, clinging to crystals, peering at visions of a crumbling reality.

"We might be destroying the cosmos," Addy whispered.

"Then let it be destroyed," Marco said. "And let it be remade. Without him."

Addy nodded, tears in her eyes. "I love you, Marco."

"I love you too, Addy. Always."

They faced the Tick-Tock King.

They shouted wordlessly and leaped toward him.

They grabbed the vestigial, dangling legs. They pulled themselves up onto the wrinkled body. The Oracle howled. He snapped his jaws and shook his head wildly, struggling to shake them off while still mending spacetime. A tooth sliced Marco's arm. His blood dripped. He kept climbing, grabbed a cable, and pulled himself onto the Oracle's back. Addy joined him. They clung to the creature, dangling here among the ring of crystals.

All around him, Marco beheld space and time.

His past. His present. His future. Mankind rising from the muck, roaming the forests, reaching for the stars. Mankind choosing paths of darkness or paths of light. Evolving into twisted, wretched beings or rising to become noble and pure. All the cosmos spread around him.

A voice rumbled deep in his mind.

You cannot kill me. You would be killing yourself.

"Then I kill myself."

You would be destroying your own species!

Marco raised his eyes. In a crystal above him, he saw a different path. A path where the grays never existed. Where humanity evolved over a million years to become noble, beautiful, custodians of a green planet. That path still lay ahead, and no paradox could touch it.

"I will not," Marco said softly. "Only yours."

He reached toward the Oracle's head. A crown of shards rose there, the crystal embedded into the skull, connecting the brain itself to the light of spacetime. Marco grabbed one of those crystals. It was cold and smooth and the size of a dagger. He yanked it back, pulling it out from the Oracle's skull.

The creature screamed.

Addy grabbed another one of the crystals that sprouted from the Oracle's head. She tugged it free.

The creature went limp and moved no more.

They removed the last of the hooks, and the deformed, wretched thing thumped onto the floor, dead.

Marco and Addy stared at it. It looked so pathetic. So withered. A deflated, pale octopus rotting on the beach.

Marco turned away from the dead Oracle. He never wanted to think of it again.

He stumbled across the chamber and knelt by Ben-Ari. The old woman was ghostly, so pale, so thin. Marco gathered her in his arms. She weighed nothing.

"Marco," she whispered.

"I'm here, Einav." His tears fell through her.

"It's over now," Ben-Ari whispered, translucent, and a smile touched her lips. "Finally this long pain ... it will never have been. All these years of agony. They will never have been. *Shalom.* Peace. Peace ..."

She grew dimmer, faded to a wisp, and was gone.

* * * * *

She pulled her derringer's trigger.

The gun jammed.

Ben-Ari lowered the weapon and stared at it, confused.

I'm still alive. I'm still in Jerusalem.

Gripping her, Nefitis cackled. "You cannot break time! My father broke your pistol, ape. I cannot be destroyed. You will be captured. You will be broken. You …"

The creature's voice faded.

Her body began withering.

Ben-Ari fell from the goddess's grip.

Nefitis screamed. Her body was coiling inward, drying up, growing translucent. Across the hills and valleys of Jerusalem, the gray army was fading to dust. Its saucers fell from the sky, vanishing on impact.

Ben-Ari raised her eyes to the sky. The portal was still there. Through it, she could see the future Earth.

It was shattering.

The pyramid was cracking open.

Ben-Ari wept.

"You did it," she whispered, sobbing. "Marco. Addy. You did it. You did it!"

Nefitis fell to her knees. The goddess's body was nearly gone now. She raised an arm, reaching up to Ben-Ari.

"Help me!" Nefitis cried. "Mother. Mother! Help me!"

Ben-Ari stared, tears on her cheeks.

"I'm sorry," she whispered. "Daughter."

Nefitis gave her a last, pleading look, and then her arm fell and shattered. She vanished from the world. She had never existed at all.

Across the battlefield, soldiers began to cheer.

"Victory! Victory!"

The last of the grays vanished. But Earth still lay in ruin. Thousands, maybe millions of humans still lay dead. They could not undo the damage the grays had wrought.

But the enemy was defeated. Earth would rebuild.

"Victory!" the soldiers cried.

Ben-Ari looked away from them. She ran across the ruins and knelt by President Petty.

He was still alive, but barely. Nefitis had cut him deeply. His hand was gone. His body was crushed. Fresh tears filled Ben-Ari's eyes to see him this way. Petty had always seemed so strong to her, impossible to hurt, the pillar of Earth. She placed a hand on his cheek.

"James," she whispered.

His eyes were hazy. He managed to reach up, to touch her cheek.

"Einav."

Her tears fell into his hair. "It's all right, James. You'll be all right."

He shook his head. "I … die in battle. I … lived to see victory. Defend Earth, Einav. Defend our world. You must lead them onward. To peace. To peace …"

She nodded. "To peace," she whispered.

"Peace …" Petty smiled softly. His eyes closed.

Ben-Ari let out a cry. She wrapped him in her arms, lowered her head, and wept for him.

A crack sounded above her.

She looked up to see the portal vanish.

The link to the future was gone.

"Addy," Ben-Ari whispered. "Marco."

She rose to her feet.

Leaving Petty behind, she ran.

She needed to find the professor. And she needed to repair her ship.

* * * * *

A *crack* sounded, loud as gunfire. Marco spun to see one of the azoth crystals in the ring shatter. Shards clattered to the floor. Another crystal burst. Soon the entire ring was collapsing. The visions of past and future vanished.

A crack raced across a wall. Another crack tore open on the floor, separating Marco and Addy. Debris began raining from the ceiling. The chamber trembled so madly he nearly fell.

"The whole pyramid is falling apart!" Marco shouted over the din.

"Save me, Captain Obvious!" Addy cried. "Come on, let's get out of here!"

Marco ran and jumped over the crack in the floor. He joined Addy. The door was still locked, but the wall was crumbling around it. They slammed against the loose door, knocking it down, and raced into the tunnel.

Stones cascaded around them. Cracks raced across the walls and ceiling. The pyramid trembled. They ran through dust and falling bricks.

They burst out of the pyramid to see a collapsing world.

Obelisks and towers were breaking and falling across the city. Great cracks loomed open on the roads like the hungry mouths of primordial beasts, swallowing grays and chariots. Saucers crumbled in the sky and rained fire. Sinkholes opened up, devouring homes. In the distance, mountains were falling.

Marco and Addy stood on the platform that thrust out from the pyramid, the place where Nefitis had once reigned. Her throne shattered into a million shards that rose as smoke. The pyramid was collapsing beneath them. The sky itself was falling.

Marco and Addy stood on the stone outcrop. The devastation spread around them. They clasped their hands.

"The world is ending," Addy whispered.

"This world," said Marco. "But not our home." Tears flowed down his cheeks, and he raised an azoth crystal taken from the Oracle's lair. "Look, Addy. Look! Green Earth. It's still there. It's saved."

They saw it in the crystal: The armies of grays vanishing off Green Earth. Human victory. Earth triumphant.

"We saved our home," Addy whispered, eyes damp.

Marco nodded. "We did it, Addy. We saved Earth."

The platform shook. Cracks raced across it. Marco and Addy fell to their knees. Their wounds kept bleeding. The cuts from the Oracle's claws were deep, and their weariness from the long journey here had left them as weak as children. They could not rise again.

Tiles were tearing free from the pyramid and falling all around them. The entire top of the pyramid tore off. The stone triangle slid down the crumbling slope, digging through the bricks. Canyons opened up beneath the pyramid, forming gaping pits of coiling, shrieking smoke. Barely anything remained of the city now. The platform tore free, fell a few meters, and landed on a jutting shard of stone. The outcrop balanced over the void. The platform tilted, and Marco reached out to grab a ledge. The crystal fell from his grasp and vanished below into the destruction.

Marco and Addy lay down on the stone slab, clinging for purchase, teetering over the ruin of the world. The pyramid was still crumbling, brick by brick tearing off and rolling down to the darkness. Any moment now, the platform would follow and they would be lost.

Marco moved closer to Addy and held her in his arms. She clung to him.

"Look into my eyes," he whispered. "Don't look at the shadows."

Addy nodded, gazing into his eyes. "I see you," she whispered.

Bricks fell around them. Stones cascaded. Smoke and dust filled the air, and the sky cracked open, ripping apart, and the void flowed.

Marco held Addy close. "Let's imagine that we're back there. On the beach in Greece. In the cove we discovered."

"Shipwreck Cove." Addy smiled through her tears. "The beach with the shipwreck in the sand. Our secret place." She wept. "I can see it, Marco. It's so beautiful. I can see the light on the water, and the seashells, and the golden sand … It's so beautiful, and I'm there with you."

"We'll always be together," he whispered, embracing her as the world fell apart. "Always. I love you, Addy Linden."

She clung to him. "I love you, Marco Emery. I'm so glad I saved the world with you. I'm so glad I'm with you here as this world ends."

They kept bleeding. They were so tired. So hurt. Marco's eyes grew hazy. Around them, the last structures of the city vanished. All was chaos. All was stone and fire. All was the void and the shadow.

And above them—a light.

A new star.

A single flicker growing brighter.

And from the shadows she emerged, glorious and beautiful, a ship of hope.

The *Lodestar*.

Marco gazed up, eyes blurred, scarcely believing his eyes. Surely it was just a vision. Just an echo from the fallen crystal. Just a dream.

The beautiful ship, shaped like the hull of an old sailing vessel, descended with beams of light. From her prow thrust out

Eos, golden and luminous. A hatch opened on the ship. A figure stood there, wreathed in light, and Marco wept. It was impossible, yet there she stood. Young again. Calling to him.

"Einav," he whispered, raising a weak hand toward her. "Einav Ben-Ari. My captain."

With blazing light and rumbling engines and storming clouds, the *Lodestar* descended to hover before the crumbling pyramid. And Ben-Ari reached out her hand.

Marco clasped it.

His captain pulled him into the airlock, then reached for Addy too.

The ship rose.

Below them, the pyramid gave a last groan, then collapsed, tearing apart into dust. Its ruins vanished into the void.

Marco lay on the floor as medics knelt above him. He reached out and clasped Addy's hand. Through the porthole he saw that they were rising, flying over storm and sea, saw the mountains falling. A glowing blue portal opened like sheets of rain under dawn, and they passed through the light, and all was shimmering raindrops and molten sunbeams. His eyes closed, and all sound faded, but he still felt Addy's hand in his, warm and gripping him, and he knew that they would never let go.

CHAPTER TWENTY-FOUR

He did not remember falling asleep.

For a long time, he floated through dreams of childhood.

Light fell upon his eyelids, and finally Marco opened his eyes and saw dawn spilling through a window, golden and warm.

Trees rustled outside the window. Robins sang.

It was Earth.

"Earth," he whispered. "We saved it."

"Poet!"

Something heavy slammed down on him, knocking out his breath. A wild beast was grabbing him, shaking him, kissing him.

"Poet, Poet, you're awake!"

He groaned. "Ow. Addy! You're poking my ribs again. God, you weigh a ton. Off! Off, wild beast!"

But she would not release him. She kept kissing him. "You're alive! God, when you lost consciousness, when the medics were all working on you, I thought ..." Addy laughed and wiped her eyes. "But you're alive."

He blinked and looked down at his body. A sheet was pulled up to his waist. His arms were thin. His legs felt so weak.

"How badly was I hurt?" he said softly.

Addy's smile vanished. Her eyes turned solemn. Sitting on the bedside, she placed a hand on his cheek.

"Poet, I'm really sorry." Her voice was somber. "They had to amputate your penis."

Marco groaned. "Addy!" He shoved her away. He checked just to be sure. Still there.

She laughed and began kissing him again. "Oh, I'd have missed it more than you." She reached under the sheets. "I love my little mini-Poet."

Marco frowned. "Not that mini, surely."

She kissed his cheek and mussed his hair. "My poor giant Poet." She leaned against him, and she held his hand. "I'm glad you're alive."

He looked at Addy in the dawn's light. Her eyes were still sunken, her hair still matted. Both had suffered along the road. Both were weak, scarred outside and inside. Both would need long to recover.

But she was beautiful. She was the most beautiful thing he had ever seen.

"We did it, Addy," he whispered, pulling her into his arms. "We did it. We're alive. We saved the world. We're still here."

"We're still here," she whispered, holding him tightly. "We'll always be here. You and me. Marco and Addy. Things will be good now." Her tears fell, and she smiled, a beautiful smile that showed her teeth. "Hockey."

"Books," he said.

Her eyes lit up. "Hot dogs!"

"You and me." He kissed her.

And then he was crying. And she cried too. Because the pain was still too real. The scars inside would never heal. They would never forget the shadows on Black Earth. Never forget the horror they had seen in Gehenna, city of the grays. Never heal from those wounds.

But it was over.

They had won this war.

And after fire and death and darkness, they had found each other. And they were happy.

The door burst open.

Lailani and Elvis raced into the room.

"Poet!" they cried.

"Not in the ribs—ow!"

Both Lailani and Elvis jumped right onto him, all hugs and kisses and poking elbows.

For a long time, they just hugged, laughed, joked.

Finally Marco asked, "Where are we anyway?"

"Switzerland, I think," Addy said. "Or is it Sweden? I keep getting those two confused."

Lailani nodded. "Yesterday you thought it was Swaziland." She looked at Marco. "It's Switzerland. The Alliance of Nations is headquartered here. We're inside the presidential chalet." She lowered her head. "President Petty fell in battle. The tough old bastard fought Nefitis hand to hand.

And the Oracle begged.

"Do not do this! You will undo an entire species! You cannot! You cannot! Please. Mercy. Mercy …"

Addy looked into Marco's eyes.

He nodded.

They both screamed and shoved down the crystals like blades, slamming them back into the Oracle's skull, driving them deep, deep into the brain, cutting, destroying, and spacetime blasted out in waves of visions and sounds from infinite realities. All around them—themselves as children, as ancients, humanity evolving and falling and rising again, nomads in the desert and navigators among the stars.

They grabbed more crystals.

They shoved them deep.

The Oracle screamed.

Addy grabbed one of the cables that held up the creature. She tore the cable free, wrapped it around the Oracle's neck, and tugged.

The creature sputtered, tried to beg, could not. His dozens of arms retracted, curling up, leaving the ring of crystals. Inside the shards, Marco saw the saucers falling, the gray army fading away.

The Oracle's tongue emerged, warty and twitching. On his many hands, his eyes bulged.

Marco took hold of the cable too. He and Addy gave a mighty tug.

The Oracle's neck snapped.

They haven't yet chosen a new president, but they said we can stay here for now." Lailani looked up, and her eyes brightened. "Come on outside if you can walk. It's pretty."

Marco rose from bed. He was still dizzy, still weak, but he managed to walk on his own. The president's chalet was a cozy wooden home, filled with portraits of previous presidents. The last two frames showed President Maria Katson and President James Petty. The hallway would need a new portrait soon.

The companions stepped outside into sunlight. Mountains rose around a lake, capped with snow. Grass swayed, flowers bloomed, and a lazy stream gurgled. Deer grazed and birds sang in a copse of pines. The air was fresh and warm, the sky without a cloud.

It was beautiful.

It was Earth.

Marco thought about the world he had seen in the future, a world without a blade of grass or flower, a world where smog hid the sky and the rain burned, a world of desolation and despair.

Here before him was a world of life. A world he had saved. A world to cherish.

"Our work is not yet done," he said softly. "We must protect this world. Make sure it lasts forever."

Addy nodded. "We will. We'll tell everyone what we saw." She squeezed his hand. "We'll take care of this place, Poet. We'll save all the baby whales." She mussed his hair and winked. "There are some trees over there if you wanna hug one."

He looked at those trees, and he saw a figure walking among them. At first his heart leaped, the old instincts kicking in, and he imagined a gray among the pines. He reached for a gun, realized he had none.

Then the figure emerged into the light. It was Ben-Ari. She wore hiking boots, cargo pants, and an HDF sweatshirt. It was so rare to see her in civilian clothes that Marco at first did a double take.

She ran up to him. Yes. It was her.

Marco pulled her into his arms.

"Captain! I mean—ma'am! I mean—Einav."

She grinned. "Marco. You and Addy did it." She squeezed him in her embrace. "I'm so proud of you. I'm so grateful." Her eyes dampened. "Oh, Marco. My dearest Marco." Her tears fell. "Thank you. Thank you."

He held her tight. He never wanted to let her go. For a long moment they stood in silence, just holding each other, saying more with tears than they ever could with words.

"How?" he finally whispered. "The *Lodestar*—"

"Professor Isaac did it," Ben-Ari said, smiling through her tears. "He studied the hourglass. It was out of sand, but the professor was able to cut new sand grains from azoth crystals, to open a new portal. To find you and Addy."

Marco looked around him. This lake was beautiful. But he had seen the saucers fly over Green Earth. In the crystals inside the pyramid, he had seen the war rage.

He spoke softly. "How bad was it? The war."

Ben-Ari lowered her head. "It was bad, Marco. Many brave warriors fell. We will never forget their sacrifice." She raised her chin. "But we will rebuild. We will heal. There is much work left to do. Across the world, governments are scrambling to maintain order. Already fascist, communist, and theocratic movements are seeking to seize control. President Petty fell in battle, and there are many who seek to shatter Earth, to plunge her into chaos. The grays are gone. But we must still battle ourselves. Perhaps that is our fate for a long while—a battle between the nobility of humanity and our darker nature. That is a battle that will, perhaps, rage for many generations." Then her face softened, and Ben-Ari smiled. "But today we rest."

But Marco frowned. "Ma'am, the Nefitians. The monks on Isfet. Won't they just evolve into the grays again? Can we kill them, or—"

"They're gone." Ben-Ari touched his cheek. "Destroyed in the paradox. We're safe, Marco." She hugged him. "So rest. You deserve it more than anyone, my friend."

Marco nodded. "I could use some rest. Some time to breathe."

"We can go fishing," Lailani said, stepping up toward them.

385385

Earth Eternal

"We can build a campfire and sing some tunes," Elvis said, joining them.

Addy ran up, eyes bright. "Does anyone have a rake?"

* * * * *

That night, they sat around the campfire, and Elvis played guitar and sang, and Addy roasted hot dogs, and Marco and Ben-Ari talked about literature and poetry and other things that made Addy roll her eyes and call them nerds. The professor joined them here in Switzerland, and the kindly man sat by HOBBS's massive metal form, talking to the robot about the physics of time travel. Epimetheus kept running up to Addy, who was quickly becoming his favorite, thanks to her generosity with sharing her hot dogs.

"So as you see, one cannot change the past," Professor Isaac was saying. "It's a law of physics. You can perhaps change things for a short while, but the universe will always correct itself, the way the universe will fill a vacuum the instant it finds air. The grays tried to change the past. They ended up vanishing."

HOBBS tilted his head. "But professor, is time travel then impossible?"

"We are all time travelers," said Isaac. "We just move forward. Very slowly."

Addy tossed a hot dog at them. "Will you two dopes stop talking science? You're boring me to tears."

"Addy, stop wasting food," Marco said.

"What?" Addy bristled. "Epi is eating it!"

"I swear, that dog will weigh three hundred pounds by the end of the night," Marco muttered.

Addy poked him in the ribs. "You need to gain a few pounds yourself. You've gotten scrawny. Eat."

Elvis approached them with his guitar. "Ah, young love! Let me serenade the couple." He began to croon. Soon the others were hooting.

It was a night of friendship. Of peace. Of joy.

But a shadow hung over Lailani. She sat quietly by the fire, watching the others, feeling empty. She only smiled thinly at the jokes, did not laugh like the others. She only nibbled on her fish, did not scarf down the food like everyone else. Her belly felt cold. Her chest was tight. Even her robot and dog could not soothe her today.

I left a rip in spacetime. I changed the past. I created a paradox.

She kept seeing it before her. The tear in space. It was far from here, all the way over at Indrani, a red giant in a different solar system. But it seemed to hover before her. A crack inside her.

Lailani felt nauseous.

She rose to her feet.

"Excuse me."

She ran to the bushes, and she threw up behind them.

She straightened and stood for a moment, gasping for air. Her head spun. From behind her, she could hear her friends. Laughing. Enjoying the night.

Lailani stood in the shadows. She walked down toward the lake, washed her face, and rinsed out her mouth. She looked up at the moon and stars.

I saw myself there, she thought. *A young girl. A monster. I went back in time and met myself. And I don't know who I am now.*

She was back on the *Miyari.*

She was digging her claws into Elvis.

A crack spread across time.

A crack was spreading inside her.

She was breaking apart. She was past and present. She was afraid.

"I don't know who I am," she whispered. She stood on a lakeside. She stood in a starship. She stood on a knife's edge between two worlds.

"Lailani?"

The voice came from behind her. She turned to see Elvis approaching her.

"Lailani, are you all right?" His voice was soft, and he joined her by the lake.

"I don't know," she whispered. "I feel like I'm in two places at once. That I'm thirty years old, a captain in the military, here by this lake. That I'm eighteen years old, a monster on a starship far away."

"You still *look* like a teenager," Elvis said. "But I assure you, you are a captain. I saw you lead a company in battle. You were amazing."

Tears filled her eyes.

"I'm scared this isn't real," she whispered. "That you aren't really here. That I broke something. Something in the universe. Something in me."

Elvis smiled. "Lailani, I assure you. I am real. I am here." He stepped toward her. "Here, feel me. Hold my hand."

He held out his hand. Lailani reached to take it, and her hand passed through him.

She stared up into his eyes, startled.

She took a step back.

Elvis frowned. He reached for her again. He tried to hold her. His arms passed through her as if he were a ghost.

"Elvis," she whispered. "Benny. Benny!"

He stared at her, eyes wide.

He was becoming translucent.

"Professor!" Lailani shouted. "Hurry! There's something wrong!"

The others all left the campfire and rushed toward her. They gathered around Elvis.

"Guys!" Elvis said, laughing nervously. "I'm fine! I'm just a little dizzy. Maybe tipsy?"

Suddenly he doubled over. He fell to the ground, not even bending the grass. They knelt above him. When they tried to touch him, their hands passed through his body. He was growing dim.

"What's happening?" Lailani cried, turning toward the professor.

Isaac lowered his head. He spoke softly. "The universal timeline is correcting itself. I'm sorry, Lailani."

She spun back toward Elvis, then toward the professor again.

"Where's he going?" she cried.

But she already knew.

Back to where she had saved him.

To die.

Her tears flowed.

She leaned over Elvis, trying to stroke his cheeks, to kiss him, but she couldn't feel him. She could barely see him anymore.

"Benny, you have to stay here," Lailani said. "You have to fight this. Do you hear me? Stay here with me!"

His eyes were damp. "It was wonderful, Lailani. To see you again. To see all of you. Poet. Addy. Ben-Ari. Everyone else. I'm so happy I got to see you all one last time."

"Don't you talk like that!" Lailani said. "You're staying right here with me." She wept. "You have to." She leaned over him, her tears falling through him. "I'm pregnant, Benny. I'm pregnant with your child."

Lying in the grass, barely visible now, Elvis gasped. His eyes lit up. He smiled.

A breeze blew from the lake, and he was gone.

Lailani knelt on the lakeside, head lowered, tears falling.

Ben-Ari knelt beside her and placed a hand on her shoulder.

"Lailani, I'm sorry," Ben-Ari said softly.

Epimetheus ran up to Lailani and nuzzled her. Addy was crying and hugging Marco. The professor and HOBBS watched, silent, heads lowered.

Lailani rose to her feet. She walked toward HOBBS. The robot knelt, bringing himself to eye level with her. She placed a hand on his chest.

"Mistress, I am sorry," HOBBS said. "All that we have been through. Our journey to find the hourglass. To save your friend. It was all for nothing. I am sorry."

Lailani kept her hand on his chest. Inside of HOBBS, she could feel it beating. The human heart. Her tears flowed. She understood.

She turned toward Isaac, and she spoke in a shaky voice. "Professor? I'm going to need my hourglass back."

* * * * *

She flew in the *Ryujin*, her small starship with the dragon painted on the hull.

She flew with only Epimetheus at her side.

She flew back to Indrani, the giant planet on the frontier.

"There it is again, Epi." Lailani ruffled the Doberman's ears. "The red giant. You ready for one last trip?"

He gave an approving bark.

"Good."

Lailani pulled out her hourglass. Professor Isaac had carved more grains of sand, each grain's facade calibrated down to the atom. The grains had let the *Lodestar* fly to save Marco and Addy. And a few grains still remained. Just the right amount. The professor had counted them himself, one by one.

With her starship orbiting the planet, *Lailani* tilted the hourglass, and she flew through the portal.

Twelve years rewound.

She saw it ahead. The starship *Miyari*. An angry, scared girl was aboard, her head shaved, her wrists scarred, an alien evil screaming inside her.

A girl who will grow into a strong woman, Lailani thought. She placed a hand on her swelling belly. *Who will become a mother.*

She wished she could hug that young girl, tell her things would be all right. But that younger Lailani, that girl in the warship ahead, would have to discover this truth on her own. She still had a long path to tread, full of darkness and danger and loss. But the path led to light.

Lailani flew closer.

She emerged from the *Ryujin* and glided through space in a spacesuit.

As she had before, once more she entered the *Miyari*.

The vision replayed before her. Young Lailani, possessed by the scum, shrieked and cackled in the engine room. This time the older Lailani did not interfere. Did not try to save Elvis. This time she merely watched as her younger self ripped the heart out of her friend, then dropped it to the floor.

And then the older Lailani crept forward.

Gently, without her younger self seeing, she lifted Elvis's heart, and she placed it in a box of ice.

She flew away.

But Lailani did not return to her own timeline. Not yet. She still had work to do here in the past.

The *Ryujin* traveled through space. It traveled to Earth.

Lailani landed her ship in a dusty, hot junkyard in Japan.

Hundreds of rusty, dented, cracked starships sat in the yard, some a century old. Signs were taped to them, original prices scratched out, bargain prices displayed in red. There were robots here too, hundreds of them, deactivated and rusting in the sun. There were serving bots to cook and clean, companion bots shaped like dogs and cats, baby bots for bereft parents, warehouse workers and farming bots, an assortment of sex bots to cater to every taste, and a handful of robotic soldiers. All were old, rusting, falling apart, some dating back to the classic age of robotics.

"Welcome, welcome to JEX's Starship Emporium!"

A rotund robot teetered toward her, shedding bolts and rust. His body was formed from a tin barrel, and he chomped on an electronic cigar made from a car's cigarette lighter.

"Whatever your price, whatever your pleasure, you will find the ride of your dreams here!" said the robot. "To take you to the stars—and beyond!"

Lailani remembered him. JEX the Junkyard Expert.

"Hello, JEX," she said. "Mind if I just browse for a bit on my own?"

JEX's face soured. But then a family strolled into the junkyard, and the father whipped out his wallet, and JEX trundled toward them, leaving a trail of oil.

"Welcome, welcome to JEX's Starship Emporium!"

As JEX and the family began haggling over a vintage moon-cruiser, Lailani walked between the rows of used robots. She was in the year 2143. Eleven years from now, a version of her will arrive here, a new chip in her head, and purchase a robot named HOBBS. A robot who would become her best friend. A robot with a human heart inside him.

But here, in 2143, he did not yet have a heart.

She passed by several warehouse robots until she saw him there.

Her eyes dampened.

Lailani came to stand before him. He stood in the dust, over seven feet tall. The words were barely visible on his chest.

HOBBS: Humanoid Offensive Biometric Battle Soldier. Her friend.

"HOBBS," Lailani whispered.

His eyes turned on, shining blue. "Hello, human. Are you interested in purchasing me?"

"Yes." Lailani nodded. "But not yet. Not for eleven more years. I have something for you, HOBBS. Something you must cherish and protect."

She did not know how HOBBS had ended up in JEX's junkyard. But she knew who had built him. It was Doctor Elliot Schroeder, serial killer and mad scientist, who had built HOBBS, creating a vessel to store the heart of a murder victim. Lailani had saved many of Schroeder's robots from his lair, releasing them to a life on Earth.

And I will save you, HOBBS. Her tears flowed. *As best I can.*

She opened HOBBS's chest. He gazed at her, curious, but did not stop her. Lailani opened her freezer box, pulled out Elvis's heart, and placed it into HOBBS's chest.

HOBBS's technology did the rest, connecting to the heart, reanimating it, letting it pump again.

Lailani closed his chest, sealing the heart within.

"I could not save you, Benny Elvis Ray," she whispered, tears falling. "But I could save your heart. And in eleven years, I will find your heart again. Your child will grow up knowing his father's heart is always with him."

HOBBS looked at her, confused, but then something akin to understanding filled his luminous eyes. He placed his hand on his chest.

"I will keep it safe," he said. "And I will wait for you to return."

Lailani reentered the *Ryujin* and sat at the helm. Epimetheus leaped onto her lap, nearly crushing her, outweighing her by a good twenty pounds. She took flight. In space, she filled her hourglass with sand from a pouch, then opened a portal.

She flew to 2155. To her true time. To her friends.

She flew home.

She rejoined the others at the lakeside chalet. Addy and Marco were fishing off a dock, while Ben-Ari and Professor Isaac sat curled up on a rocking chair, drinking hot chocolate. HOBBS was standing guard over the group, a little older here, a little more dented, but still her dear friend.

Lailani ran up toward him. HOBBS greeted her with a nod. His mouth could not move, but she swore that somehow he was smiling.

"Hello again, mistress," he said. "I have waited for a long time."

She embraced him. She could hear the heart beating within.

"You always knew," she whispered. "Whose heart is inside you."

HOBBS nodded. "Yes, mistress. I had to wait for you to find out on your own."

"Call me Lailani," she whispered, holding him close.

He wrapped his metal arms around her. "Lailani."

And in addition to his heartbeat, there was another heart beating. A small heartbeat, fast inside her.

You will have a father, little one, she thought, placing her hand on her belly. *Your mother and father will always love you.*

The professor approached Lailani. His eyes were solemn.

"Lailani, it's time," he said softly.

"Soon," Lailani whispered. "I must do one more thing first."

The professor nodded.

Lailani took the hourglass into the copse of trees. She wanted privacy. From her pocket, she pulled out a single grain of azoth sand. It twinkled on her fingertip. She dropped it into the hourglass and flipped the bulb.

The portal was small. A mere sparkle of blue light in the air.

But it was enough.

Lailani peered into the gleaming drop of light, and she saw herself last year, walking among the rice paddies in the Philippines.

"Find the hourglass," she whispered.

The younger her looked up, confused.

"Who are you?" the younger Lailani whispered.

"One who is here to help you," Lailani said.

She deactivated the chip in her head. And she sent the message into her younger self's mind, showing her the constellation, the planet she must reach, the place to seek the hourglass.

The portal closed.

Her message was sent.

Standing in the grove, Lailani smiled shakily. Last year, when she had received this message, it had shocked her, scared her. She had thought it a message from an alien power. Only now did she realize: *It was, has always been, a message from myself.*

There were still many mysteries. Which gray had betrayed his nation, had taught the Mahatekis to build the hourglass? What had happened to the scroll of Nefitis? Would the crack in the universe she had caused ever mend?

Lailani did not know. Perhaps it was good that some mysteries remained. The cosmos was a strange place, always flowing, reforming, breaking and healing again. Perhaps it was like her life.

She left the trees. She returned to her friends by the lake. It was time.

Her friends gathered around her, and Lailani placed the hourglass on a tree stump. She turned toward her friends.

"We cannot change the past," Lailani said. "The grays learned that. We did too. But we can still change our future.

The future that Marco and Addy visited is not set in stone. We will protect our planet. Always. Earth is eternal."

She raised her rifle and aimed at the hourglass. She hit it on her first try. The hourglass shattered into countless pieces, and the shards scattered across the grass and shone like stars.

* * * * *

That night, Lailani sat alone by the lake. The Milky Way shone above. The others were asleep in the chalet, even Epimetheus. She sat here alone, gazing at the water.

For a long time, she merely watched the water and the stars, just breathing with the world.

Footsteps padded behind her, and she turned to see Ben-Ari approach. Her officer sat down beside her. They sat in silence for a moment, watching the moonlight reflect on the lake.

"Can't sleep?" Lailani finally said.

Ben-Ari spoke softly. "Noah asked me to marry him."

"Who's Noah?" Lailani asked. "Oh! You mean the professor?" She smiled. "Congratulations, ma'am! I'm happy for you." She frowned. "You said yes, of course."

Ben-Ari smiled too. She nodded. She held Lailani's hand.

"Lailani." Ben-Ari spoke carefully as if considering each word. "I never forgot that night we shared. On that planet inside the black hole. When we made love."

"Me neither," Lailani said softly.

Ben-Ari stroked her short black hair. "You will always be dear to me, Lailani. I will always love you. Marco told me that you plan to return to your country. To keep building schools. Know this. Wherever your path takes you, you are loved. Whenever you need me, I am here for you. Always."

Ben-Ari kissed Lailani's cheek.

"Thank you, Einav," Lailani whispered. "I think I'll be fine now. I've learned a lot. I've grown. I'm stronger. I have HOBBS and Epi. And soon I'll have my child." She grinned. "And I have the *Ryujin*, so I'll come visit you and the professor a lot."

Ben-Ari hugged her, kissed her forehead, and returned to the chalet. Lailani remained by the lake for a long time, gazing at the stars and water. Finally she rose to her feet, stepped indoors, and lay on her bed. Epimetheus hopped up beside her and curled up on her feet.

When Lailani placed her hand on her belly, she saw her scars in the moonlight. The scars on her wrist. The scars from her suicide attempt.

I was a child in the slums. I was a youth in a war. I was a woman torn and broken. And for the first time in my life, at age thirty, soon to be a mother, I am happy.

CHAPTER TWENTY-FIVE

They offered her the job.

When Ben-Ari heard, she stared in shock.

"You want *me* to be the new president of the Alliance of Nations?" She couldn't believe her ears. "You want *me* to lead Earth?"

The delegation stared back, somber. They nodded. A dozen men and women in suits, they had come to see her at the presidential chalet.

"It was Petty's wish," one of the men said. "He wrote it in his will. In three years we'll have an election. Until then, the job is yours. Petty was convinced—as we all are—that you are the most qualified to lead us, Einav Ben-Ari."

Ben-Ari blinked. Just last week, she had finally—after years of night classes—completed her bachelor's degree from Galactica University, majoring in history. She had never imagined the job offers would roll in this quickly. Let alone *this* job offer.

She rubbed her eyes and blinked. "I'm only thirty-two."

They nodded. "Half the average age of the previous presidents. Yet how many other thirtysomethings have defeated alien empires, have flown to the depths of space and back, and saved Earth more times than we can count?"

"Every living soldier in my platoon," she said.

They just stared back, waiting for an answer.

Ben-Ari looked away. She closed her eyes.

She thought of time.

She remembered a young girl, losing her mother.

She remembered bouncing from military base to military base, her homeland destroyed.

She remembered a rebellious youth, running away from her father, remembered booze and trysts with boys.

She remembered a cadet, dedicating herself to Earth, to sacrifice.

My ancestors fought the Nazis in the forests, so I decided to fight the enemies of humanity. And for fourteen years, I fought them as a soldier, rising from cadet to captain of a flagship.

She took a deep breath.

But saving the world is not a one-time job. Saving the world is like tending to a garden. It requires continuous work, devotion, love. The weeds are always growing. We must always be uprooting them, preserving the beauty of our garden. More weeds will rise. More pestilence will plague this world that I love. I am a custodian of this planet. I am a gardener in this garden. I will never stop fighting for Earth. Because I've flown across the galaxy, and I've seen countless worlds, and I know that Earth is just a pale blue marble in the darkness. But Earth is my home. Earth is beautiful. Earth is eternal.

She opened her eyes. She looked at the men and women from the Alliance. She nodded.

"Yes," she whispered.

I was a broken girl. I was a soldier. I was a captain. She looked at the mountains outside the chalet, at the blue sky, at the forests and fields. *I will be Earth's protector. I will not let Earth fall to evil and despair. I will cherish our world. Always.*

* * * * *

Marco was still in Switzerland, staying with Ben-Ari at her chalet, when Tomiko sent him a message. He read it on his phone. She wanted to meet him in the nearby town.

"It's obviously a trap," Addy said. "She'll say she divorced her new husband, that she wants you back." She grabbed Marco. "But you are mine, Poet."

He pulled himself free. "First of all, I belong to nobody. Second—"

Addy wrestled him into a headlock. "Mine!"

He groaned and shoved her off. "For God's sake! Get a pet."

"I had one! The fish. Remember?" Addy lowered her head. "I named him George. And I used to cuddle him and cherish him and love him forever and ever. At least until I threw him onto a gray's face and lit him on fire."

Marco sighed and left the chalet.

He rode a bike along a dirt path. After so many years in roaring rockets and clattering starships, it felt good to ride in the open air. He carried no weapons. He wore no uniform. It was a two-hour ride, and he spent it in Deep Being, allowing his thoughts to flow by, merely soaking in the sunlight, the fresh air, the verdant landscapes.

After so long as a soldier, as a machine of war, he felt like a man again.

His body bore new wounds. He would carry new scars for the rest of his life. The horrors he had seen, the pain he had endured—they would forever linger inside him, forever rise in his sleep as nightmares. He would always miss those he had lost. His parents. Elvis. Caveman and Beast. Anisha. Perhaps more than all—Kemi. Those holes would always fill his heart. There was peace here in this world, here on this bike among the mountains, but he was a broken man.

And yet I have Deep Being. I have a method to cope. I have Addy. I can find some peace.

He reached the town, a picturesque little place with medieval houses, cobbled streets, gardens lush with flowers, and cafes that bustled with visitors. The war had not touched this place. It was a pocket of paradise from a more innocent time.

He went to the cafe where Tomiko had asked to meet him. He was early. He sat at a patio table. They didn't have North American-style coffee, just black and brewed straight from the pot, so he ordered something with steamed milk and a flower drawn into the foam. He was thankful Addy wasn't here to see him drink it; she would have mocked him mercilessly.

He had almost finished his drink, and he was wondering if Tomiko would show up at all, when engines rumbled above. A rickety starship, probably a good fifteen years old and the size of a bus, descended and landed on the street, belching out smoke. The cafe's patrons scowled.

The starship's airlock opened. Marco glimpsed Tomiko's second husband at the helm, an older man with graying hair. He did not look Marco's way. Tomiko emerged, wearing a summer dress, and ran across the street. She joined Marco at the cafe.

He rose from his seat and hugged her. For a moment they just stood holding each other.

"How are you?" Marco finally said. "Are you all right?"

Tomiko sniffed and nodded. She smiled at him shakily. "I'm all right."

Visions flashed before Marco's eyes. He remembered Tomiko in Gehenna, the city of the grays. He remembered the creatures tearing her clothes, carrying her into the brothel, preparing to rape her. But here she stood before him, healthy, beautiful, safe. She had broken his heart, but he loved her, and he forgave her, and her happiness was as important to him as his own.

"They don't have real coffee," he told her. "But they draw adorable little flowers in steamed milk. Remember to lift your pinky as you raise the cup!"

Tomiko laughed. "I won't order anything. I'm not staying long. Craig and I have a starship to catch, a bigger one than this old clunker." She gestured at the ship on the road. "We're moving to a new world, Marco. To a new colony they just founded. It's a world similar to Earth. Craig has a job there waiting for him. I came here ... to say goodbye."

"I'm happy for you, Tomiko." He held her hand. "Be happy there. Make it a good future."

She smiled, lowered her head, and wiped her damp eyes. "Marco, take your house back. The house in Greece. It's yours. Move in there with Addy if you want to. And ... the book royalties too. I'm giving it all back." She touched his cheek. "I want us to be okay."

He nodded. His throat was tight. "We're okay, Tomiko. Everything is okay."

She hugged him and kissed his cheek.

"Love you," she whispered, then ran off. When the starship took off, she waved from the porthole. He waved back.

"Goodbye, Tomiko," he said softly, watching her ship fly away.

He ordered another drink. He sat for a while, watching the people come and go. Then he got on his bike and rode back to the chalet. Back to his friends. Back to Addy.

* * * * *

A year after the Gray War began, Marco and Addy came home.

They walked along the beach, heading toward their old house.

"Poet!" Addy leaped onto his back. "Carry me."

He shoved her off. "No, Addy. You weigh a metric ton."

"But I'm tired!" She jumped onto his back again.

He shoved her off again. "Addy, for Chrissake! We walked across the desolate plains of Black Earth. You can handle a stroll on the beach."

She pouted. "Black Earth didn't have sand."

They kept walking, their backpacks filled with their belongings—a change of clothes, a few medals from the war, a gray's helmet Addy had kept as a souvenir, a bit of food. It was all they owned.

These backpacks—and their house.

Finally he saw it ahead. Addy and he ran.

They burst through the front door into their home.

"We're home!" Addy cried, running around like a madwoman. "We're home! We're home!"

She leaped over the couch, rolled across the floor, ran rings around the living room table, burst into the kitchen, raced upstairs, and darted in and out of every room.

"Poet, we're home, we're home!" She leaped around, head tossed back, arms raised. "We're home!"

He stared at her. It was like staring at a typhoon.

"I thought you were tired."

She ran toward him, leaped onto him, and wrapped all four limbs around him. She squeezed him and showered him with kisses, nearly knocking him down the stairs.

"We're home, Poet! Our home. Finally. You and me." She shed tears. "We're home." Her eyes lit up, and she gasped. "Do you think Tomiko kept my corn dogs in the freezer?"

She leaped off Marco and ran into the kitchen. Her whoops of joy filled the house.

Marco explored the house more quietly and slowly. He entered the living room. Tomiko had kept his and Addy's mementos from the military: their medals in shadowboxes, a scum's claw, their first berets, and framed photographs from their service. Marco paused and gazed at one photograph, the one from boot camp twelve years ago. The entire platoon was there. Eighteen and scrawny, Marco was trying to look somber, but Addy was holding up two fingers like rabbit ears behind his head. Lailani had her cheeks puffed out, her eyes crossed, and Elvis had his arm around her shoulder.

So many friends lost. So many faces now only in memory. Elvis. Caveman. Jackass. Beast. Sergeant Singh. Corporal Diaz. Corporal St-Pierre. Corporal Webb. Sheriff. Pinky. They had all fallen. And Marco would never forget them. They were all his brothers and sisters in arms.

He went upstairs. His bedroom was as he had left it. The library still had all his old books, mostly books from authors he loved, but also his own books. *Loggerhead. Le Kill. The Dragons of Yesteryear* trilogy. *Under the Stairs* and its sequels. His hopes and dreams and fears, there within the pages. The collection was only missing *The Clockwork Rose*, the novel he had written on the flight to Durmia.

He stepped into his studio, the little room with a view of the sea, the place where he wrote. Where he would write again. He placed his hand on the desk. A framed photo of Kemi was still on the wall.

Let me never be a soldier again, he thought. *Let me spend the next fifty years here, in this home. Writing. Living with Addy. Forgetting the terror and remembering the friends I lost.*

He stepped back downstairs. Addy and he had built this home years ago, planning it for themselves and their friends. It was a large house, too large for just the two of them.

Though maybe someday, he thought, two would become three. Or four. The thought tickled him.

"Poet." Addy approached him, calmer now, and took his hands. "I don't want to sleep here tonight."

"What?" He tilted his head. "Addy! You were running around like a maniac for the past fifteen minutes, shouting that you want to dump me and marry the house."

"I know." She nodded. "But … there's a place I've been waiting to return to even more." She grinned. "Grab a blanket."

Marco smiled. He nodded. He understood.

A semicircle of cliffs surrounded the cove. The beach was hidden from the rest of the island, accessible only by boat. They rowed there. The cove's water was sparkling azure, warm and shallow, and waves rarely disturbed it. They dropped anchor and walked toward the beach, the water rising to their knees. Fish flitted between their legs, and seashells shone. They reached the golden sand. The old shipwreck still lay here, aging gracefully in the sunlight, its hold filled with sand and crabs.

Marco and Addy reached the beach. They gazed around them at the white cliffs, the golden beach, the shipwreck, the pale water. It was beautiful. It was just as they had remembered it.

Addy placed an arm around Marco. She spoke in a soft voice.

"In the darkness, in the desolation of Black Earth, we often dreamed of this place. We imagined that we were back here." She wiped her eyes. "But I never believed, not really. I didn't think we'd ever make it back. Is this real, Poet? Are we really here?"

He held her close. "We're really here, Addy."

She smiled. "Shipwreck Cove. The most beautiful place in the world. *Our* place. The place where you first told me you're madly in love with me."

They stood in the sand, kissing.

"I love you, Marco." Addy touched his cheek. "I love you so much. I can't imagine life without you. Do you love me too? Forever and ever? You'll never leave me, right? Even if you become a famous, distinguished author and I become a fat, old ugly cow?"

"Addy!" He held the small of her back and stared into her eyes. "I'm already a famous, distinguished author, and you're already a—"

"Watch it!" She raised her fist.

He laughed and kissed her cheek. "Ads, I will never stop loving you. I will never leave you. You are beautiful. You've been my best friend for twenty years. You are my other half. We'll be together from now on. Here. On this island. We'll never leave again."

She nearly crushed him in her embrace. She wept against his shoulder, and they were tears of joy.

The sun set, and they lay down on their blanket. They did not bother looking up at the stars. They had gazed upon those lights enough times. They lay facing each other, gazing into each other's eyes in the moonlight, laughing, tickling, joking, kissing, making love, then whispering softly of many things.

I am happy, Marco thought. *After so many years of pain, I am happy—a true, deep, full happiness.*

"Poet?" Addy said. "Do you wanna get married?"

He blinked. "What, right now? Right here?"

She groaned. "Is that really the best response you could think of?"

He bit his lip. He grinned. "Yes."

"It is?" Addy said. "You can't think of *anything* better to say, even though you're a writer, and—"

"I mean yes, Addy, I want to get married."

"Oh." She looked at him. She grinned. "Okay. Let's do it. Right now. Right here."

He laughed.

They waited a while longer—until the next day, that was.

They brought a priest over in a little boat. And he married them in this cove by the shipwreck. They invited no guests. They wanted their marriage to be private, something just about them, just for them. They didn't need a big gathering or party. They just needed this cove, this beautiful place, and each other.

Husband and wife, they walked back to their house.

"So here we are!" Addy said. "Addy Linden and Marco Linden."

He frowned. "Hey. Wait a minute. We're Marco and Addy Emery."

She snorted. "You wish."

He froze. "Addy!"

She groaned. "Fine. Can we be the Emery-Lindens?"

"No!" he said. "It's against tradition. I'm the man, and— ow! Ow! Addy, stop kicking me! Not in the crotch! Fine. Fine! The Emery-Lindens!"

She grinned and mussed his hair. "I knew you'd see reason."

Daniel Arenson

He sighed and opened the front door. "This'll be a long fifty years."

"Wait, before you enter!" Addy leaped into his arms. "Carry me."

He groaned. "You weigh a ton!"

"Yeah, well, you're short."

"We're *the same height*!"

But he carried her into their home. He kicked the door shut behind him. He didn't even make it upstairs. He made love to her on the living room floor. Twice. And then he lay by her side, stroking her golden hair. He was with his best friend. With his wife. With Addison Elizabeth Emery-Linden. His Addy. They had been through hell, and here they found heaven.

* * * * *

He lifted his pen.

He wrote two more words in his notebook.

The End.

"It's done," Marco said. "My twelfth novel."

He gazed at his pile of notebooks. It was a tale of a goblin girl and her adventures in a magical land. The other

races in this world—the humans, the elves, the dwarves—all
thought goblins were twisted, evil creatures, hunched over,
hook-nosed, hoarding treasure in dank tunnels. In truth, goblins
were friendly—if shy—beings who lived in peaceful forests.
They looked much like elves, fair and pointy-eared, though
shorter and more humble. Throughout the novel, the young
goblin heroine met many other misunderstood races. Trolls.
Orcs. Kobolds. All demonized and shunned. Yet together these
misfits saved the world.

Perhaps Marco himself had often felt like a goblin.
When he had returned from fighting the scum, many had called
him a war criminal. He still felt uncomfortable among other
people, even today. He liked being alone or just with Addy. He
liked being at home or walking on a quiet beach. He found it
difficult to connect with others. With people who hadn't lived
through battles. Who hadn't seen the hives on Abaddon or the
terrors of the marauders. Who hadn't suffered for many days on
the desolate plains of Black Earth, slowly starving, and—

He winced, sudden pain stabbing him. It was a chilly
morning. His old wounds still ached in the cold. He took
several deep breaths, sinking into Deep Being. He still practiced
the art most days. He reached into his drawer, and he pulled out
two bottles. He swallowed two pills. One to reduce the pain in
his wounds. Another to drown the nightmares in his mind. He
took both daily. Both helped.

It was two years since Black Earth. Two years since
Ben-Ari had arrived on the *Lodestar* to save him and Addy. The

nightmares had never fully gone away. He knew they never would. But he had Deep Being. He had his writing and his medicine. He had his beautiful family. He was thirty-two years old. He was finally beginning his life.

"Poet!" Addy cried from downstairs. "For God's sake, Poet, it's your turn! Two stinky, poopy diapers down here!"

Marco put down his pen. He went downstairs.

Addy was in the living room, holding a stinky baby in each arm.

"Your turn," Addy said.

Marco smiled. "All right, all right!"

He took the twins from her and kissed their heads. Roza and Sam were both little clones of Addy, blond of hair, blue of eyes, fierce of heart. They had inherited nothing from Marco, it seemed, and yet he loved them both with all his heart. His little girl and his little boy. His bright lights.

Addy had named their girl. She had chosen the name Roza after Roza Shanina, a heroine of the Second World War. Marco had named their boy, choosing Sam after Samwise Gamgee, his favorite character in literature.

"Are you stinky, Roza and Sam?" Marco tickled them, and they giggled. "All right. Your old man will change you. No crawling away without a fresh diaper."

Sam peed on him while Marco was changing him. The little bastard laughed.

"Poet! Poet!" Addy shouted from outside.

"I'm doing it!" he cried back. "Jesus, Ads, I'm changing them!"

"Not that," Addy said. "They're here! Come on, hurry, they're landing!"

Marco could hear it now. His hearing had never fully recovered from the war, but this sound was *loud*. Engines rumbling. He quickly finished diapering the twins, lifted both, and hurried outside.

The starship came flying down. The *Ryujin* had been patched up, and the dragon and rainbow on her hull had been repainted.

The *Ryujin* landed on the beach, and the airlock opened. Epimetheus emerged first, racing across the sand toward Marco and his family. HOBBS climbed out next, careful as he walked across the beach, mumbling something about getting sand in his gears. Finally Lailani emerged. She had let her hair grow during the past year, and she wore shorts and sandals. In her arms she carried a baby.

Marco and Addy rushed toward her.

Lailani smiled at them. She looked happy. For the first time since Marco had met her, she looked truly happy.

She held out her baby. "Meet Tala de la Rosa, my little goddess. Her name means 'goddess of stars' in my language."

Addy's eyes widened. "She looks just like you. She's a mini-Lailani! And that's saying something, given how mini you already are."

Lailani laughed and admired the twins, speaking of how they looked like Addy. The two women shared stories of motherhood and cooed over the little ones.

Marco watched Lailani as she spoke, her eyes bright.

Years ago, I fell in love with you, Lailani, he thought. *I asked you to marry me. You said no. You broke my heart. I wonder what might have been. If that could have been my child ...*

Lailani raised her eyes and met his gaze. She smiled and placed a hand on his arm.

Marco's line of thought faded. Silliness.

He kissed Lailani's cheek. "She's beautiful. And she does look like you."

Another engine rumbled. A shadow fell. They looked up to see a second starship. This one was larger, newer, far more expensive than the *Ryujin*. On her white hull appeared the blue Earth and the silver moon—symbol of the Alliance of Nations. The starship landed on the beach too, scattering sand. A hatch opened. Two guards emerged, stood at attention, and saluted.

And out she came, President Einav Ben-Ari.

Addy and Lailani gazed in awe. Their commanding officer, the twenty-year-old ensign they had met in the desert long ago, had become the leader of Earth. At first the sight of her emerging from that starship seemed almost holy. Marco wasn't sure if to salute, to bow, or even to kneel.

Instead, he smiled. And that smile turned into a grin. And he ran toward his officer, his president, his friend.

"Einav."

She smiled and hugged him. "Marco."

Professor Isaac emerged from the starship next, and he carried a baby. Marco's eyes widened.

"Meet little Carl," Ben-Ari said. "Our son."

The baby had dark hair like the professor's, but his eyes were green like his mother's. He did not cry nor fuss, simply gazed around with wide, curious eyes.

"He's beautiful," Marco said. "And he seems wise."

Ben-Ari laughed. "Wise?"

Marco nodded. "Yes. The way he looks around. I can tell."

It was two years—to the day—since their campfire by that lake in Switzerland. They built another campfire here in Greece. They vowed to meet every year on this date, no matter where their lives took them, for a campfire, for friendship, for memory.

They spent the evening roasting hot dogs, potatoes, and marshmallows. Ben-Ari and Marco discussed the books they had read over the past year, and Lailani showed them all photographs from her school. Little Tala de la Rosa, oldest among the babies, showed off by saying "mama" and "HOBBA" while hearts melted. It was an evening full of joy, of laughter.

But also of pain.

Sometimes when Marco glanced into Ben-Ari's eyes, he saw the deep trauma, the ghosts that still haunted her.

Sometimes Lailani grew very quiet and just gazed into the fire, and she seemed so sad.

We all have too many memories, Marco thought. *We meet once a year to be joyous. But we will forever be scarred.*

He lifted Roza and Sam, and he held the twins close. They gazed up at him, smiling softly.

"We did this for you," Marco whispered to his children. "So that you will have a better world than we did. We bled. We killed. We suffered. We cried out in so much anguish, and we lost so much, because we were waiting for you. Because we love you. Because we needed to build you a home."

He realized that his friends had heard him, that they were watching him, and Marco's cheeks flushed. Lailani shifted closer and leaned against his side. Ben-Ari moved to sit beside Marco too, leaning against his other side. They too held their children. Four curious, beautiful babies. Four new souls.

"May you never know fear," Marco said to their children. "May you never know pain. May you never see friends die. May you never kill. May yours be lives of joy. Of love. Of peace."

His tears fell, but he smiled. His friends embraced him. The fire crackled and the stars shone above. There was so much pain, so much terror up there. But right now, down here, there was light and life. And life was beautiful.

"Hey!" Addy said, suddenly bolting to her feet. "I forgot my rake!"

She rushed toward the house, then returned to the campfire with her ceremonial rake, and soon she was roasting hot dogs, and everyone was laughing again. Marco laughed too.

Fourteen years ago, a rocket had taken him to a military base in a desert. Fourteen years ago, his war had begun. Often he had not thought he would survive. He was thirty-two, and he had never thought he'd live so long.

When I look back upon those years, he thought, *let me forget the terror and pain. Let me remember the good times we had, the friendships we made. We cannot change the past. But the future is ours to forge. May our lives be filled with laughter and love. May we all know nothing but peace.*

The End

NOVELS BY DANIEL ARENSON

Earthrise:
Earth Alone
Earth Lost
Earth Rising
Earth Fire
Earth Shadows
Earth Valor
Earth Reborn
Earth Honor
Earth Eternal

Alien Hunters:
Alien Hunters
Alien Sky
Alien Shadows

The Moth Saga:
Moth
Empires of Moth
Secrets of Moth
Daughter of Moth
Shadows of Moth
Legacy of Moth

KEEP IN TOUCH

www.DanielArenson.com
Daniel@DanielArenson.com
Facebook.com/DanielArenson
Twitter.com/DanielArenson

Made in the USA
Middletown, DE
11 January 2018